FOREWORD

This book is dedicated to the young people of America, who are rebelling because they know something is very wrong in their country, but do not know just what it is. I hope this book will help to enlighten them.

There is not, to my knowledge, any family like the 'Armagh Family' in America, nor has there ever been, and all characters, except those obviously historical, are my own invention. However, the historical background and the political background of this novel are authentic. The 'Committee for Foreign Studies' does indeed exist, today as of yesterday, and so does the 'Scardo Society', but not by these names.

There is indeed a 'plot against the people', and probably always will be, for government has always been hostile towards the governed. It is not a new story, and the conspirators and conspiracies have varied from era to era, depending on the political or economic situation in their various countries.

But it was not until the era of the League of Just Men and Karl Marx that conspirators and conspiracies become one, with one aim, one objective, and one determination. This has nothing to do with any 'ideology' or form of government, or ideals or 'materialism' or any other catch-phrases generously fed to the unthinking masses. It has absolutely nothing to do with races or religions, for the conspirators are beyond what they call 'such trivialities'. They are also beyond good and evil. The Caesars they put into power are their creatures, whether they know it or not, and the peoples of all nations are helpless, whether they live in America, Europe, Russia, China, Africa or South America. They will always be helpless until they are aware of their real enemy.

President John F. Kennedy knew what he was talking about when he spoke of 'the Gnomes of Zürich'. Perhaps he knew too much! Coups d'état are an old story, but they are now growing too numerous. This is probably the last hour for mankind as a rational species, before it becomes the slave of a 'planned society'. A bibliography ends this book, and I hope many of my readers will avail themselves of the facts. That is all the hope I have.

TAYLOR CALDWELL

'The tumult and the shouting dies;
The Captains and the Kings depart:
Still stands Thine ancient Sacrifice,
An humble and a contrite heart.

'Lord God of Hosts, be with us yet,
Lest we forget – lest we forget!'

Rudyard Kipling

Captains and the Kings

TAYLOR CALDWELL, an Englishwoman by birth, has lived in America since 1906 when her family emigrated to New York State. After many years of research, writing and discouragement, her novel *Dynasty of Death* was published in 1938: an immediate bestseller, it launched her on a spectacularly successful writing career.

Since then she has published over thirty more books, with settings ranging from modern and nineteenth-century America back to the golden age of Athens and the legendary kingdom of Atlantis. Two of her most famous bestsellers, *Captains and the Kings* and *Testimony of Two Men*, were made into successful television series

TAYLOR CALDWELL

Captains and the Kings

FONTANA/Collins

First published in Great Britain in 1972 by
William Collins Sons & Co. Ltd
First issued in Fontana Paperbacks 1975
Sixteenth impression September 1985

Made and printed in Great Britain by
Richard Clay (The Chaucer Press) Ltd,
Bungay, Suffolk

PART ONE

Joseph Francis Xavier Armagh

'Much memory or memory of many things, is called experience.'

Thomas Hobbes, OF MAN

CHAPTER ONE

'JOEY, Joey? Oh God! Joey?' his mother cried out of her extremity and pain.

'I'm here, Mum,' said Joseph, holding her thin small hand tighter. 'I won't leave you, Mum.' She stared at him in the dimness, her eyes bright and distended with terror. Joseph bent over her, the stool on which he sat rocking with the heavy labouring of the anchored ship. Her fingers squeezed his hand until they were tight on his flesh. 'Oh, Mum,' he murmured. 'You'll be well, Mum.' He was thirteen years old.

'I'm dying, Joey,' she said, and her weary young voice was hardly audible. 'There's Sean, Joey, and the little colleen. You'll take care of them, Joey, for himself? You'll mind them?'

'Sure, and I'll mind them, Mum,' he said. 'Dad will meet us. You'll be well then.'

'Good Joey,' she whispered. 'You were always a good boy-een. You're a man, Joey.'

'Yes, Mum,' he said. The fingers that clutched his hand had become icy, and not only the tips. His mother's thick black hair faintly shone in the light of the stinking and swaying lantern which hung from the wooden ceiling. That ceiling and the wet wooden walls sweated and the big masted ship creaked all about them. It was still light outside the four small portholes but little light entered here in the rancid steerage where fifty women and children slept on noxious bunks under thin blankets. The broken floor was soiled with the urine of children and scattered with sawdust. It was very cold. The portholes were blurred with spray. The ship was a four-master which had left Queenstown, Ireland, over six weeks ago. By standing on tiptoe the tallest could see the shoreline of New York, the faint gloomy illumination of lamps. Some of the steerage passengers had been rejected twenty-four hours ago in Boston. They were Irish.

The majority of women and children on the hard bunks were sick with cholera, famine fever, tuberculosis and pneumonia. Joseph Francis Xavier Armagh felt and saw nothing but his dying mother, who was hardly thirty years old. He heard bitter crying near him and he knew it was his little brother, Sean, who was scarcely six. Sean was crying because he was perpetually hungry and cold and frightened. He had had his supper ten minutes before, a bowl of thin oatmeal and a slice of coarse dry bread which smelled of mice.

Joseph did not turn to Sean. He did not hear the wailing of children and the weeping of the sick women in the steerage. His mind and his passionate determination were fixed on his mother. Joseph had eaten no supper at all, and had pushed aside the bowl which Sister Mary Bridget had entreated him to take. If he thought of anything but his mother now she would die. If he took his hand from hers and his eyes from her face, she would die. 'They' would have killed her at last, Moira Armagh, who laughed when there was no occasion to laugh and valiantly prayed when there was no God to hear her.

But Joseph dared not remember that there was no God, and he was afraid of mortal sin, and only a God could help Moira now – and the will of her son. The new baby had been born at midnight, and the Sisters had taken her, and the old priest in the steerage had baptised the child and had named her, on Moira's whispered word, Mary Regina. The child was too weak to cry; a young nun sat on the bunk near her and stood up as Father O'Leary pushed aside the curtain and entered the quarters of the women and young children. The long passage became silent; even the sick children stopped crying. Mothers reached from the narrow bunks to touch his frayed black cassock. He had been summoned by a Sister aboard, Sister Teresa, and he carried, very carefully, a worn and ancient leather bag in his hand.

One of the six nuns in the steerage had produced a small splintered table and this she set near Moira Armagh's head. 'Joey,' said Sister Mary Bridget in his ear, 'you won't deny your own mother Extreme Unction, will you, and deprive her of the comforting? She has made her confession . . .'

Joseph's voice, as hard and ruthless as his nature, rose on a great cry. 'And what has she to confess, my Mum?' he almost screamed. 'What has she done in her life to make God hate her? How has she ever sinned? It is God who should confess!'

A nun who had been spreading the table with an anonymous square of white cloth drew in her breath at this blasphemy, and blessed herself. Vermin ran up and down the curved wooden walls of the deck. The children began to wail again.

Fetid air blew through the curtain at the end of the deck and now some man on a bunk beyond the curtain began to play on a mouth organ, a dolorous Irish ballad, and a few hoarse voices hummed the chorus. The kneeling nuns began to murmur: 'Holy Mary, Mother of God, pray for us sinners now and at the hour of our death . . .'

'No, no, no!' shouted Joseph, and he beat the side of his mother's bunk with one clenched fist. But he did not release his other hand from hers. Moira Armagh lay in mute exhaustion.

The priest silently opened his case and his ancient hands trembled with age and sorrow and reverence. Joseph's eyes now fastened on him and his pale lips lifted from his big teeth in a soundless snarl.

'Joey,' said Moira in the faintest of dying voices.

'Go away,' Joseph said to the priest. 'If she receives she will die.' He could not forgive God. He could no longer believe. He had only hate and despair to sustain him now, to give him courage.

A heavy mist was rising from the cold sea and melancholy horns began to moan in the harbour. The ship rocked. 'I'll take ye to your home again,' sang the men beyond the curtain, 'to where the grass is fresh and green!' They sang of the land they had left because there was no bread there any longer to satisfy the body, and only rotting and blackened potatoes in the wet and ravished fields.

A murmurous sound rose, the Litany for the Dying. The priest administered the Sacrament of Extreme Unction and Viaticum to the dying woman, whose white lips barely moved in her extremity. Then the priest said, 'Go forth from this world, O Christian soul . . .'

Joseph did not hear this. He was saying to his father, Daniel, who was to meet them in New York, 'I brought her to you, Dad, and Sean and the little colleen, and now you and I will take care of them, in the house you provided, and we'll be free and never hungry or homeless again. No one will hate us and drive us from our land and tell us to starve . . . Dad, we've come home to you.'

It was real to him, for he had dreamt that scene a thousand times on this sorrowful voyage. His father would meet his family on the dock and enfold them all, and then he would take them to the 'flat' in the Bowery where he lived with his brother, Jack, and it would be warm and there would be soft beds and a hot stove and joy and the fragrance of boiling potatoes and turnips and beef or lamb and safety and comfort and peace and hope. Had they not received letters from him, and money, and had he not told them of this? He had a good job as janitor in a small hotel. He ate to repletion for the first time in years. He worked hard, and he received money for his labour. He would provide for his family, and no more would they be hunted like vermin and despised and execrated for their Faith, and thrown from their land to die on the highways of exposure and hunger. 'Ah, and it is a land for free men,' Daniel had written in his careful hand. 'The lads will go to school, and the little one will be born in America, and we will be Americans together, and never part again.'

The dying woman suddenly moved so convulsively that Joseph's dream abruptly ended, and he lifted his head. His mother's eyes, no longer filmed and dull, were gazing over his shoulder with an expression of profound joy. 'Danny, Danny!' she cried. 'Oh Danny, you've come for us!' Then the light faded from her eyes and her face, and she died between one breath and another.

CHAPTER TWO

JOSEPH, now sitting on the edge of the bunk where his little brother Sean slept with tears on his wan cheeks, remembered all the dolorous suffering of Ireland and his father who waited for his family. He remembered, also, that the English Queen had contemptuously offered multitudes of the Irish free passage to America to escape starvation and oppression; it was evident that she considered America still a penal colony as her grandfather had so considered it, and still a British possession though a worthless one. The multitudes who had no alternative but death and brutality and starvation had fled their stricken land. But Daniel's brother had sent passage money for the steerage.

Joseph sat in the deepening cold of the men's portion of the deck, and thought. The sick moaned in their pain-racked sleep. The men no longer sang, but sat mutely side by side on the lower bunks. The cattle below lowed uneasily. Joseph sat near his sleeping brother, his eyes fixed, almost without blinking, on the gritty deck beneath his feet. Where would they be permitted to land? Joseph knew of the many little ships that had been turned back at various ports in America: they were not wanted. They were the destitute and the starveling, and they were 'Romans' and Irish and trouble-makers and strange. The Religious were especially despised and secretly feared.

Was Daniel Armagh still waiting for his family on the wharf in New York? Did he know they might be rejected, not permitted to land? It was winter: was he standing at the door of one of the sheds and staring hopelessly at the big anchored ship with its slack sails and its wet fortress-like hull? Was he doing, thought Joseph with an acrid taste of bitterness in his mouth, anything at all for his imprisoned family except praying? Did he know that his young wife was dead? Dead. Joseph squeezed his dry eyes shut and his chest became tight and smothering with his huge hatred and sorrow. Oh Mum, he said in himself. They could not consign her to the ocean in the harbour. They would wait until they were at sea again. They would bind her in a ragged blanket and fasten her body to a thin frame of wood, and she would go into the cold and blackness of the water just as her soul was in the cold blackness of nothingness now.

But he dared not think of this yet. There was the immediate calamity to be faced. Would they be returned to Ireland, and would they then all perish inevitably on the way back, or on landing? The real question confronted him: How was he to assure the survival of his brother and infant sister, and himself? If he were alone or had only Sean to consider he might contrive, in the morning just before dawn, to steal from the ship when it moved to the wharfs to unload the cattle and the passengers who comfortably travelled on the upper decks, from which steerage passengers were excluded. Authorities were not too difficult to circumvent, if one assumed a confident and assured appearance and was clean and quiet. However, there was the baby and even the dullest of authorities would be curious about a youth with an infant in his arms, and accompanied by a young child also, with no apparent guardians. Though he, Joseph, could doubtless manage to provide some food and shelter for two boys, the little girl needed

13

womanly comfort and care, and where were these to be found for the derelict?

The four portholes began to emerge greyly from the gloom as dawn approached. The stench from unwashed and dying bodies and from the latrines filled the cold dank air. The wooden ceiling dripped. The sawdust on the floor was smeared ominously with the blood from diseased lungs. Joseph traced the stain on his knee with rising quickness. His strong russet hair hung in ragged points over his forehead and ears and neck.

He felt a touch on his shoulder and looked up with blank and sunken eyes. Old Father O'Leary was standing before him, in his long nightshirt. 'You haven't been to bed,' said the priest. 'Sure, and you will be sick, too, if ye do not rest, Joey.'

'How will we let my father know if we cannot leave the ship?' asked Joseph.

'In the morning, I will go ashore – it is permitted for me for an hour – and I will find Danny and tell him, and we should know, then, where we are going. It is to Philadelphia, I think, and let us pray that they will permit us to land there. Joey, you must rest for a bit.'

'Philadelphia?' said Joseph. 'Is it far from New York? It has a pretty sound.'

The old priest smiled painfully, his ancient and haggard face falling into deep grey lines. His shock of white hair was dishevelled and as ragged as Joseph's, and his nightshirt dragged on his skeleton body. 'Philadelphia,' he said. 'It means the city of Brotherly Love. Pray they will have some "love" for us, Joey. We must trust in God . . .'

'There are steam-cars from Philadelphia to New York, are there not?' said Joseph.

'To be sure, Joey. All will be well, if we trust in Our Lord. Joey, it is cold. Put on your coat. And the seamen will be bringing our breakfast before we sail.'

He helplessly patted the boy's shoulder, then sighing he turned away, for a sick man had weakly called him in his extremity. He wore old carpet slippers and he shuffled on the sooty floor. Joseph felt for the packet which hung on a string around his neck, and against his chest. The gold certificates were safe. Fifteen dollars. Three pounds. It was a lot of money which his father had sent to the family before they had left Ireland. And his wages were but two pounds a week. It had taken Daniel Armagh several months to accumulate such a sum.

One porthole was suddenly rosy with dawn, and Joseph stood up on his tiptoes and looked outside. Almost imperceptibly the ship was moving to a pier among a forest of bare masts and crowded hulls. Sailors were already working on the anchored ships, and their voices came faintly to Joseph whose face was pressed against the salt-crusted thick glass of the porthole The slow oily water of the harbour was black and sluggish, but its small crests were lighted with cold pink. Now Joseph saw the long piers and wharfs and warehouses in the growing light, and beyond them crowded brick houses and other low buildings. Their roofs were wet with moisture and here and there a street could be seen from the ship, narrow and cobbled and winding, with patches of grey leprous snow piled along the kerbs. Drays and wagons were beginning to move along those streets, horses straining.

Foot by foot the *Irish Queen* moved to the docks and Joseph strained fiercely to see the faces of the lonely crowds gathered on the wooden wharf. Was his father among them? There were many there, including some women, and they were weeping, for they already knew that the steerage passengers would not be permitted to land. Some forlorn hands waved in greeting. A man was raising a flag on a staff nearby and for the first time in his life Joseph saw the stars and stripes whipping wetly in the cold wind of winter and unfurling heavily to the new and hopeless day.

'So, and that is the brave flag,' said a man at another porthole, and other men joined him to gaze at the forbidden land. One laughed derisively, then burst into a fit of coughing. Others joined him, as if a signal had been given. 'They don't want the likes of us,' said another voice. 'Sure, and they do, and we go to Philadelphia,' said still another. 'I have heard it, meself, with these ears, from the Father.'

The door at the end of the deck opened and three seamen appeared with a cart on which steamed bowls of oatmeal and fresh tea, and there were tin plates of hard biscuits and bread. The men and boys rushed eagerly to seize the food but Joseph did not move. Was that his father there, that tall man whose fair hair showed under his workman's cap? Joseph struggled for a moment with the fastening of the porthole, but the iron

15

had corroded and it could not be moved. Ah, yes, it was surely Daniel Armagh there waiting, for the quickening light showed his fine features and Joseph's eyes were keen. Joseph's thin fist beat impotently on the porthole, and he shouted. His cries awakened Sean, who began to whimper, and Joseph pulled him upright in the bunk and forced his face against the porthole.

'There!' he cried. 'There is Dada, Sean, waiting for us!'

Sean wailed. 'It's not Dada,' he protested. 'I want my brekky.'

Joseph had forgotten. He looked about him anxiously. The cart with its steaming but depleted load was about to pass behind the curtain to the women. Joseph raced after it. 'My little brother,' he said. 'He has not eaten.'

The seamen glared at him suspiciously. 'You'll not be wanting extra for yourself, then?' one demanded. 'There's not enough.'

'I don't want it for myself,' said Joseph. He pointed at Sean. 'My brother. Give him mine, too.'

A hot bowl was thrust into his hands and a hunk of mouldy bread, and he was pushed away. He carried the breakfast to Sean who looked at it and whimpered again. 'I don't want it,' he wailed, and retched.

Joseph's heart clenched in fresh dread. 'Sean!' he exclaimed. 'You must eat your breakfast or you will be ill, and there is no time.'

'I want Mum,' said Sean and turned away his pretty face.

'But first, you must eat,' said Joseph, with sternness. Was that indeed fever on Sean's thin cheeks? 'Oh God,' Joseph muttered with hatred between his clenched teeth. He felt Sean's brow. It was cool but sweaty. 'Eat,' Joseph commanded, and the new note in his voice frightened his little brother who began to cry again and sniffle. But he accepted the tin bowl and the big spoon and, sobbing, forced the porridge into his mouth.

'Good boyeen,' said Joseph. He looked at the bread in his hand and hesitated. There was a gaunt hollow in him. But if he sickened, himself, then there would be no help for the other children. He began to chew on the hard bread, and now and then he rose on tiptoe to watch the slow moving of the ship to the wharfs.

There were hurrying loud footsteps on the decks above, and calls, and Joseph knew that the fortunate passengers were disembarking and their trunks and boxes with them. By straining he could see the first passengers leaving, the women in furs, the men in thick greatcoats and tall beaver hats. Carriages were appearing on the wharfs, with coachmen. The wind whipped coats and the men, laughing, held their hats to their heads and helped their ladies against the blast and to the carriages. The horses' sleek bodies smoked. The water smoked. The sky appeared to smoke. And the morning steadily darkened.

Luggage was taken ashore, and waiting crowds embraced the passengers, and even from the closed steerage Joseph could hear laughter and excited twitterings, and could see the happy movements of snugly clad bodies. The crowd waiting for steerage passengers had retreated like a frightened band of cattle, and huddled together to let the fortunate pass to their carriages, followed by carts of leather luggage and trunks banded in iron and brass. These were not those whom the Queen called 'the Irish peasantry', but were landed gentry or Americans returning from sojourns abroad. Joseph watched them enter their closed carriages, laughing at the wind, the ladies' bonnets whirling with ribbons, their skirts ballooning. The carriages rumbled away at last, and now there was only the wretched crowd who would not be permitted to enter the ship nor even to see their relatives in the steerage, for fear of contagion.

For the first time in his life Joseph felt the awful sickness of humiliation. True, in Ireland, the Irish were despised and reviled and persecuted by the Sassenach, but then one in turn stoutly despised and reviled the Sassenach, himself. No Irishman ever felt inferior even to his 'betters', or to the English. He walked and lived proudly, even when starving. He never raised a piteous cry for succour and sympathy. He was a man.

But Joseph now guessed that in America the Irishman was not a man. Here he would be permitted no pride in his race and in his Faith. He would meet only with indifference or contempt or rejection, less than the cattle which were now clambering down the oily wet gangplank, accompanied by amorphous figures huddled against cold and storm.

CHAPTER THREE

A LITTLE later Father O'Leary was sitting on the edge of Sean's bunk, and he held the little boy on his knee and stroked his bright hair with a tender and shaking hand. He saw Joseph approaching. He saw the strength in the thin rigid body, the set of the shoulders, the fixed hardness of the young face, and the freckles that seemed to protrude on the white cheeks, and the mouth that was as firm as stone, and as implacable.

Joseph reached him and stood before him. 'Well, and you must tell me,' he said, and his voice was the voice of a man who can endure. 'And is it my Dad?'

'Yes,' said the priest. He patted Sean's cheek and piteously smiled. 'It's a good boyeen, this,' he said. 'He will not cry while Joey and I speak together.' He fumbled in the pocket of his frayed habit and brought forth an apple and held it high, and Sean looked at it with wonderment, his mouth opening.

The priest put it with a flourish in Sean's hands, and the little fingers stroked it with awe, and puzzlement, for he had never seen an apple before. 'It is good, Sean,' said Father O'Leary. 'Eat it slowly. It is sweeter than honey.' Sean stared at him and then at Joseph, and clutched the fruit as if in fear that his brother would take it from him. The priest said, 'I bought it on the wharf, for Sean.' His old voice strived for lightness, and pride. 'Fifty cents, and that would be two shillings, I am thinking, for it is not the season and it was in gilt paper.'

The priest stood up, and then he staggered with weakness and he bowed his head as he caught at the edge of the upper bunk to steady himself. Only yesterday Joseph would have helped him, but now he held himself away, and stiffly, as if he feared he would shatter and this was no time to shatter. 'Come,' said the priest, and led the way down the deck to the end near the door where they could have a small privacy. Once there Joseph said in a rough voice, 'You did not see my Dad.'

'No,' said the priest. He lifted his head and his eyes were filled with tears. Joseph considered him without pity or emotion.

18

'You saw my Uncle Jack,' said Joseph. 'It was him I saw, on the wharf.'

'Yes,' said Father O'Leary. He wet his lips with the tip of his tongue. He studied the floor. Then he reached into his pocket again and brought out a crumpled green bill. 'Two dollars, almost half a pound,' said the priest. 'It is all your uncle could spare.' He pushed the money into Joseph's hand.

Joseph leaned against the door and folded his arms across his bony chest. He surveyed the priest with what the old man knew for cold hate and revulsion.

'And my Dad?' he said at last, when the priest did not speak.

The priest's mouth shook, and he squeezed his eyes together. 'You will be remembering, Joey,' he said in a very low voice, 'that your mother, before she was taken, and after she had received, looked beyond us and cried out to your Dad, as if he were there, and she smiled and died with a smile of joy, recognising him.' He paused. The coughers had begun again, drearily.

Joseph did not move. 'You are telling me, I think, that my father is dead, too?'

The priest spread out his hands humbly, but could not meet the boy's stare. 'I believe she saw his soul, and he was waiting for her,' he whispered. 'It was a joyful reunion, and you must not grieve. They are safe with God.' Now he looked at Joseph and what he saw made him wince. 'It was two months ago, Joey. He died of the lung fever.'

I must not think, yet, thought Joseph. I must hear and know it all. 'And my uncle, Father?'

The priest hesitated. 'He has married, Joey.'

'And he has no room for us.'

'Joey. You must understand. He is a poor man. The two dollars he sent you is a sacrifice. This is not a land of gold at all, at all. It is a land of bitter labour, and the worker is driven like cattle. It is all your uncle can do for you.'

Joseph chewed his underlip and the priest wondered at his impassiveness. Joseph said, 'Then I need not spend the fifteen dollars to come back to New York from Philadelphia. There is nought to return to. There is no one.'

The priest spoke with compassionate eagerness. 'You must keep the money, Joey. There is an orphanage in Philadelphia, managed by the Sisters of Charity, where these with us are bound. I, too, am to live there. They will welcome the children of Danny Armagh and love them as their own.'

He paused. 'And it is possible that some good man, with money, will be joyful to adopt the little colleen, and Sean, and give them rich homes with warm fires and fine food and clothing.'

For the first time Joseph stirred and showed emotion. He stared at the priest in outraged fury. 'And is it mad you are, Father?' he exclaimed. 'My brother, and my sister, my flesh and blood, given to strangers so that I will not know how they fare or where they are? Is that permitted in this America, that my kin be taken from me? If so, we will return to Ireland.'

'Joey,' said the priest, sadly, 'I have the paper from your uncle, consenting.'

Joseph said, 'And let me see that famous paper.'

Father O'Leary hesitated again, then felt inside his habit and brought forth a paper and silently gave it to Joseph. The boy read: 'I hereby grant to religious authorities the privilege of conveying adoption in the matter of my deceased brother's children, Daniel Padraic Armagh, for they have neither father nor mother. Signed, John Sean Armagh.' The paper was written poorly but clearly, and dated this morning, March 1st, and signed.

Joseph, slowly and deliberately, and watching the priest balefully all the while, tore the paper into shreds, over and over, and then stuffed the remnants in his pocket.

The priest shook his head. 'Joey, Joey. That will do no good. I have but to send to your uncle for another paper. Ah, Joey, you are not dull. I taught you myself for nine years. You are but thirteen. How can you care for Sean and the babe?'

The blows of the last hours now began to ache agonisingly in Joseph, but he held himself still. His voice was stifled and gasping when he spoke. 'Father, I will work. I am strong. I will find work in this America. The children will be with the Sisters until I can provide a home for them. I will pay the Sisters. They will not be on charity. I will pay. And if I pay they cannot be taken from me.'

The priest could have wept. 'And what can you do, Joey?'

'I can write a fine hand, and that you taught me, Father. I can work in the fields and in the manufactories. Perhaps there will be work in the orphanage a strong man can do, fires to keep, walls and roofs to repair. I have worked, Father, and I know what work is, and I do not fear it. But you must not take my brother and my sister from me! If you do, Father, I will kill myself, and that I swear to you!'

'Joey, Joey!' cried the priest in horror. 'It is a mortal sin even to speak of that!'

'Mortal sin or not, that I shall do,' said Joseph, and the priest, with dread, knew that he was not speaking as a child but as a man. 'And you will be responsible for my lost soul.'

'You do not fear God,' said the priest, and blessed himself.

'I never feared anything,' said the boy. 'I shall not begin now. But mark me, Father, what I must do I will do.' He looked at the priest with renewed hatred. 'And that was what you were doing so long, Father, with my uncle this morning, while I waited. You were plotting against the children of Daniel Armagh, and telling my uncle how to write the letter. You were uncommonly sly, Father, but it has come to nothing.'

The priest studied him with both pity and dread. 'We thought it best,' he murmured. 'It was no wickedness we plotted against you, Joey. But if it is your will, then so be it.'

He left Joseph then and returned to Sean who was licking his fingers after eating the apple. The priest's eyes filled with tears again, and he held Sean to his breast.

'Mum?' said Sean, and his face twisted as he began to cry. 'I want my Mum.'

Joseph stood beside the priest. He thrust the two-dollar bill into his hand. 'This I owe you,' he said. 'I take no charity. Say a Mass for my mother for what is left.' He looked at the priest with daunting strength and aversion. Then he took his brother from the priest's knee and held his two hands in his own and looked down into the large tearful eyes.

'Sean,' he said, 'I am your father, and your mother now, and we are alone together. I will never leave you.' He lifted his hand less in a vow than an imprecation, thought the priest with a dim terror.

The ship was weighing anchor. It began to move from the harbour and the snow and rain hissed at the portholes and the wind howled in the lifted sails, and their last hope gone, the men and women in the steerage put their faces in their hands.

CHAPTER FOUR

'No,' said Joseph Francis Xavier Armagh, 'I am not Irish. I am a Scotsman.'

'Well, you don't look Irish, that's for sure. But that's a funny name, Armagh. What is it?'

'Scots,' said Joseph. 'An old Scots name. I am of the Established Church of Scotland.'

'Well, that's better than Irish,' said the fat man, with a smirk. 'Still and all, you're a foreigner. We don't like foreigners in this country. What do you mean, the Established Church?'

'Presbyterian,' said Joseph.

'I'm nothing, myself, though I'm no atheist,' said the fat man. 'Anyway, you're not a Roman. Hate Romans. Trying to take this country over for the Pope.' The fat man tilted his cigar and chuckled. 'Well, anyways, how old are you?'

'Eighteen,' said Joseph, who was sixteen.

The fat man nodded. 'Big strong fella, too. And you got the mean look I like. Hold your own. That's what I need, driving these big wagons. Know anything about horses?'

'Yes.'

'Don't talk much, do you? Just yes or no. Like that, too. Well, now. You know how these blue-noses in Pennsylvania are: agin drink of any kind.' The fat man spat into a spittoon lavishly. 'So the po-leese don't like wagons hauling beer and such on Sundays. Godless.' The fat man laughed again. 'But there's folks who need their drinks on Sundays, and who should be agin them? And saloons run short. So we haul the beer and likker on Sundays when we get calls. Saloons ain't supposed to stay open on Sundays, but they do a good back-door business. That's where we come in. You haul the beer and likker in a nice respectable-looking wagon with "grain-feed" on it, and you deliver and collect, and that's all there is to it.'

'Except the police,' said Joseph.

'Yeh,' said the fat man, suddenly and sharply scrutinising the boy again. ''Cept the po-leese. Ain't likely to bother you, though. Just drive sober and straight. Farm boy going home or something. Just don't lose your head. You don't look the kind, though, that would. Feed bags on top of the stuff. Let 'em look if they want to. Invite 'em to. That makes them sure it's all right. Then you drive on.'

'And if they do more than just take a look?'

The fat man shrugged. 'That's why I'm paying you a whole four dollars for one day's work, son. You get stupid. Someone gave you a little money to drive down a few streets. You don't know where, and you're supposed to meet a fella somewheres on a corner, and he's supposed to take over. That's all you know, see? The po-leese confiscates the stuff, and you get thrown in the pokey for a couple days, and that's all. When you get out you get ten dollars, from me. And the next Sunday you're on the job again. Simple. On a different route.'

Joseph considered. Four dollars a week! He made but four for six days a week, twelve hours a day, in a saw-mill on the river. It would come to eight dollars a week, a fortune. He looked at the fat man and loathed him.

'If you're thinking that I wouldn't pay you the ten dollars,' said the man.

'I've no fear of that,' said Joseph. 'After all, if you didn't, I'd go to the police, myself, and let my tongue wag.'

The fat man howled with laughter and slapped Joseph's knee. 'That's what I like! A man with spirit. Loyal, that's what it is. I treat you fair, you treat me fair. And you'll deliver right, too. I'm a man that keeps my word. And I got friends that help me, if a man does me wrong. Understand?'

Joseph stood up. 'Thank you. I will be here at six next Sunday, Mr Squibbs.'

He walked out of the gloomy anonymous little building that stood on the edge of the small town of Winfield, Pennsylvania. It was a wooden building and held but two offices and two desks and a few tables and chairs. On the side in huge whitewashed letters was the legend: 'Squibbs Bros. Dealers in wholesale grain and feed. Harness.' Behind the office building was a vast and well-kept stable of big dappled horses and vans. Behind this building was a warehouse of bagged corn and other grains, and harness. It was seemingly very legitimate. The warehouse and stables were full of men, not openly working – for that was forbidden on the Sabbath in Pennsylvania – but merely caring for the horses and watering and grooming and feeding them. Some saw Joseph emerge from the offices and studied him acutely, smoking their pipes, their caps pulled down over their brows. New fellow. Tall and hard-looking, and steady. Trust old Squibbs to pick them right. Never made but one mistake, and that was a smooth Federal-spy – and nobody ever saw that one again anywhere. Nobody.

And trust old Squibbs, too. If a wagon was ever traced back to him – and that was easy, his name was on the wagons, he didn't know nothing, either. Some trusted employee had taken advantage of him, that's all, doing some illegal work for some bootlegger or somebody on Sundays. Old Squibbs had the chief of police in his pocket, and was a big contributor to the Party. Even knew the Mayor, Tom Hennessey. Of course, the police, and everybody, knew it was old Squibbs all the time, but he never got hauled in, no sir. And none of his men ever served more than a day in the pokey, either.

Winfield was one hundred and fifty miles from Pittsburgh, a dull little town which had no major industry but the saw-mills on the river. Yet, it was a rich town, for many of its men dealt in illegalities, including slave-running, and other vices such as the transportation of farm girls and women to the large cities. The inhabitants preferred that the town seem to be poverty-stricken and humble, unworthy of notice and scrutiny, supported by its mills and the prosperous farmers beyond its confines. All spoke of 'tolerance' and 'brotherly love' and honoured William Penn, and no community was more ruthless and exploitative and bigoted than Winfield.

To Joseph Armagh, Winfield was repulsive, alien and lightless. Its ugliness and lack of colour disgusted him. The voices he heard were strange and discordant. Its lack of human diversity and lively movement depressed him. It was a grey prison and often he felt that he was smothering. His loneliness frequently overwhelmed him with despair of so active a nature that it was like an ague. He had lived here for three years and knew no one but the Sisters in the St Agnes Orphanage, and he had little conversation with his fellow-workers in the saw-mill.

The Sabbath evening was closing in this late November day while Joseph walked towards the orphanage which he visited once a week. He hurried, for it would soon be too late for visitors. He walked proudly, not bowing his head before the drizzle. He could smell the wet dust of the streets, and the

24

dead leaves in the gutter. The river wind exhaled an odour of fishy cold water, and a rancid stench of oil blew from somewhere. His pale young face was set but otherwise it expressed no emotion. He had learned that he must endure, and the Irish genius for endurance was strong in him. He passed a small livery stable in which a yellow light burned, and he saw the accustomed sign on the closed doors: 'No Irish Hired.' With this, too, he was familiar. He felt himself fortunate that he had his job on the river saw-mills and never could regret that he had called himself a Scotsman in order to obtain work.

He passed the filthy little saloons with the shut doors and the dark windows, and knew that in the rear revelry 'on the Sabbath' was in full voice. He hesitated. He was thirsty, and a mug of beer would be satisfying. But he had but fifty cents in one pocket and payday was not until Tuesday, and in the meantime he had to give his aching stomach some sustenance. In another pocket, pinned securely, were three dollar bills which he would give to the Sister Superior tonight for the weekly board of his brother and sister. So long as he supported Sean and Regina they could never be taken from him on the plea that they were indigent orphans.

He was recovering from a cold. He coughed harshly and noisily once or twice, and then spat. The rain was now pelting. He began a half-run. Against a sky becoming steadily darker he could see the steeple of St Agnes's Church, a miserable little building which had once been a barn, all grey walls and peeling paint and narrow plain glass windows and shingled roof which leaked during bad storms. It was open only for Sunday Mass and for the morning Mass during the week-days. Otherwise it was locked, for fear of vandals. Next to the church stood an equally miserable building, a little smaller, which had also been a big barn long ago, but which now housed five nuns and some forty children without homes or guardians. Somehow the nuns had gathered together enough money to enlarge the barn and make it a two-storey and ramshackle affair of wood and odds and ends of curious lumber, and somehow they had furnished it cleanly if meagrely. It stood, with the church, on a small plot of land which the men of the parish kept green and neat in the summer.

The people of the parish, to the rest of the inhabitants of Winfield, were pariah dogs, fit only for the dirtiest work. They were also the poorest paid. Their women worked in the houses of their superiors for small rations of food and two or three dollars a month. They brought the food home nightly to their families. The only joy any of them possessed was an occasional mug of beer, and their Church, and their Faith. Joseph Armagh never entered that church. He never mingled with the people. They had nothing to do with him, and his life, and the thoughts he thought, and the stony determination that lived in him like a dark fire. Once Father Barton, accosting him as he left the orphanage, had asked Joseph why he never attended Mass, and Joseph said nothing.

'Ah, I know it is the Irish bitterness in you,' said the young priest with sadness. 'You remember Ireland, and the English. But here, in America, we are free.'

'Free – for what, Father?'

The priest had looked at him earnestly, and then had winced at the sight of Joseph's face. 'To live,' he had murmured.

Joseph had burst out into ugly laughter, then, and had left him.

The priest then spoke of Joseph to the Superior of the combined convent and orphanage, Sister Elizabeth, a small, portly, middle-aged woman with gentle eyes, but also with a grim mouth and a will that, Father Barton suspected, not even God could bend. She was not the conventional docile and obedient nun. She feared no one – and possibly not even God, the priest also suspected with some interior misgivings, and she had a worldly, brief smile and an impatient air of tolerance when he delivered some small homily or pious aphorism to her. When he became particularly ethereal she would say quickly and with an abrupt motion of her small fat hand, 'Yes, yes, Father, but that will not buy any potatoes, I am thinking.' It was her famous reply to any maudlin remark or sentimental dithering on the part of anyone.

Father Barton had said to her, 'Joseph Armagh, Sister. I confess that he troubles me, for though he is very young he seems to have had experiences far beyond his age, and has become hard and vindictive over them, and unforgiving, and perhaps even vengeful.'

Sister Elizabeth considered, fixing her eyes upon the priest for several moments. Then she said, 'He has his reasons, Father, with which you and I may not agree, but they are his reasons, born out of sorrow, and he must find his way alone.'

'He needs the help of his Church, and his God,' said the priest.

'Father, has it ever occurred to you that Joseph has no Church, and no God?'

'At so young an age?' The priest's voice trembled.

'Father, he is not young, and it is possible that he never was.' With that reply she had closed the conversation and had bustled away, her wooden beads clicking.

Joseph reached the orphanage with its faint yellow lamps shining through the clean bare windows, and its whitened stone steps and its bare façade. Then he paused. Standing at the kerb was a wonderful equipage which he had never seen before in America but only coming or going to the great houses of the landed gentry in Ireland. It was a sleek and blackly polished closed carriage, with a coachman on its high seat, and with glittering windows and varnished wheels. Two horses drew it, as black as the carriage itself, and as sleek, and their harness gleamed like silver in the faint lamplight nearby.

The first curiosity Joseph had felt for years stirred him, but he shrugged and went up the shallow steps of the orphanage and pulled the bell. A young nun, Sister Frances, opened the door and smiled at him, though he never smiled in answer. 'And it's very late, Joseph,' she said. 'The children have supped and are at their prayers before bed.'

Joseph entered the damp hall without reply, though he wiped his feet on the bristled rug at the door very carefully. The nun closed the door after him. 'Only five minutes, Joseph,' she said. 'You'll wait in the parlour, as usual, and then I'll see.'

Joseph went into the little reception room which was as chill as death and dank, and smelled of beeswax and generous amounts of soap. The walls were white-plastered, and nothing the nuns could do could remove the stains of damp permanently. The floor was polished to brightness, and the room contained a table covered with a coarse linen cloth bordered with coarser lace and held the convent's cherished Bible bound in mouldering red leather, and nothing else except a lighted kerosene lamp. A tiny window near the ceiling let in the only daylight but never any sun, and there were four straight kitchen chairs ranged stiffly against the walls.

He sat on one of the stiff chairs and shivered, and he wondered, with alarm, if he had got another chill in the rain. The only fear that he ever allowed himself was the fear of desperate illness and unemployment and beggary, for he believed that in that event he would never see his brother and sister again, and they would be given for adoption to strangers whose names he would never know. None in Winfield had ever mentioned or hinted it, but he was convinced of it, remembering old Father O'Leary who had brought the family to this place and then had died a month later.

Joseph waited for his family, and he shivered again and remembered that he had had but one small meal today – all he could afford – and that a poor one of bread and cold bacon and black coffee in his boarding house. He was also cramped by pangs of hunger, and he rubbed his cold hands together and tried not to think of food. He raised his eyes and they encountered the crucifix, and for the first time he was aware of it clearly and there was a sudden and darkly violent convulsion in him.

'Sure, and You never helped anyone,' he said aloud. 'It is all lies, and that I am knowing and none can tell me anything else.'

The door opened and he looked at it eagerly, for what he would see was his only comfort and the source of his desperate cold determination. But it was Sister Elizabeth who was entering and he slowly rose to his feet and his face was as neutral and closed as always.

CHAPTER FIVE

'J o s e p h lad,' said the nun and held out her hand to him. It was a hand calloused and scored by endless hard work, but warm and strong. His own was cold and flaccid in it, and the nun was aware of the fact. But she smiled.

'Where is Sean, and Regina?' Joseph asked with no replying smile.

'Joey, sit down, do, and let me talk to you,' said Sister Elizabeth. 'Have no fear. The little ones are expecting you and they will be here presently. But I have something important to tell you.'

'They are sick!' said Joseph in a loud accusatory voice.

'Not at all,' said Sister Elizabeth, and no longer smiled. Her face became stern and commanding. 'Stand, if you will, and not sit. You are a very stubborn lad, Joey, and I am displeased with you. I thought I would speak to you as I would to a sensible man but I am afraid there is little hope of that! Ah, well. Did you notice that handsome carriage and all, outside, waiting?'

'What has it to do with me?' demanded Joseph.

She regarded him with compassion. 'Well, I must tell you. There is a beautiful young lady here, the wife of a gentleman of excellent prospects. She is, herself, rich and it is her house in which they live, and her servants, and she is almost the sole support of our church in Winfield, and it is she who pays for our food and shelter and clothing and boots, and she gives to the Missions and a seminary. But there is a bottom to every purse, I have heard, and she does all she can.

'She has a little daughter, the age of Mary Regina, but alas, she can have no more children. Her great heart longs for another little one, but it is not to be. It is God's will. So she wishes to adopt . . .'

'Regina?' said Joseph in a tone like a curse. 'Is that what you would tell me?'

'Joey . . .'

'How dared you show Regina to her!' His voice rose to a broken shout of rage and affront. 'Do I not pay for my sister? You would steal her from me, in spite of your mealy promises. You lied to me!'

She reached out, her face as hard as his, and she caught his thin arm and shook him. 'Speak to me not like that, Joey, or I shall leave you and say no more. In truth, I would leave you now were it not for Mary Regina and her future. I did not show your sister to this lady, whom I must call Mrs Smith, for you are not to know her name. She saw the child on one of her missions of mercy to this orphanage, bringing us rolls of wool and flannel, and some money, and she loved the child at once and thought of her as a sister for her own little one.

'Hark, Joey. Let the madness go from your mind a moment. What future has Mary Regina here, and in this city? You are only sixteen, poor lad. You are half-starved and live miserably, and though you have not told me I know. You have a brother, also. Life is not good for the Irish now in America, as you have discovered for yourself, and it may never be.' She lifted her eyes to the crucifix on the wall, and her face was pale. But she continued to talk quietly and resolutely.

'What life opens before Mary Regina, who needs a home and a mother's love and care and a future of peace and comfort, and education? At the best you may make some higher wages, but short of a miracle you will be hard pressed to support yourself and Sean for many years. In the meantime, you will live as you live, and there will be no hope for Mary Regina, and little for yourself and Sean.

'Do not the children of your dead parents deserve more than this? You are a man, Joey, and Sean will soon be a man, and life is not so hard for men as it is for women, and that we know. You will manage for yourselves. But what of Mary Regina? We can teach her her letters and domestic duties, but when she is fourteen we can no longer keep her here, for her place must be given to a younger girl. We have no choice. So Mary Regina must go into service and be a despised servant the rest of her life.

'You have told me, Joey, that when Mary Regina is fourteen you will be able to give her a good home of your own making. That is in less than eleven years. Do you believe this truly, Joey?'

'Yes,' said Joseph.

The nun sighed again and looked down at her clasped hands. 'You do not know the world, Joey, in spite of what you have already endured. You are very young, and so to you nothing is impossible. But, Joey, almost all of the dreams of the young come to nothing, and I have seen that for myself. I have seen hundreds of high young hearts broken, and die in the breaking. And I have heard the silence of despair, more times than I dare think of.' Her round voice, usually so full and assured, now sank into melancholy.

'Joey,' she continued after a moment, 'I do not deny that you may make your way, and well. But not with a sister to care for and protect. You must also think of Sean. Do not deprive Mary Regina of the mother and the love and the home this beautiful lady has offered her out of the goodness and tenderness of her heart. You dare not, Joey.'

His deep-set blue eyes fixed themselves with unmoving intensity upon the nun, and his wide thin mouth was like a blade.

'Think, Joey, before you speak,' said Sister Elizabeth.

Joseph began to walk up and down the little room, firmly and slowly, his hands in his pockets, his stare fixed blindly ahead of him. He suddenly halted before the nun. 'Let me see this precious lady,' he said.

Almost crying out in her joy Sister Elizabeth bounced to her feet and waddled swiftly from the room. Alone again Joseph turned and surveyed the crucifix. It seemed to flicker with life as the waning and brightening of the lamplight washed across it in waves.

The door opened and Sister Elizabeth entered, and a young lady with her. Joseph opened his eyes – they were sunken now as if from a profound illness.

'Mrs – Smith,' said the nun. 'This is Joseph Armagh, Mary Regina's brother, of whom I have told you. Joey?' She looked with dismay at the boy. Joseph was leaning against the wall and did not move and gave no response. But he was gazing with complete fixity at the young woman who stood near Sister Elizabeth.

She was young, possibly nineteen or twenty, tall and slender, with large dark eyes and a scarlet mouth. Under a bonnet of rich pink velvet, tied with pink satin ribbons, her hair curled. She wore a short jacket of some smooth dark fur, shining and expensive, and her elegant hooped skirt was of black velvet trimmed with gilt braid. She carried a muff in her gloved hands. There were diamond and ruby earrings in her ears. Her slippers were of velvet, with low heels, and beneath her skirt there was a hint of pantalettes of lace and silk.

Joseph had never seen any woman so lovely, nor one so richly clad. A faint odour of violets floated from her, and his nostrils distended, and not with pleasure. She was as far removed from him as any point in space that he could think of, and as alien as another species. He hated her and the hatred was like acid in his throat. They regarded each other in silence, and Sister Elizabeth earnestly looked from one to the other and prayed inwardly. Then Joseph said, 'And so you would buy my sister?'

Sister Elizabeth caught her breath. 'Joey,' she said with quiet sternness, 'that is most uncivil and wicked. There has been no talk of "buying", and that you know.' She tried to meet Joseph's eyes to command and reprove him, but he did not look away from Mrs Smith. It was as if he had not heard.

'Would you have my sister as a toy, a servant, for your own child?' Joseph asked.

Sister Elizabeth was aghast. Her round full face deepened in colour and her eyes were wide behind her glasses. But Mrs Smith, to her amazement, pleadingly touched her arm and said, 'Sister, I will answer Mr Armagh.'

Mrs Smith faced Joseph again and drew a long breath and her eyes met his widely. 'Not as a toy but as my own loved daughter, sister to my own Bernadette, cherished, guarded, protected with tenderness and devotion. She will inherit as my daughter will inherit. I have seen her but once and I loved her immediately, and it seemed to me that she was my very own, Mr Armagh, and my arms ached for her, and all my heart. Beyond that, I can say no more.'

Joseph's voice was quiet. 'Then you will give me a paper,' he said, 'written as I say, or there will be no more talk. My sister will keep her name, though you take her, for it is a great name in Ireland and proud I am of it, and my sister will be proud. She must always know that she has two brothers, and that one day we will claim her, and until that day I must see her as I see her now, and Sean must see her also. I will lend her, then, for the advantages you can give her now, as a companion to your own child, but only lend her.'

'But that is impossible!' exclaimed Sister Elizabeth. 'An adopted child takes the name of the adoptive parents and her new sister, and she is of the family and has no other, and must know no other! It is a protection for the child, herself, so that her heart is not divided nor her thoughts troubled. You must understand that, Joey.'

Joseph turned to the nun with repudiation. 'It is my flesh and blood we are speaking of, is it not, Sister? The flesh and blood of my own parents, the body of my sister Regina! It is you who cannot understand, I am thinking. A man does not give away what is of his flesh and blood and turn and never see it again, as if it was the family pig or goat going off to market! Regina is mine, as Sean is mine, and we belong to each other and never shall we be parted from each other. That is my final say, Sister, and if Mrs Smith refuses, then that is the end of it.'

Mrs Smith spoke again in her timid voice. 'Do you think, Mr Armagh, that you are being just to Regina to condemn her to live in an orphanage with no hope for her future? Do you think your mother would wish that?'

'My mother would wish her children to know each other and remain together,' said Joseph, and he made a gesture of dismissal.

'Wait. Please,' said Mrs Smith, and she put out her small gloved hand to him. 'My husband and I – we are leaving Winfield, and it may be that we shall never return. We are going to – to a distant city – for my husband is a man of consequence and has many ambitions. Regina would have to go with us . . .'

'No,' said Joseph and his voice was loud. 'We have talked too much. I have nothing more to say. I am here to see my brother and my sister, and I will see them alone – if you please.'

Mrs Smith bent her head, fumbled in her muff and brought forth a scented handkerchief which she put to her eyes. She burst into soft weeping.

'Joey,' said Sister Elizabeth, and she was very touched. 'It's a proud lad you are, and of proud blood as you have said yourself. But be careful that it does not lead you astray. And now, you cannot dispose of Mary Regina's fate as lightly as this.'

'There is more than money, Sister. There is a man's family, and he does not sell that family. I have nothing more to say.'

Sister Elizabeth put her arm about the sobbing young woman and led her away, murmuring consoling words.

The door opened and the two children came in, running, and calling his name, and he could not get up as yet to greet them, but held out his arms to them without a word and they ran to him. He lifted, with an enormous effort, the little girl to his knee and put an arm about Sean, Sean tall and very thin and fair and nine years old, and Regina but three.

'They made us wait a long time to see you, Joey,' said Sean, and leaned against his brother's shoulder.

'I had affairs to discuss with Sister,' he said, and turned all his attention to Regina, and his deep-set dark-blue eyes softened. For Regina, as the Sisters all said, was a delightful, grave child who seldom smiled, and who was unusually beautiful, with her long curling glossy black hair, white skin and rosy cheeks and lips, and eyes as dark a blue as Joseph's, but larger and rounder.

She was, to Joseph, dear above all other things in the world, dearer even than Sean, and far dearer than his own life. As if she knew that Joseph had undergone some recent travail she looked up silently into his face, and then she touched his cheek lightly. Sean was moving restlessly up and down the room, and endlessly chattering and questioning, but Joseph held his sister to him and felt that he had rescued her from something direful.

Sean stopped before his brother, jealously. 'And where is that fine home you have been promising us, Joey?' he demanded.

'Soon,' said Joseph, and he thought of the three years he had been in this country. Three years, and there was no home as he had promised his mother and then these children, but only an orphanage for Sean and Regina, and only a miserable tiny room for himself under the eaves of a widow's decaying house more than a mile from the orphanage.

He remembered that next Sunday he would receive four dollars for twelve hours of somewhat dangerous work, and he felt a sudden relief. He said to Sean again, 'Soon. It will not be long, now. I will bring you a cake next Sunday, and a cake for Regina.'

He put his arm about Sean again and held him to his side, and he held Regina to him also, and the children were silent now, watching him with quiet curiosity for they felt the hard concentration in him. None heard the door open and none saw Sister Elizabeth for a moment or two, on the threshold, and she stood there, her eyes burning with tears. Then she said, briskly, 'And it's still up, are you, Sean and Mary Regina, when you should be in bed? Off with you, and kiss your brother good night for he is tired, too.'

She bustled into the room keeping her mouth pressed tightly together for fear of its trembling, and she ruffled Sean's light hair with her plump hand, affectionately, and smoothed Regina's curls. Then, as if annoyed with herself, she hurried them out and closed the door smartly after them, grumbling. She had placed two parcels on one chair as she had entered. Joseph stood before her with cold and silent hostility, and she sighed.

'Well, Joey, all's been said that could be said, and I pray that you will not be regretting it. And now, we are not going to be silly tonight, are we, and refuse the little dinner Sister Mary Margaret packed for you, saying you are not hungry when I know you are, and raising the pride up in you again? For it's very thin and sickly you are, with your cold, and if you fall ill, who then will care for the little ones?'

It was an artful plea and Joseph glanced at the parcel on the chair and tried to prevent himself from shivering.

'And I have the usual books for you, too, Joey, left for you by a good man.'

Joseph went to the parcel and tried to ignore the thick bread and cheese and slice of fried pork fat, though his mouth watered for them instantly. He looked at the books in their separate parcel, wrapped in newspaper. There were four of them. There was always at least one every Sunday, and some he sold for a penny or two after he had read them and some he kept for re-reading. Tonight the parcel contained a book of pious reading with a frontispiece of a group of asexual angels standing on a pillar of white fire, a volume of Shakespeare's Sonnets, Charles Darwin's *Voyage of the Beagle*, which he examined with sharp intentness, and a volume of the philosophies of Descartes, Voltaire, Rousseau and Hobbes. As always, he felt a deep thrill of anticipation and excitement at the sight of books and the feel of them in his hand and the rustle of paper. They were like food and drink to him. He put down the book of pious readings with a small gesture of scorn, and wrapped up the other three books in the newspaper. Then he hesitated. Finally, with real reluctance, he lifted the parcel of food also. He said, 'Thank you, Sister.' But his white cheek-bones flushed with mortification. 'I can afford my dinners, Sister, but I am hungry tonight, and so I thank you.'

He tucked the parcels under his arm and removed his cap from the table.

'Joey,' said Sister Elizabeth, 'God go with you, my child.'

He was surprised at the emotion he saw on her face, for she was always so full of common-sense and never uttered pious aphorisms and blessings. He was not sure that what he felt in response was contempt or embarrassment, but he ducked his head and passed her with a final 'thank you'. She watched him go, not moving for a few moments. As he went by her secluded 'parlour' he heard Mrs Smith's soft mourning and now the voice of a man comforting her. He left the convent-orphanage, and the fine coach was still waiting. He walked slowly towards it, smiling as pleasantly as he could, and the coachman watched him come with sharp alertness and clutched his whip. Joseph stopped near him and stood back on his heels, and laughed.

'A noble carriage for Winfield,' he jeered. 'Does the gentleman keep it for his lady-love, perhaps, but not to be seen on the streets in the day?'

'It's a foul tongue you have in your head, boyeen!' shouted the coachman, and glared down at the haggard face below him and raised his whip. 'This is the carriage of himself, the Mayor of Winfield, and his lady, Mrs Tom Hennessey, and it's not in Winfield they live,' and he spat, 'but in Green Hills where the likes of you would skulk at the back door begging for bread! And be kicked off, down the road!'

Now Joseph's alarm reached icy terror, but he merely stood there and grinned up at the coachman. Then he finally shrugged, gave the carriage a last sneering glance and walked off. The Mayor of Winfield, and his lady, and they coveted Regina and would steal her if they could, like a picaninny in the hands of a blackbirder! Joseph hurried through the streets, panting, clutching his parcels, senseless fright snapping at his heels. It was not until he was near his rooming house, in the darkest and most poverty-stricken part of Winfield, that he was able to control himself.

He needed more money. Money was the answer to all things. Had he not read that somewhere, probably in the Bible his father had cherished at home, and which had gone with all the other Armagh treasures – 'A rich man's wealth is his strong city.' He had been determined from the beginning to be rich some day, but now his determination was complete. He thought of his mother, given to the sea after the ship had left New York, and his father in a pauper's grave, without stone or remembrance, and Joseph's mouth became a slit of pain in his stark face. He must have money. He no longer cared how he would obtain, not a comfortable wage, but money in profusion. It was a matter from this night on of discovering the secret, and he would find it. He would surely find it.

He thought of Mr Tom Hennessey, the Irishman who had made his fortune, it was said with truth, in blackbirding, and he had many interests in the great Commonwealth of Pennsylvania, and all of them, it was hinted, equally nefarious. It was his money which had made him mayor of this town, and which had given him a luxurious home in Green Hills, he the son of an Irish immigrant like Joseph Armagh, himself. The townsmen spoke in awe of him, while they sneered at his origins – but with a sort of indulgent fawning. Even an Irishman with money was to be respected and honoured, and caps lifted at his passing. What was it his lady had said? They would be going to another city, far away. Joseph could not afford the penny for a newspaper but he had heard the men at the saw-mill discussing that 'Papist' who had just been appointed by the State legislature as one of the two Senators to go to Washington. They pretended to despise him, but they were proud that a Senator – something like a member of the House of Lords, Joseph had thought – would be from their town and so add polish and pride to it. Besides, he had been born here, and he had been a less venal mayor than most, and had often expressed his 'fraternal interest' in the poor working man 'and the conditions of his work'. The fact that he had done nothing to help either was not held against him, and in spite of the general loathing and fear of 'Popery' Tom Hennessey was not suspected of secret unspeakable crimes except the ones less appalling, which were at least understandable and even to be admired as 'cuteness', and obsequiously envied.

Joseph crossed the mean town square. A street led off it, named Philadelphia Terrace, and here was the gritty and forlorn rooming house in which Joseph Armagh lived. It was a little woeful house, more decayed than its neighbours, and sagging and dilapidated, its clapboards pulling from the walls. One street-lamp lighted it feebly. It was past eight o'clock and all decent folk were in bed for the work tomorrow. Joseph pushed upon the unlocked door and made his way to the table on which his own lamp stood, filled and cleaned and ready to be carried up the creaking stairs which reeked of mould and dust and rodents and cabbage.

His room was hardly more than a cupboard and smelled of sifting dust and damp. He put the lamp on the commode. He looked about the hopeless dreariness of his 'home', and at the pile of books neatly stacked in one corner. Sudden heavy sleet began to hiss and rattle against the little window. Joseph took off his coat and covered the one blanket on his sagging bed with it, for extra warmth. Autumnal thunder, one loud and explosive clap, followed on a brilliant flare of lightning, and the wind rose and the glass in the window shook and one loose shutter banged somewhere.

Joseph was conscious of a nauseating ravenousness, and he sat on the edge of his bed and unwrapped the parcel of food.

He stuffed the stale bread and sour cheese and cold pork into his mouth rapidly, hardly chewing, so great was his hunger. He licked the crumbs of bread and cheese and fat from his fingers, voraciously, and was immediately strengthened.

The oily newspaper lay on his bed. An item caught his quick attention. He read it again and again. Then he lay back with his arms under his head, and thought for at least an hour. He thought only of money, and he had found the first step towards it. It was a matter, now, only of a little more patience, a little more knowledge, and much planning. Even when he blew out his lamp he continued to think, for once unaware of the sick smell of his flat pillow and the hammock-sag of his bed and the thinness of the blanket and coat which covered him. Out of terror and despair and hatred he had found the way. If it was not the one extolled in theology, it held, for Joseph Francis Xavier Armagh, far more truth and practicality.

CHAPTER SIX

THE names of the seven seceding Southern States of the Union, the initial affair at Fort Sumter, the agony of President Lincoln, were all unimportant to Joseph Armagh while the winter deepened. The world of men except as it pertained to himself and his family was unimportant. He wasted no penny on a newspaper; he never stopped in the streets of the town to hear the shouts and angry words of new crowds; he did not listen to his fellow-workers. They were aliens in an alien world, to him, which concerned him not at all: The language they spoke did not resound in him, their lives did not touch his nor did he permit them to touch his. When his landlady, Mrs Marshall, said to him once, fearfully, 'Oh, is it not terrible, Mr Armagh, this threat of war between the States?' he had replied with impatience, 'I am not interested, Mistress Marshall. I have too much to do.'

Mr Lincoln's train passed through Winfield on the route to Pittsburgh, and a holiday was given so that men could go to the depot for a brief glimpse of the melancholy man who was on his way to Washington for his inaugural as President. The majority wished him well, especially now that the threat of war was increasing, but the hint of assassination excited them and they would not have been too grieved had it come to pass. Their lives were so dingy, so obscure and so lacking in gaiety or any joy or notable event, that a national calamity would have titillated them. But Joseph Armagh, as indifferent to Mr Lincoln as he was to the existence of the farthest star, did not go to the depot. He had no interest in events except as they threatened him and Sean and Regina, for too deeply and at too young an age had he experienced anguish and frenzy and grief, and if he thought of his relationship to the world at all it was as its enemy.

Each Sunday, armed with a truncheon that never left the seat beside him, he drove a van or a wagon of ostensible feed and grain to the various saloons in the town. Each Sunday he collected the forty or fifty or sixty or even the one hundred dollars in payment for the true illicit load he carried under the burlap bags. The money was given him in brown paper, which he kept in his pockets – tight rolls tied with thick string. He delivered the money to Mr Squibbs, who was highly satisfied with his latest employee, and to such an extent that after the first few months he did not even count the money in Joseph's presence. He allowed his 'Sunday lads' fifty cents extra for a lunch, but Joseph did not spend it. He saved it, along with two of the four dollars he made on Sunday, and he had contrived a money-belt of sorts to tie about his waist, for he would not leave the bills in his boarding-house. Nor did he consider the bank, and for a reason pertinent to him.

The police never stopped or questioned him, and he was too indifferent to wonder why, though the ten dollars promised by Mr Squibbs would have been welcome even at the cost of a night in gaol. But for some reason he was not halted.

'He looks stupid, like a dummy,' said Mr Squibbs's brother. 'That's why the po-leese don't even see him. If they did they'd think we'd have more sense than to hire him to carry likker.'

Mr Squibbs chuckled. 'All the better. But he don't look stupid. Looks kind of like he don't even live here. Got a mean look in his eye, though, if you just try to be pleasant or make a joke, and he looks at you like you're pizen or somebody from the moon.'

The thoughts of Joseph Armagh were long thoughts, which would have appalled Sister Elizabeth. The money increased in his money-belt. He counted it every day or two, greasy bills of a great size which were more precious to him than his own life. They were the passports which guaranteed entry into living for his brother and sister. Without them, they would be barred for ever from the world in which they must live — which would never be his world. And as the months passed that which was within him became more taut and rigid, and more dangerous.

The Confederacy was making active plans for war. Not long after Mr Lincoln's inauguration three members of a Southern commission went to Washington to discuss with the President a more or less amiable agreement concerning public debts and public property, agreements which would go into effect after total separation of the Confederacy from the Union. They informed Mr Lincoln that 'we are the representatives of an independent nation, *de facto* and *de jure,* and we possess our own government perfect in all its parts and endowed with all the means of self-support, and we desire only a speedy adjustment of all questions in dispute on terms of amity, good-will and mutual interest.' To which Mr Lincoln sorrowfully replied that his new Secretary of State, William Seward of New York, would answer in due time.

The President understood the pride and the deep anger and affront which the South cherished, and he knew that according to the Constitution it had every right to secede from the Union. To object, to use force against the South, was unconstitutional, and none knew this better than the President. But as he loved his country, both North and South, he was as terrified as any man of his character could be.

On the warm April day when Captain George James fired on Ft Sumter, Joseph Armagh, after his day's work, set out on the three-mile walk to Green Hills, where the Mayor of Winfield lived. The roaring excitement in the town was, to him, like the far barking of dogs, and just as significant.

He knew that Mayor Hennessey lived on Willoughby Terrace, and he watched for discreet board signs as roads were increasingly named. Then he came on it to his right and he turned off the rough main road on to a narrower but smoother road, very winding and overhung with oaks and elms and maples. A low greystone wall followed the road instead of iron fences and gates and over this he could see the mansions, some sunken below the rising ground of the distance, some bold and standing like monarchs on their land. Dogs barked warningly, and some collies raced across lawns to the stone walls and challenged Joseph's passing. He did not pause or even look at them. He was watching for an iron shield embedded in the wall with the number eighteen upon it in Gothic scroll. He finally found it, and stopped to look past the lawns which rolled and spread serenely over several acres.

The Mayor's white house was the largest and most imposing of any which Joseph had seen so far, and the most opulent and pretentious. Its centre was of the classic outdoor portico type of ancient Roman fashion with smooth white pillars and Corinthian capitals and frescoes and ponderous carved bases. The floor within was of white stone, gleaming and polished as marble, leading to mighty double bronze doors of Italian origin. On each side of the tall porticoed entrance structure stretched a two-storeyed wing, broad as well as high, with ornamental friezes near the eaves and a wide balcony at the end, extending from the upper floor. Every window was partly shaded by shirred grey silk, glimmering as silver; flowering spring shrubs, yellow and snowy, pressed against the shining walls. Great pruned trees were scattered in groups of twos and threes on the lawn, and every blade of grass had its own iridescence in the lowering light of early evening.

So, thought Joseph, himself lives here and his money came from human misery and death and despair, as always it does. Yet, there is none to reproach him, neither God nor man, and all fawn upon him and he will be a Senator and crowds will laud him and he will have the ear of the President and all will honour his riches and consider him worthier than other men because of it. I, too, honour him, for he is a thief and a murderer and a mountebank and a whoremonger – and does the world not prefer such to an honest and devoted man? It can only be that the good and noble man is a fool, despised by God, for does not the Bible say, 'The wicked flourish like a green bay tree' and their children dance with joy in the streets? It is true.

He leaned his elbows on the wall and contemplated the grounds and the mansion and listened to the evensong of the birds. Here would his sister, Regina, have lived had he permitted it, slowly forgetting that she was of another family, lost to him and Sean for ever. She would have slept in one of those chambers of the upper storey, and would have run on these lawns. But, she would no longer be Mary Regina Armagh of a prouder name than Hennessey and it would be as if she had died, and she would finally have believed that those within were her family and she had no other, and her love would be for unworthy strangers.

Not for an instant did Joseph regret his decision concerning his sister. He could only smile grimly at the house and nod his head over and over again as in secret agreement with himself.

He heard the shrill ringing sound of a young child's voice, and a very little girl came suddenly running across the grass towards the wall where he stood, and she was followed by an elderly woman in the blue cotton dress, white apron and cap of a nursemaid. Joseph stood in brushy shadow and he looked at the child, who was about Regina's age and screaming with malicious mirth. She was somewhat smaller than Regina, but plump, and she wore a frock of white silk and a jacket of blue velvet trimmed with silver embroidery and as her tiny petticoats swayed they revealed the ruffles of lace pantalettes and black slippers and white silk stockings.

She had a round golden face, saucy and rather flat, and merry hazel eyes, and her smooth brown hair had been trained into glistening curls that reached almost to her shoulders. Her lips were full and red and showed bright teeth, and her nose was tilted. It was not a pretty face, but she had a look of constant mirth that was very attractive and even fascinating. Regina was grave and thoughtful. This child – Bernadette, is it? – had probably never wept for fear in her life and probably had no thoughts but of her own babyish satisfaction. Like Regina, she was four years old.

She had almost reached the wall but did not see the watching Joseph in the shadows. She looked about her with gleeful mischief, and as the nursemaid, uttering loud reproaches, was almost upon her, she darted away like a squirrel, squealing with impish laughter, showing her pantalettes up to her fat thighs. She ran very fast and soon she was lost among the trees and the panting old nursemaid stopped to catch her breath and shake her head.

The long spring twilight began to flow over the lawns and Joseph turned away and began his long walk back to Winfield. A mist was rising over the ground now and the joyous cries of the peepers were louder and more insistent. The sky was a pure soft green and the orange of the west had turned to scarlet. A wind came up, heavily scented by warming pines and living plants.

Joseph had just reached the intersection of the private road with the main road when he heard the rattling of wheels and the rapid pound of hoofs. He looked down the broad road and saw an open Victoria approaching, pulled by two beautiful white horses. A coachman, young and in fine livery, was driving the horses and he looked at Joseph out of a broad and bellicose face, snapping his whip, as the carriage turned in on Willoughby Terrace. But Joseph did not look at him. He was staring at the occupant of the Victoria, and he had no doubt at all that this was Mayor Tom Hennessey, for he had once seen his likeness in a newspaper which had enclosed his lunch.

As Mrs Hennessey was young, Joseph had thought to see a young husband, for the likeness had been flattering. But Tom Hennessey appeared to be a man approaching forty at least, a big, wide, handsome man with a wenching and florid face and slate-grey, narrow eyes, and an exigent, even brutal, mouth. He had the Irish long lip, as Joseph had also, but a thick ridge of a nose protruded above it, giving his face an arrogant and scoundrelly expression. His chin was smooth-shaven, as was his lip, and heavy and dimpled, and it indicated common blood.

He was clad in fawn broadcloth with a greatcoat of brown velvety cloth, and his waistcoat was richly embroidered. He wore a tall and shining hat, and from under it flowed his brown and waving hair and his brown sideburns. He looked potent and virile and cruel, though his mouth was automatically arranged in a look of amity and humour. His gloved hands rested on an ebony walking-stick with a gold head, and his jewellery was flashing and considerably vulgar.

Foot travellers were few on Willoughby Terrace and Tom Hennessey's attention was caught by the sight of this tall, thin youth with the beggarly clothing and workman's boots and woollen cap. A servant? A gardening hand? Tom Hennessey had the born politician's powers of keen observation and he missed nothing, no matter how unimportant. The sunken blue eyes of Joseph were met squarely in sudden confrontation with the merciless grey eyes of the older man. It was absurd to the Mayor, but something which had quickened shot between them and the Mayor was fully conscious of it as was

43

Joseph. The Mayor touched the rump of his coachman with the tip of his cane and the man brought the horse to a halt very close to the stranger.

The Mayor had a round and sonorous voice, the voice of a blackguard politician, and it was mellifluous and fruity in addition, trained as it was by ruthless guile. He said to Joseph, 'Do you live on these estates, my lad?'

Joseph wanted to go on with a mumble but his own interest in the Mayor held him near to the horses' heads. 'No,' he said, 'I do not.'

Tom Hennessey had been born in Pennsylvania, but his father had been born in Ireland and he well remembered the rich brogue and it echoed now in Joseph's voice. Tom's eyes sharpened. He studied Joseph calmly from his seat in the Victoria.

'What is it, then, that you do?' he asked and smiled his engaging smile.

Joseph looked at him in silence and not with trepidation. 'It's out for a walk, I am,' he replied. Now he became wary. If this man spoke to his wife of Joseph's appearance, and his Irish intonations, then she would immediately suspect Joseph's identity. There would be no danger in that, but to Joseph the whole world was dangerous and should not be informed. He added, 'I am a gardener's helper.'

'Hum,' said the Mayor. Had not the news been so portentous today, and were he not turning hurriedly home from Winfield to pack for a fast journey to Washington – as a Senator just confirmed by the State legislature – he would have taken the time to satisfy his curiosity about Joseph. Abruptly, he ordered the coachman to drive on. But Joseph stood and watched the vehicle until it was out of sight beyond a bend in the road. He smiled a little. His conviction that he had been only too right concerning Regina's adoption was confirmed. A father like that – he would inevitably have poisoned that young soul with his own sensuality and coarseness. Shanty Irish, commented Joseph to himself, in scorn, as he walked rapidly towards town. Did America, then, have no pride that she should honour such as Tom Hennessey and raise them to high estate? Joseph, for the first time in years, began to whistle as he walked back to Winfield, and his young heart was lighter than it had been since he had been a child. If the Tom Hennesseys could become rich and famous and honoured in this America, then an Armagh could also, and easier.

It was dark when he reached his boarding-house and again he read what he had first read last November on a black and sleeting night in the midst of his suffering, and he thought and said to himself: It will be next Sunday.

CHAPTER SEVEN

O N Saturday night, after work, Joseph counted up the money he had saved. It amounted to seventy-two dollars, after nearly six months of Sunday work, and sacrifice and the payment of three dollars a week to the orphanage. It seemed an enormous sum to Joseph, but he knew it was not enough.

He carefully wrote a letter, bought a stamp at the post-office, near the depot, and mailed it. It was the first posted letter he had ever written in America. Absently, he noted the large poster in brilliant red, white and blue on the post-office walls, urgently calling for volunteers for the army and the cavalry and the navy, but it meant nothing to him though he was surrounded by men who excitedly discussed it. He went out, unseen and himself indifferent.

He went to the orphanage, though this was but Saturday night, and Sister Elizabeth was surprised to see him. 'The children are in bed,' she said. 'But I will ask Sister to bring them to you if you cannot see them tomorrow, Joey.'

'No,' he said. If he saw his brother and sister now it would be a weakness he could not afford, and might hold him back.

He said, 'Sister, I am going away for a little while, a few months, perhaps a year. I have another job, in Pittsburgh, which will pay me better.'

'Capital, Joey!' she said, and looked at him searchingly. 'Oh, Joey, you are going to join the army?'

'No.' The idea amused him, and he gave the nun his dark, unmirthful smile. 'But it is connected in some fashion, Sister. It will pay me very well – in Pittsburgh.'

'You must write as soon as you are settled,' said Sister Elizabeth.

45

'I will.' He looked down into her shrewd eyes, and hesitated a moment. 'I hope, in the near future, to send for Sean and Regina.'

'I see,' said the nun. 'You will send your address?'

Joseph paused. 'I will not be staying, Sister, at one place, but I will send money now and then.' He put a roll of bills into her hand. 'There is fifty dollars here, Sister, for Sean and Regina, for their board. When that is gone there will be more from me.'

Her peculiar uneasiness sharpened. 'I wish I could know that all will be well for you, Joey.'

'Sister, your meaning of "well" may not be mine, I am thinking.'

He went out into the early night, unaware that Sister Elizabeth was watching him from the doorway, and he looked back at the façade of the convent-orphanage for the last time. He knew he would never see it again, and he was thankful. He thought of his brother and sister asleep behind those frail wooden walls, and he pressed his lips together against a wince of pain that he was leaving them without a good-bye.

He returned to his boarding-house and looked at his few belongings. He would have to leave his beloved books. He laid out his one change of clothing beyond what he already wore. He packed these tightly in a cardboard box, pitifully small, even though it included another pair of mended boots. He was glad that it was still cool enough, at night, to wear his patched greatcoat. He lay down on his bed and went to sleep at once, for long ago he had taught himself to sleep immediately and on demand. The violet twilight deepened outside and the swallows flew against a purpling sky, and the town murmured with the excitement of threatened war. But Joseph Armagh slept with resolution for it had nothing to do with him.

It was only faintly light when Joseph awoke in the morning. The silence was total, for it was too early even for church bells. The air, he was pleased to feel, was a little chilly and so his greatcoat would excite no attention. He wrote a note on a piece of brown paper to Mrs Marshall: 'I am sorry to leave you, Mistress Marshall, but I have been offered an excellent post in Pittsburgh and will leave for it today. I could not give you notice, but kindly accept, with my compliments, this ten-dollar gold certificate. I will not be returning. I am grateful for your kindness to me in the past. Your obedient Servant, Joseph Armagh.'

He looked at his books. He lifted the thin volume of Shakespeare's Sonnets and pushed it under his blue cotton shirt. He picked up his cardboard box and stole silently from the house, never looking back. Like Sister Elizabeth, it no longer existed for him. The street lost its familiarity. He was done with it. Again, he was an absolute alien in an alien land.

He had always carried his lunch in the cardboard box which now held his few possessions, so no one at Squibbs Bros. noted it as he arrived at the stables and office. His wagon and the horses were waiting for him. The first pale sun was touching high chimneys and the tops of trees, but the earth was still in morning twilight. There was a hint of the coming hot summer in the air.

'Good load today, Scottie,' said the foreman. 'People are thirsty, thinking of the war,' and he chuckled. He gave Joseph the customary few cents for his lunch and Joseph nodded, tucked the coins in his pocket and lifted the reins. 'Big load,' said the foreman. 'Could be you'll be getting back late.'

'It doesn't matter,' said Joseph. 'But do not forget the extra fifty cents if I am.'

The town was still silent though here and there flutters of grey smoke were rising from chimneys. Not even the horsecars were running as yet. Joseph tied up the horses six streets from the depot, then ran swiftly. The railroad depot was just opening, for the seven-ten was expected in an hour from Philadelphia. He hurried to the counter and asked for a ticket to Pittsburgh on the late afternoon train, and paid for it: two dollars from his store. He put the ticket in his pocket. The old station-master would remember, if asked, that a young man he had never seen before had that morning bought a ticket to Pittsburgh for two dollars. But it was very improbable that he would be asked. Moreover, Joseph had carefully tucked the last thread of his russet hair under his workman's cap and he appeared insignificant enough, and the station-master had seen no wagon and no horses. Ah, thought Joseph, poverty is marvellously anonymous.

He raced back to his tethered horses and found them peacefully cropping some blades of grass that had forced them-

47

selves through the bricks of the road. He climbed on to his seat and set about his deliveries. By ten o'clock he had collected sixty dollars. At this time the people were going to church in the quiet and sunlit town, most on foot, a number in buggies or carry-alls or shabby surries, and all dressed respectably and all with pious, downcast eyes. They did not notice the heavy wagon lumbering slowly along the kerb or if they did they ignored it. They did not speak of the approaching conflict or even of the beset President, for such was 'unseemly' on the Sabbath. Church bells began to ring, competing stridently from steeple to steeple, and Joseph could hear the solemn murmurings of organs through doors open to the warming air.

By three o'clock he had collected over one hundred and fifty dollars and had watered his horses at a street trough and had fed them their oats in the bags. He had also eaten his dry lunch. At four he admitted to a furtive saloon-keeper that he was thirsty and hungry and accepted, for thirty cents, two large mugs of foaming yellow beer and a package of hard-boiled eggs, four ham sandwiches, a German sausage in a long bun, and two pickles and one salt herring and two slices of seed-cake, including a package of potato salad, a German delicacy he had never eaten before. He complained about the price, and so the saloon-keeper returned five cents and magnanimously included another mug of beer. He gave Joseph forty dollars. At the next saloon, at five, Joseph collected another fifty dollars. It had been a very successful day, and the load had been twice as much as usual as Mr Squibbs had learned to trust his newest 'Sunday lad'.

Two hundred and forty dollars. With the twelve dollars in his money-belt it reached the enormous sum of two hundred and fifty-two dollars. At half past five he turned his wagon about, reached a street of warehouses completely barren on this Sunday of any passers-by or vehicles, abandoned the horses after patting them, and ran for the depot. He reached it just as a train in the station, with its gigantic funnel and blinking headlight, was shrilly sounding its bell and letting off painful shrieks of steam. Its wheels were already grinding as Joseph leaped aboard the last coach. The conductor, about to shut the door, growled at him, 'Almost got kilt, you did, and where's your ticket?' He suspiciously examined it front and back and glared at Joseph who muttered something in what he hoped would pass as a foreign language. The conductor sniffed, said, 'Foreigners! Cain't even speak a word of English!' Joseph humbly touched his cap, gabbled again pleadingly. The conductor roughly pushed him inside the coach and forgot him.

Joseph, whose breath was short from his long run, found the coach partly empty and so he chose a seat in the rear and huddled down, pulling his cap as far over his eyes as he could. He did not take off his cap but he loosened his greatcoat. He discovered that he had not only taken his cardboard box with his belongings, but had accidentally included his protective truncheon as well. This amused him. Cautiously, watching his fellow-passengers all the while, he pushed the weapon into the long side-pocket of his coat. It seemed, to his Irish soul, that this was some sort of an omen, though he usually despised superstition.

He hoped that the horses, intelligent beasts, would eventually grow tired of waiting for him – for he had not tethered them – and would find their way back to their stables. By now it was past time when he should be arriving at the stables, himself, with that great sum of money. He knew that the other men would be looking up the street for him. By eight o'clock they would be searching and would be making the rounds of the saloons. By ten they would be convinced that he had departed with the collections. By eight tomorrow Mr Squibbs would receive his letter:

'I have not stolen your money, sir, but have only borrowed it, on my honour. I have been offered a fine post in Pittsburgh and needed some money to tide me over until I have become settled. You may find this very reprehensible, sir, but I beg of you to trust me for a few months, when I will return your money with six per cent interest. I am no thief, sir, but only a poor Scotsman in desperate circumstances. Resp'y your Servant, Joseph Armagh.'

Mr Squibbs would not dare to go to the police for a variety of reasons, and his thugs would not find a Joseph Armagh in the big city of Pittsburgh, for the simple reason that Joseph's destination was not Pittsburgh at all. He felt in his pocket for the worn newspaper clipping he had kept these long months and re-read it:

'More and more fine oil wells are being drilled at Titusville

49

monthly and are richly yielding, some of them thousands of barrels a week at least. The little town is booming as the Klondike in '45, and workers are receiving unbelievable wages. Men are flocking from all over Pennsylvania and other States to work in the fields, and regrettable Vice is accompanying them as it always does Riches. Incredible wages of up to twelve and even fifteen dollars a week are being paid for mean labour such as hauling the oil barrels to the flat-boats and loading them. Those engaged in drilling, it is rumoured, receive far more. So close to the surface is the Rich Oil Deposit that it gushes out of the ground on mere drilling. But a few of the wells are much deeper, and these have the best of oil, more refined. So some are being "blown" by nitro-glycerine, though not many, and it is quite a novelty. Intrepid young men, with apparently no regard for their Lives, are willing to haul nitro-glycerine, a very dangerous Element, for the wells, and it is said that they can receive up to twenty dollars a week, unheard-of Recompense. No wonder Corruption is an inevitable Companion, and there are now more saloons in Titusville than there are churches, impossible though this may be in the opinion of Our Readers. It is fortunate that Titusville still has only one train a week, on Sunday night, but it is expected that in a few months it will have daily runs and our Fears mount accordingly. It is hoped that young Men of Decorum in other sections of the State will not rush to Titusville to make their fortunes but to imperil their Souls.

'It is rumoured that Pithole, a few miles from Titusville, has even more astounding Oil deposits, but it is in rough country and is arduous to reach over some formidable hills and rude territory. Men from Titusville and other parts of the State, it is said, are buying up land near Pithole and hope to do what, in their parlance, is called "wild-catting". It is said that "oil lies on the very ground and in holes and pits, ready for the taking, without drilling, in Pithole". Alas, if it is so, for a quiet and God-fearing community of a few souls. If enough oil is discovered there a shuttle may be run to Pithole, but that, we hope, will never transpire. There are enough ruthless Entrepreneurs and Gamblers already in Titusville, with eyes on Pithole, and are selling stock certificates hand over fist for Enormous Sums. Yet the Standard Oil Company, we have heard, is evincing interest. So far the owners of the oil-fields in Titusville have resisted the blandishments of the Standard Oil

Company, so the battle continues for control of the new wealth which will soon entirely eliminate, it is believed, the market for whale and other oils. We are not that sanguine, for we have heard that the odour of crude natural oil is beyond bearing and creates Hazards of smoke and fire.

'While we all rejoice at the abounding wealth of our Great Commonwealth, we must also mourn that its Cohorts abound also, women of unspeakable morals and card-sharps and the vendors of liquors and beer, and dance-halls and opera houses and other dens of Vice. We pray with the deepest piety and apprehension, for the Souls of . . .' But Joseph had torn off the rest and had kept the clipping.

He tucked the paper in his pocket again. Months ago he had decided to become an 'Evil Entrepreneur' as soon as possible. Men do not get rich by honest labour, he had often thought. They study and then gamble cautiously, but not too cautiously. He knew the danger of failure, but he did not intend to fail. He thought of Pithole as well as Titusville, and the oil which lay there for the taking. He had no grandiloquent dreams of sudden fortune, but he had the intuition of the Irish for the place of eventual fortunes, if a man used his intelligence and overlooked no opportunity.

It was dark beyond the train window. Joseph opened his parcel of food and devoured three hard-boiled eggs, all the ham sandwiches and pickles and herring and the sausage and its bun, and then finished the meal with the cake. The whistle howled as the train pounded through the hidden countryside and past little villages and tiny lighted depots where it did not stop. The steam and soot spewing past the window were lighted with red sparks, and some of the filth found its way even into the shut coach and the murk and smoke set all to coughing. Joseph saw that his hands were already blackened and he suspected that his face was, also. He had no watch. He did not know the time and dared not ask the trainman for fear of revealing that he understood English. But he knew that the train stopped at a small town in about two hours, and had a shuttle to Titusville, and that it met this train before it turned east towards Pittsburgh.

He thought of Corland, twenty miles from Titusville, and he said to himself, 'I have found a way to be rich, and nothing will stop me!' It needed only what Americans called 'a stake', and that he would have in a very short time. It needed con-

CHAPTER EIGHT

The train for Titusville had not yet arrived when Joseph's train reached the little town of Wheatfield. So, with others, he left his train, pulled his cap down lower on his forehead and tried to appear as inconspicuous as possible as he entered the hot little depot, which was well lighted and crowded to its walls. Joseph had never seen such a bewildering gathering of men as he saw now. There were men in silk and tall beaver hats, rich greatcoats and florid waistcoats and splendidly pinned cravats and fawn pantaloons, men fat and red and sweating of face and with flowing hair and sideburns and exquisitely trimmed beards and moustaches, and carrying Malacca canes with gold or carved silver heads and with fat fingers loaded with sparkling rings and with watch-chains embellished with jewelled charms. They all smoked thick cigars or cheroots and they smelled of bay rum or racier perfumes, and their boots shone daintily. Among them milled workmen in cloth caps and patched coats and blue shirts stained with sweat and oil and dirt. There were also the quiet and deadly men in subdued but rich clothing along the walls, watching all newcomers closely, their rings shining, their shirts ruffled and fluted, their cravats and pantaloons and waistcoats elegant. These were the hunters and gamblers.

Posters imploring enlistments covered the dirty stained walls of the little depot and in one corner stood a young lieutenant in blue with his forage cap smartly over his forehead, a little table before him and two soldiers soliciting the younger men to join 'the patriotic service of your choice'.

The uproar was appalling with the constant crescendoes of masculine voices arguing, wheedling, boasting, promising, and raucous. Spittoons were ignored. The floor was almost covered with blackish-brown slime. The stench and the heat overpowered Joseph and he kept near the door in spite of the jostling he received. Men shouldered others aside, were cursed or clapped on the back. There was an odour of raw whisky as men tilted bottles to their mouths. The depot was like an enormous monkey-house, seething with heat and movement and restiveness and vehement roars and impassioned shouts and great belly-laughter and good-humoured imprecations. Men fell over luggage on the dirty floor, cursed, laughed or kicked aside the portmanteaux and bags. The young army lieutenant surveyed the dazing movement in genteel bafflement, for it was apparent that he was a gentleman among men who were certainly not gentlemen. He had been taught goodwill by his mother and his mentors, and he struggled to maintain it, keeping a reserved but friendly half-smile fixed on his boyish moustached face. But his expression was becoming haunted. The flag at his right hung limply in the suffocating and noxious air.

After a little Joseph could endure it no longer and he went out on the platform and looked down the tracks which were silvered by the moonlight. Here, at least, there was the cleaner smell of steel and cinders and dust and warmed wood and rock. The lights of Wheatfield glimmered dimly in the distance. The moon rode in a black sky seemingly without stars. Occasionally the platform vibrated as clots of men exploded from the depot to look down the tracks also.

At last Joseph became aware that someone had been standing silently beside him for several minutes and would not move away. He ignored the presence, continuing to stare glumly down the tracks. He was very tired after his long day, and he knew he would have a miserable ride to Titusville, and he was becoming afraid that if he were not vigilant there would be no room on the train for him.

'Got a lucifer, Mister?' the presence asked at last in a very young voice.

Joseph did not turn. 'No,' he said in his usual short fashion when approached by strangers. Fear came to him. Had he been followed after all? It was this fear and not mere curiosity which made him cautiously move his head a little and glance sideways through the corner of his eyes. But what he saw reassured him. The presence was smaller than he, and infinitely more shabby, even ragged, and it was only a boy about fifteen years old, a boy without a cap or hat or coat, and

53

very thin. He had a starveling appearance but not one of degradation nor had he spoken with the snivelling importunity such as the very poor affected.

His whole appearance and manner were astonishingly lively, even gay and light-hearted, as if he were perpetually happy and interested and cheerful. Joseph, accustomed to the bland anonymity of the Anglo-Saxon appearance in Winfield, was surprised at the elfish face which hardly rose to his shoulder, a dark face, almost brown, the black eyes gleaming through lashes silken and glimmering, and the mop of vital black curls and the prominent 'hooked' nose. The undisciplined and obviously uncombed hair spilled over the low brown forehead. A pointed chin with a dimple, and a smiling red mouth, added reckless gaiety to the impudent face, and white teeth shone eagerly between moist lips.

'I don't even have a cheroot or a stub,' said the boy, with actual glee. 'I just wanted to talk.' His voice was light, almost as light as a girl's, and faintly and exotically accented. He laughed at himself. But when he saw Joseph's truculent expression and his cold, half-averted ironic eyes, he stopped laughing though he continued to smile hopefully. 'I just wanted to talk,' he repeated.

'I just don't want to talk,' said Joseph, and turned aside and studied the rails again.

There was a little silence. Then the boy said, 'My name's Haroun. You goin' to Titusville, too?'

Joseph's mouth tightened. He debated a lie. But this strange boy might be on the same train and he would appear foolish or a suspicious runaway or a criminal in flight. So he nodded his head.

'Me too,' said Haroun. Joseph permitted himself to glance swiftly at that remarkable young face again. The boy was encouraged. He gave Joseph a very large smile. 'You can make lots of money in Titusville,' he said. 'If you've got a mind to, and I don't have nothin' else to put my mind to so I am goin' to make money!' He laughed joyously and Joseph, to his own amazement, felt his face move into a smile.

'I can say that, too,' he said, and was again amazed at himself.

'All I got in this world is six bits,' said Haroun. 'All I make is two dollars a week in the blacksmith shop, and a bed in the hay-loft and some bread and bacon in the mornin'. It wasn't bad, though. Learnt how to shoe horses and that's a good trade, yes sir, and you can always make a livin' at it. I'd'a saved money from that two dollars but I had my old granny to take care of, and she was sick and there was medicine, and then she died. God rest her soul,' added Haroun with no melancholy in his voice but only affection. 'Took care of me after my people died, here in Wheatfield, when I was a little shaver, washin' clothes for the quality folk when she could get work. Anyway, she died, and she's buried in Potter's Field, but I think like this: where does it matter where you're buried? You're dead, ain't you? And your soul's gone off some place but I don't believe up in any heaven as my granny told it to me. Anyway, after I bought my ticket today I've got six bits until I can find work in Titusville, or maybe Corland.'

The recital was so artless yet so explicit and so full of confidence and inner surety that Joseph was reluctantly intrigued. Here was one who totally loved life and believed in it and found it blithe, and even Joseph in his youth could recognise the soul which was not only indomitable but light-hearted.

Haroun permitted himself, without resentment or uneasiness, to be inspected. He even seemed amused.

Joseph said, 'How far do you think you can go on six bits?'

Haroun listened acutely to his voice. 'Hey, you're a foreigner, like me, ain't you?' He stuck out his small brown hand frankly and Joseph found himself taking it. It was like hard warm wood in his fingers. 'Where you from?'

Joseph hesitated. His associates at work in Winfield had known him as a Scotsman. Now he said, 'Ireland. A long time ago. And you?'

The boy answered, shrugging eloquently. 'Don't know where it is, but I heard it was Lebanon. A funny place, near Egypt or maybe it was China. One of them places. What does it matter where you're born?'

Joseph, the proud, looked at him coldly then decided that one so ignorant deserved no rebuke but only indifference. He was about to turn finally away and into the depot to escape the boy when Haroun said, 'Hey, I'll share my six bits with you if you want to.'

Joseph was freshly amazed. He looked over his shoulder and halted and said, 'Why should you do that? You don't even know me.'

Haroun grinned whitely and the great black eyes laughed.

'It'd be Christian, wouldn't it?' And his voice rippled with mischief.

'I'm not a Christian,' said Joseph. 'Are you?'

'Greek Orthodox. That's what my folks were, from Lebanon. That's where I was baptised. Haroun Zieff. I was only a year old when they come here, to Wheatfield. My Pa was a weaver, but he and my Ma got sick here and died, and so there was just me and Granny.'

Joseph considered him again, half turning. 'Why are you telling me all this?' he asked. 'Do you tell every stranger your whole history? It's dangerous, that it is.'

'Why? Why's it dangerous? Who'd hurt me?'

'Best to keep your own counsel,' said Joseph. 'The less people know about you the less harm they can do you.'

'You talk like an old man,' said Haroun, kindly and with no rancour. 'You can't sit around all the time and wait for someone to knife you, can you?'

'No. Just be prepared, that's all.' Joseph could not help smiling a little.

Haroun shook his head violently. 'I'd hate to live like that,' he said. Then he laughed. 'Maybe nobody ever hurt me bad because I didn't have anything they wanted.'

One of the young soldiers sauntered out on the platform, taking off his forage cap to wipe his wet forehead. He saw Joseph and Haroun and brightened. He said, 'You men want to join up? Looks like we're going to have a war.'

'No, sir,' said Haroun with much politeness, but Joseph showed only contempt.

'Pay's good,' said the soldier mendaciously.

'No, sir,' repeated Haroun. The soldier peered at him with suspicion, at the dark face and the mass of black curls. Haroun's appearance made him namelessly uneasy. He turned to Joseph who had listened to this exchange with harsh amusement. Joseph's face and manner appeased the soldier. 'How about you, sir?'

'I'm not interested in wars,' said Joseph.

'Don't anything matter to you?' Haroun asked.

Joseph was startled at the perceptiveness of one so young and he retreated in himself. 'Why do you ask that?' he said. 'That's impertinent, I'm thinking.'

'Now, I didn't mean anything,' said Haroun, spreading out his hands in a gesture Joseph had never seen before. 'You just don't seem to care, that's all.'

'You are quite right. I don't care,' said Joseph. A group of bellowing men erupted on to the platform and they glared up the tracks and cursed futilely. They were very drunk. 'Won't get in 'til noon, now!' one bawled. 'And got a derrick to deliver 'fore that! Ought to sue the railroad!'

They returned in a sweaty rout to the depot. Joseph followed them with his eyes. He said, as if to himself, 'Who are all these people?'

'Why, they're prospectors – oil,' said Haroun. 'They're going to Titusville to stake out a claim or buy land around there and start to drill. That's what you're going there to work for, ain't you?'

'Yes.' Joseph looked at Haroun fully for the first time. 'Do you know anything about it?'

'Well, I heard a lot. There's not much work in Wheatfield, with the Panic, and people don't even keep their horses shod right, and I'd like to make more than two dollars a week,' said Haroun, cheerful again. 'I aim to be a millionaire, like everybody else who goes to Titusville. I'm going to drive one of them wagons with nitro-glycerine, and when I got a stake I'm going to buy a drill myself or go into partnership with somebody, and take options on the land. You can do that, if you can't buy the land, and be sure nobody around Titusville or even Corland is selling out his land right now! You take options, and if you strike oil then you give the owner of the land royalties. I heard all about it in Wheatfield. Lots of men going there now, to work in the oil-fields. Some of the men in the depot already struck it rich, real rich, and they're here to buy more machinery cheap, and hire help. I'm already hired,' he added, with pride. 'Seven dollars a week and board to work in the fields, but I'm going to drive the hot wagons. That's what they call 'em.'

Suddenly there was a howling and clanging like an outbreak of furious metallic madness. A blinding white eye roared out of the darkness around the bend and the rails trembled. Joseph could hear the hiss of escaping steam as brakes were applied, and there was the train to Titusville screaming towards the depot, the squat black engine dwarfed by the gigantic smoke-stack which was retching smoke and fire into the night.

Now the platform was boiling with masses of men. They exploded in masses towards the coaches and the two thin youths were no matches for their strength. They struggled to board the train. Joseph found Haroun clinging desperately to his arm and he restrained the angry impulse to shake him off. Once Haroun fell to his knees, punched in the back by a swearing brute of a man, and Joseph felt instinctively for his truncheon. Then he knew that neither he nor Haroun would be able to board except by extreme and punitive measures, so he pulled out his truncheon and literally beat his way through the masses, his young arm flailing. Some of the men fell back, howling, and Joseph pulled his companion through the narrow passage between heavy bodies and helped Haroun to climb the narrow, steep steps. The train was already snorting for departure. The coaches were loaded now with seated and bawling and laughing men, and the aisles were crowded and smotheringly hot. There was no place in the coaches for Joseph and Haroun, though men continued to push by them to try to enter the coaches and then clot about the open doors, which could not be shut.

Joseph was panting. He muttered, 'God damn them.' The sleeves of his greatcoat were torn and he had lost his cap. Haroun was sallow with pain. But he tried to smile. His breath was heavy and painful and he was holding his thin back in the region of his kidneys, where he had been punched. 'Lucky we got this far,' he said, 'thanks to you. What's your name?'

'Joe,' said Joseph. The train started with a lurch. The two boys were marooned on the sliding platform between two coaches. An attempt had been made to overcome the danger to those standing on the platform, a new invention over the coupling and its pin: two moving plates of metal which met occasionally then slid back with the movement of the train. The plates were slippery, and Joseph had to cling to the handhold of the coach ahead. Haroun leaned against the coach behind, his face running with cold sweat, his breath loud and wheezing and irregular, his feet holding to the moving plate under them. But he still smiled with admiration at Joseph. 'You got us aboard,' he said. 'Never thought we'd make it.'

'We may be sorry we did,' Joseph grunted. 'We'll have to stand out here all the way to Titusville, I am thinking.'

Then Haroun uttered a desolate cry. 'My bag! I dropped my bag. Now I got no clothes!'

Joseph said nothing. He clung to the iron hand-hold of the open coach ahead. He must shake off this importunate boy who had apparently decided to adopt him. He would only hamper and make demands and intrude his friendship and so weaken him, Joseph.

'You should never let go of what belongs to you,' he said indifferently.

If he could just find a corner into which he could flee from Haroun! But not even a garter snake could have entered either of the stuffed coaches. Then Haroun screamed, a scream of mortal pain and terror and Joseph turned back to him.

One of Haroun's thin feet, in its broken boot, had been seized at the ankle between the jostling and sliding steel plates on the platform, and he had fallen on his knees. Light spilled from the coaches and Joseph saw the boy's anguished and terrified face and then the blood oozing from his captured foot. The plates still slid backwards and forwards but now they did not entirely close because of the frail flesh and bone caught between them.

'My God! You fool! Why didn't you hang on?' Joseph shouted with mingled rage and fear. He dropped his box and fell to his knees beside the screaming boy. When a plate receded slightly he tugged at the caught foot, but it was wedged. The opening was not wide enough, and each lurch of the pounding train and each sway around a curve and each of Joseph's tugs only enhanced Haroun's agony, and he screamed without let.

Then Joseph thought of his truncheon. He pulled it from his pocket; he waited until the plates slid apart at their widest aperture and thrust the truncheon between them. Then he wedged the steel-shod heel of his sturdy boot into the opening also, and pulled it from his foot. He looked down into the grey darkness between the plates, closing his ears to Haroun's shrieks. He bit his lip. He would have to reach down into the forced opening and push off Haroun's shoe, which was hopelessly caught in the metal. In doing so he risked having his own hand caught and perhaps losing it between the jaws of the plates. He hesitated and a lightning thought rushed through his mind, 'Why should I risk this for a stranger who is nothing to me?'

The edges of the stout leather and steel truncheon were already being chewed by the plates, and so was the heel of Joseph's boot. He would have to act at once. He closed his eyes and pushed his hand between the plates, caught the back of Haroun's shoe and waited for an instant until the orifice widened slightly again. Then in one rapid motion he pushed off the shoe and tore Haroun's foot from the aperture and released his own boot. The truncheon broke and fell down upon the track. A moment later and it would have been too late.

Haroun lay on his face on the sliding plates. Shock had overcome him. He lay flaccid and prone, his meagre body moving rhythmically on the sliding plates. The train shrieked into the night. Clouds of smoke gushed on to the platform. The feeble light of a small depot fled by the train. Wheels pounded. Joseph's breathing began to slow.

Then a rough coarse voice sounded over Joseph's shoulder. 'What's all this, eh? What's wrong here?'

A stout, short man had appeared in the doorway of the coach ahead, a man of about forty, a man richly dressed but with a bald head like a huge pear rising from broad, thick shoulders. His wide face was florid and jowled above a folded silken cravat held with a diamond pin. He had tiny eyes like wet raisins, and restless, and enormous pink ears and a fat pursed mouth. A watch-chain loaded with gemmed trinkets spread across a bulging waistcoat dazzling in its brocaded colours. His plump hands, which clung to each side of the doorway, glittered with jewelled rings.

He was a man of authority and importance, for the men he had pushed aside stood behind him, still grinning, but respectful. Joseph looked up at the glistening and well-fed face. 'He caught his foot. He hurt his ankle. He's bleeding. I got him out just in time,' said Joseph with hard and contemptuous curtness. 'His foot's hurt. He needs attention.'

The man's face quickened at the sound of Joseph's voice. A big cigar was held between stained teeth. He removed the cigar with his sparkling fingers. He grunted then. He looked down at the prostrate Haroun. He said, 'Got him out, did you?' Then he suddenly shouted in a voice louder than the uproar in the coaches and the howling of the train. 'Come on, here!' he bellowed, looking over his shoulder. 'Clear another seat, damn you all! Lift this boy and take him inside, or I'll have your lights and livers, damn you!'

No one contested or argued. Men rose in the billows of cigar smoke and a seat was miraculously vacated. The stranger gestured. Two of the men picked up Haroun and bore him inside the coach and sat him on the seat. The boy's eyes, nooding with tears, remained closed. Blood dripped from his torn ankle. 'And in with you, too, boyeen,' said the stranger. Joseph fell into the space beside Haroun. The back of the seat ahead was reversed and the stranger sat down ponderously upon it and surveyed the two boys. Crowded faces peered. The stench of sweat and smoke and pomade and whisky choked Joseph's breath.

'Well, now,' said the stranger, planting his fat hands on his knees. 'We gotta do something for this spalpeen, don't we? Don't want him bleeding to death. Where you lads from?'

'Wheatfield. Going to Titusville,' said Joseph. 'To work.'

The man bellowed again, without looking away from Joseph and Haroun. 'Whisky, damn your hides, lots of it, and clean kerchiefs! Fast!' There was a flurry behind and about him. He smiled at Joseph. 'And what's your moniker, eh? And his?'

His teeth were small and stained and crooked, but there was a certain rude geniality in his smile.

Joseph said, 'Joe Francis.' He nodded at Haroun. 'He says his name is Haroun Zieff.'

But the stranger was staring at Joseph intently. 'Joseph Francis Xavier – what?'

Joseph's muscles contracted. He looked more closely at the broad and glistening face opposite him and at the little dark eyes, so shrewd and cynical. 'Just Joe Francis,' he said.

The stranger grinned knowingly. 'Now then,' he said, 'I'm an Irisher, meself, though born in this country. Dad came from County Cork. Name's Ed Healey. Never been on the ould sod, but heard enough from Dada. So I know an Irisher when I meet one. Afraid to say you are, is that it? Don't blame you, in this country. But an Irisher is match enough for anybody, ain't he? But don't never be ashamed of your name, boyeen.'

'I'm not,' said Joseph.

'But you're running from something, is that it?'

'Perhaps,' said Joseph, and thought of Ireland and not of Mr Squibbs.

'Not a long tongue in you, is there?' said Mr Healey, in a tone of approval. 'That's what I like: a man of few words. So, Joseph Francis Xavier something-or-other, you're going to Titusville with this lad with the heathen name?'

'He is no heathen. He's a Christian,' said Joseph.

Large clean kerchiefs had been produced in profusion. Mr

Healey kept them folded on his knee. He gave Joseph a tin cup with swirling pale liquid in it, a considerable amount. 'Bourbon, best white mule,' said Mr Healey. 'Make him drink every drop.' He held a large jug in his hand and nodded at Haroun and smiled encouragingly.

'It'll kill him,' said Joseph.

'Life's no bargain,' said Mr Healey in a voice of reason. 'But never heard of a man dying of good ole Kentucky brew. Not even anybody with a heathen name.'

Joseph said to Haroun, 'You must drink this. Quick, now.'

'Yes, Joe,' said Haroun in such a meek and trusting voice that Mr Healey blinked. Haroun held his breath and drank quickly. After the cup was empty his face bulged and his great black eyes started from his head, and he strangled and held his throat. Mr Healey chuckled. 'In a minute he won't have no pain,' he commented.

Mr Healey, smiling widely, soaked two or three kerchiefs in whisky from the jug he held.

'Why do you do this for us?' asked Joseph. 'We're nothing to you.'

Mr Healey studied Haroun keenly, but he said to Joseph, 'It's like that, eh? If you don't know, boyo, don't you ask.'

Joseph was silent. Mr Healey still studied Haroun, lying in the circle of Joseph's arms. He said, 'This heathen ain't anything to you either, is he? But you got his foot out and saved it. Why? Don't you tell me, now. You think on it.'

Haroun's eyes closed. He lay limp in Joseph's arms. Then Mr Healey became brisk. He leaned forward, muttering, and wiped the dirty and bloody ankle quickly and expertly. Haroun moaned once, but did not move. 'Best thing for anything,' said Mr Healey. 'Beats the devil for curing.' The kerchief was soon soaked with blood and filth. Mr Healey wet another. 'Don't think there's anything broken,' he said. 'Just tore up. Bad, though. Could have been cut off. Now, it's clean.'

He deftly swathed the lacerated ankle in fresh white kerchiefs and generously poured raw whisky on them. 'Well,' he said, 'seems I heard that the meek'll inherit the earth, and maybe the helpless, but not until the rest of us have eaten the lion's share and don't want no more. But no use quarrelling with things as they are. Only a fool does that.' He looked at Joseph. 'You ain't no fool, and that's for sure, boyo.'

'I am going to survive,' said Joseph, and suddenly, his head fell back against the rattan seat and he slept. The train screamed on into the night like a triumphant banshee. Flickering red fire glared briefly at the windows.

CHAPTER NINE

JOSEPH was awakened by brilliant sunshine lying on his eyes and face. Stiff and aching and weary, he moved on the rattan seat where he and Haroun had spent the night in heavy slumber. The younger boy's head lay on Joseph's right shoulder, as a child's head lies, his dusky face empty of everything but innocence and pain. His thick curling hair, black as coal and as shining, spilled on Joseph's arm and neck. One of his hands had fallen on Joseph's knee.

Joseph's eyes narrowed thoughtfully as he studied Mr Healey. His instincts told him that his benefactor was a rascal, but unlike Tom Hennessey's rascality Mr Healey's was open and frank and in a way admirable and a sign of strength. He was a man who would use but probably could not be used. There was a strong shrewdness in him, an alert intelligence, a benign implacability – in short, a man to be feared, a capricious man perhaps, a man who had authority of his own and therefore did not fear authority and could outwit it, and who had little regard for stringent opinions concerning wrong and right. Mr Healey, it was possible, ran his affairs dangerously close to the cutting edge of the law, and no doubt he had defeated it many a time.

As soon as the train reached Titusville he, Joseph, would immediately abandon Haroun. Mr Healey was another matter. He exuded wealth, competence, authority and strength. Joseph continued his study.

'And what will you be thinking, with that look on your face?' Mr Healey inquired. Joseph flushed. Apparently Mr Healey had awakened recently and had studied Joseph in his turn. 'Joseph Francis Xavier What?'

'Joe Francis. That is all,' said Joseph.

Mr Healey yawned vastly. He appeared amused. He leaned

forward to inspect the sleeping Haroun's foot. It was swathed in kerchiefs no longer immaculately white, and it was badly swollen and appeared red and hot. 'Got to do something about your friend,' Mr Healey remarked.

'He is not my friend,' said Joseph. 'I met him on the platform last night, and that is all. And why should you help him?'

'Well,' said Mr Healey, still examining Haroun's foot, 'what do you think? Out of the goodness of my heart? Brotherly love or something? Touched by a lad so young and his plight? Wanting to help the unfortunate? Kindness of my big soul? Or maybe I can use him? You pays your money and you takes your choice, as the horse-race fellers say. You figure it out, Joe.'

He looked at his gold watch, then clicked it shut. 'Soon be in Titusville. I am a Grand Panjandrum, Joe. A man with lots of affairs. Finger in every pie. Politics. Oil. River boats. Retailer. Name it. I'm it. Never turn down an honest penny and maybe never turn down a dishonest one, either.'

'So you are a politician, too?'

'No, sir. Too dirty for me. But I control politicians, and that's better.'

Joseph was becoming extremely interested in spite of his aloofness. 'Do you know Senator Hennessey?'

'Ole Tom?' Mr Healey laughed richly. 'I made Ole Tom! Knew half a dozen of the Pennsylvania legislature. Been living in Pittsburgh and Philadelphia last twenty years or so. Worked like hell to stop that yokel, Abe Lincoln, but it didn't turn out. Anyways, all for the best. We're in a war now and there's always a lot of money to be made out of wars. Know them all. Did a lot of business in wars in Mexico and other places. People say they hate wars, but governments never made a war and nobody came. That's human nature. And when we win this war, there's going to be lots of good fat pickings in the South, too. That, boyo, is what the war's about, though you hear a lot of drivel about slavery and the Rights of Man, et cetera. Lot of dung. It's money, that's all. South too prosperous. North in an industrial panic. Simple as that.'

'I'm not interested in wars,' said Joseph.

'Now that,' said Mr Healey, 'is one goddamned stupid remark. If you want to make your mark, boyo, you've got to be interested in every last goddamn thing the world does, and see where it will turn a profit for you if you're smart. You got to learn a lot, Joseph Francis Xavier.'

'And you intend to teach me?' said Joseph, with contempt.

Mr Healey studied him and his eyes narrowed so much that they almost disappeared. 'If I do, son, it'll be the luckiest day of your life, sure and it will. You think you're tough and ornery. You ain't. Not yet you ain't. Tough and ornery folks don't appear to be. It's the soft ones who put on the front of toughness and hardness, to sort of protect themselves from the real murderers, who are all sweet talk and kind smiles and helpfulness. It don't do them no good, though. The tough fellers can see right through all that shell to the tasty oyster inside.'

'And you think I'm a tasty oyster?'

Mr Healey burst out laughing. He pointed his cigar at Joseph, and he laughed so heartily that tears filled his little eyes and spilled out on to his fat full cheeks. He shook his head over and over in uncontrolled mirth. Joseph watched him with mortified and furious anger.

'Son,' gasped Mr Healey, 'you ain't even a morsel of shrimp!' He pulled out another scented and folded kerchief from his hip pocket and wiped his eyes and moaned with delight. 'Oh, my God. Oh, my God!' he groaned with rich feeling and pleasure. 'You're killing me, son.'

He looked at Joseph and tried to control himself. His whole body quaked with joyous laughter, and he belched and gulped. Then he pointed the cigar at Joseph again.

'Son,' he said in a strangled voice, 'I'm interested in you because you got the makings of a scoundrel. Besides, you're an Irisher, and always had a soft spot for an Irisher, feckless or not. You can do something with the Irish. And you can depend on their loyalty, too, if they like you. If they don't, you're a dead man. Now, look here, you helped this boy, though he's no kin or friend of yours. Maybe saved his life. I'm not asking for an explanation, because you can't explain it. But I liked that in you, though I don't say I admired it. What is he, anyways – a Turk?'

Joseph, in his silent rage, could not speak for a moment. 'No,' he said at last, in a voice full of hate for Mr Healey, 'he's a Lebanese. I told you he was a Christian, if that means anything. Do you know,' said Joseph with unusual malice, 'what a Lebanese is?'

But Mr Healey was not humiliated or annoyed. 'No, boyo,

I don't. Don't even want to know. Never heard of anyone like that, though, come to think of it. He looks like life dealt him a dirty hand, too. Know anything about that?'

'A little,' said Joseph.

'Bad as your own, eh?'

'Perhaps.'

'But he don't look sour like you, boyo, and maybe there's something in that for me, too. Think you'd like to join up with me?'

'Depends on the pay, Mr Healey.'

Mr Healey nodded again with great approval. 'That's what I like to hear. If you'd said that it depends on anything else I wouldn't waste my time on you. Money: that's the ticket. Looks like your Turk is waking up. What you say his name is, his moniker? Haroun Zieff? Heathen name. From now on he's – let me see. Harry Zeff. That's what we'll call him. Sounds more American. German. Lots of Germans in Pennsylvania. Good stuff in them. Know how to work, they do, and how to turn a profit, and never heard them whining, either. If there's anything I hate it's a whiner. What's your Turk trying to say to you?'

He looked at Joseph with a contented and important expression but Joseph was distastefully examining Haroun. Haroun's dark face was deeply flushed and very hot. His whole body moved restlessly with pain and distress, and sometimes he groaned. His toes extruded through the kerchiefs which swathed them. Mr Healey looked at him with interest, leaning forward.

'Now Joseph Francis Xavier What,' he said, 'what do you propose we do with this boyeen – who's no concern of ours, eh? No friend of yours. Never saw him before, myself. Leave him on the train for the conductor to dispose of like rubbish?'

Joseph did not move. He looked up at Mr Healey. His eyes were blue and enraged fire.

'I don't know anyone in Titusville,' he said. 'Maybe you know somebody who'd take him in and care for him until he's better. I can give them the money.'

'Son,' said Mr Healey, standing up, 'you don't know Titusville. It's like a jungle, it is that. I seen many a man, young as this and you, dying on the streets from cholera or ague or something and nobody cared. Black gold fever: that's what's got this town. And when men are after gold, the devil take the hindmost, specially the sick and the weak. Everybody's too busy filling his pockets and robbing his neighbour. There ain't an inn or hotel in Titusville that ain't crowded to the door, and no new-fangled hospital, if that's what you're thinking about. You take people who are living peaceful in town or country and they'll help a stranger – sometimes – out of Christian charity, but you take a mad-house like Titusville, a stranger is just a dog unless he's got two good hands and a good back to work with, or a stake. Now, if your Turk was a girl I'd know just the place who'd take him in. Own four or five, myself,' and Mr Healey chuckled. The train was moving very slowly now and the men in the coach were gathering up their bags and talking and laughing with the exuberance only the thought of money can induce. The coach was hurtfully glaring with sunlight but the wind that invaded the coach was very cool.

Joseph closed his eyes and bit his lip so hard it turned white. Haroun's restless hands were moving over him, as hot as coals.

'Well, Joe, here we are, depot riding right in. Coming?'

Joseph said, 'I can't leave him. I'll find a way.'

'Now,' said Mr Healey, 'that's what I like to hear a man say: "I'll find a way." None of that, "For the love of dear Jaysus, sir, help me, 'cause I'm too damned lazy and stupid and no-account to do it meself. I appeal to your Christian charity, sir." Any man says that to me,' said Mr Healey with real pent emotion, 'I say to him, "Get off your ass and help yourself as I did and millions afore you, damn you." Wouldn't trust a psalm-singer or a beggar with a two-cent piece, no sir. They'd eat you alive, come they had the chance.'

The train had halted at a dismal makeshift depot and the men were running from it with shouts to acquaintances and friends they had seen from the windows.

Mr Healey waited. But Joseph had not been listening closely. He saw that Haroun had begun to shiver and that his child's face had suddenly turned grey. He tugged off his old great-coat and clumsily wrapped Haroun in it. A trainman was coming down the aisle with a basket, in which he was depositing the empty bottles on the floor. Joseph called to him. 'Hey, there, I need a hand with my sick friend! I've got to find a place for him to stay. Know of any?'

The trainman stood up straight and scowled. Mr Healey

uttered an astonished grunt. 'What the hell's the matter with you, Joe?' he demanded. 'Ain't I here? Too proud to ask, eh, and me your old friend, Ed Healey!'

The trainman recognised Mr Healey, and came forward, bowing his head and tugging at his cap. He looked at the two boys. 'Friends of yours, sir?' he asked in a grovelling whine. He looked more closely, and was astonished at the sight of the two ragged youths, one of whom was obviously almost moribund.

'Bet your life they are, Jim,' said Mr Healey. 'My carry-all out there with my shiftless Bill?'

'Sure is, Mr Healey, I'll run get him and he can help you with – with your friends,' he added in a weak voice. 'Give you a hand too. Glad to do it, sir. Anythin' for Mr Healey, any-thin'!' He looked again at Joseph and Haroun and blinked incredulously.

'Capital,' said Mr Healey, and shook hands with the train-man and the dazed Joseph saw the gleam of silver before it disappeared. The trainman ran, like a boy off the train, shout-ing to someone and calling.

The air was chill and bright outside the train, and the new rough depot platform milled with excited men carrying their wicker luggage and portmanteaux.

Titusville, set among circling hills and valleys the colour and gleaming texture of emerald velvet, was hardly a frontier town, though the normal and settled population was just in excess of one thousand, more or less. It was about forty miles from Lake Erie, and had been prosperous even before oil, being noted for its lumber production and its saw-mills and its busy flat-boats carrying wood down Oil Creek for distant parts. The farmers were prosperous also, for the land was rich and fertile, and life, to the people of the pretty village, had always been good and never arduous. But the newcomers from nearby States, and the oil frenzy, gave it the air of an exploding frontier town of the West, in spite of noble old mansions scattered at intervals throughout the town behind great oaks and elms and smooth lawns, and proud old families who pretended not to notice the raw newcomers and their frantic ways and their bawling voices.

Mr Healey's 'Bill' was a William Strickland from the stark hills of Appalachia, a Kentuckian. Joseph had never seen a man so tall and so excessively thin and lank. He was like a skeleton tree, narrow and fleshless and without juice. He had a face like the head of an axe, and hardly wider, and a shock of black hair stiff and lifeless like the quills of a porcupine, and as erect. His eyes, though not intelligent, were brilliantly intent and hazel, the eyes of an avid and predatory beast. His shoulders, including his neck, were no more than sixteen inches broad, and his hips appeared even more meagre. But he had gigantic hands, the hands of a strangler, and feet resembling long slabs of wood crudely fashioned. His skin was withered and deeply lined, and he possessed few teeth and those like fangs and stained with tobacco juice. He could have been aged from thirty to fifty. His impression on Joseph was of a creature of witless ferocity.

But Bill was strong. A word from Mr Healey and he lifted the delirious Haroun in his arms without strain and carried him from the depot. He smelled of dirt and rancid sow belly. His voice was soft and subservient to Mr Healey, and never questioning. He wore a filthy dark blue shirt, the sleeves rolled up over brown tendons and elongated muscles, and blackish overalls, and nothing else. His feet were bare. A thin stream of tobacco saliva dribbled from a corner of his mouth. He had glanced once at Joseph and that glance was as opaque as wood, and as interested. He showed no wonder at the sight of Haroun. Apparently what Mr Healey ordained was sufficient for him, however strange or foreign, and Joseph thought, 'He would kill on command.' When he found out later that Bill had indeed killed he was not surprised.

Everyone appeared to know Mr Healey's fine carry-all with its fringed top, for there was an empty circle about it. Bill tenderly helped Mr Healey into the carry-all, then laid Haroun along one side. He seemed startled when Joseph followed as if the youth had not been encountered before. Then he climbed to his seat, struck the mares with his whip and the iron-shod wheels rolled off smartly.

Seeing that Haroun rocked on the long opposite seat and was in danger of rolling off, Joseph braced the boy's middle with his boots. Haroun never ceased his feverish moaning, and Joseph watched him with an inscrutable expression.

'He'll live, strong and healthy, and if he don't there's no loss,' remarked Mr Healey. 'Look about you, Irish, you're in Titus-ville now and ain't that where you want to be? We brought some life to this hick town, and you'd think they'd be grateful, wouldn't you?'

Joseph thought that Winfield had been barren and repulsive enough, but he saw that what the 'outsiders' had made of a once lovely and charming village was nothing short of desecration – in the name of progress and money. An apparently new and raw community had grown up swiftly in the vicinity of the depot, and the cold northern sun gripped without the softening effect of trees and grass on wooden walks. The carriage rolled over broken slabs of stone and long dusty planks laid roughly and in a haphazard fashion on bare packed earth. Cheap houses, still unpainted, fashioned of crude siding or logs, huddled sheepishly between noxious saloons and tawdry shops. Small copses of trees had been chopped down to make plots of grassless clay, waiting for new and ugly buildings, a number of them in various stages of construction, and being built without regard for gracious space, inviting vistas or even regularity. Some had already been finished and Mr Healey pointed to them and said, 'Our new op'ry houses. Lively every night 'til early morning. Liveliest places in town, 'cept for the whore-houses, which does a good business all the time. Saloons never empty, neither. Even Sundays,' and he chuckled fatly. 'We put this town on the railroad, that we did.'

He said to Mr Healey, 'Do you live here, sir?'

'Me? Hell, no. Got a house here where I stay in town, bought it cheap from some high-and-mighty snot-nose never worked a day in his life and went bankrupt. Hard to believe in this here territory where there's so much lumber, and salt mines and good land, but he managed, that he did. Feckless. That was before the oil came in. I live in Philadelphia and sometimes Pittsburgh, where I got a lot of interests, too.'

Joseph reflected that Mr Healey told as little about his affairs as did he, Joseph, and he smiled sourly to himself.

'Now here's the square, as they call it, and the City Hall, and the best stores and the law fellers' offices, and the doctors,' said Mr Healey as the carry-all entered the square. It was apparent that once this small section of land had been as entrancing and gently lovely as any other spot in the vicinity, for trees still stood on it in cool dark clusters, their leaves glittering in the sunlight, and there were gravel paths winding through dead earth which formerly had been green and soft. There was a broken fountain in the centre, and a stone plinth

70

with carved words on it, and nothing else except clay and weeds. The square was surrounded by buildings which still hinted of grace before the 'outsiders' had come, ravening here, of fieldstone, and the windows were still bravely polished, but there was a sad look about them as if they were shrinking.

The carry-all moved briskly towards the opposite end of the square and suddenly Joseph, half disbelieving, caught the scent of grass and fresh trees and roses and honeysuckle. The carry-all swung down the far street and at once everything changed abruptly. Pretty, small houses and lawns and gardens and tall elms and oaks appeared as if one walked from a prison yard into comparative and blooming heaven. The cobbled street began to broaden, as if smiling as it revealed treasures, and the houses became bigger and taller, the lawns wider, the trees higher and more profuse and the gardens luxurious. This area was not Green Hills in the least, but to Joseph it was a refreshment to the eye and a green touch on the spirit.

'Pretty, ain't it?' said Mr Healey, who noticed everything. 'Old families. Own lots of farmland, good rich lumber farms, and fields where we're drilling. Been here before the Revolution, and sometimes I think none of them ever died but just live on like mummies or something, or what is that thing that turns to stone?'

'Petrified wood,' said Joseph.

'You're right smart, ain't you?' said Mr Healey, with a little friendly rancour. 'Never held it against a man, though. What else do you know besides everything, Joe?'

'I've read a lot most of my life,' said Joseph. 'And I write a fine hand.'

'Is that so? Need an honest man to keep my books. Maybe you'll do.'

'No,' said Joseph. 'I'm not going to be a clerk in some dark office. I am going to drive one of the wagons to the oil-fields. I hear the wages are very good.'

'You want to blow all those brains of yours to kingdom-come, eh?'

Joseph shrugged. 'Better that than live the way I have been living, Mr Healey. I need a great deal of money. I want to make my fortune. The little life is not for me. That is why I came to Titusville. As I told you before, I'll do anything – for money.'

71

Mr Healey squinted at him. 'It's that way, eh?'

'Yes,' said Joseph.

'Reckon I can use you,' said Mr Healey. 'I'll think on it. But don' despise ledgers. You can learn a lot that way.'

He thought a moment or two, as he clung, swaying, to the straps of the vehicle. Then he said with a positive air, 'The law for you, boyo. That's the ticket.'

'Law?' said Joseph, his small blue eyes widening in incredulity.

'Why not? Legal plunder, that's what it is. Don't dirty your hands, and gold sticks to 'em. Other people's gold.' His body shook with his fruity laughter. 'It ain't necessary to be a lawyer to go into politics, but it helps. Don't look at me as if I'm demented, boyo. I know what I'm talking about. We'll put you to study law with some fine thief of a lawyer, and your fortune's made.' He slapped his fat thighs happily. 'I need a private lawyer, that I do.

'Of course,' said Mr Healey, 'that ain't tomorrow. In the meantime, we can make a good thing together, you working for me.'

'At what?'

'My interests,' said Mr Healey. 'Collecting, managing and such. Had a feller up to a month ago and he stole me blind. Almost. Got sent up for twenty years and he was almost hanged.' He looked at Joseph intently. 'In places like this, they ain't soft on thieves – except legal ones. Ever stole anything, Joe?'

Joseph immediately thought of Mr Squibbs. He said, 'I borrowed some money – once. At six per cent interest.'

'All cleared up now?' He winked knowingly. But Joseph remained without expression.

'No. And that is why I've got to make a lot of money, soon.'

'Why'd you borrow the money?'

Joseph considered him. 'Mr Healey,' he said at last, 'that is my own affair. I've not questioned you about your affairs.'

'Sassy tongue on you, don't you?' said Mr Healey. 'Well, I like a man with spirit. Knew you had guts minute I saw you. Hate snivellers. Would you say you was an honest man, Joe?'

Joseph smiled his cold and ironic smile. 'If it is to my interest, yes.'

Mr Healey laughed. 'Knew you was a born lawyer! Well, here we are.'

It was a ponderous three-storey house, 'baronial', in Joseph's first appraisal, of rose brick and white stone, tall if narrow, with pedimented windows and white shutters, and a wide *porte-cochère* of brick and snowy pillars. It did not have the smooth grandeur of Tom Hennessey's house in warm Green Hills, but it had a hard and compact strength, and lace curtains and velvet hung against polished glass and the doors were double and white and high.

'Nice, ain't it?' said Mr Healey as the carry-all rolled towards the *porte-cochère*. 'It does me well when I'm here. Got it for a song.'

The carry-all passed under the roof of the *porte-cochère* and the door flew open and on the threshold stood a young lady of uncommon beauty and obvious vivacity. Joseph's mouth opened in surprise. Mr Healey's daughter? She was no more than twenty, if even of those years, and had a lovely figure which her rich gown of wine-red merino draped over enormous hoops could not entirely hide. She had a look of intense life and gusto, and she stood on the middle step of a white flight of four, laughingly holding out her arms and regarding Mr Healey with radiant glee. He climbed from the carry-all and bowed and lifted his hat, and shouted, 'Miss Emmy! God bless you, my child!'

Joseph had not been prepared for such a house nor for such a girl, and he stood dumbly beside Mr Healey, conscious as never before of his shabby state and dirty boots and soiled shirt and scarf, and hatless head, his cardboard box under his arm. The girl looked at him with open surprise, at his shaggy mass of russet hair tumbled and uncombed, at his pale and freckled face, at his general air of indigence. Then she ran down the rest of the stairs and flung herself, laughing and trilling, into Mr Healey's arms. He kissed and embraced her with enthusiasm, then smacked her on the backside with pleasure.

'Miss Emmy,' he said, 'this here is Joe. My new friend, Joe, who's thrown in his lot with me. Look at him, now: gawking like a chicken with the croup. Never saw such a pretty sight as you, Miss Emmy, as he sees now, and his mouth's awatering.'

'Pish!' exclaimed Miss Emmy, in the prettiest voice, like that of a happy child. 'I swear, sir, that you make me blush!' She dropped a light little curtsy, full of demureness, in Joseph's general direction, and he bowed his head stiffly, full of silent bewilderment.

'Joe,' said Mr Healey, 'this here is Miss Emmy. Miss Emmy, love, I don't rightly know his name, but he calls himself Joe Francis, and he's got a close mouth and so we make the best of it.'

Sunlight flashed on the glossiness of Miss Emmy's ringlets and on the side of her bright cheek and now she looked at Joseph with more interest, seeing, as Mr Healey had already seen, the latent young virility of him and the capacity for violence about his eyes and wide thin mouth. 'Mr Francis,' she murmured.

Bill appeared with the unconscious Haroun in his arms, Joseph's greatcoat swathing the slight body. Miss Emmy was astounded. She looked to Mr Healey for enlightenment. 'Just a young spalpeen, penniless beggar from the train,' he explained. 'Joe here's friend. Think we got a bed for him, and a bed for Joe?'

'Why, Mr Healey, sir, it is your house and there is room for all – for all your friends,' said the girl. But her fair brow puckered in bafflement. 'I will tell Miz Murray.' She swung about, hoops and ringlets and lace swaying, and ran up the stairs and into the house, as blithely as a kitten. Mr Healey watched her go, fondly, his face suffused and contented, and he went up the steps motioning for Joseph and Bill to follow.

'Bought Miss Emmy from a whore-house when she was fifteen, three years ago,' said Mr Healey over his shoulder, and without the slightest embarrassment. 'Come from Covington, Kentucky, raw as an egg. Cost me three hundred dollars, but cheap enough for a piece like that, wouldn't you say, Joe?'

Mr Healey had reached the door. 'That's what the madam said she was worth, but more, and I own the whore-house and Miss Emmy drew a lot of money and she was young, and the madam had cleaned her up and dressed her and taught her manners like a lady, and so she was worth the money. Not that I own her like you mean, boyo, like a nigger, but I own her, by God I do! And God help the man who looks at her now and licks his lips!'

The hall was dim after the glare of sunlight outside, but

after a moment Joseph could see that the tall walls were covered with red silk damask – he had read of such in romantic novels – and were profusely covered with landscapes, seascapes and classical subjects, very decorous, in heavy gilt frames. The walls were also lined with handsome sofas and chairs in blue and green and red and velvet, and the floor under Joseph's feet was soft and he saw the Persian rug in many different hues and of a tortuous pattern. At the end of the hall an overpowering staircase of mahogany rose and turned upwards in the direction of the second and third storeys. Joseph could smell beeswax and old potpourri and cinnamon and cloves, and something else which he could not as yet define but which he later learned was gas from the oil-wells of Titusville. Behind him waited, in that sinister and patient silence of his, Bill Strickland with Haroun still in his arms.

A door banged open in one of the walls, and Joseph heard Miss Emmy's teasing and laughing voice, and another voice, rough and strident and protesting, and he was taken aback when he saw the owner of the voice for he had thought it had come from a man. But a middle-aged woman was entering the hall with a rocking tread. Joseph's first impression of her was that she was a troll, short and wide and muscular, the torso like two big balls superimposed one above the other, the billowing black taffeta skirts made huge by many petticoats, the two balls parted by a white frilled apron. There was, too, the third ball which was her oversized head set squarely on corpulent shoulders straining against black silk. A white ruffle puffed out under the roll of flesh which was her chin, and jet buttons winked over her truly awesome bosom.

But it was her face that immediately caught Joseph's attention. He decided he had never seen an uglier, more belligerent or more repellent countenance, for the coarse flesh was the colour and texture of a dead flounder, the nose bulbous, the tiny eyes pale and vicious, the mouth gross and malignant. Her hair was iron-grey and like unravelled rope, only partly seen from under a mob cap of fine white linen and lace. Her peasant's hands were as broad as they were long, and swollen.

'Miz Murray, ma'am, it's home I am,' said Mr Healey in a most genial voice, and he doffed his hat in a gesture both mocking and elaborate. 'Now, Miz Murray, these are my friends, Joe Francis here, who's joined up with me, and little

Harry Zeff you see in Bill's arms. It's ill, he is, and needs care, and so Bill will go for the doctor when the lad's in bed.' Mr Healey spoke genially as always, but now his own face had become rosy rock and the woman's stare faltered. 'You'll do your best, as my housekeeper, Miz Murray, and ask no questions.'

The woman turned and marched towards the staircase, followed by her master and the sad little procession led by Joseph. She walked heavily on her heels and her manner suggested that she was marching towards the scaffold with determined courage and valour. Mr Healey chuckled, and they all walked up stairs padded with Persian carpets. Smooth mahogany slid under Joseph's hand in the duskiness of the stairwell. Now he was beginning to feel his familiar harsh amusement again, and a loathing for Mrs Murray.

The upper hall was dim also, lighted only by a skylight of coloured glass set high in the ceiling of the third storey. The passage-way was narrower than the one downstairs, and coloured light from the skylight splashed on thick Oriental runners and on walls covered with blue silk damask. A line of polished mahogany doors lined the walls, their brass knobs faintly gleaming in the diffused light. And now, a very thin and frightened little housemaid, in black and with a white apron and cap, bounced into the hall by way of the rear staircase, all eyes and moist mouth, and cringing. She was hardly more than thirteen, and there was not a single curve on her flat body.

'Liza!' roared Mrs Murray, seeing an object for her rage. 'Where were you? You need a strapping agin, within an inch of your worthless life! We got company, hear? Open those two back rooms, the blue one and the green one, and quick about it, my girl!'

'Yes'm,' whispered the child and raced to one door, throwing it open and then to another, and Joseph thought: And this is what Regina will come to if I do not make money for her, and very soon. Liza stood aside, cowering and with bent head, but her humble attitude did not save her from a resounding slap on her cheek, bestowed by Mrs Murray. The girl whimpered, but did not lift her eyes. Joseph now saw pockmarks on her thin pale cheeks, and her young face was plain and fearful. In about eight years, thought Joseph, who had seen scores of abused children in America, Regina will be her age, and only I stand between my sister and this.

'Now, here you are, Joe, my lad,' said Mr Healey, and waved majestically at one open door. 'You'll do with a good wash, and then we'll have our breakfast like decent Christians, and Bill here will put little Harry down and go for the doctor.'

Joseph fumbled at his pinned pocket and took out his treasured twenty-dollar gold piece. He held it out to Mr Healey and even Mrs Murray's malign attention was caught.

'What's this, what's this?' asked Mr Healey in surprise.

'For our expenses, Mr Healey,' said Joseph. 'I told you I take no charity.'

Mr Healey lifted his hand in protest. Then he saw Joseph's face. Mrs Murray had sucked in her vindictive mouth, and was staring blankly at the youth, while behind him Bill waited with that sinister patience of his and appeared to see nothing.

'All right,' said Mr Healey, and he took the shimmering golden coin and tossed it in his hand. 'I like a man with pride, and have no quarrel with it.' Now he looked more closely at Joseph, and with curiosity. 'Some of the money you—borrowed?'

'No,' said Joseph. 'I earned it.'

'Hum,' said Mr Healey, and put the coin in his pocket, and Mrs Murray regarded Joseph with squinted and wicked eyes and nodded her head in affirmation of some invidious remark she had made silently to herself. Liza gaped abjectly at Joseph as at an apparition, for now she saw his ragged appearance and his shock of hair like a dull blaze under the skylight.

Mr Healey turned. 'In half an hour, Joe, in half an hour.'

Mrs Murray followed Mr Healey to the door of his own room and then stood on the threshold.

'That one's a thief, sir,' she said. 'Plain as day.'

Mr Healey began to loosen his cravat. He looked at himself in a long mirror on the silken wall. He said, 'Possibly, ma'am, very possible. And now please close the door behind you. Unless you'd like to see me nekkid, like Miss Emmy does.' He looked at her blandly, and she rumbled away.

CHAPTER TEN

AFTER dinner that night Mr Healey gallantly dismissed Miss Emmy and invited Joseph into his 'lib-ry to talk business'. It was indeed a handsome library and Joseph immediately noticed that the walls were filled with books, and that the leather furniture gleamed softly and the tables glowed. Here was a room, like his upstairs, which soothed his abraded sensitivity, and he resented Mr Healey who sat behind a low long table and proceeded to preside, his cigar smoke blue in the rays of sunlight which came between long blue velvet curtains.

'Do all my business here,' said Mr Healey, leaning back in his chair. His rings glittered and so did the trinkets on his watch-chain. 'Now then. I don't do business with mysteries. I got to have answers to my questions. You see that, don't you, Joe? I like open things, before I hire a man. So, I'll ask the questions, and I'll take it kindly if you answer them in the spirit they're asked.' He was no longer so easily affable. His little dark eyes pointed. His mouth had assumed a tight look, though he smiled.

'Yes,' said Joseph, and hid his hard amusement.

'I got to trust a man,' said Mr Healey, admiringly inspecting the long ash on his cigar. 'Can't trust anybody right off the street. I got interests, confidential, and I got to trust. That's understood.'

'Yes,' said Joseph.

'Shut-mouthed, and that's what I like,' said Mr Healey. 'Never did like a wagging tongue. All right. How old are you, Joe?'

'I'll soon be eighteen.'

Mr Healey nodded. 'Not too old, not too young. Can be trained. All right, Joe, what's your full moniker?'

'For the present,' said Joseph, 'I am Joe Francis.'

Mr Healey pursed his lips. 'Police looking for you, Joe?'

Joe thought of Mr Squibbs. 'No.'

'Nobody else?'

'No.'

'What've you been working at?'

'Saw-mills. Taking care of horses. Driving wagons.'

'Where you from, Joe?'

'Wheatfield.'

'How'd you get there?'

Joseph could not help himself. 'On the train,' he said, and smiled his short and taciturn smile.

'Getting things out of you, Joe, is like digging with a bowie knife in a coal mine,' said Mr Healey. 'Got any reason for not opening up, like?'

'Just my nature,' said Joseph, and smiled again.

'No kin?'

Joseph's face became shut. 'No,' he said. 'I am an orphan.'

'Not married, and running away?'

'No.'

'That's sensible. I'm not married, myself,' said Mr Healey, and chuckled. 'Never did believe in it. Here, Joe. Write something on this paper. Anything.'

Joseph picked up the quill pen with the new steel tip which Mr Healey had rolled towards him across the burnished table. He considered Mr Healey, and with growing and amused contempt. Yet, for some reason even he could not understand, he felt a stab of unfamiliar pity. He considered, his ruddy brows drawn together.

He wrote: 'No man is contented until at least one person knows how dangerous he is.' He was careful with flourishes and neatness and artistic shading. Then he pushed what he had written on fine vellum to Mr Healey, who read it slowly, his fat mouth moving over every syllable.

'Right smart sentiment,' said Mr Healey at last, with heartiness. But he glowered a little at Joseph. 'Your own sentiments, eh?'

'No. Henry Haskins.'

'That feller,' said Mr Healey, who had never heard of Henry Haskins. 'Now, I never wanted any feller to think I was dangerous. It's bad for business. Ain't no place in business for dangerous fellers. Word gets around. Can't be trusted.'

'I thought you said it was a smart sentiment,' said Joseph.

'For city slickers. I ain't one.' He scrutinised the writing closely. 'You write a fine hand, Joe.'

'I am not a clerk,' said Joseph. 'I do not intend to be one.'

'Joe, how much money did you make at your last job?'

'I worked a full week, and I received eight dollars a week. That isn't enough.'

Mr Healey's mouth made a soundless whistle. 'Nearly eighteen, and eight dollars a week ain't enough! A man with a family's mighty lucky, Joe, to make that. Hard labour, too.

'Not enough,' said Joseph.

'What do you aim to make?'

'A million dollars.' His square white teeth suddenly flashed in his face.

'You're mad,' said Mr Healey, with simplicity.

'Mr Healey, don't you want to make a million dollars?'

'I'm older'n you. Got more experience.'

'I am younger than you, sir, and so I have much more time. And experience comes with living, and doing.'

'Hum.' They regarded each other in a short silence.

'You're a hard customer,' said Mr Healey.

'If I weren't, I'd be no use to you.'

'You never said a truer word, I am thinking,' said Mr Healey. 'I see we understand each other. Here's my ideas: I show you around, you help manage my business. You study law with a smart lawyer feller. I pay you seven dollars a week until you're worth more.'

'No,' said Joseph.

Mr Healey leaned back in his chair and smiled sweetly. 'That includes room and board.'

Joseph wanted to be, as always, his own man, and not 'be holden' to anyone else. But he thought of the books in this house, to which he would have access, and he hesitated. Then he said again, 'No. I want eighteen dollars a week, and to pay five for my board. In one month I want a four-dollar raise – a week. Then we'll discuss just how valuable I am to you.'

Mr Healey ruminated, his beefy face as closed as Joseph's own. He said, 'You got a right high opinion of yourself, don't you, Irish? Well, I like that, too. How about the boyeen upstairs?' and he tilted his head at the ceiling.

'I've paid you for his room and board, until he can work.'

'And who's he going to work for?'

Joseph shrugged. 'He said he has a job in this town.'

'How about him working for me, too?'

'Mr Healey, that is entirely your affair, and Haroun's not mine.'

'You don't want no burdens?'

'That is right.'

Mr Healey smoked thoughtfully. He said, 'Eighteen years old, and talks like a sharpie with pockets full of gold. Well, how do you expect to make a million dollars?'

'When I have enough money I intend to buy a string of tools, myself, and drill.'

'In competition with me and the other lads?'

'Mr Healey, I'll never cheat you. On that you can rely.'

Mr Healey nodded and said again, 'We understand each other.' He considered. 'All right, eighteen dollars a week, and you pay five for board. For yourself. Then I'll find out if you're worth a corncob to wipe my ass. If you ain't, we part. If you are, we'll talk again. Now –' and he leaned back in his chair and assumed a very open expression, candid and even a little pious – 'I believe in laying my cards out on the table so a feller can see them. They call me "sincere" around here.'

Joseph immediately became wary.

'So you can trust me, Joe.'

Joseph said nothing. Mr Healey laughed gently. 'A real sharpie. You don't trust nobody. You must've had a hard life, Joe.'

'I did.'

'Want to tell me about it?'

'No. It isn't important.'

'You got to trust some people, Joe, or you won't get nowhere.'

'Mr Healey, the less we confide in each other about our private affairs the better friends we'll be. We'll just discuss our work together, frankly.'

'You ain't even prepared to trust me, and I've laid everything on the line to you, Joe. I'm sorry you think everybody's a rascal.'

Joseph could not help smiling. 'Let's say,' he said, 'that we may learn to trust each other.'

'Good enough,' said Mr Healey, with heartiness, and slapped his fat hand on the table. 'Let's get down to business. I'm the president of eight oil companies. Ever since 1855. Started in Pithole, with the oil coming right out of the ground. No need to drill. Pithole ain't developed yet. But I got my options out there; first one to do it. Just scoop it up off'n the water and out of the holes. For twenty-five dollars I sell twenty-five thousand shares in my companies. Can't get out the certifi-

81

cates fast enough, that's how good business is, in Titusville. And I've got three distilleries, too, right on Oil Creek. Up to date, we've been shipping out the barrels on flat-boats all over the State and country. Kerosene. And just the crude oil to distilleries elsewhere. Kerosene's going to replace all other fuel for lamps, and the crude oil's being used for lubricants instead of the more expensive oils being used. I got part of a patent for burning kerosene – since 1857. Saw the possibilities at once. I call that the Healey Kerosene Company. And helped develop better lamps than the old ones burning whale oil and such.

'When they run the railroad regular from Titusville in a few months, instead of one train on Sunday, my business will be ten times as much. Quicker and more than the flat-boats. I got an interest in the railroad, too. You might say I got many interests. Did a lot of business in Mexico not long ago.' He stared expressionlessly at Joseph.

'Legal, sir?'

'Well, it wasn't oil. I told you: I never miss a chance at turning a penny.'

Joseph thought. He remembered reading, in a newspaper, of men like Mr Healey who had made fortunes gun-running in Mexico. But he held his tongue. It was none of his affair just yet.

'I own salt mines here, too,' said Mr Healey. 'And I do a good business in lumber. Lumber's what made this town, before oil. Wide interests, Joe. All in all, I got about two hundred men working for me, townsmen and outsiders. I'm a director in the new bank, too. Own a couple of lawyers, but they ain't smart. But one of them can teach you what you need to practise law, yourself. If I was you, Joe – ' and Mr Healey leaned forward in a most paternal and confidential manner, as one speaking to a beloved young relative, perhaps a son – 'I'd concentrate on patent laws, criminal laws.'

'Especially criminal law,' said Joseph.

Mr Healey laughed expansively, and leaned back. 'Well, I don't do nothing downright criminal, you understand. But every businessman runs close to the edge, or why else is he a businessman? Couldn't make a living if he didn't. Now law's law; you got to have laws, or the country wouldn't hold together. But sometimes law can be – well, can be . . .'

'Ambiguous,' said Joseph, with a little malice.

Mr Healey frowned. He did not understand the word. 'Well, anyways. I mean you take two lawyers, and they can't agree what's legal and what ain't, and that goes for judges and juries, too. Laws're written funny, sometimes. And it's the funny part that's profitable, if you're smart.'

Joseph nodded. 'And if you have a good lawyer.'

Mr Healey nodded and smiled also. 'And there's this here war I hear we're going into, right now. Lots of profit there for a smart man. I hear there's a patent in England for a six- or eight-chamber rifle . . . but that ain't for tomorrow, Joe.'

Joseph suddenly became intensely interested. 'And Washington will buy the rifle from England? Which is the most prosperous side, the Union or the South?'

'The South, son, the South. South wasn't hit by the Panic that's here, like the North. King Cotton. Slave labour. Farming. The South's where the money is. And that's what makes the Northern factory owners and businessmen madder'n a hornet. They ain't worried about slave labour because it ain't moral, or something. They just wish they could have slave labour, themselves, though that's just about what they have right now, with the foreign labour they're importing from Europe, foreigners can't speak English, and starving. Still, they got to pay some wages, and that's killing them. It's the cost of labour. Profits. Joe, if you want to use just one word,' and Mr Healey wagged a huge finger at Joseph, 'to describe wars and the making of wars, it's profits. Nothing else. Profits.'

'And this war, too?'

'Joe! What else? Sure, and Mr Lincoln talks about saving the Union, and a house divided against itself must fall, and the immorality of slavery, and from what I've seen of him I reckon he speaks without lying and hypocrisy. He's kind of simple, in a way. Businessmen always like simple politicians; they're easier to manage and persuade. So they give Mr Lincoln high-falutin' slogans and talk moral-like to him. But all it is is profits. King Profits. Kill off slavery in the South and the South ain't got the big factories and businessmen, and where does that leave the South? The South's where gentlemen live, and gentlemen ain't up to managing business. And so the Northerners can go down there and get rich. Profits, again. Do you follow me?'

'Yes' said Joseph. 'Who do you think will win?'

Mr Healey winked. 'Well, the North, of course. They got

the factories for munitions. It ain't fair, it ain't. Somebody ought to even up the balance.'

Joseph nodded solemnly. 'Only fair,' said Mr Healey. 'Provided there ain't no interference in honest trade. But we won't know about that for a little while.'

'And Mr Lincoln wants to abolish slavery?'

'Well, not rightly. That ain't exactly what he's saying. It's preserving the Union. Did hear he said that if slavery would preserve the Union he wouldn't interfere with it. But the South's sick and tired of all them howling preachers up North screaming for abolition, and the hungry businessmen and factory owners, and interference, and being called names, such as murderers and Simon Legrees. As I told you, the Southerners are gentlemen. The South wasn't used much for the dumping of English whores and thiefs like the North was. Easier to ship them here, the Sassenach thought, than hanging all of them. So the South sort of despises the North besides being mad at the interference. The South knows what it's all about, and they want an aristocratic nation of their own. Of course, that ain't democracy, and me, Ed Healey, I'm for democracy, too. Didn't vote for Lincoln, myself, that Republican.' He nodded virtuously. Then he stood up, and pulled down his florid waistcoat and took out his thick gold watch and sounded the repeater. 'Well, Joe, tomorrow we go out and look around a little, so you get the feel of the town and some of my business. Right?'

They went downstairs. Joseph saw the almost mute Bill Strickland sitting like an image in the hall, waiting. He stood up, galvanised, when he saw his master, and Joseph observed the absolute devotion and blind dedication on the man's ugly face. The back of his neck prickled for no reason he could feel consciously. Then Bill turned his head slowly in Joseph's direction and stared at him emptily.

Joseph saw the killer's fervid eyes and an icy finger touched him between the shoulder-blades. Mr Healey laid his hand with affection on Bill's incredibly narrow shoulder, and he smiled at Joseph.

'Bill,' he said, 'would do anything for me. Anything.' His smile widened as he and Joseph regarded each other in a little silence.

The surrey was standing on the wooden bridge overlooking

Oil Creek. They drove out into the countryside, which was, to Joseph, no countryside at all but a raped Eden. Derricks and well-houses filled a landscape once placid and silent. Here and there at a distance he could see rich fields filled with black and white cattle, and the shine of a blue pond and meadows with rising corn and clumps of trees. But the air was permeated with the sick and pungent stench of crude oil; smoke, black and oily, poured from the steeples of the well-houses which, incongruously, resembled miniature brown churches. The new God, thought Joseph, and oil is His prophet.

'Well, here we are,' said Mr Healey. They had arrived at a large cluster of housed oil-wells and Joseph could hear the rhythm, like mechanical heartbeats, of machinery.

He followed Mr Healey into one of the housed oil-wells. He saw the great wheels being turned by leather belts and the sweating attendants and heard the monotonous pound of the pumps as they sucked up the black blood of the earth. He saw the donkey-engine being fed sedulously by young men, naked to the waist. The workers had the intense and dedicated appearance of priests, their faces and their bare arms stained with streaming wet moisture as black as coal, their brows sooted. They looked at Mr Healey and their white teeth glittered in their young faces. They were just as avid as he, but they were also subservient. 'Hundred barrels so far today!' one of them shouted at Mr Healey. 'And more to come, sir.'

Mr Healey nodded. He said to Joseph, 'It's all surface oil; just pump it out. Maybe lakes of it. Perhaps the whole damned world is filled with oil. Never can tell.' He smiled widely at Joseph and his small dark eyes squinted.

They returned to the town and Mr Healey took Joseph into a three-storey building near the square. The wooden steps were gritty and dusty; the halls were narrow and lightless. Splintered doors lined them, and Mr Healey flung one open. 'Here's where I really conduct my business,' he said. 'My house is just for important folks.'

The door opened on what Joseph immediately saw was a series of small adjoining rooms. The dirty windows were shut tightly and the air was heavy with heat and smoke, and if these rooms had ever been cleaned in a decade it was not evident. The floors were filthy with tobacco-spittle, though cuspidors were placed here and there, and the walls were a dull brown and the ceilings were of dark-brown tin. Every room held a roll-top desk stuffed with papers and a high book-keeping desk with a stool, and a dilapidated chair or two. Mr Healey's own office was little better but it did have a long table as well as a desk and a comfortable leather chair. The light that seeped in through the grey smeared windows was like light struggling through fog. Joseph also noticed that the windows were barred, as if the offices held prisoners, and that the door leading into the series of rooms was steel-sheathed on the inside and had a number of complicated locks. Garish calendars hung on some walls, and Mr Healey's room held a bookcase full of law books.

But what caught Joseph's interest at once was not so much the decrepit and ugly and polluted atmosphere of the rooms as the inhabitants of them. He saw at least fourteen men there, and not one was over forty, the youngest being in his early twenties. However, they had various things in common, so that they seemed of one family, one breed, one blood and mind: they were all tall, slender, elegant and deadly and dispassionate, and their faces were as unreadable as his own. They were richly dressed, though they had discarded their long coats because of the heat.

They did not move as Mr Healey entered with Joseph, though those who had been sitting rose and stood. They said nothing. They did not smile. It was as if the king wolf had come among them and they waited for his orders, which would be obeyed instantly and without question. Some of them were smoking the long thick cigars Mr Healey favoured, and they removed them from their mouths and held them in their long and extraordinarily aristocratic hands. Their black boots twinkled in the muted light from the dirty windows. Their thick hair, of many different shades, was fashionably long, covering their napes, and marvellously burnished and sleekly waving. With the exception of neat sideburns they were all clean-shaven, and all complexions were uniformly pale and unblemished and displayed minute care. From them all exuded faint perfumes and the scent of expensive hair tonics.

Mr Healey boomed affectionately, 'Lads, I want you to meet this here spalpeen, Joe Francis he calls himself, and he's going to help keep the books while I'm off making money for all of us!' He laughed happily. 'Then I won't have to strain my eyes over all those details. You just tell him. He'll boil it down. Smart, and sure he is. Fine hand, too. He'll give me in an hour what takes me, now, a whole day to get into my head,' and he tapped his rosy and glistening temple. His attitude was affable and easy. 'My manager, you can call him. Kind of young, but he ain't young in his mind, are you, Joe?'

Joseph saw no signal, but the men came together in a thin-hipped queue and held out their soft gamblers' hands to him and bowed a little. He took their hands. He still felt the incredulity of the whole affair. There were a few men here old enough to be his father, yet they lowered their tall heads in respect. They felt his lack of fear for them, but if they guessed it was because he did not know exactly what he should fear, they did not show it.

A young man gracefully offered him a cigar, but Joseph shook his head. He looked at the man and said, 'I do not smoke. I never intend to smoke. I don't want to waste my time and my money.' Mr Healey overheard this and sauntered back, beaming and chuckling. 'And that, boyo, is just my senti-ments, too. But everybody to his own pizen, I say.' He beamed and patted his enormous paunch. 'But I don't drink the booze when I'm working, and you know my sentiments about that, too. No whisky in these offices. Pistols yes, but no whisky. And no hang-overs tolerated. This is just for Joe's information, lads. And now, I want Joe to have my office, beginning tomorrow, and my desk, but not my table. That's mine. He'll be on hand at seven in the morning.'

He looked at Joseph, then indicated the man nearest him. 'This here is Mr Montrose. We never call each other by Christian names, Joe. Just Mister, and God knows if their monikers is the ones they were born with. Don't matter, anyway. Mr Montrose will take you to the shops tomorrow morning and buy you clothing fitten my men.'

'Not unless I can pay for it myself,' said Joseph.

Mr Healey waved his cigar. 'That's understood. Get off your high horse, Joe,' but he was pleased and looked at the others with a self-congratulatory smirk.

He took Joseph by the arm, nodded to his employees, and led the young man out into the gritty corridor. 'Finest lads in the world,' he said. 'Smart as turpentine, too. Don't fear God or man, or the police. Just fear me. I reckon there's not one but police are looking for them somewheres. Maybe like you, Joe, eh?'

Joseph said, 'No police are looking for me, Mr Healey. I've told you that before. Nor am I running away from anyone, nor have I ever been in gaol. Nor will I ever be.'

They drove home. Mr Healey went to his own quarters in the front of the second storey and Joseph walked down the hall to his own room. He was about to open his door when he heard a weak and fretful voice behind the door of the green room, and a soft young female voice answering. He said to himself, 'It's none of my business any longer what happens to Haroun. I have my own self to consider, and no involvements.' But still he hesitated. He remembered what he had felt outside this house a few minutes ago, and then with an imprecation against himself he went to Haroun's room and opened the door, throwing it open angrily as if driven not by his own will but by the power of a stupid stranger.

Vivid red sunlight poured into the room and Joseph noticed at once that this room was as beautifully serene and as austere as his own, but in green shades. Haroun was lying in a magnificently carved poster bed made of some black wood, and he was resting on plump white pillows. Beside him sat Liza, holding his hand and soothing him and talking to him in the gentlest and sweetest of voices. They were both children, and Joseph, in spite of himself, thought of Sean and Regina.

Liza jumped to her feet in obvious terror when she saw Joseph, her thin flat body quaking in its black cotton uniform, her starved face tremulous. She shrank; she tried to make herself invisible, and cowered. She dropped her head as if awaiting a blow.

But Haroun's fevered face, the huge black eyes shining, brightened with delight. He was ominously sick; he appeared to have dwindled in size and shape. He held out his dusky hand and quavered, 'Joe!'

Joseph looked at Liza. He said, 'Thank you for taking care of – for taking care of . . .' She lifted her head a little and glanced with fearful timidity at him. 'I just been talkin' to Mr Zeff, sir. I didn't do no harm. I'll bring him his supper,' and she fled from the room.

Haroun still held out his hand and Joseph was forced to take it. 'I don't know how I got here, Joe,' said Haroun. 'But I reckon you did it.'

'It was Mr Healey. This is his house, not mine.'

'But you did it,' said Haroun with the most absolute conviction. 'He'd never look at me 'cept for you.'

'Well, get well, Haroun, and you can repay Mr Healey. I did nothing.'

'You saved my life, Joe. I remember the train.'

It was then that Haroun looked up at Joseph with a glowing look, a deep and intense devotion, a total trust, a passionate fervour. It was the look which Bill Strickland gave Mr Healey, unquestioning, dedicated. It was not to be shaken, that faith. It was beyond reason.

'I am your man,' said Haroun, in a whisper. 'For all my life.'

Joseph pulled his hand from Haroun's. 'Be your own man, for life,' he said in a harsh tone. But Haroun still glowed upon him, and Joseph almost ran from the room.

CHAPTER ELEVEN

JOSEPH discovered that Mr Healey had been somewhat modest about his holdings and activities and financial worth and prospects. Mr Healey's steel files were kept in a room next to his 'suite of offices', as he called the dirty and dingy rooms he rented, or owned. There were bars on the windows here, too. There was a cot with blankets. In this room each man in his employ slept for two nights a month, or at least dozed, with pistols and a shotgun. Mr Healey dealt with banks in Pittsburgh and Philadelphia, and with a new one in Titusville, but he always kept a large sum in gold in the enormous iron and steel safe in that central arsenal in his offices. His men had orders to shoot to kill any intruder, and this was known well in the township. Each of his men was an expert marksman, and practised in the country at frequent intervals. Joseph was not exempt. His immediate mentor, Mr Montrose, was his teacher, and Mr Montrose reported to Mr Healey that 'that boy has an eye like a hawk, and never missed from the beginning'.

For Mr Healey all the men had devotion. Joseph had at

first thought they only feared him, but Mr Montrose enlightened him.

'The man they fear and detest and who is the subject of their nightmares is not Mr Healey, who is a considerate gentleman,' Mr Montrose told Joseph. 'They know he is human as they are human themselves, and is frequently sentimental. They trust him. Certainly, they will avoid any opportunity to annoy him – for various reasons. Their real hate and fear is for Bill Strickland, the white trash with the soul of a tiger.' (It was the first time that Joseph had heard the term 'white trash' but he understood it at once.) 'Mr Bill Strickland,' Montrose continued, with the first glare Joseph had ever seen in his eyes, 'is atavistic. He is mindless, as you have possibly observed yourself, Mr Francis. He is a living and murderous weapon and Mr Healey holds the trigger. Creatures like Bill Strickland are outside humanity, and are incapable of even the most distorted reason. They kill impersonally without malice or enmity or rage – and that is something other men cannot comprehend. They ask no questions. They do not even demand money for their slaughter. They simply – are. Do you understand me?'

'Yes,' said Joseph. 'Is he an idiot, or feeble-minded?'

Mr Montrose smiled, showing his excellent teeth. 'I have told you: he is an atavism. Once, I have read, all men were like that, before they became fully men, homo sapiens. The alarming thing is that their number is not small. You will find them among the mercenaries, and you will even find them in the best of families. You will find them everywhere, though frequently they are disguised as men.'

Mr Montrose smoked reflectively. 'I have never feared any man in my life. But I confess to fearing Bill Strickland – if he is behind my back. He makes my flesh crawl.'

'And Mr Healey employs him.'

Mr Montrose laughed, and touched Joseph lightly on his shoulder. 'Mr Francis, he employs him as men employ guards or guns. He is a weapon. If Mr Healey carried a pistol you would not fault him, would you? You would say he is a man careful of his safety. Mr Healey does not carry a pistol. He has Bill Strickland.'

It came as a mortifying shock to Joseph, who had reached his conclusions about Bill Strickland through his own reason and observation and the conversation with Mr Montrose, that young Haroun Zieff knew all about Bill by pure and artless instinct. Yet Haroun was the only one of Mr Healey's entourage who felt no mystic horror of the man or instinctive revulsion and loathing. 'I'd never cross him, and I'd stay away from his muzzle,' he told Joseph. His eyes shone with a light that Joseph could not interpret. 'But I wouldn't run away from him. You don't do that – with a jackal.' For the first time Joseph encountered the quiet courage and peculiar ferocity of the desert-born. 'Don't you ever be afraid of him, Joe. I'm here, your friend.'

Haroun now occupied a small but comfortable room over Mr Healey's stables. His wounds had healed, though sometimes he limped. He never complained. He accepted life with high-heartedness and a simple wisdom which was beyond Joseph's capabilities. He was never resentful nor grudging. He gave largely of himself and his big glowing smiles, and his native merriment.

Mr Healey, on Joseph's insistence, paid Haroun ten dollars a week to haul nitro-glycerine from the depot in Titusville to the deeper-drilled wells. Mr Healey had looked with smiling meditation at Joseph. That had been ten months ago. Haroun was now earning eighteen dollars a week and Joseph – who did not consider it surprising though his associates did – was receiving thirty-eight dollars a week. In a town where a doctor or a lawyer felt affluent if his earnings were thirty-five dollars a week this was remarkable. Joseph paid Mr Healey five dollars a week for his board, something which Mr Healey found hilarious though Joseph could see no occasion for amusement. He put his savings in the bank. He would not have spent money on clothing had not Mr Healey been insistent. 'I'll have no ragged beggars working for me!' So he dressed sombrely and plainly and cleanly.

In an effort to awaken Joseph's joy in living – which Mr Healey fully believed lay latent in every man – he gave Joseph a silver token which would admit him to any brothel he desired in Titusville, and to the prettiest girl, and at no cost. 'I've got the handsomest wenches in the whole Commonwealth,' he said. 'Never one over sixteen, youngest about twelve. Farm-fed, rich with butter and cream, plump as doves. Makes a man smack his lips. They know all the tricks. I've got madams who teach 'em. No gutter drabs in my houses! All clean and scented and healthy, and not cheap. You go and have a good time, boyo.'

'No,' said Joseph.

Mr Healey frowned. 'You ain't got a hankering for . . .? No, reckon not, though you never can tell. Well, you're only nineteen still. Well, they say that's the hottest time. Think so, myself. Couldn't stay away from the wenches, when I was eighteen, nineteen. Just about used myself up.' He chuckled. 'You keep that token. One of these days, you damned monk you, you'll look at it, spit on it, and polish it, and off you'll go just like everybody else.'

On three nights a week after supper at five o'clock, Joseph went to the office of Mr James Spaulding, a lawyer whom Mr Healey 'owned'. He also spent two hours on Saturday afternoon there, and half a day on Sunday. Here he studied law with Mr Spaulding as his teacher.

Once Mr Spaulding said to Joseph, 'It is not what the Law *says* that is important. It is how it is interpreted, how it is used . . .'

'Yes,' said Joseph. 'Law is a harlot.'

Joseph soon discovered in full why Mr Spaulding was so necessary to Mr Healey. The evidence was in the files in the locked room. He often found himself sickened at the evidence of collusion between Mr Healey and Mr Spaulding and the two local judges. For certain favours the judges owed their elections to Mr Healey, and Mr Healey owed considerable to the judges, and all this was presided over by the massive realism of Mr Spaulding. He once said to Joseph, in a rare moment of vulgarity, 'It's a case, dear boy, of you scratching my back, and me scratching yours, and what is wrong with a little proper scratching at the right time and in the right place? You can't always reach the itch, yourself, and you need help, and in a way it is Christian reciprocity. Joseph, if we all adhered to the letter of the Law, which I think Christ Himself condemned, there would be precious few of us left free in this world, and very little joy. Or profit.'

The months went by and Joseph learned in the offices of Mr Healey and in the richer office of Mr Spaulding, and what he learned, in spite of himself, made his nature harsher than it was even by birth, and bitterer than he could ever have imagined. More and more he was convinced that as an inhabitant of 'this world, for which he was not guilty, he must live by its laws and its exigencies if he were to survive and save his family. His last chance for personal happiness winked out and the ponderous darkness settled upon his spirit.

CHAPTER TWELVE

JOSEPH, out of desperate necessity, had finally been forced to trust the first person, with the exception of his mother, he had ever trusted in his life. It was a trust that was really only partial mistrust, but it had to be risked.

He needed to send money to Sister Elizabeth for his brother and sister. He knew that there was only a slight chance that Mr Squibbs would ever discover that 'Scottie' was really an Irishman and that he had a family in St Agnes Orphanage, and that through them he could trace the man who had absconded with his money. Still, there was that chance, and life was grotesque enough to permit it, and Joseph dared not risk such Hogarthian jokes. He was saving everything he could, and soon he would have enough for Mr Squibbs, plus interest. In the meantime there was Sean, and Regina and his unshaken belief that in the event money was not received by Sister Elizabeth they would be separated and adopted, or worse.

He considered. Every two months or so Mr Healey sent Haroun and two older men to Wheatfield to buy equipment for his wells, or other of his enterprises, or to deliver messages. (Mr Healey did not trust the United States Post Office, nor even the Wells Fargo Express.) Joseph had once suggested that he would not mind such a journey occasionally, himself, but Mr Healey assured him that his time was too valuable in Titusville. So Joseph had recourse to Haroun, whose dedication to him was frequently embarrassing. ('You've got yourself your own Bill Strickland, ain't you?' Mr Healey asked once, with immense amusement.)

Joseph wrote a letter to Sister Elizabeth in which he said he sometimes 'passed through' Wheatfield on business from Pittsburgh, and he enclosed a full year's payment for his family in gold bills, and extra money for small luxuries for them for the coming Christmas and their birthdays. He added that he was sealing the letter in red wax in three places, and that he'd be obliged if Sister Elizabeth would inform him if the letter had been tampered with and if anything had been taken from the envelope. Then he went to the stables over which Haroun slept and lived in a small hay-scented and manure-pungent room, and Haroun was happy to see him for never before had Joseph visited him here. Joseph sat with the letter in his hand and studied Haroun with the intensity he always gave those he was judging and weighing.

Joseph sat on the edge of Haroun's narrow cot and Haroun sat on the wooden crate which was his only chair and which held his few belongings, and in the light of the kerosene lamp Haroun's delight at this visit was embarrassing to the older man. He held the letter to Sister Elizabeth in his hand, and he looked into Haroun's eyes and said, 'I want you to mail this letter in Wheatfield tomorrow, when you go there early in the morning.'

'Yes,' said Haroun, and held out his small brown hand for the letter. But Joseph still held it. Would Haroun ask why it should be posted in Wheatfield? If he did then he could not be entrusted with the posting. But Haroun did not ask. He only waited, his hand still extended. If Joseph wished something it was enough for him, and he almost palpitated with the pleasure of the thought that he would be helping his friend.

'You must not let anyone else see this letter,' said Joseph.

'No!' exclaimed Haroun, shaking his curls until they flew.

'You will take it to the post-office,' said Joseph. 'And there you will arrange for a postal box for me, Joseph Francis. I will give you the two dollars rent for the year.'

For the first time Haroun was puzzled. 'I do not understand this, about a box,' he said. 'You must tell me so I can be sure.'

So Joseph explained and Haroun listened with the older boy's own intensity and concentration, and then Joseph made him repeat the instructions at least twice. Then he gave the letter to Haroun who tied it in a kerchief and stuffed it into the pocket of his only coat. Joseph watched him closely, but the boy showed no curiosity, no slyness, no speculation. He was only happy that Joseph was with him.

'How do you like your work for Mr Healey, Harry?'

Joseph asked, not with interest for he could feel none, but he felt that some amenities should be concluded.

'I like it,' said Haroun. 'I am making money, and isn't that enough?' He laughed and his white teeth shone in the lamp-light. 'I will soon be a rich man, like Mr Healey.'

Joseph could not resist smiling. 'And how do you think you'll manage that?'

Haroun looked wise. 'I save almost all, and when I have enough I will buy a string of tools for myself. One of these days.'

'Good,' said Joseph.

'Nothing like a good war for prosperity!' said Mr Healey to Mr Montrose, showing him an advance cheque on a British bank for delivery of four thousand eight-chamber repeating rifles which had been manufactured by Barbour & Bouchard, munitions makers in Pennsylvania. 'And this is just the beginning,' added Mr Healey with satisfaction. 'What's four thousand rifles? Hardly a flea-bite. Of course, Barbour & Bouchard are doing their own gun-running and arrangements with the Confederacy, and making millions. Maybe they want to be generous and let me and other small fry make an honest dollar.' He chuckled.

'And perhaps,' said the elegant Mr Montrose, 'Barbour & Bouchard are testing us to see if we can be entirely trusted with the gun-running, and perhaps they have heard that so far we have been discreet and bold enough to do the running to the Confederacy of contraband, without being caught once.'

Barbour & Bouchard sold the eight-chamber repeating rifles in enormous quantities to the Federal Government in Wash-ington. Whether or not the four thousand rifles now waiting in New York in a discreet warehouse – the boxes labelled 'machine parts' – were rifles stolen by interested parties from the Federal allotment, or whether Barbour & Bouchard had delivered those weapons themselves to that warehouse, was something Mr Healey would not have dreamed of speculat-ing about. That would have been uncivil, ungrateful, unrealistic and unworthy of a businessman. Besides, the bank draft was solely for successful delivery and demanded no investment of Mr Healey beyond the lives or liberty of his agents. Never-theless, one had to be careful in choosing those agents.

'It is time to break young Francis in,' said Mr Montrose. 'I have kept my counsel for two years about him, giving him only temperate commendations to you, but now I am certain not only were you completely correct about him in the beginning but that he has improved so he is, himself, a formidable weapon, or henchman, or whatever you may wish to call him. My trust is rarely given in full, but I think we can trust young Mr Francis to the utmost – so long as we continue to pay him well and he can pick our brains.'

'Um,' said Mr Healey. He considered the ash on his cigar as he and Mr Montrose sat in his study over brandy. 'Perhaps it is right you are. I sent him to Corland to buy up some leases, but before he went he said to me, "Mr Healey, I want to buy some leases on my own, and next to the leases you want. I do not yet have the money. Would you lend me two thousand dollars?"

'Well, sir, I thought that was mighty cool on the part of the spalpeen, to whom I pay forty dollars a week now – under duress, you might say.' Mr Healey smiled, but not with annoyance. 'Mighty cool. Twenty dollars a week to be returned from his pay, with six per cent interest. Well, sir, I did.'

'I know,' said Mr Montrose.

Mr Healey was not surprised. What Mr Montrose did not know was of the very least significance.

'I had a small talk with him,' Mr Montrose said. He preferred narrow and scented cheroots to the thick and robust cigars Mr Healey favoured. 'No, he did not tell me of the loan. I said to him, "All leases, to be legal, must be in your full and correct name in the courthouse, or later – er, scoundrels – might dispute the matter." I like the young man, and wished to help him and prevent him from doing himself a grave mischief. He appeared somewhat disturbed at this. To make certain he visited the courthouse himself. He trusts no one, and that is in itself commendable. Apparently he discovered that I had given him correct information.'

Mr Healey sat up. 'Yes? And what is his correct name?' Mr Healey knew Mr Montrose too well to question how he had come by the information.

'Joseph Francis Xavier Armagh. That is a strange name.'

'A high-nosed Irish name!' said Mr Healey, delighted. 'County Armagh. Not your County Mayo or Cork or such. High-nosed. Damn me if I don't have a lordship working for me! I always knew it.'

Mr Montrose said, 'Certainly we will not betray to young Mr Francis that we know his true and full name. That would be most vulgar of us. It is none of our business, as you know, sir.'

They settled down to business. Gun-running to the embattled South was somewhat different from running in food supplies, wool lengths, tools and such, in which Mr Healey had been heavily and profitably engaged since the outbreak of the war. For contraband such as weapons Washington had threatened the death-penalty.

'I don't want anybody killed, or caught,' said Mr Healey. 'Or anybody who would talk. You are right, you are. I'll have a talk with Joe Francis Xavier. Sound him out.'

'I want you to do something for me,' said Mr Healey to Joseph, after he had called him into the study. 'A little – dangerous. And no questions.'

'What?' asked Joseph, frowning.

Mr Healey raised a pacific hand. 'Now, now, don't get on your high horse. I'm not asking you this time to look about you in Pittsburgh and bring some nice pretty little girls to some of my boarding-houses, where they'll be well-fed and protected and make a bit of solid cash. I don't understand you,' complained Mr Healey. 'The girls I have always – protected, call it – come from wretched homes or have no homes, or are in slavey service, starving and what not. What's the harm in their earning some good money and having a gay time with many a spark? But not you, you monk, you Joe St Francis Xavier, not you. It ain't moral, or something, you think. But I have my ears out, and you didn't find it amiss just lately to use that there little token I gave you, did you?'

Joseph was silent. Mr Healey laughed, leaned across his table and slapped Joseph on one of the cold, slender hands which rested tensely on the wood. 'Don't give it a second thought, Joe. You're young, and it's only envious I am. What it is to be young! Never mind. The job I have in mind for you, Joe, is something you never dreamed of before, and I never engaged in it, myself. Not out of your morality, you righteous humbug, but out of lack of opportunity. Now, no questions. It's gun-running down to a little port in Ole Virginny, as they call it.'

Joe studied him. His expression did not change. He said,

'And how will I manage that?'

Mr Healey, before replying, opened his desk drawer and removed a packet of gold bills from it and a new pistol and a box of ammunition. 'Now here,' he said, 'is what you will use to grease your way, if things get a little sticky, which we hope they won't. Never saw a man whose eyes don't shine when he sees these. And this here gun is for you. It's yours, for always. Fine gun, isn't it? Best made; Barbour & Bouchard, right here in this here Commonwealth. They made those four thousand eight-chamber rifles you'll be delivering down South. Mr Montrose will go with you. Time you faced a little danger, took on some of the responsibilities my other lads have been doing right along, as you know only too well. But you've been snug in my offices, like a flea in a dog's ear, and the only danger you ever had was when you spent those two nights a month in the file room. My lads're not getting younger, and you're young, and it's hard to recruit the proper men for the proper jobs. Haven't found anyone but you in three – four long years, and that's a compliment, sir, that's a compliment.'

Joseph thought of his brother and his sister, and then he took the pistol in his hand and tested it. It had a fine balance, an excellent 'feel', a certain competent smoothness, a certain deadly reassurance. 'You've said no questions,' said Joseph. 'But I need to ask a few.'

'Go ahead,' said Mr Healey, with a large wave of his hand. 'But that don't mean I have to answer them.'

'Is there any chance I may be killed, or caught?'

Mr Healey watched him closely, then nodded. 'I'll be honest with you. Yes. Not a big chance, but some. Depends on what you do, what you say, how you conduct yourself, and your luck. But you got the luck of the Irish, don't you?'

Joe's hands caressed the pistol but he looked silently at Mr Healey for several moments. He said, 'And how much will you pay me for this?'

Mr Healey affected incredulous astonishment. 'You get your pay, don't you? Pay my other lads didn't get until they'd worked for me at least ten whole years, and you've been around only little over two. It's the soft heart I have, and I'm getting sentimental in my old age. I'll forget you ever asked that question.'

Joseph smiled faintly. 'I owe you one thousand eight hundred dollars still. You've treated me fair and square, as you call it, Mr Healey, and you've collected your interest, too, which is only right. So, to be brief, when I return after this job you will cancel the balance of my debt to you.' He lifted his own hand. 'I take care of your books, Mr Healey. You do pay the men a handsome salary, but for certain tricky jobs you give them a fine gift. I know. I write out the cheques myself, for your signature. I may be your eyes and your ears, as you have kindly mentioned yourself several times, but I do have eyes and ears of my own, too, though I keep my tongue to myself.'

'You're mad, that you are,' said Mr Healey.

Joseph said nothing, but waited.

'Your first important job, and God knows if you'll do it right, and you want one thousand eight hundred dollars for it!'

'Mr Healey, there is a good chance, and that I know, that I may never come back. I will leave a letter with – someone – who will deliver my options to another person in another city, if I am killed or caught. You need have no anxieties. I will not tell that – someone – where I am going or what I am going to do. I will only tell him that if I don't return he is to go to you and you will give him the cancelled agreement, and he will send it off to another person. You see, Mr Healey,' and Joseph smiled his grimace of a smile again, 'I am giving you my absolute trust that you will act honourably.'

Mr Healey was alarmed. He sat up straight, his face swelling and turning crimson. 'And who, may I ask, is that person in another city?'

Joseph almost laughed. 'Only a nun, sir, only a nun.'

'A nun!'

'Yes. A harmless old nun – she once did me a great favour.'

'I think,' said Mr Healey with awe, 'that you're daft. A nun! You! And who's your messenger right here, who'll take papers to that nun, not that I believe a word of it.'

'Harry Zeff.'

'And he knows that nun?' Mr Healey slapped his forehead in despair.

'No, he does not. He won't even need to know her or see her. He will only send her the papers when he reads her address in the letter I will leave him.'

'Good God, why all these secrets?'

'No secrets, Mr Healey. A nun is not a secret, and we Irish do have a penchant for the Religious, don't we?'

'So, you want to be charitable, to an old nun who probably never saw twenty dollars in her life!'

'No. Not charitable. Just a – remembrance, I'll call it.'

Mr Healey repeated, 'I think you're daft.' He chewed furiously on his cigar, then spat. He glared at Joseph. 'You're deeper than a well,' he said. 'Maybe deeper than hell, even. Any connection of yours, that nun?'

'No.'

'I don't believe any of this,' said Mr Healey.

'Nobody, sir, is going to force you to believe anything. I just want your word of honour that you will deliver that cancelled agreement to Harry Zeff to be sent to that nun, if I don't return.'

'All I know is,' said Mr Healey, 'is that in some way you outsmarted me and got me to say you can have that money I lent you. I didn't intend to. All right, get on with you. Get out of this room.'

Joseph stood up and said, 'Thank you, Mr Healey. You are a gentleman.'

Mr Healey watched the young man leave the room and silently close the door after him. He ruminated. He began to smile, and it was both a rueful and affectionate smile, and then he shook his head as if laughing at himself. 'The damned Irish!' he said aloud. 'You can't beat us.'

CHAPTER THIRTEEN

JOSEPH wrote the letter to Sister Elizabeth, and enclosed the deeds to the options he had bought near Corland. He wrote that the options were to be held for his brother and sister, and then offered for sale in a year for a certain price to Mr Healey. He mentioned that a cheque would be reaching her shortly in the amount of several hundred dollars, for the board of his family. 'This will protect their future, which I leave in your hands,' he wrote, 'for if you receive this letter I will probably be dead.' He sealed the letter carefully and wrapped paper about it, which he sealed also.

Then he wrote a short note to Haroun Zieff and sealed it also, the hot red wax dripping on his fingers. The candle he had lighted for this purpose flickered and smoked. On the envelope he wrote, 'Not to be opened unless I am dead.' He blew out the candle and the wan and sharper light of his table lamp filled his bedroom. A fire burned quietly in the grate. It was April 1, 1863, a cold bleak April after a desperately bitter winter. Joseph put the two packets together, placed them in a drawer of the rosewood desk and turned the key and pocketed it. The packets would be given to Haroun on the day he left for New York.

He threw more coals on the fire and opened a book and began to read. He had marked a place with Sister Elizabeth's last letter. He would re-read it again, then burn it. He never left any incriminating item behind him. He had put the thought of his coming mission to New York, and then Virginia, out of his mind for there was no need to think of it at present.

Joseph had sent her ten dollars extra in his last letter and in accordance with his request Sister Elizabeth had sent him a daguerreotype of Sean and one of Mary Regina, somewhat highly coloured, by hand, by the photographer. But not even the too-florid and vivid touches could conceal the smiling and poetic face of Sean Armagh, over-sensitive and refined, and the shining gaze and immaculate countenance of Regina, fragile yet exquisitely strong and softly ardent.

He believed that he would always have to protect Sean but that Regina was beyond his protection and had no need of it. What nonsense, he thought with some anger. I will make a man of my brother if I have to kill him doing it, but Regina will always need me, my darling, my sister.

He went to his coat which hung with his other few items of clothing in the rosewood wardrobe and brought out his leather pocket-book and he put the portraits of his brother and his sister in one side and tried, with sternness, to control the sudden turbulence of his foolish thoughts. He returned to his chair and gloomily studied the fire, then re-read the final page of Sister Elizabeth's letter.

'Among our dearest and most devoted helpers is Mrs Tom Hennessey, the wife of our Senator. So kind and gracious a lady, so dedicated and tireless! Sometimes she brings her little girl, Bernadette, to our orphanage, for you cannot instil too soon a spirit of charity and love and kindness in a Child, and

Bernadette, a most charming Child, is as thoughtful as her mother and brings gifts to the Little Ones who have no one to remember them. She and Mary Regina have become friends, for all Mary Regina's natural reserve and reticence, and it is well for Mary Regina to have so blithe a spirit sometimes near her, for she is often too grave. I have often heard Mary Regina laugh, her quiet laugh, and it is music to my heart. We love her dearly.'

Looking at the fire now he said to himself that time was growing short and that when he returned from his mission he would go on business for Mr Healey to Pittsburgh and have another conversation with a man he had met there. Having decided this, he picked up his book, closed his mind to all other thoughts, and read. The carved clock below in the hall struck one, two and then three, and the fire died down and the room became cold and Joseph still read.

Mr Healey did not come to his offices the next day as was his usual custom. Nor had he been present at breakfast with Joseph. Little Liza timidly informed Joseph, on his indifferent question, that no, Mr Healey was not sick. He had but gone to the depot to meet an Important Personage who would be a guest in this house for a few days, a very Important Personage. No, she did not know his name. (Joseph had not asked.) But Miz Murray said that before she, Liza, had come here the Personage had been a frequent visitor, though now Mr Healey visited him instead. As Liza sounded somewhat breathless at the honour about to be bestowed on this household, Joseph glanced up at the girl and saw that she was quite flushed with importance and that her colour made her plainness attractive and even appealing.

The April morning had suddenly turned warm and balmy, and Joseph put his greatcoat over his arm, and then settled his tall sober hat over his brows. Mrs Murray came into the hall and said in her sullen fashion that he was not to go to Mr Spaulding's office tonight but to return to this house at half past four. There was a visitor and lateness on Joseph's part would be uncivil if not unpardonable. Joseph said nothing, and did not acknowledge this message from Mr Healey. He ran down the steps outside and began to walk rapidly. Mrs Murray stood in the doorway and watched him, and her face took on its usual grey malevolent look when she encountered the young man. Joseph knew that she hated him, but did not ask himself why, and he knew that Bill Strickland, in his mindless way, was also aware of him and hated him also. But Joseph had encountered too much hatred in his life to be concerned at this, in Mr Healey's house. He accepted unmotivated malice as part of human existence.

After Mrs Murray shut the door, muttering in a malign undertone, she went upstairs to her daily task before Liza or the other little maid began theirs: she entered Joseph's room and carefully and quickly searched every drawer in his commode, deftly opened the locked desk with a similar key and started at encountering within the drawer a thick sheaf of gold notes and a new pistol and a box of ammunition. 'Ahah!' she cried aloud. Then to her immense disappointment she saw Mr Healey's handwriting on the band which held the notes and the words, 'Joe Francis.' She re-locked the drawer and her thick, whitish lips moved in and out surlily and with resentment. Mr Healey should have told her last night. She moved to the wardrobe and searched every pocket lingeringly, and felt every seam, hoping for some evidence which would convince Mr Healey that his protégé was a thief or perhaps a murderer, or some other kind of criminal. Diligently, she ran her hand over the tops of books, almost praying for a forgotten and incriminating letter. She shook Joseph's book which he had left on his bedside table. She turned up the mattress and felt between it and the bed boards, then looked hopefully under the bed itself. She felt the pillows, examined the seams for an entrance. She lifted the corners of the rug, felt behind the one large picture on the wall which depicted a pale woodland scene. She examined the backing. She searched behind the draperies at the window, and at the window ledge on top. All this was familiar to her and she searched deftly. More and more disappointed – though she was positive that on one of these days she would uncover some baleful proof of her intuition regarding Joseph – she glanced down into the cold fireplace. Aha, he had burned another letter, as he had burned others, the sly, cunning fox! She crouched fatly and with difficulty on the hearth and turned the black flakes over with the poker. Her breath stopped when she found a torn piece which had been only charred at the edges, a small but clear piece with chaste writing upon it. Snatching up the scrap she read it: 'Sister Elizabeth.'

So, he had a sister, had he, hidden away probably in gaol, or perhaps in a brothel. Yet he had told poor, trusting Mr Healey that he had no kin! Men did not conceal the existence of blameless sisters or deny that they possessed any. The drab had been kept out of sight, though she probably advised and guided her brother into plots and schemes and infamy. Why, they could be conspiring together at this very minute to rob and murder Mr Healey in his bed! Why else would a man hide such a relative? Trembling with triumph and joy she carefully wrapped the scrap of paper in her kerchief and rumbled rapidly out of the room. She met Miss Emmy in the hall and abruptly came to a halt.

Miss Emmy smiled at her bewitchingly. 'Anything found today?' she asked.

Mrs Murray said in a surly voice, 'I don't know what you're talking about, Miss Emmy. I was just making certain that the girls do not fault their cleaning.' Then she could not contain herself. 'I always knew he was a sly, deep one, probably a thief or a murderer! I did find part of a letter he had burned, but he overlooked this! See it!' She gave the scrap to Miss Emmy who examined it curiously: Then the girl laughed and returned it. She said, 'Why Mr Francis is Irish and a Catholic, Mr Healey told me, and "Sister Elizabeth" is probably a nun! He'd know them, just as Mr Healey knows some in Pittsburgh. He even sends them money at Christmas for orphanages and such.'

Seeing Mrs Murray's bloated face becoming greyer and greyer with frustration, and her eyes blinking rapidly, the girl asked with sharper curiosity, 'Why do you hate Mr Francis so much? I've seen you looking at him, and you'd like to stick a knife in him.'

Mrs Murray lifted a massive hand and shook a finger at the girl. 'I've lived a life, Miss Emmy, and I can tell a criminal when I see one, and you mark it – it will all come out one of these days, and maybe then you'll be sorry you laughed at me.' She trundled off with her behemoth tread and the floorboards shook and her whole thick body expressed her malignance and hate.

When Joseph arrived at Mr Healey's offices Mr Montrose accosted him and invited him for a consultation in an empty room. Mr Montrose said, 'We leave, as you know, very soon. We are to travel on the railroad in Mr Healey's private coach, at Mr Healey's order, for are we humble and unknown travellers?' Mr Montrose smiled, and his cat's eyes gleamed at Joseph. 'We are gentlemen, and important as Mr Healey's employees. When we arrive in New York we will stay at the best hotel. Our wardrobe will be irreproachable.'

'My wardrobe is sufficient,' said Joseph, thinking of his saved money.

'No,' said Mr Montrose. 'What is it Shakespeare said? I believe it was something regarding the glass of fashion, rich but not gaudy. Mr Healey has commissioned me to be certain that you are attired so. It is not "charity", Mr Francis, for I, too, must dress for the occasion, at Mr Healey's expense.'

'I thought,' said Joseph, 'that dangerous work demands anonymity.'

Mr Montrose looked at him as one looks at a child. 'Mr Francis, when we travel for Mr Healey we are not on dangerous work. We are agents travelling on his very respectable business, and so we stay at respectable hotels and conduct ourselves respectably and noticeably in New York, or wherever. We consult with others concerned in Mr Healey's affairs; we dine with them; we converse with them; we walk with them. Mr Healey is not unknown in New York, Mr Francis. When we do our other – shall I say manipulations – we do it quietly and unseen, and who is to suspect us, we who are on important business in New York, admired and esteemed, above reproach or suspicion?'

Joseph spent the rest of the day studying and searching the reports of Mr Healey's men who worked for his various enterprises. Eight thousand dollars' income the last ten days from the brothels of Titusville and vicinity, over and above expenses. Illicit gambling was another huge source of income, and there were discreet notations to the effect that 'drinking supplies' were vastly increasing, also the incomes of saloons. These did not include revenues from Pittsburgh and Philadelphia and New York and Boston, which were separate items and kept under lock and key, nor the income from oil-wells. Joseph summarised the ones on his desk; it was a monthly task. The April day was becoming warm and stuffy and though the sun shone brightly there was a dull mutter of thunder in the air.

He left early, remembering Mr Healey's message. Mrs Murray met him in the hall with hateful rebuke. 'You are late,' she said. 'You have kept the gentlemen waiting.' Even as she spoke the clock chimed the half hour.

CHAPTER FOURTEEN

'THREE HUNDRED and one men you wish to keep from the draft,' said the Important Personage. 'That will be very costly, Ed. You will have to buy substitutes for them. The price is high. One hundred dollars apiece, at the very least. That is what they are asking now in New York. Some ask for as much as five hundred dollars and find five offers.' He laughed. 'I have heard that some millionaires are offering as much as five thousand dollars for a substitute for their sons! Yet you offer twenty dollars. Come, Ed, you must be jesting.'

He sipped the excellent whisky and looked at Mr Healey with humour. 'What are you saving it for? Neither wife nor children nor kin.'

'I was poor once,' said Mr Healey. 'You were never that, and you don't know what it means. I do. I can understand why men offer their souls to the devil. You don't.'

They sat in Mr Healey's library. 'I think,' said the Personage, admiring one of Mr Healey's cigars which was held in his fingers, 'that every man, if he could, and knew how, would sell his soul to the devil. That is why the devil is discreet. He'd have too many customers if he proclaimed that he was in the market for souls. Well, Ed, are you ready to put up the money?'

'To you? Or to the substitutes?'

'Now, now, Ed, no need to be uncivil.'

'You owe me a lot,' said Mr Healey. 'I don't want to mention how much. That would be "uncivil", as you call it, and impolite. I helped you. You wasn't too smart in many ways. I didn't ask you to meet me here to discuss money for substitutes. I asked for your influence in Washington.'

The Personage inclined his head. 'The price of my influence comes high, Ed. We have Mr Lincoln to deal with and he abhors the reality of substitutes, though he has to accept it.

The army needs men. We've suffered great losses. Recruiting does not fill the ranks any longer. People are realising now that war is no lark. Its price is blood and death. When you buy a substitute you buy the probability of a man's life, and a life is all a man has. Call it a worthless life – it is still the man's life and all he knows. Now don't be huffy. It is true I have influence, as do others. But this is a dangerous and delicate business, Ed, and needs the aplomb of a thousand Philadelphia lawyers, not to mention their fee. If I should undertake this for you I would put myself into jeopardy. There are already disagreeable rumours about others in my position, and Mr Lincoln is getting wrathy, to put it very mildly. If the axe falls – I don't want it to be my head, and I am sure you will understand.'

Mr Healey looked at him with blunt rudeness. 'How much do you want?'

'Two hundred thousand dollars, in gold, not bills, not in notes, nor cheques.'

'You are daft,' said Mr Healey. His visitor shrugged fine brown broadcloth shoulders. 'One hundred thousand.'

'For my whole career, if it is found out?'

'For your whole career – which I could stop on a word.'

The visitor laughed gently. 'You are not the only one who has a Bill Strickland, Ed.'

'But you have more to lose than I do. As you said, I have neither wife nor child.'

There was a sudden black chill in the library though the golden light increased in intensity against the walls.

Then the visitor said in a soft voice. 'Are you threatening me, Ed?'

'I think we are threatening each other. Let's be sensible. I will make it one hundred thousand but not a penny more. Take it or leave it.'

The visitor frowned as if with pensive pain, as if musing on the infidelity of old and beloved friends who are hinting at betrayal. His face became sad. Mr Healey smiled and refilled their glasses.

The visitor sighed and said, 'I will do what I can, Ed. I can't promise success. . . .'

'For one hundred thousand dollars any man would cut his wife's throat, turn traitor, become an assassin, blow up the White House. Anything. I don't pay for promises of doing one's "best". I've been robbed too many times by the "best" a man can do. I pay on delivery. I will pay when all my men receive notice that a substitute has offered himself to the army in his place, and that the substitute has been accepted. Is that clear?'

'Ed, you have always made yourself eminently clear. You've never been obscure.'

'Is it a bargain, then?'

The visitor reflected, then with an air of indulgent surrender and deep brotherhood and affection, he reached across the table and shook hands with Mr Healey. 'A bargain, though God knows what it will cost me.'

'You mean what it will cost me, I am thinking,' said Mr Healey. 'What the hell. I wonder if my lads are worth it.' Mr Healey smiled without illusion at his visitor. Then he turned his large rosy head. 'I think the boyo is here now. Not that you can change my opinion, but I'd like yours, honest, if it isn't too much to ask.'

There was a knock on the door and Mr Healey bellowed genially, 'Come in, come in!' He shifted his great bulk on his chair. The door opened and Joseph stood on the threshold and he saw the visitor, after his first glance of greeting at Mr Healey and the first inclination of his head.

Mr Healey said, 'This here's my right hand, Tom, Joe Francis Xavier I call him. Joe, be on your mark: this gentleman is our esteemed Senator, Tom Hennessey, come to visit his old friend.'

Joseph did not stir or even appear to breathe for a moment or two. He did not look away from the Senator. Then, stiffly, as if he had become wood, he bowed a little and murmured a respectful greeting, to which the Senator replied with a gracious inclination of his head and a winning smile. But now the expression on his large and sensual face was puzzled. He said in his fruitiest tones. 'Happy to meet you, Mr Francis. I have heard very flattering remarks about you from our dear friend, Mr Healey.'

The Senator leaned his still handsome body back in his chair, with easy negligence, and he smiled at Joseph with all his captivating charm.

'Mr Francis,' he said, and his voice was as soft and lulling as down, 'haven't we met before? I never forget a face.'

Joseph faced the Senator. 'No, sir,' he replied. 'We have

never met.' His eyes met the Senator's straightly.

The Senator's ears were keener even than his eyes and he said to himself: I've heard that voice, not recently, but I have heard it. It is an Irish voice, and there is the Irish accent like my father's, and it is a strong voice and I have an impression of trees. But where, when?

Now, then, this is very interesting, thought Mr Healey and watched with acute attention.

'Were you ever in Winfield, Mr Francis?' asked the Senator, leaning forward now so as not to miss the slightest change of expression on Joseph's face, the slightest hesitation in his voice.

'Winfield?' said Joseph. He wondered if the savage pounding of his heart was audible in this room. His whole body felt numb and cold and prickling.

He's afraid, thought the Senator.

'Ain't Winfield near Pittsburgh?' Mr Healey asked Joseph, who turned to him as if he were afraid that he would break if he moved rapidly.

'I think so, Mr Healey.'

You damned well know so, thought the Senator. Now, how could I be dangerous to a fellow like this? he wondered. Recognition of him? Exposure of him? He can't be much over twenty, and I think that it must be several years since I first saw him.

'You were born in Ireland, I believe, Mr Francis?' said the Senator.

'Yes, sir.' The voice was stronger than before, and the challenge was there also. 'In Carney.'

The Senator quickened. 'Carney? My father spoke of it once or twice County Armagh.'

It was Mr Healey's turn to quicken, and he stared at Joseph openly.

The dread was on Joseph again, and he felt hatred for himself that he had been so indiscreet. But he said with quietness, 'Armagh. Yes.'

The Senator gazed at him, musing. Armagh. Where had he heard that as a personal name before? He would remember soon; he always remembered. He would remember where he had seen Joseph before, too. Their eyes did not move from each other and Mr Healey watched. Then he was surprised. The Senator was a mountebank and could assume any expression at will, all of them lying and hypocritical, as needed for the occasion. But the expression now on the Senator's face was unguarded and, for the first time, honest, and Mr Healey recognised this astutely. It was as if he were remembering someone for whom he had had some genuine affection, some close emotion, some unforgotten fondness. Then, as if conscious of his own self-revealment the Senator's face almost immediately changed and became false again.

Joseph rose and turned to Mr Healey. 'If you will excuse me, Mr Healey, before supper? I must wash and change.'

Then he half-turned to the Senator and bowed in his direction and said, 'I am happy to make your acquaintance, sir.'

I bet you are, thought the Senator, but without contempt and even with humour. I don't think you are a thief or a scoundrel, now, or hiding from the law. But you are hiding, my lad, and I will know why, and from what and from whom. He inclined his own head graciously. 'And I am happy to make your acquaintance too, Mr Francis.'

They watched Joseph leave the room and shut the door behind him. 'Now,' said Mr Healey, 'what was all that?'

'I could swear I've seen him before, and heard his voice, Ed. But I can't remember.'

'We don't get younger, Tom.'

The Senator gave him an unfriendly look. 'I'm not senile yet, Ed. Yes, I've seen him before. I'll probably remember.'

'You don't think he can be trusted? I want your opinion, Tom.'

'You mean you want my corroboration. Very well. He won't knife you in the back. I've – known – one or two, one at least, like that. He won't sell you out, Ed. But he's his own man. He'll never be anyone else's. When the time comes for him to move, he'll move, but he'll give you warning.'

Joseph did not speak a dozen words at the table that night and avoided direct glances at the Senator. But Miss Emmy preened coquettishly and smiled at the Senator, for she knew he admired her. She hoped Joseph was watching. Joseph was watching only the Senator from the corner of his eye. So, the bastard hadn't remembered yet. It was possible he never would. In a few years it would not matter if he remembered. He, Joseph, would be safe, no longer vulnerable to idle malice, no longer vulnerable to Mr Healey's anger at being deceived if only by a name.

At the end of the dinner Mr Healey laid his hand in a fatherly fashion on Joseph's shoulder and said, 'I'd like a minute of your time, Joe, in the lib'ry.'

For an instant Joseph stiffened, but there was nothing in Mr Healey's face which was false or unkind, and he followed him into the study, or the library.

Mr Healey sat down at his table and faced Joseph, and smoked contemplatively on his cigar.

'Joe,' he said, as if asking the most innocent question, 'who is Sister Elizabeth?'

Again Joseph's heart jolted in his chest. He looked at Mr Healey, and now all his caution returned to him. 'Sister Elizabeth?' he repeated. What Mr Healey said next would reveal what he really knew.

'Come on, Joe, you know very well who Sister Elizabeth is.'

'If you know that name, Mr Healey, why do you ask me about it? Where did you hear it, and from whom?' Now Joseph understood that in some way Mr Healey had learned of the name, but knew nothing else. Joseph's thought ran to Haroun, then dismissed it. He suddenly remembered burning the letter last night. It had never been out of his hands or his pockets since Haroun had delivered it to him, fully sealed. Joseph could see the fireplace. Had a scrap remained, a shred of paper? He kept his face still. He waited.

'Now, Joe, don't you trust me?'

So, he doesn't know anything but the name, and how did that come about?

Then he recalled that Miss Emmy had told him weeks ago that Mrs Murray searched his room every morning for some unknown reason. She could have found only a scrap of paper in the fireplace, and he cursed his carelessness in not making certain as he usually did.

He said to Mr Healey, 'You remember our conversation last night, Mr Healey. I told you of a nun I know, to whom my money will be delivered if I did not return from my – mission. She is Sister Elizabeth.'

'Where does she live? Where's her convent?'

Joseph simulated profound surprise. 'What does that matter to you. Mr Healey? That is my own affair. But I will tell you a little. She was kind to me when I was a boy fresh from Ireland.'

Mr Healey considered. That damned old whore, Miz

111

Murray, and her whispered message to him tonight, and her triumphant showing to him of that little scrap of paper! Now he might lose Joe, that damned proud Irisher, and all at once, to his baffled amazement, Mr Healey felt a bereavement so sharp that he was frightened.

'Nothing to do with me, eh, Joe?'

'None at all, Mr Healey.'

'You never told me your real name.'

'Joseph Francis is my name. That is no lie.'

Mr Healey smiled. He almost laughed. 'Joe, you're always up on your high horse. Climb down. Never mind how I knew about Sister Elizabeth. It'll be our own secret, eh? And one of these days maybe you'll tell me all about it – confiding like.'

So, Joseph thought for the first time, the Senator had not remembered. Had he remembered and told Mr Healey the latter would not now be so paternal and kind, even wistful. It was the wistfulness that astonished Joseph.

CHAPTER FIFTEEN

JOSEPH and Mr Montrose travelled in Mr Healey's private coach and arrived in New York in the early morning. Joseph had watched the red morning light on the peaceful Hudson River and on the green Palisades with their white and grey mansions and great gardens overhung by enormous glistening trees. The river was full of steam-boats and small sailing vessels and flat-boats, their reflections gliding with them on the water, so still was it. It is a beautiful world, thought Joseph, with that mystic deep melancholy of his which had no name.

The station in New York at 26th Street and 4th Avenue was even more tumultuous than the stations in Pittsburgh and Philadelphia, and far larger. The noise of bells, whistles, voices and trundling carts and leaving and departing trains was overpowering. Joseph saw a vast welter of confusion, of running men, of lanterns, of gaslight, and the sides of coaches sliding past his window, rumbling and squealing. And, as usual these days, troops were climbing into standing trains.

The station platforms were heaped with wooden boxes and cartons and luggage, and men in crude workmen's clothing sweated them on to flat wagons and struggled with larger pieces. Steam gushed from the wheels of trains, screaming thinly. Smoke from stacks billowed in black gushes through the station. Somewhere a bugle sounded, then a rattle of drums, and somewhere a whole group of people laughed. Everywhere hung the red, blue and white bunting, and the limp lengths of flags, sluggishly stirring in the wind created by movement of trains and people. Now, through far distant doors the morning brightened and with it entered unseasonable heat on an almost visible wave of soot-speckled air. And always the hurrying groups, entering or leaving, the thrusting heads, the portmanteaux, the wicker suitcases, the scurrying carts filled with anonymous objects, the shouting of porters, and the sudden splitting howl of a train on the move.

As detached as inhabitants of another earth Joseph and Mr Montrose left the train to be met at once by a uniformed coachman who touched his hat and took their luggage. A fine closed carriage awaited the two men from Titusville. The coachman fought his way to Fifth Avenue with lashings of a whip and the strong menace of his two huge black horses. Mr Montrose lit a cheroot and leaned back on crimson leather cushions. The harness of the horses was so polished and so brilliant in the sun that it shot back lances of light into the carriage and Joseph's eyes smarted. Then they turned into Fifth Avenue, 'as famous, in its way, as the Strand in London,' said Mr Montrose.

When they arrived at the ostentatious pile of the Fifth Avenue Hotel Mr Montrose left the carriage with the agility of a youth and Joseph followed, bending his angular body from his lean waist. They entered the lobby and Joseph felt himself immediately inundated by an enormous redness and at once the air, to his senses at least, was far hotter and more overwhelming than on the street. The walls were of dark mahogany and red satin damask under a domed ceiling of gilded wood. The carpet was scarlet, the great chairs of mahogany were cushioned in the same colour. The lobby was one movement of men and women coming and going, laughing and talking, greeting and saying farewell. There was such an air of festival here that Joseph wondered if there was a holiday in progress peculiar to New York alone. Then he

113

remembered that this was the joyful air of war prosperity, despite the shortages of goods and food, and the new income tax which Washington had desperately imposed to pay for the conflict. From behind some gilded screens came the soft singing of violins and a piano, unobtrusive but adding their own sweet comment to the happiness and gaiety here, the air of well-being and riches and importance and excitement. All the ladies were beautifully and expensively dressed, their silk hoops draped with contrasting colours, and beaded and embroidered, their mantles bordered with gold or silver ornamentations, their ears and necks jewelled, their parasols of many bright colours, and all were scented so that the lobby seemed to be one hot flower-garden blowing in full sun. Young or not so young, every face was beautiful and every woman, apparently, tried to resemble a soubrette. Their gestures were pretty and animated, their voices like birds. Their fans fluttered; embroidered reticules swayed on their gloved wrists. There was not a sad or anxious countenance among them. Their gentlemen were equally splendid and as marvellously arrayed and dashing, and when they were not speaking they were laughing or bowing to some lady or displaying a handsome leg in tight pantaloons.

As if the lobby were empty Mr Montrose moved smoothly to the desk where at least two of the gentlemen recognised him at once, and bowed. He said, 'Mr Francis, my associate, is with me, gentlemen, and I will have the customary suite.' One man produced a thick book and wrote in it swiftly, nodding his head with respect at Joseph. Behind them stood two men in the yellow uniforms which Joseph had seen outside, holding their luggage.

They entered one of the gilded caged and grilled elevators, and the operator pulled on his rope easily and they ascended. 'How do you like it, Mr Francis?' asked Mr Montrose. Joseph considered. He looked down through the grille at the red falling lobby and its many-coloured and milling inhabitants. 'I don't think I do,' he said.

The two men and their two escorts with the luggage left the elevator at the fourth floor, and they walked down a corridor paved with red carpeting and bounded by walls of polished mahogany. One carved door was unlocked and flung open. Mr Montrose was about to enter when an army officer, apparently in haste, suddenly left the room opposite and collided with the small caravan in his way. He was a short youngish man with a full clean-shaven and pugnacious face and eyes of a darting and restless intelligence, and of a peculiar sharp and piercing blue.

He halted and bowed to Mr Montrose. 'My abject apologies sir,' he said.

'Accepted, sir,' said Mr Montrose with a responding bow.

The officer looked swiftly at Joseph, inclined his head, then raced down the corridor in the direction of the elevators. 'These soldiers,' said Mr Montrose. 'They move as though there is a battlefield around the corner.' His voice was indulgent. But Joseph remembered the searching and penetrating glance the man had given him, as if judging him.

The expansive suite was mercifully decorated in dove grey and soft green silk and velvet, with not a single touch of red, for which Joseph was grateful. The uniformed attendants quickly and expertly unpacked the gentlemen's luggage, and put the contents in wardrobes and chests with gilt handles. Joseph went to the window and stared down at the welter of Fifth Avenue and its small front lawns and iridescent trees and its endlessly moving crowds on the pavements and its fiercely congested traffic. As so many ladies had opened coloured parasols against the sun it was like looking down on a hanging garden on a rampage. Suddenly Joseph felt that he was being suffocated. He closed the windows, and the noise was muted. He felt Mr Montrose near him, and he turned and saw that he had opened his hand and consulted the merest scrap of white paper in it. 'We shall have a visitor in exactly five minutes. Perhaps you would care for a glass of this water, and then a quick wash?'

Joseph thought: But we were very late on the train and no one knew when we would arrive, and so there could have been no definite appointment, and no messages were asked for or delivered at the desk downstairs. Nor did I see a paper or an envelope in these rooms. Yet a visitor will be here in exactly five minutes!

He went into the bathroom and washed himself. He went over the last hour or so in his mind. No one had given Mr Montrose an envelope; he had spoken to no one except on the business of obtaining this suite. No one had discreetly passed him a paper, not even in passing –

Joseph wiped his hands slowly. Except that one had collided

115

with him and spoken to him in the corridor outside: the army officer. One had apologised, one had accepted the apology, and then they had disentangled themselves. Joseph smiled. He went into the parlour again and looked at Mr Montrose who was as fresh as if he had just arisen. Joseph hesitated. He wondered if Mr Montrose was waiting for him to comment, and to approve the comment, or if he would be vexed if Joseph spoke, and would think the less of him. But Joseph, still perturbed about the collision, said, 'Ah, yes, our visitor is the army officer, I assume?'

Mr Montrose looked up alertly. He said, 'Were we that clumsy or obvious?' But he seemed capriciously pleased.

'No, not at all,' said Joseph. 'It is just my deduction from the events of this morning.'

CHAPTER SIXTEEN

COLONEL Elbert Braithwaite literally burst into the room when Mr Montrose opened the door, and he threw a last blazing blue glance over his shoulder as he bounced over the threshold. The air in the suite was far cooler than on the avenue below, but the Colonel was sweating profusely and his pugnacious face gleamed. He shook hands heartily with Mr Montrose and bowed and grinned, showing a vast amount of large and glistening white teeth. His manner was boyish and happy and excited. 'I waited all day yesterday and all night!' he exclaimed, and looked at Mr Montrose with laughing reproach. 'I assume, sir, that the train was very late due to the troop trains and such.'

The Colonel had ignored Joseph's presence, and Joseph waited. Finally Mr Montrose detached himself from his friend and gestured towards Joseph. 'Colonel Braithwaite,' he said, 'this is my new associate, Mr Francis. He is also in my utmost confidence and so you can trust him. Mr Healey, who never makes a mistake, as you know, chose him.'

The Colonel swung at once to Joseph, bowed deeply, and held out his strong, short hand in utmost fellowship and greeting. 'My compliments, sir!' he exclaimed. 'I am happy to make your acquaintance!' His teeth, like white porcelain, glowed.

Joseph bowed also, touched the hand quickly and withdrew. He repeated, 'I am happy to make your acquaintance.'

The Colonel listened acutely. It was his theory that you could discover a lot by listening to a man's voice and not his words. His thick pink ears seemed to peak as he heard Joseph's lilting accent. Then a quick look of incredulity ran over his face. He had heard that accent tens of thousands of times in his native Boston. He heard it every day among his men. His nostrils twitched with distaste and the broad good humour of his countenance hardened.

'You are from Boston, sir?' he asked.

Mr Montrose's ever-ready deviltry came to the surface and he said, 'Mr Francis also comes from Ireland, I believe.'

'I thought so,' said the Colonel, with mingled self-satisfaction and a contempt which was so obvious that Mr Montrose's usually serene and aloof face became somewhat stern. 'I can always pick them out.'

He then turned his back on Joseph and began his fast chattering again with Mr Montrose, giving him news of the city and the war. Then he said more slowly and with loud emphasis. 'You will be glad to know, sir, that we have finally put down the Irish Rebellion in this city. It was not done, however, until we were given orders to shoot rioters on the spot. Excellent! They soon enough retired to their hovels and gutters and caves in Central Park with their rats' tails between their legs!'

The insult was so palpable, and so intended, that Joseph's fists clenched and he started blindly towards the Colonel. and the lust to kill he had felt in the past rose up in him and reddened his eyesight. The Colonel had the soldier's instinct, and he turned immediately and said with the most open and happiest smile, 'Present company excepted, of course, Mr Francis!'

Joseph stopped, shaking with his cold anger. He looked down into those mocking but contemptuous eyes and said, 'Present company is not excepted, sir, when I say soldiers are brutes and not men, and that they are incapable of reason and have no capacity for thought and obey orders as mindlessly as a gun. They are never masters; they are slaves.'

'Come, come, gentlemen,' said Mr Montrose. 'I am certain that no one intended to insult anyone else in this room. Are we not gentlemen here? Do we not have business to transact, and is not business transcendent over mere pique and misunderstandings?' He looked at the Colonel straightly and there was an expression on his face which Joseph had never seen before, but the Colonel's figure seemed to diminish. 'I have told you, sir,' said Mr Montrose, 'that Mr Healey has chosen Mr Francis, and he would be extremely – disturbed – if he heard that his choice has been deprecated. I am sure, Colonel, that that was not your intention?'

'Not at all!' cried the Colonel. 'I was merely remarking on outlaws in this city, and if I implied that they were Irish my implication was quite true, unfortunately. Mr Francis is too sensitive. My compliments and apologies, sir,' and he bowed to Joseph again, a little too emphatically. 'I am your servant.' The Colonel's teeth flared and glowed again, and Joseph was disgusted. The Colonel said, 'You must convey my compliments to Mr Healey and my pleasure in serving him, sir. I deduce this is another shipment similar to the ones before.' He added, 'Did you say that Mr Healey is prepared to be even more generous?' His face became eagerly alerted and leaned towards Mr Montrose.

'Much more generous,' said Mr Montrose. 'I might even add that it will take your breath away, sir.'

'Ah!' cried the soldier with joy, and he slapped the table. 'Then Mr Healey has finally realised the danger!'

Mr Montrose arched his brows. 'Was it so dangerous, Colonel, to give clearance to the clipper *Isabel* in the port? After all, you are military authority of the port of New York, are you not?'

'The *Isabel*,' said the Colonel, and now there was the slightest scowl on his low and sweating forehead, 'is a commercial vessel operating between Boston and New York, and sails openly, with the tide, day or night. When she takes a different tack, shall we say, it takes the utmost discretion and – consideration – to avoid the Federal patrols. This is not without danger.'

'But beyond the limits of the patrols – who believe she is on the way to Boston or other Union ports – there is not much surveillance?'

The Colonel again slapped the table vigorously. 'You have

118

not heard. The surveillance has become very close, and sleepless, far from the coast. You are not the only ones engaged in – commerce – Mr Montrose, sir. And different tacks, frequently observed, are usually questioned, and papers beforehand, at the home port, have been minutely examined recently.'

He added, 'There is perhaps another thing you have not heard. British vessels, leaving this port more or less innocently, have been observed by the Russian Czar's patrols, who are determined that the British do not help the Confederacy.'

'The Russians have not dared to halt the British vessels?' said Mr Montrose.

'No. They dare not. The British vessels have the most remarkable – protection. They are very valiant seamen, sir, the British, and I am proud to belong to their race . . .' He glanced out of the corner of his eye at Joseph, who stirred.

Joseph said, with hard clear precision. 'I assume, sir, when you speak of the "British" you mean my fellow Celts? And not Her Germanic Majesty, Queen Victoria's, former bondsmen and slaves, the English?'

'Come, come,' said Mr Montrose, smiling sweetly, 'we are not about to begin a discussion of racial origins, are we, sirs? I have read that once the vast majority of us were slaves from the beginning, owned by but a few masters.' He gave Joseph a cryptic glance.

'There is nothing I dislike more,' said the Colonel, with an attempt at a quelling glance, 'than the discussion of irrelevancies . . .'

'Between businessmen,' said Mr Montrose. 'Let us continue.' He noticed that the Colonel was not only angry but sullen. 'We were discussing, I think, the slight contretemps between the – ah – Russians and the English.'

'The Russians,' said the Colonel, 'have been reporting erratic courses taken by obviously innocent British vessels plying between Union ports. This has led to the outrageous seizure of British vessels by the Federal government, and some very warm international exchanges between diplomats. The Russians only desire to embarrass the British, for, one day, they will contest for empire.'

'And so shall we,' said Mr Montrose. 'That is inevitable with empires. Shall we continue? What time can the *Isabel* sail tomorrow?'

'At midnight,' said the Colonel, sullenly. 'The usual cargo, I assume?'

Mr Montrose leaned back in his chair and contemplated the smoke from his cheroot. 'We will need more men. There will be sixty very large crates and some two hundred smaller crates. They will be very heavy.'

The Colonel whistled. His eyes squinted at Mr Montrose. Mr Montrose smiled shyly. 'This is a first run. If it succeeds there will be larger runs – and more profit for you, Colonel.'

The Colonel said, 'How are the crates marked?'

'Tools for Boston and Philadelphia and various other ports. They are marked Barbour & Bouchard.'

He wrote quickly on a slip of paper. 'The wharf,' he said. The Colonel read it and then Mr Montrose burned the paper. 'You will see that the wharf number has been changed, Colonel.'

The Colonel was silent. He stared at the ceiling. He seemed deflated. He finally said, 'Execution is the punishment for clearing such contraband.'

'If caught,' said Mr Montrose. 'An intelligent man is rarely if ever caught. I am Mr Montrose of Titusville, and this is Mr Francis, also of Titusville. Under no circumstances will any other name be mentioned. It is settled, then? There will be enough men to handle the crates, and the *Isabel* will sail tomorrow at midnight, fully cleared. It is not the affair of the military authority to open and examine each and every crate. Crate number thirty-one contains nothing but machine tools, and the crates are openly marked with the name of the respected manufacturers. In short, this is a safer run than for mere food, clothing and the essentials of life. Too, the payment is far greater.'

The Colonel assumed a serious and even virtuous expression. 'It is quite a different matter, sir, to supply innocent women and children with food and covering than gun-running . . .'

Mr Montrose lifted a fine hand in warning. 'I have said the payment is far greater.'

Joseph stared at the Colonel's profile with larger disgust.

'How much more?' asked the Colonel with blunt avarice.

'Twice as much.'

'Not enough.'

Mr Montrose shrugged. He turned to a leather case on the table and opened it. It was filled with bills of large denominations and the Colonel leaned forward to look at them and his face expressed total greed and delight, and even humble worship. Mr Montrose slowly removed half the packets of bills – which were tied with coloured string – and laid them on the table. 'Count them,' he said.

There was silence in the room while the Colonel counted the bills. His fingers clung to them lovingly; he released the crackling packets with reluctance. His hard mouth trembled with a kind of sexual passion. His fingers began to quiver. Mr Montrose smiled as the last packet was laid on the table.

'The second half,' he said, 'will be given to you when the *Isabel* returns safely. Take these with you now, Colonel. I have another case which I am happy to present to you.'

He brought another case, empty, from his bedroom and the Colonel watched him closely as he laid the money within it, then fastened the straps. He pushed the case towards the Colonel. Slowly, the Colonel lifted his hands and then let them rest on it tightly as he would rest his hands on the breast of a beloved woman. 'I am satisfied,' he said, and his voice was hoarse. He looked at the case with the remaining money and his fierce eyes bulged. Then he licked the corner of his lips.

'The extra men,' said Mr Montrose, 'will be paid by us. It will not be necessary this time for you or any agent to pay them. This is another safeguard for you, Colonel. So, all the profit is yours.'

'I am satisfied,' repeated the soldier. His forehead was hugely beaded with moisture.

Mr Montrose closed the other case. 'We hope this will not be the last time you will be satisfied, sir.'

Only Joseph saw the merest little flicker run over the Colonel's face, and he thought about it. The Colonel said with enthusiasm. 'I trust not!' He did not wait for Mr Montrose to refill his glass. He filled it himself and drank it down at once with a flourish, and his face flushed.

'We will meet here again in eight days,' said Mr Montrose. He drank a small glass of wine. 'I suggest you return to your own rooms at once, Colonel. It is not sensible to remain here any longer.'

The Colonel stood up, saluted, and laughed a little recklessly. Mr Montrose opened the door and cautiously glanced up and down the corridor. 'Now!' he said. The Colonel snatched up his case and ran from the room and Mr Montrose closed the door after him. He turned to Joseph.

'What do you think of our boisterous soldier, who is so useful to us?'

'I don't trust him,' said Joseph. 'If possible, I'd put a guard on him.'

Mr Montrose raised his brows. 'We have trusted him for nearly three years and have had no occasion to doubt him.' He sipped his wine and looked over the brim at Joseph. 'Are you not speaking solely from natural dislike, Mr Francis?'

Joseph considered. He rubbed one dark-red eyebrow with his index finger. 'I think not,' he said at last. 'I never permitted dislike to interfere with business, or expediency. It is just – perhaps I should say intuition. Smile if you will, Mr Montrose.'

But Mr Montrose did not smile. He looked a little grave. 'I have respect for intuition, Mr Francis. No intelligent man deprecates it. However, we must operate empirically. The Colonel has been very valuable to us in the past. There is no reason to think he will not continue to be valuable.' He looked at Joseph questioningly, and then when Joseph made no comment he said, 'We have no other choice. There is no time. Besides, the Colonel is the military authority of the port of New York. What would you do if you were in charge of this, Mr Francis?'

'I would let the *Isabel* be cleared by the Colonel, and then I would not sail. I would wait a few days – after he believed we had already sailed, and then I would sail.'

'But he has informers. Come, come. Why should he deprive himself of future profits, Mr Francis? One betrayal, and he would have cut off his nose to spite his face. I am sure we are not the only ones who use him. One word, and he would get no more money from anyone. The news would spread.'

'I don't know,' said Joseph. 'It is just a feeling I have.'

Mr Montrose studied him again in silence. Then he went to his room and brought out an extra pistol and another box of ammunition. He put them on the table and pushed them towards Joseph. 'Load the pistol,' he said. 'This is for you As I said, I do not deprecate intuition though I confess I do not feel it now. I have my own and it has never betrayed me. Nonetheless, I believe you will feel safer with the extra protection.'

'I will,' said Joseph .He loaded the pistol expertly. 'A detest-

able man,' he said. 'And a hypocrite. I never trusted a hypocrite.' He smiled thinly at Mr Montrose. 'Mr Healey is often
a hypocrite, Mr Montrose, but he never pretends that you
must take him seriously.'

'Yes,' said Mr Montrose. 'Endearing. It is a joke with him.
Remarkable that you should know that.' He continued, 'Tonight we are serene gentlemen in New York, whose business
has been satisfactorily concluded. Therefore, we shall dine in
state in the dining-room of this hotel, and we shall then
repair to the Academy of Music where we will hear Chopin, a
most delectable composer, and newly celebrated.'

The dining-room was at least as flamboyant as the lobby, and
appeared even larger in its blaze of crystal, its glimmer of
gilt, its rococo carpet and upholstery. Even the stiff white
tablecloths blazed, and the heavy silver and glass sparkled.
Here, as it was evening, the gaiety had increased to louder
and more feverish laughter and a constant rustle, ululation, trip-
ping and shrillness of eager and excited babble. Here, too,
was the same light-hearted music from behind a screen, empha-
sising without intrusion the happiness of the diners and their
joy in war. The waiters were clad as English footmen, with
powdered wigs, scarlet coats and breeches adorned with
twinkling brass buttons, ruffled shirts and white silk stockings.
The head waiter, recognising Mr Montrose, led him and
Joseph to a secluded table near the rose-damask wall where
they could see and yet be somewhat secluded. The ladies at the
tables were sumptuously clad in colourful velvet, lace, silk and
satin, their beautiful half-naked shoulders and breasts rising
like Dresden porcelain from their billowing hoops, their hair
of many hues and shades elaborately dressed and falling in
long ringlets and curls far down their delicate backs, their
coiffures glittering with diamonds or daintily entwined with
fresh flowers. Flowers, too, stood in vases and bowls on all
the tables and the hot scent of them, and the breeze of perfume which constantly swept through the room, and the
sweetness of rice-powder and cosmetics and the inciting odour
of young flesh, almost overpowered the austere Joseph, but
Mr Montrose leaned back negligently in his red plush chair
and surveyed and savoured it all with a smile of ostensible
pleasure. His eyes wandered from one pretty face to another,
considering, rejecting, approving, admiring.

Joseph noticed the merest scrap of folded white paper close to Mr Montrose's plate, and wondered how it had arrived and who had placed it there. Mr Montrose saw Joseph's eyes directed on the paper and he took it at once, unfolded and read it. He passed it to Joseph and said calmly, 'It would seem our plans are changed. We must, unfortunately, leave the concert a little earlier, and this is awkward, for one of my precepts, very valuable, is that one should never attract attention.'

Joseph read the slip of paper: 'Plans changed. Tonight at midnight, not tomorrow.' Mr Montrose deftly retrieved the paper and carefully burned it with the tip of his cheroot and deposited the ashes into the tray and then stirred them thoroughly. At Joseph's inquiring look he said, 'We never question how messages are delivered. It may seem melodramatic to you but melodrama is a natural side of life, however pragmatists may deplore it.'

He sighed. 'Now I must leave my own message to our banker friends tonight, regretting the delay for a few days. It is a nuisance. You may think I am a little too cautious, Mr Francis, but delays can be dangerous. We must go to the concert, for the tickets are in my name, and I have the customary seats, and absence would be noted and commented upon. I suggest that we do not converse at the concert, and that I leave a few moments before you, and I will wait and then you will join me.' He poured the wine just brought to the table and savoured his own glass. 'Excellent,' he said. 'A splendid rosé.'

Joseph knew that he must not ask questions. He considered the wild duck placed before him, and its exotic sauce, and took up his knife and fork. The meat was too pungent for his ascetic tastes and the sauce unpleasant. But he had long ago schooled himself to accept food of any kind, remembering his years of starvation. He forced himself to eat, and forced himself to sip at the wine. The hysterically happy babble and laughter all about him was unbearably intrusive, and his deep Irish melancholy, without a reason he could fathom, fell on him again. The music of the distant ballroom enhanced his gloom.

He said, in an effort to disperse it and because something constantly worried him, 'The Colonel, Mr Montrose. You mentioned to him that Mr Healey had chosen me, and therefore implied that he should treat me with consideration. Yet, on our immediate meeting he insulted me, and so insulted Mr Healey. Would that not show a disregard for Mr Healey, such as he had never shown before?'

Mr Montrose drank musingly and gazed at Joseph over his glass. Then he put it down. 'That is very astute of you. What conclusions would you draw?'

'That he intends to betray us, as I said before.'

Joseph was surprised to see Mr Montrose's eyes brighten at the thought of danger and he said to himself that though he would never retreat from it if an advantage was involved he would never like it or be pleased at the prospect. But Mr Montrose, he suspected, loved danger for itself and would even court it, as a wild mistress wooed at extraordinary times, in spite of his concern for caution.

Mr Montrose said, 'You believe he has had a rush of conscience to the head or the heart?'

'No, I don't think he has either. It is something else, and has nothing to do with us personally.'

'Um,' said Mr Montrose, and thoughtfully puffed at his cheroot. 'That is interesting. You may be wrong, you know, and you may be right. I have considerable respect for your intuitions. I think I will go doubly armed and make some changes by messenger to the docks.'

He lifted his glass again. 'Is this duck not delightful? Let us enjoy ourselves.' He smiled at Joseph and there was a little subtle excitement in his smile and a tensing, catlike, in his body. Then Joseph, with his powerful Irish intuition, understood that in many men there is a suicidal urge, not without delight, and this explained a considerable number of those who worked for Mr Healey. He, himself, was not among them though he had no love for life as they, themselves, obviously did.

CHAPTER SEVENTEEN

THEY left the hotel after dinner, now clad in discreetly dark clothing, and carrying with them leather cases. Joseph, as did Mr Montrose, wore a pistol holster under his long black coat and in a pocket in the coat he carried the extra pistol. The coachman was waiting for them, as mute as before, and they entered the carriage in silence.

Joseph had read of halls of music but he had never seen such baroque grandeur, such lavishness of velvet and crystal, such gilt bulging of boxes and such silken brilliant movement as he saw in the Academy of Music tonight. The hall roared with laughter, with voices, with eager banter. Throngs moved down the narrow aisles, the ladies smiling when they recognised friends in the orchestra seats, the men bowing deeply. Everyone glanced up at the crowded boxes filled with women in many-hued Worth dresses, lavishly arrayed gentlemen, feathers, fans, flowers and constant vivacity. Down in the orchestra pit could be faintly heard the glittering and tentative notes of a harp, the testing run of a violin, the boom of a 'cello, the rumble of a drum. The whole hall seethed with joyous animation. Programmes fluttered; lorgnettes flashed in the light of the immense crystal chandeliers; jewels blazed, tiaras were rings of fire on pretty heads; white bare shoulders were illuminated. The hot hall was smotheringly heavy with the effluvia of perfume and powder and gas. Everyone seemed excited, too noisily elated, too lively.

Mr Montrose and Joseph were led by an usher with gloves and programmes to seats midway down the orchestra level to purple-plush seats. They delicately climbed over the huge hoops of seated ladies, while the gentlemen rose and bowed politely and a word was murmured here and there: 'Mr Montrose, sir. Happy to greet you again. Delightful evening, is it not? No, pray don't apologise. My fault, sir.' They looked with curiosity at Joseph, but as Mr Montrose did not introduce him nor appear to know him they only slightly bowed and turned from him.

Joseph read the programme. He looked at the vast stage with its looped purple velvet curtains fringed with gold. It was empty, hardly lit. Two grand pianos stood back to back, waiting. The gaslights, dimmed in front, rose and fell. He looked at his watch. It was seven o'clock. The *Isabel* sailed at midnight. The hubbub all about him faded from his senses. He began to think, frowning. His premonitions were stronger than ever. He thought of his family. Then he glanced up, to evade his thoughts, at a box just above him.

Mrs Tom Hennessey – 'Mrs Smith' – sat there, wan and

strained in a lilac silk dress with a deep yoke of creamy lace hardly concealing her breast. Her tawny hair, undressed and without jewels, feathers or flowers, hung down her back. Her beautiful face was set in a pleasant and amiable expression, for she was surrounded by men and women obviously her friends, but her eyes were sunken in dark hollows and her lovely mouth was pale and a little tremulous. She kept touching her lips and brows with a lace kerchief, and her expression, when unwatched, was remote and tragic, and her eyes kept roving in a kind of mute despair. She wore no gems but the dazzle of diamonds and emeralds he had seen on her hand before.

A heavy shock ran through Joseph. He stared up at her. Feeling, perhaps, the focus of his eyes, she looked down at him but her own eyes were blinded with misery and she evidently did not really see him. Someone in the box spoke to her. Joseph could see the soft whiteness of her tilted chin, the pearly perfection of her colourless face, the star-like shadow of the lashes on her cheek, the tender cleft between her young breasts. She was speaking softly and politely, but her weariness was evident. Her round white arms and gloved hands were listless, and her fingers held a large fan of multi-coloured feathers but did not move it. Suddenly and helplessly, her eyes closed. She leaned back in the chair and apparently sank into a doze, her lips parted like the lips of a child, the lilac silk crumpling and glowing over her collapsed figure.

A young gentleman in the box emerged from the dimness behind and carefully laid a silvery mantle over the girl. Some of the ladies leaned forward, and one or two winked and tittered behind their fans. The other gentlemen leaned forward and spoke in concerned voices. The girl slept in her exhaustion, her head thrown back against the purple velvet of her deep chair, her chin raised pathetically.

Mr Montrose sat next to Joseph but not by the smallest gesture or glance did he convey knowledge of him. However, so acute was he that he felt some disturbance and glanced through the corner of his eye at the younger man. Joseph appeared to be in a state of frozen shock. Mr Montrose wondered, but did not speak to him. Then he saw that Joseph was staring up at the sleeping girl in the box above, and he was intrigued. A pretty enough piece, there, and a lady, but she was evidently sleeping off too much wine and too much rich food, and had probably danced too late into this morning. Mr Montrose had no objection to silly frivolous women, but he was surprised that Joseph should be looking up at her so fixedly. He had thought better of the young man.

She seems to be dying, thought Joseph, and the women around her titter and look knowing. Where is her abominable husband? Why is it not possible for me to go to her, to carry her from this place and let her sleep in peace? In some quiet spot where I could sit beside her and watch over her . . . away from blood and death and wounds . . . He looks entranced, thought Mr Montrose. She must be at least three years older than he. Does he know her? Impossible. She seemed familiar to Mr Montrose. He had seen her before, at a distance. Then it came to him. Tom Hennessey's wife, and Mr Montrose could have laughed aloud.

The chandeliers began to dim slowly but steadily, and in laughing protest the roar of voices rose higher. The stage brightened. There were various perfumed flurries in the aisles and smothered mirth as coveys of late arrivals tripped to their seats, exuding fresh warmth, stirring the air with flutters and gestures and ribbons and laces and quick whispers and soft little sounds and coy apologies as they subsided. Joseph watched the stage; his hands gripped the arms of his chair. He said to himself that he was a fool, a puling imbecile, for he had lost control of himself in one devastating moment, and he realised with considerable inward terror that he was not as invulnerable as he had believed and that he, too, could be weak.

Two young men in elaborate clothing and ruffled shirts stepped silently from the wings. They might have been twins, with their thin white faces, large dark eyes, tensed mouths and long dark hair swept over their brows and down over their ears, and they were impeccable, their boots slim and shining. They halted at mid-stage and bowed to the audience, which was barely quieting, and there was a condescending spatter of applause and the ladies patted their gloved hands together graciously. Now the hall was in almost complete darkness and the stage was full of light. The two young pianists seated themselves on their respective benches and glanced over the pianos at each other then lifted their hands and brought their long fingers down on the keys . . .

The streets were not so crowded when they left the concert. The carriage began to clatter and clop its way through narrower streets and darker ones, and the houses became smaller and dilapidated with little yellowish glimmers at the windows, and there was a noxious smell and a hollow emptiness and fewer and fewer people. Eventually even these dwindled and what few men there were seemed to skulk and the buildings were blind and the lamplight became feebler and there was an odour which haunted Joseph but which he could not immediately recognise. Finally it came to him. It was the odour of the sea, and Joseph clearly saw an ashen winter morning of snow and wind and black docks and oily water, and felt again the almost forgotten dread and despair and hopelessness. Mr Montrose reached across Joseph and locked the carriage door without a comment.

The carriage turned on the docks, past clusters of great and small vessels, some with their sails raised, some with empty masts, and all the ships heaved and bobbed and splashed, and feeble lanterns gleamed from wet docks. There was an air of desertion everywhere. Then Joseph saw, beyond the harbour, out at sea, shifting light and dim shadowy forms of large vessels. 'Federal patrols,' said Mr Montrose, as if commenting on nothing significant. An occasional ship spewed black smoke and the smell of burning coal on the air, and at intervals vessels moved away from piers in a quiet that was sinister. Yet Joseph became aware, in spite of the quiet, that here was an intense busyness and commerce, both of war and peace.

The carriage stopped. Joseph saw the bow of a large clipper, and, in the lantern-light which fought the darkness on the deck, the name *Isabel*. The sails were already up. Joseph heard, rather than saw, the activity of many men aboard, for figures could hardly be discerned. They were loading huge cartons and crates from this wharf, which was covered rather than open, and larger than other wharfs they had passed. The grating and squealing of iron-wheeled vehicles seemed suddenly very loud on the dock.

The open doors of the wharf were immense, and were capable of admitting two large teams of horses and their wagons side by side. Dollies and great carts could be seen inside, being heaped with the material to be loaded. Mr Montrose nodded with satisfaction. 'They have worked fast. Another half an hour, and we will be ready.'

He was about to get out of the carriage when he saw a military patrol smartly moving on the dock. A young officer approached the carriage and saluted. Mr Montrose smiled at him genially, and opened the window and showed him the copy of the clearance which Colonel Braithwaite had given him, the original of which was in the hands of the captain on board. 'We are going on the clipper to Boston,' he said. 'Is it a good night for sailing, captain?'

The captain was obviously a lieutenant, and he saluted again. 'A good night, sir,' he said. 'Are you, and this gentleman, the only passengers?'

'Indeed, yes. Our first journey to Boston. I am afraid it is going to be rigorous.' One soldier held up a lantern to scrutinise Joseph. 'But,' said Mr Montrose, 'as representatives of Barbour & Bouchard, we must do our duty to aid in the war, must we not?'

The young man saluted again, and he moved off with his troop. Suddenly a tall young man approached them and Joseph's first thought – from his reading of sea stories – was that here was truly a pirate in the great tradition, a true brigand and murderous adventurer. He was not more than thirty-seven, tall and lean and as lithe as a panther, and he walked with the same grace and economy of movement as did Mr Montrose. He was obviously the captain, from his uniform and his cap, and he had a narrow dark face, so dark that Joseph at first thought he was either Negro or Indian, and black shining eyes as predatory as an animal's, a great nose and an almost lipless mouth. He had a controlled but reckless air, and he looked at Mr Montrose with smiling affection and removed his cap. His black hair was thick and curling and unkempt, and he extended a dark thin hand to the other man and he shook Mr Montrose's hand warmly. He hesitated only a moment, then he put his hands on Mr Montrose's shoulders in an embracing gesture. In spite of his somewhat casual uniform and his intimation of enormous strength he was obviously a man of breeding as well as deviltry and courage.

'I have news for you!' he exclaimed. Then added, as he saw Joseph, 'Mr Montrose. Great news.'

'Excellent, Edmund,' said Mr Montrose. He turned to Joseph. 'Edmund, this is my new associate, Joseph Francis. Mr Francis, Captain Oglethorpe.'

Joseph had detected, in the captain's slow speech, the same

soft accents he had heard in the voice of Mr Montrose. The captain bowed ceremoniously. 'Happy to have you aboard, Mr Francis.' He gave his hand to Joseph, and his eyes vividly ran over Joseph's face and body like the flash of a knife in lightning. Then Joseph knew that here was a man at least as dangerous as Mr Montrose and as ruthless if not more so, and he guessed that killing was not beyond him. Yet he had such a gay dark appearance, such a zest, that Joseph was intrigued as well as wary, and he knew that his first impression had been correct. Captain Oglethorpe was, in soul at any rate, a pirate and a brigand, utterly without mercy when necessary, and totally without fear. He carried no weapons, as if his own power were enough for him. Joseph saw that his eyes were restless and mirthful and very intelligent and piercing, and that nothing was unobserved by him. After his brief and in some way frightening survey of Joseph, he turned to Mr Montrose and nodded.

'I dismissed the extra men fifteen minutes ago,' he said. 'They were good workers. These remaining are our regular crew. We will leave, on the hour, with no delay.' He looked with smiling satisfaction—it seemed he was almost always smiling—at the scurrying men. His large white teeth glittered in his dusky face.

'No trouble at all, Edmund?' asked Mr Montrose.

'None.' Joseph noticed that he did not speak to Mr Montrose with the word 'sir'. He spoke to the other man as an equal. 'The clearance from our friend came here promptly four hours ago.'

Mr Montrose inclined his head. He stood on the littered wharf, out of place here in his elegance. 'Mr Francis, Edmund, has expressed some suspicions of our friend, whom he had not seen before.'

'Oh?' said the captain. He turned again to Joseph and again scrutinised him. He said, 'May I ask why, sir?'

Joseph said, 'I don't know why. There was something about him which made me suspicious. I may have been wrong.'

The captain considered. He accepted one of Mr Montrose's cheroots and lit it with a lucifer, his lively face somewhat thoughtful. He said, 'I like first impressions. They are usually true. Still, we have the clearances. There has been only one inspection, crate number thirty-one. It required special tools to open. I invited the military inspector to open others, but he declined. We then went on board for a little refreshment.'

He turned again to Joseph. 'Was there anything in particular, sir, which alarmed you about our friend?'

'His lack of courtesy to me, a stranger, an employee of Mr Healey.'

The captain raised thick black eyebrows, which met above his nose, and glanced at Mr Montrose, who nodded. 'I never dismiss a man's intuitions,' said the captain. He looked at the huge remaining crates. 'It may be best to move at once, before midnight.'

'Is that possible?'

'I will see. I will go on board again and watch the loading. My men are working very fast but perhaps I can induce them to work even faster.' He paused. 'Will you and Mr Francis go to your quarters now, Mr Montrose? They are comfortable, as you know.'

'If you are going aboard again, Edmund, Mr Francis and I will remain here until the last crate is loaded. I prefer to be easy in my mind. Too, I should like Mr Francis to become familiar with our – operations.'

The captain smiled, as always, saluted and walked with his easy and gliding rapidity to the end of the wharf and then up the ramp to the deck. Joseph, peculiarly sensitive to cold since his childhood, shivered, for the wind rushing in from sea and dock was becoming bitter this early spring evening. But Mr Montrose smoked pleasantly and watched the men. He looked with interest at the monolithic remaining boxes and crates. 'Cannon,' he said. 'This is a new invention of Barbour & Bouchard, far superior to conventional cannon. It is said they will kill twenty men to the others' five, and can bore through a yard-thick wall of brick as easily as a knife through bread. Better still, the balls shatter very prettily, and each fragment is as deadly as a bayonet, sharp as a razor. I believe they stole the patent from their British colleagues.'

'Is the Union receiving the same cannon?' asked Joseph.

'Certainly, my dear Mr Francis. That was a very naïve question. Munitions makers are the most impartial of men, the most neutral, the most indiscriminating. Their business is profits, and you must have learned by this time that profits are what make civilisation possible. Remove profits and you remove incentive, and barbarism results. It is human nature to work for rewards. Even animals do so. Men are not angels.

They will not, unless they are saints or insane, work for anything but their own advantage, and that is sensible. Without rewards the work of the world would come to an end. It is as simple as that. We would be individually grubbing for roots and berries and hunting raw meat, as once we did æons ago. If I were a law-maker I would insist that every idealist, every lofty bourgeois, work with his hands at a desperate living, in field and mine and factory, before he even wrote a word or uttered one on "behalf of mankind".'

Joseph listened intently, now unaware of the activity about him and the emptying wharf. Much of what he had just heard appeared to him eminently logical, and he could not deny the truth of it. But he said, 'There are, though, inequities.'

Mr Montrose shook his head at him indulgently. 'Mr Francis, I never knew of a superior man, an intelligent man, who wanted for bread, and I say this despite the tales of artists in garrets and starveling geniuses. While they are indulging their art it surely would be sensible of them to work for a living also, at least for their daily sustenance.'

Joseph became aware that only two huge boxes remained, to his right, and that the wharf was empty but for himself and Mr Montrose, and two workmen who were pushing dollies up the ramp. Mr Montrose had wandered away. He was inspecting, with interest, the innocent proclamations on the crates, and their destination in Boston and Philadelphia. He was hidden from the doors of the wharf, and smoking idly. Only Joseph was visible from the doors. The lanterns on the ship at the end of the wharf were dancing and hoarse faint calls came from the decks, at a considerable distance. The wind was keener, and the smells of the harbour more insistent. Joseph shivered again. His and Mr Montrose's leather cases stood aside, near one of the crates, shining brownly in the shifting light, their fine brass locks gleaming like gold, incongruous in that rude open space and on the dirty floor.

He heard a sudden sharp sound of running feet outside, and then in the doorway appeared an army lieutenant and three civilians, roughly dressed, with bestial faces. Mr Montrose had heard also, and he thrust his head and half of his body beyond the boxes. Joseph saw that the lieutenant held a double-barrelled pistol in his gloved hand, and that the civilians held rifles. Joseph became as still and as rigid as stone as he saw three weapons directed at him, and one at the shoulder of Mr

Montrose. Murder had brightened, as if by a superior light, the faces of the lieutenant and his thugs, and every feature shone with an evil radiance.

The lieutenant, a young man with a fair complexion and with waves of golden hair under his cap, said in a very clear and quiet voice, 'We don't want any trouble. Quick, if you please. Step back from those cases with your arms raised, Mr Montrose. We want the money in those cases.' His air was compact and business-like and he showed no nervousness.

'The money?' said Joseph, in a bewildered voice.

'No nonsense, please,' said the lieutenant in his disciplined accents. 'Colonel Braithwaite wants it at once. Your rooms were searched after you left to dine. There was no money-case left behind. If you please, sir – ' and he stared at Joseph – 'kindly kick those cases towards me. We are not jesting. If you do not obey you are dead men.'

He glanced swiftly at Mr Montrose. He said, 'Step back, Mr Montrose, with your arms raised above your head. We know you are armed. But one movement to your pistol and it will be your last. Come, sir. Move quickly. We mean you no personal harm, but we want that money.'

Mr Montrose moved entirely from the shelter of the box with his arms raised. He looked at Joseph, the perfect example of the very young and confused man confronted with imminent violence. But he saw something else. Joseph's face had become hollow, like a skull, and inhumanly dangerous, and his small blue eyes had flattened. The lieutenant was not so perceptive.

'What of the cargo?' asked Mr Montrose.

The lieutenant, as he was young, could not resist grinning maliciously. 'You will not pass the patrols,' he said. 'We will, sir, take the clearances with us as well as the money.'

'Colonel Braithwaite,' said Mr Montrose. It was evident that he was delaying in the hope the captain would appear, and reinforcements, and the lieutenant knew at once. He laughed shortly. 'Do not try to forestall me, please, Mr Montrose. The colonel leaves for Philadelphia tomorrow. He has been trans-ferred. The cases, sir,' he said to Joseph. 'The colonel will become impatient.'

But the diversion had been enough. The lieutenant had hardly spoken when Joseph rapidly drew and fired his pistol. He had directed the weapon not at the body of the young soldier but precisely at his right thigh. He had fired with total deadliness and care, with not a single tremor or hesitancy, or even a thought.

Before the lieutenant had begun his shocked crumpling to the floor Joseph had swung on the civilians with their rifles and Mr Montrose had found his pistol. It was evident, in an instant, that the men were aghast at the attack on their leader, that they had expected no resistance, and that they were not prepared to fight to the death. They turned as one man and fled into the night with their rifles. One even dropped his weapon in his flight. It struck the floor of the wharf at the instant the lieutenant dropped, his pistol flying from his hand and clanging and bouncing on the wood.

CHAPTER EIGHTEEN

JOSEPH'S shot had raised thunderous and bounding echoes in the cavernous depths of the wharf, and the men at the top of the ramp had halted, looking back over their shoulders. They saw at once what had happened and they raced their vehicle into the ship and scattered like mice, shouting.

Captain Oglethorpe suddenly appeared on the ramp, and then he ran down it into the wharf, a black and avenging figure. He reached Mr Montrose, and exclaimed, 'Clair! Are you hurt?'

'No, no, not in the least, Edmund,' said Mr Montrose and frowned slightly at the other man. 'We were attacked by this gentleman here – ' he indicated the fallen soldier with a delicate movement of his foot – 'and Mr Francis heroically disposed of him at once. A perfect shot. We were about to be robbed of our funds. Worse, we were about to be robbed of our clearances. Mr Francis's intuitions were only too true.'

He turned to Joseph, smiling calmly. Joseph still held his pistol. He stood over the groaning and bleeding and writhing lieutenant in silent menace. The swaying lantern-light showed the soldier's white and sweating face, distorted with pain, and the blood that ran from his injured leg, and it showed his terror. His large blue eyes swiftly roved from face to face. He expected instant death, but he did not speak.

Captain Oglethorpe moved to Joseph's side. His face showed

no anger or viciousness, but only interest. He said to Joseph, 'Finish him off. We have no time to waste, I see.'

A few men were cautiously filtering back into the wharf from the clipper, but they stood warily at a distance, watching and listening intently. Mr Montrose pursed his lips and considered the groaning soldier. He said at last, 'No. There are some questions to which I need the answers. Besides to kill him and leave him here would be, I am afraid, rather difficult to explain on our return, and now indeed we have no time to waste. The patrols may have already been alerted by the other robbers who accompanied our brave military friend. Take him into the ship, Edmund, and staunch his bleeding so he will not die before he has given us some necessary information.'

The soldier lay, still writhing, but silent now. The sweat glistened on his face. He gritted his teeth. Death had passed him by, temporarily. But he could still feel its coldness in his flesh.

The captain looked at his distant men, whistled to them and waved his arm, and they came at once. He gave them their orders. They looked down incredulously at the soldier but made no comment. They lifted him, and he suddenly shrieked with agony, but they were indifferent and hurried with him to the ship. The three men on the wharf watched them go in silence. Joseph still held his pistol, and occasionally he glanced swiftly at the doors of the wharf.

'Let me congratulate you, Mr Francis,' said Mr Montrose. 'I could not even detect a movement on your part before you fired.' He looked at Joseph consideringly and with a faint smile. 'I take it that you did not intend to kill him?'

'No,' said Joseph.

'May I ask why not?'

Joseph's face still retained its hollow gauntness, but he drew a deep breath. 'I have no objection to killing, if it is necessary. I did not believe it necessary in this instance.'

But Mr Montrose, still smiling faintly, did not entirely believe him. He said, 'A most remarkable shot. I could not have done half so well, nor could you, Edmund. It was admirable.'

The captain was dissatisfied. 'We could have killed him here, taken his body aboard and then dropped him into the sea. What information can you expect from him?'

Mr Montrose said, 'He called me by name. He mentioned Braithwaite, and the search of our rooms for the money. This was well-planned – by our friend. It was to be his last coup, for he is being transferred. Moreover, I suspect he did not love us, and plotted to betray us as well as rob us. No doubt he hoped we would be captured by the patrol or killed by them, beyond the harbour.'

The captain nodded reluctantly. 'That could well happen, without the clearances. We could, however, if captured, involve Braithwaite in our confessions.'

'Be sure he had thought of that, and that is why I need to question our captive.'

Joseph was thinking. He had, himself, felt the presence of death. He said, 'I do not think that even if we had kept the clearances we would have sailed. That man intended to kill us after robbing us, so that we could not embroil the Colonel.'

Mr Montrose considered this, then inclined his head. 'That is probably true, Mr Francis. He wished the clearances not so that we would be captured by the patrol out of the harbour but just so that there would be no evidence against our gallant Colonel. It is well he had no trained soldiers with him, but only ruffians from the gutters of the city whom he could bribe. Had he shot one of us the others would have had the courage, then, to shoot me, and Edmund, but your amazing action, Mr Francis, startled and frightened them and drove them to panic. Moreover, they had seen their leader fall, and without a leader such animals become mindless. It is well that the soldier was young and could not resist wasting time in baiting us. Otherwise we should now be dead.'

In the meantime the final boxes and crates had disappeared with tremendous speed into the clipper. The wharf stood empty, the light was uncertain, and everywhere there were booming echoes. The three men walked quickly towards the ship. 'We sail at once,' said Edmund Oglethorpe. 'We dare not wait until midnight.' He looked with friendly curiosity at Joseph, and with some admiration. 'I am honoured, sir,' he said, 'to have you aboard my ship, for above all things I like brave men.' He put his hand briefly on Joseph's shoulder. 'I am grateful that you saved the life of Mr Montrose, even more than my life.'

Mr Montrose smiled affectionately at the captain. 'The soldier knew that when he fired at us it would draw your attention, if you were not already on the wharf, and that would have been the end of you also, Edmund. Still, it was an audacious and courageous thing for him to do, though he had probably watched and waited until we were alone. He was more brave, in this instance, than I suspect he would be on the battlefield. But then, money is a great inspirer.'

'On our return, we shall find the Colonel,' said the captain, as they all walked up the wet and greasy ramp to the deck. He spoke with casualness and almost indifferently.

'Certainly,' said Mr Montrose. Joseph felt a chill touch on the back of his neck. Mr Montrose continued: 'Men like the Colonel are not often found on the battlefield. They are much too clever and adroit, so he will not die in battle.'

Captain Oglethorpe laughed. 'But he will surely die, just the same.' Joseph saw the flash of his white teeth in the semi-darkness.

Mr Montrose sat with Captain Oglethorpe in the latter's warm cabin, and they sipped brandy.

'The news, Edmund,' said Mr Montrose. 'I know you must go on deck almost immediately. But I must have the news.'

'I sent a brave and trustworthy man up near Richmond,' said the captain. His smiling lips smiled wider. 'To our home, Kentville.'

Mr Montrose considered him. 'That brave and trustworthy man was you, dear Edmund.'

'Come to think of it, it was,' said Edmund, with a vast air of surprise. 'After all, I did not want to endanger one of my men, and I wanted no garbled accounts.'

'You might have been caught, and killed, as a spy or something.'

'I? Dear Clair! Who am I but a humble returning seaman, a wanderer, a no-account and shiftless man, one who has drifted? One who had only returned from foreign parts recently and had heard only rumours of this war, and just wanted to see his kin again.'

'A likely story,' said Mr Montrose. 'But you are such a rascal that you probably could deceive General Sherman himself. I take it you encountered no great difficulties with patrols or bands of Union soldiers, or military occupance?'

'A mite,' said the captain. 'It was a little chancy a few times, and it took longer than I expected. But I have been a seaman since I was twenty, as you know, and weather does not disturb me, and sleeping in burned houses and abandoned barns, or even in the open, is nothing to an experienced seaman. I haven't forgotten how to ride a horse, and there were horses here and there—'

'Which you stole,' said Mr Montrose.

The captain looked hurt. 'To whom do those horses belong? To us or the damned Yankees who really stole them? God damn me if I don't hate them!'

'Did you have to kill very often?'

The captain looked bashful, and grinned. 'A few,' he admitted. 'But what's a Yankee? I did it only when necessary— and when I needed ammunition, or a fresh horse. Your Dad said many times to me, when I was only an ornery young 'un, that a gentleman kills only when he is compelled to do so, and he told you that, too, and I have a great respect for your Dad, even if you never had. After all, he was my uncle, and my own Pa had died when I was small, and he took care of Mama and me and sent me to school, and if he talked too damned much and too piously all the time he had his virtues.'

'A true Southern gentleman,' said Mr Montrose. 'I know.'

The captain looked pained. 'You never had any respect for anybody, Clair. Not even for your dainty Mama. You were always a rogue, and you have the audacity to call me a rascal. At least I honoured my elders and didn't mock them to their faces, as you did. And I went to church with them, of a Sunday, which you refused to do since you were a shaver of five. There was always something a little flighty about you.'

Mr Montrose nodded. 'There's nothing to choose between us, Edmund. We have the same pirate blood, inherited through our saintly Mamas. And what ladies they were! I used to wonder if Mama ever shat. I am sure Daddy believed she did not. But, the news, Edmund, the news.'

The captain refilled his glass. The ship was gathering speed and the lantern on the ceiling swayed. 'Luane,' said Edmund, 'never received any of your letters except the first two.'

'Daddy confiscated them.'

'No,' said Edmund. 'It was your Mama. All for Luane's good, certainly. It distresses me to remember that you loved your Mama even less than you did your Daddy, and she such a fragile and lovely lady who never raised her voice not even to a slave. No, it was Mama, I regret to confess.'

Mr Montrose's feline face changed. He leaned forward. 'You

have seen Luane? Quick, you must tell me!'

The captain stared at him then said abruptly, 'The Yanks burned down the house, where we both were born, and where your father was born. They burned the fields and the cotton. They drove off the cattle. What they could not take they destroyed – everything. Gardens, hen-houses, horses, barns. There's only a chimney or two left, Clair. They burned down everything but the slave quarters. Now even the slaves are gone.'

Mr Montrose's eyes glowed like the eyes of a great cat. 'Luane?'

'Luane stayed. She hid your mother in the woods and when the Yankees went off she brought her into the slave quarters.'

'Did they hurt Luane?'

'No. That's a right smart wench of yours, Clair. They never found her. She hid with your mother – for a whole week. She knew what the Yankees did to the slave women, and how they shot the bucks and even the pic'ninnies after they drank up your Dad's wine and whisky. I heard the same stories all over Virginia. Can you imagine a Southerner shooting helpless folks, even black ones?'

'Yes, of course,' said Mr Montrose. 'Not as readily as a Yankee, however.' He sipped brandy. 'You saw Luane.'

'Yes. I hollered when I got there, and looked around. Sounded like I was calling the hogs. A mite distressed, you could say. And Luane came out of the slave quarters, and she recognised me and ran to me and shouted out, "Master Clair! Tell me about Master Clair!" She was fitten to be tied, almost out of her mind. She took me by the arm and shook me and screamed your name over and over. I got right bothered by her hollering, wondering if Yankees were still around, and if you and I hadn't played with her when we were young 'uns together I might have fetched her one, just to shut her up. It was surely Luane, and she doesn't look a day over twenty, and she in her thirties at that.'

He shook his head. 'A fine wench, still, with those big grey eyes of hers, and a skin like new cream and a mouth – I used to think when I was a stripling – like a dark rose. I would dream at night of bedding her myself, but you got there first, Clair, and she only thirteen. I had dreams of murdering you,' and the captain laughed and shook his head again. 'Trouble was, your Dad was against white folks messing around with their slaves. He kept slaves, but to give him his due he never abused them, and respected them as human beings with those inalienable rights he was always quoting from the Declaration of Independence, though that proclamation somehow didn't mean he believed in freeing the slaves, or felt it had anything to do with the darkies. Contradictory. No mind, Clair. You will remember that when your Dad found out about you and Luane he carried on as if Luane was his precious only daughter and you a dirty ravisher who should be horse-whipped and hanged. Kind of a simple fellow, your Dad. Luane was only a slave wench, and you were his only son. He almost had a seizure.'

Mr Montrose smiled unpleasantly. 'Perhaps he remembered that Luane was his second cousin, daughter of his cousin, Will, who didn't hold anything against one who messed around with the darkies.'

'Well, Cousin Will, your cousin Will, not mine, was purely white trash, Clair. Shiftless, no-account bastard. Never had anything but a grubby little farm, and not a slave to call his own. He had no right bedding down with Luane's Mammy, who was owned by your Dad. But he was a right handsome man, Cousin Will, and Luane has his eyes, and his nose, and her Mammy was a pretty wench, herself, a high-yeller as they call them. Luane could pass as white, anywhere.'

'I suppose that is a compliment,' said Mr Montrose.

'I reckon it is, Clair, and don't you talk Yankee talk to me. I am a Southern gentleman, sir,' and the captain laughed. 'Well, I shut up Luane's mouth and so I got the news. Now, you must think kindly of your Dad. Before your son was born your Dad freed Luane, so her child was freeborn, and not a freedman. And now this will make you, I hope, feel even more kindly about your Dad. He loves that grandson of his. He put him in his will. Luane told me.'

'I don't even know his name,' said Mr Montrose.

The captain threw back his head and laughed a high and whinnying laugh. 'He gave your son his own name, by God! Charles!'

Mr Montrose stared with numb incredulity and the captain laughed again and slapped his knees.

'Clair,' he said, 'trouble with you is that you are a very complex man and so how can anyone as stupid as a complex man understand the simple-minded, like your Dad? You think just about everybody has subtle thoughts and such, and is complicated himself. But your Dad's as simple as clean crick-water and never had a thought in his head. Why, I knew that when I was six years old. But then I'm not a man of intellect like you, Clair. I could see things right out, but you were always looking for significant shadows and finding your own foolishness instead. Though you didn't think it was foolishness. You thought you were smart.'

Mr Montrose rubbed his fingers through his thick hair. The captain said, grinning wider than ever, 'Your boy looks like Luane, though he's yellow-headed like you. Of course, everybody knew he was yours, but nobody ever dared to laugh at your Dad, except you. Not one of his friends would have dared even to smile behind his back. A right brave gentleman, your Dad, and he'd have killed a mocker. Besides, he is proud of the boy. More than he was ever proud of you, at that. Charles was his kin. He looks like a Devereaux, and Luane has Devereaux blood, too. Those folks are prouder than the Devil himself.'

Mr Montrose was silent. His elegant features expressed nothing.

The captain refilled his cousin's glass, shaking his head as at a huge joke which only he could appreciate. 'Luane told me about those two letters she had from you. You didn't know she had been freed. You sent her money. Now, how the hell did you think a darkie pregnant wench, though she looks white, only thirteen-fourteen years old, could run away from her home, and she a slave, and get up North? I tell you, Clair, you intellectual men are right feeble-minded most of the time. True, you weren't even nineteen yourself, but you should have known better.'

'I wrote her we could be married up North,' said Mr Montrose.

'And Luane's got better sense than you have, Clair.'

When Mr Montrose said nothing, the captain went on, 'Yes, Luane's got sense. You're a Southerner born. She knew you'd remember that, some day, and that she had been a slave, with nigger blood. You'd remember you're a Devereaux.'

'And Luane has Devereaux blood.'

The captain smiled triumphantly. 'Now there, you surely showed yourself, Clair. You used to laugh at the Devereaux, but they're right in you in spite of everything. Luane knew

142

all about you. She still does. If I didn't know what I know about her I'd swear up and down that she was a lady-born, a high-born lady. There's another thing: she was always devoted to your Ma, especially after the baby was born. You never appreciated your Ma, either. Lady of principles, like your Dad, and better even than a Devereaux in spite of the pirate in the ancestry. Brought up Luane almost like her own kin, though she never showed her true feelings. Only Luane knew.'

The captain looked at Mr Montrose thoughtfully. He also glanced at his watch. 'Clair, I'll make it short. Your Ma died, in the slave quarters, with Luane caring for her like a loving daughter, two months ago. Luane wouldn't leave her, not for a minute. And when your Ma was dead Luane dug her grave for her, at the end of what was once the gardens, and wrapped her in one of her own shawls, and mourned her like a daughter.' He paused. 'Aunt Elinor was a lady, a fine lady, like her sister, my Mama, even if she wasn't any smarter than your Dad. You never could forgive fools, Clair, and yet fools often have dignity.'

'What of Luane? How is she living?'

'She's still living in the slave quarters. I gave her money. I brought four hundred dollars with me. I told her you sent it. I said you wanted her to come North, any way she could, and join you. That girl said, "Tell Master Clair that here's my country and here's my people, and I will never leave them. But I send him my love, and when this war is over I pray he'll come home and live on his own land again." And she's setting up a garden, and is right thankful for the money and she'll buy a cow or two and horses. You owe me four hundred damn Yankee dollars.'

Mr Montrose rubbed his forehead and bent his head and stared at the floor. 'Where is my son?' he asked.

The captain laughed even louder than before. 'Your Dad, Clair, is a Colonel in the army of the Confederacy, and where the hell he is now I don't know. But he took your son with him as his personal aide, and I reckon no one in that man's army knows that the boy has any nigger blood in him at all. Luane told him, but I hear he told her, his own Ma, that it was of no account and that God didn't look at a man's colour but only at his soul. Luane's right smart and knows better and I reckon she thinks your boy is as big a fool as his

143

grandad, and don't have any more sense.' He stood up. 'That Luane's a lady, and a proud lady, and has a high spirit, and she's waiting for you, which I don't think is very clever of her.'

He put his hand on Mr Montrose's shoulder and shook him as if rallying him. 'This goddam war won't last forever, Clair. Go back to your own land and your own people. Go back to Luane.'

'I can never marry her in Virginia,' said Mr Montrose as if to himself.

'Hell, what's marrying? The wench is waiting for you. If I had a wench like that waiting for me, damned if I wouldn't go to her even through the whole damned Union army. I thought I told you: Luane's proud, too. After all, she's a Devereaux even if from the wrong side of the blanket.' He pushed Mr Montrose's shoulder.

'Now, what do we do with the bastard in the brig?'

Mr Montrose stood up. He looked absent and a little dazed. He said, after a moment, 'I will talk with him now. And I want young Francis with me. He's been blooded, as my Dad used to say, after he pushed a bleeding fox-tail in my face. I want him to hear what is said.'

He looked at his cousin. 'Thank you, Edmund. That is all I can say. Thank you.' And he held out his hand. He smiled. 'You're only an Oglethorpe, but I reckon I admire you.'

'Go to hell,' said the captain, and laughed his high laugh.

CHAPTER NINETEEN

'YOU don't dare kill me, an officer of the Union army,' said the young lieutenant. He had sustained only a flesh wound, though a serious one, and had been expertly attended by a trained man on the ship. He lay on the cot in the brig and stared derisively in the lantern-light at Mr Montrose, who sat on the only chair, and then at Joseph, who stood near him with his pistol in his hand.

'You may be due for an unpleasant surprise,' said Mr Montrose with amiability. 'Just because the gentleman near you did not kill you does not mean that we shall hesitate now when we are at sea. It was only expediency which preserved your life and made us bring you aboard. Do not try my patience, Mr . . .?'

The soldier spat at him. Joseph aimed the pistol at his temple, and the soldier shrank. He looked up at Joseph's face and saw the hollow danger of it and the flat small eyes and contracted mouth. 'You don't dare,' he repeated, but it was a trembling question.

'I am losing patience,' said Mr Montrose 'You have heard our questions. Answer them immediately or, sir, you will die before another minute has passed. If you are candid with us we may spare your life. If not, you will be dead and in the sea, as soon as we have passed the patrols.'

The soldier was a young man, a very young man, and now he became hysterical both with pain and fear. He began to speak in a rushing and gasping voice. It was almost as Joseph had speculated. Colonel Braithwaite had ordered him to hire ruffians of the city and then, at the right moment, to rob Mr Montrose on the wharf, take the clearances, and then murder Mr Montrose, the captain and Joseph. After that he was to notify the port authorities that he had heard shots, had investigated, and found the three bodies. He was not to go near the ship, but 'run for my life', and call for help. The cargo would then be confiscated, after investigation, and the matter closed and labelled 'treason'. The clipper would also have been confiscated by the government.

In this manner the amenable Colonel Braithwaite would have his huge sum of money before his transfer to Philadelphia, and a malicious man's revenge, over which he would gloat.

Joseph said, 'But why "revenge"? What had our employer, or ourselves, done to him to make him our enemy?'

Mr Montrose looked at him with immense and unaffected surprise, and seeing this at one quick glance Joseph felt jejune yet confused. 'My dear Mr Francis,' the older man gently protested. 'Have you not learned as yet that it is not always necessary to injure a man to incur his enmity? In truth, the majority of enemies are made by no effort on a man's part. They are made through envy and malice and the incurable evil which lives in a man's spirit, which makes him by nature the enemy of his fellows, without a single provocation. My deadliest enemy was a man I had believed was my best friend, on whom I had conferred favours and disinterested kind-

145

nesses, and unsolicited gifts.' He reflected, smiling. 'I have come to believe that those are provocations enough, and deserving of enmity.'

The young soldier, whose face was slimy with sweat and very pale, listened with closed eyes. Mr Montrose prodded him with a light finger. 'But perhaps Colonel Braithwaite had another reason for betraying us.'

It appeared he had. The lieutenant was to tell authorities that Colonel Braithwaite's suspicions had been aroused concerning the *Isabel,* and had sent his subordinate to investigate at the last hour. Colonel Braithwaite would maintain that he had given no clearances to the ship, in the event both copies had been found, or if not found that he had been deceived by 'traitors' and gun-runners, and finally becoming uneasy had ordered another investigation. For his perspicacity and prompt action he would be soundly rewarded by the government, and advanced to Brigadier General at the least.

Mr Montrose listened to this without any emotion at all, but Joseph was sickened, and seeing this Mr Montrose faintly shook his head and smiled. 'You will observe that men do not stay bought, Mr Francis. They need constant bribes, and not only of money, to remain your friends. A bigger reward, a bigger bribe, was open to Colonel Braithwaite, and so he accepted it. Had he not been transferred to Philadelphia but had remained here as port military authority, we could have continued to do business with him.'

He said to the soldier, 'Aside from the fact that the Colonel was your superior officer and gave your orders, how did he suborn you?'

'Two thousand dollars, part of the reward, and the Colonel's recommendation that I be made Captain.' The young man spoke in a dim voice, overcome with pain. He added, 'He is also my mother's brother.'

Mr Montrose nodded. 'So, he was comparatively safe from blackmail in the future, and bound you with his own perfidy and crimes.'

He turned now to Joseph and said, 'What do you now suggest, Mr Francis?'

Joseph's heart gave a great sick leap, and he was silent. The gun was suddenly wet in his hand.

'You promised not to kill me!' cried the soldier and opened

146

his eyes, young, blue and terrified eyes large and starting in their sockets.

'I gave you no such promise,' said Mr Montrose. 'Well, Mr Francis? I leave the conclusion in your hands.'

Joseph's throat and mouth were as dry as hot stone. He said to Mr Montrose, 'I think I have a more just punishment.' He did not know that there was a sound of pleading in his voice. 'When we arrive in Virginia his wound will be almost healed. He is in the uniform of a Union officer. We will put him ashore and let him fend for himself.'

Mr Montrose laughed aloud with frank delight. 'Excellent!' he exclaimed. 'Let him elucidate to our friends in Virginia how a Union officer came to be among them suddenly, in uniform. He will be seized at once for a spy, or if he attempts to explain he will be greeted with happy laughter, and it will seem a mighty joke to our friends. If he is not hanged he will be imprisoned. If he is later rescued by his compatriots, he will not dare to explain to them, nor to mention Colonel Braithwaite. I should love to be present when he tries to rationalise his presence alone in that part of unconquered Virginia, to my people, or when he tries to justify himself to his own friends.'

He touched Joseph on the arm. 'I greatly admire a man of ingenuity and not merely of force, Mr Francis.'

'You might as well kill me now and have done with it,' said the soldier in a miserable voice.

Mr Montrose surveyed him kindly. 'Young sir, if I were your age I would accept any alternative to death. As you are a thief and a willing murderer, you may go far after all, if your life is spared. So, it is spared. Under other circumstances I would recommend you highly to Mr Healey.'

They heard shouts above and hurrying feet and the captain opened the barred door. 'We are being challenged by a patrol boat,' he said.

This had happened before and was routine, as the patrols occasionally challenged ships leaving the harbour and examined clearances. The captain looked at the soldier. 'Good God,' he said, 'is he still alive? Now we can't dispose of him before the patrols have released us, and we dare not shoot. Mr Montrose, you have been careless.'

'I think not,' said Mr Montrose. He stood up and fastidiously brushed a cheroot ash from his coat. 'We shall leave Mr Francis with our friend here, with orders to kill if he even opens his mouth. I suggest strangling or smothering, so no sound is heard. You understand, Mr Francis?'

'Yes,' said Joseph, and now his voice was resolute. The soldier had been granted mercy. If he violated that mercy he would die. Joseph doubted that he would prefer execution to life.

The captain dimmed the light of the lantern in the cell, looked searchingly at Joseph, then accompanied Mr Montrose outside. The door clanged shut and was locked. Joseph sat down in the chair and looked at the soldier. 'I will surely kill you if you make a single sound or as much as lift your hand,' he said.

There was no porthole in the cell, but Joseph could actually feel the large dark presence of the patrol boat near at hand. He heard the clipper being boarded and the voices of naval men of authority. The clipper had come to a standstill. He and the soldier waited in absolute silence. The soldier had fixed his eyes with fear on Joseph, understanding that this time Joseph would kill him no matter the consequences, and with his bare hands, if he even whispered. The soldier wanted to cry. It had all seemed such a profitable adventure, though dangerous, as explained by his uncle. Money, advancement, honour. Now he was helpless. He suppressed a whimper, and listened acutely to the voice above. He had only one hope: that the authorities would search the ship as sometimes they did. In that event Joseph would not dare combine murder with high treason. Let the authorities merely approach this cell, and he, Joshua Temple, would make a final effort, throw himself on Joseph, and shout, before the other man could kill him.

So the two young men sat or lay in utter quiet, listening intently. No one descended the stairs. No one approached the cell. The soldier lay with clenched fists, looking only at Joseph, waiting, almost praying. Long minutes passed. Then there was laughter, hoarse jesting voices, the sound of a dinghy leaving the clipper, the weighing of anchors, calls of farewell. The soldier became limp. Joseph relaxed a little. The clipper began to move, sighing, gently groaning in her timbers, swaying, the wind thunderous in her sails as they spread themselves under the moon.

Mr Montrose entered the cell. 'We are under way again,'

he said. 'Now, Mr Francis, we shall have a light supper with the captain, then retire to bed.'

The journey took six days, for a storm came up which almost wrecked the *Isabel* and made even the stout captain apprehensive. The *Isabel* was overloaded; there was danger of her foundering in blackish green waves which Joseph found unbelievable, so tremendous they were. Mr Montrose at one point suggested jettisoning some of the cargo but the captain said, 'No.' He grinned. 'I'd rather jettison some of my men.'

'You are an incurable romanticist,' said Mr Montrose. 'In spite of everything I fear you are devoted to the Confederacy.'

The captain's eyes glinted. 'There are worse devotions,' he said and Mr Montrose laughed. 'I won't repeat that to Mr Healey who has no devotions to anything but profits.'

They landed in hushed darkness at night in a little deserted bay. The keel of the *Isabel* barely escaped coming to rest on a reef under the shallowing water. Everything was silent and seemingly without life when the *Isabel* dropped anchor, but at that very instant the dock, unlighted except for starlight and stormy moonlight, came alive with silent men who, with the help of men aboard, swiftly unloaded her contraband. No one spoke except when absolutely necessary, and then frequently in whispers. Everyone was pressed into service, including the captain, Mr Montrose and Joseph. Only the lookouts held their posts, surveying everything through swinging binoculars. The transaction took several hours. Joseph felt the unbearable haste and tension, and laboured until he was soaking with sweat. The night was hot and breathless and threatening. Lightning sometimes flashed in the black clouds that raced across the moon, hiding and then revealing her. Thunder rumbled. There were brief and drenching showers and the deck became slippery.

For the second time Joseph was aware of war and its impingement on him.

At the last the soldier, Joshua Temple, unspeaking, white-faced, was put ashore. He could walk now, limping. Joseph saw him being forced down the ramp and he heard subdued laughter. At the foot of the ramp and on the dock, the soldier looked back despairingly, but was rudely pushed. He disappeared into the night.

Finally the ramp was pulled aboard, the doors locked. The

Isabel raised anchor, and silently drifted out to sea, nimble and dancing, her sails filled with moonlight. Joseph experienced a sense of enormous relief, which disgusted him. As if he understood Mr Montrose said, 'There are men who love danger for itself and could not live without it, and search for it. And there are men who do not love danger, but will face it as bravely as the others. I do not know, in all honesty, which I prefer, but if it came to the question of my life I would choose the men who do not seek danger though they will not run from it.'

CHAPTER TWENTY

' S o,' said Mr Montrose to Mr Healey, 'he is not only absolutely brave and ruthless, but is prudent, too. He won't run to danger or recklessness, but he won't avoid them when necessary. I have come to have a great affection for young Joseph Francis Xavier Armagh, and I think you are justified, sir. He can be trusted.'

Mr Healey sat expansively in his study and smoked deeply on his cigar. 'I never make a mistake,' he said, with happy self-satisfaction. 'Minute I saw him on that train I kind of knew. Well, he's coming to see me on a matter of importance, he says. Got in last night from Pittsburgh, and I think he took a trip to Philadelphia, too. So, it all depends . . .'

Mr Healey waited for Joseph's appearance, and when the young man entered the study, soberly dressed in black almost to the point of being funereal, Mr Healey saw that he carried with him a roll of blueprints. Mr Healey unaccountably sighed, as if in immense relief. 'Sit down, sit down, Joseph Francis What!' he exclaimed. 'Happy to see you home, boyo. Got good reports about you, too. Handled it well, though you're still a little rough around the edges. Takes time. Sit down, sit down. Well, what is all this?'

Joseph had laid the blueprints on the desk, though he kept his hand on the roll. He looked at Mr Healey with a fierce concentration, and he became paler. It was all very well to tell yourself, he thought, that you must have courage – when you are not face to face with the actual situation – but it is quite another when that situation confronts you. In five minutes or so he would either be booted out permanently, or Mr Healey would understand. Joseph was not too optimistic. He had frequently told himself that he was a fool to consider Mr Healey, and that he, himself, was a milksop and a weakling and a man of no real resolution and fortitude, willing to gamble everything.

He said, never taking his eyes from Mr Healey's red face, 'First of all, sir, I went to Philadelphia before coming home. I have heard rumours for a long time that the oil in the southern part of the State, just being drilled, is far superior to the oil of Titusville, for it is so far underground that it is partially refined, and naturally. So, I invested in options.' He smiled slightly. 'And in consequence I am not exactly solvent any longer.'

Mr Healey nodded. 'I heard those rumours, too. Only a couple of wells drilled. A thousand feet or more, sometimes. I didn't invest.' He smiled rosily at Joseph. 'Should I?'

Joseph hesitated. 'I don't know, sir. It's all speculation. You surely have better information than I have.'

"Course I do.' Mr Healey waved a fat red hand. 'But you invested without information, eh?'

Joseph looked at the table. He said, 'Mr Healey, I have to be rich very soon.'

'Not something to be ashamed of,' said Mr Healey. 'You got your reasons, I reckon. But you should have asked me for advice. Ain't always right to put all your chips on one number. Well, that's for the young, and you're young. Kind of a reckless boyo, ain't you?'

'Necessity sometimes makes a man reckless,' said Joseph. and again Mr Healey nodded. 'Happened to me many times,' he said. 'Sometimes being too damned prudent can cost you all your cakes.'

Joseph looked up sharply. Mr Healey chuckled. 'Oh, Mr Montrose told me all about it. Thought you did the right thing. I don't believe in murder, either, unless it's absolutely necessary. You can get a bad reputation that way, killing,' said Mr Healey.

Joseph, without warning, felt a hysterical urge to burst out into wild laughter, but he restrained it. His small blue eyes glinted and sparkled under his auburn brows and Mr Healey chuckled in appreciation. He said, 'Well, so you're bankrupt.

151

You ain't here to ask for a loan again, are you, Irish?'

'No,' said Joseph. He looked down at the roll again under his hand. 'I don't think it's important, sir, but you don't know my full name.'

Mr Healey shifted his fat bulk in his chair. 'I always knew I didn't. Want to tell me what it is?'

'Joseph Francis Xavier Armagh.'

This was the first dangerous step. Joseph waited for Mr Healey to frown, to lean forward, to glower. But to his astonishment Mr Healey merely leaned back in his creaking chair, blew out a cloud of smoke, and said, 'Right sound name, I'm thinking.'

'It doesn't matter, sir?'

'Now, boyo, why should it? Do you think for a minute Mr Montrose is Mr Montrose? You got better sense than that. You knew all the time the men who work for me don't use their real monikers. Why should I hold it against you that you didn't tell, either.'

'You always seemed to want to know,' said Joseph, baffled. The palms of his hands were wet.

'Oh, just curiosity. But you don't go around satisfying curiosity, Joe, without getting yourself in a mighty peck of trouble. Don't tell anybody anything, unless its necessary, and think on it first.'

'I thought this was necessary,' said Joseph. 'You see, I had to give my full name – on these – and I thought you ought to know.'

'Got something to show me?' Mr Healey leaned forward again with an air of great interest.

Now even Joseph's mouth was deathly pale. 'Yes. But first let me explain, sir. I've been watching the wells and the drilling all these years, and the donkey-engines, and the wood-burning. And it came to me that, as kerosene burns, why shouldn't it be burned for fuel, and not just for lamps? I'm not a mechanic, sir, nor an inventor. But I talked it over with Harry Zeff, and he was interested. We went out into the country once, with some kerosene in a pot and we set it afire and we put a pan over the pot and it became steam almost as soon as it boiled.'

'No great discovery, that,' said Mr Healey in a tone of indulgence. 'The lads at the wells do that all the time.'

'But no one has thought of firing engines with it, sir. Any

engines, not only donkey-engines.' He remembered what he had thought then. He had become dizzy with his thoughts. 'Kerosene steam engines for industry. It could be used in place of coal and wood. Harry knows a great deal about machinery, now. He helped me draw some rudimentary sketches. I took them to Pittsburgh.' He looked at Mr Healey, but Mr Healey waited in inscrutable patience, his hands folded across his belly.

'Well,' said Joseph, 'I found someone there who could put my ideas and my sketches into patentable order. And I patented it, and it was accepted.' His heart was pounding heavily and now there was a painful pulsing in his head. He could not read Mr Healey's attentive face. 'There were other patents, I discovered, along the same lines, but mine was the simplest and the cheapest.' He was finding it hard to breathe. Damn him, he thought of Mr Healey, why doesn't he say something?

Mr Healey waited, watching the young man's white and haggard face. 'Well,' he said at last, 'go on.'

'Last autumn I met, out in the fields, Mr Jason Handell, the rich oil man who is contending with Rockefeller for the control of the oil industry in Pennsylvania. He owns all the options, wells and refineries next to the Parker farm, which was sold for only fifty thousand dollars to Jonathan Watson, William F. Hansell, Standish Hanell, Mr Keen, and Mr Gillett and Henry E. Rood, who organised their own oil company. Mr Handell owns just about as much of the land and options and wells in lower Pennsylvania as does Mr Rockefeller. Mr Handell's first and only interest is oil, Mr Healey. He has no other interests and he has a very large oil company . . .'

'So you showed him your patent?' Mr Healey was most affable.

Joseph's tight face trembled a little. 'I did, sir. As I have said, his only interest is oil and the exploitation of oil, and he is a very rich man . . .'

'Richer than I am,' Mr Healey agreed, amiably.

'I – I thought so, sir. And he has the facilities to put inventions into use, as you do not. In fact, inventions utilising oil are of great interest to him. He – invited me to go to Pittsburgh to discuss – things – more fully with him. I did.' Joseph bent his head. He continued, 'He told me that it is not as yet feasible to use my patent, as there is a war and the

153

patent must be tested in the field. But he wanted to buy my patent. I said no. If Mr Handell was truly interested in it, and wanted to buy the patent, it was probably worth much more to me than fifteen thousand dollars for all the rights.'

'A right smart sum,' said Mr Healey. 'Maybe you should have taken it.'

Joseph said, and he was a little less pale now, 'No, sir. Mr Handell wouldn't have given me his time and made me that offer if the patent was worth little or nothing, or was only conjectural. Incidentally, I learned that he did test it, though he never told me, and it was not only workable but heated steam far faster and more efficiently than either wood or coal.'

'Who told you that?' said Mr Healey with bland interest.

Joseph shook his head. 'The man who drew up the blueprints for me. I gave him one hundred dollars for the information.'

'You should have given him more than that, Joe.'

'I intend to, sir. In the future.' Joseph paused. He was amazed. Mr Healey seemed quite at ease and only mildly interested and very calm, an attitude which could only have been termed paternal.

'Mr Handell,' said Joseph, 'was the one who suggested I invest in a pipeline for the transportation of oil, which will be built after the war. I did. I am,' said Joseph with a wan smile, 'pretty well up to my neck in investments, now.'

'Handell kind of favours you, eh, Joe?'

Joseph, who was inwardly trembling, considered this. 'No,' he said at last, 'I don't think Mr Handell favours anybody, sir. They say he is as hard and ruthless as Mr Rockefeller, if not more so. Nothing except for a profit. At any rate, part of the digging for the pipeline is already under way, and the rights are really owned by Samual Van Syckel of Titusville. But he didn't have all the money he needed. Mr Handell is lending him the money: It will run to Pithole.'

Mr Healey yawned. 'Yes, Irish, I know. I'm invested in it, too. I'm going to build the pumping stations. Got the rights to those pieces of land. Handell's tough. Don't know how you handled him.'

'I didn't,' said Joseph.

Mr Healey sat up. 'No?' he exclaimed. 'He got the better of you, Joe?'

'Not exactly, sir. We were at a stalemate. When he agreed to pay me royalties for my kerosene-driven engine – he says it couldn't be put to practical use at once – I told him when he issued shares he must give you the option of buying at least one-third at the private price. Of the subsidiary which will manufacture and sell the engine.'

Mr Healey's little dark eyes became protuberant. 'Irish! What the hell . . . Did he throw you out and the blueprints with you?'

'No,' said Joseph. 'I believe you know Mr Handell, sir. He isn't an impetuous man. He just laughed at me, and asked me why.'

'Well, well. Why, Joe? Why consider me at all?'

Joseph looked aside at the gleaming panelled walls. He took a long time to answer and during that pause Mr Healey began to pass his hand over and over his mouth.

'I – I tried, sir, to forget. What you did for me and for Harry. You took us in when we had nowhere to go. You – you've treated me honestly and decently, sir.' Joseph stared at Mr Healey with a kind of hopeless despair. 'I don't know! I just had to do it! Perhaps I'm a fool, but I couldn't go on with it, unless . . .'

A silence fell in the study and Joseph sat on the edge of his chair, trembling.

Mr Healey took out his handkerchief. He blew his nose. 'Damn this smoke,' he said. He put away the handkerchief, and resumed smoking. He studied Joseph.

'Know something, Irish,' he said at last, 'you sure are a fool. You worked for me honest and square and so don't owe me anything. You repaid me hundreds of times, with your loyalty. I could trust you. So why this, Irish, why this?'

Joseph clasped his hands together on the desk so tightly that the knuckles whitened. He stared down at them. 'I haven't an explanation, sir, except that I had to do it.' He was freshly amazed. 'And I don't know why, either, Mr Healey, no more than you do!'

'Thought you'd be cheating me, or something, if you didn't?'

Joseph reflected on this. 'Yes. I believe that is it. Though it wouldn't be cheating, truly. Say, perhaps, it might have been gratitude . . .'

'Nothing wrong with gratitude, Irish.'

Joseph looked up quickly. 'You don't mind, sir, that I didn't tell you at once?'

'Now, let's be reasonable, Joe. It was all up in the air. I'm not in the oil business except for investments and such. Just one of my interests. You got the best man for yourself. But when it came down firm you told me. Well, go on. That's not all of it, is it?'

'No,' said Joseph. 'Mr Handell told me to think about it. The one-third, he said, was ridiculous. Besides, I had put in for Harry, too. After all, Harry in a way gave me the original idea – it was a remark he made two years ago, out in the field. So, I thought about it. Then –' and Joseph coloured – 'I wrote to Mr Rockefeller. He asked me to come to meet him. I had told him about Mr Handell's offer and interest . . .'

'Good,' said Mr Healey. 'Play one rascal against another, but watch they don't cuddle up together against you. And then you wrote Mr Handell that Mr Rockefeller was interested.'

'Yes. So, on this trip I went to Mr Handell again and told him to make up his mind at once.'

'You told Bob Handell that, right to his face, right in his own big offices?' Mr Healey's face danced with enjoyment and pleasure. 'Wonder he didn't kick you out! He's got a mean cold temper.'

'He didn't kick me out. He just told me I was an inexperienced, gullible, contemptuous, ridiculous greenhorn.'

'And you stuck to your guns.'

'That I did, Mr Healey.'

Mr Healey leaned back and laughed aloud. 'Trouble with Handell, he ain't Irish. Don't understand how mad we are, I'm thinking. Crazy as loons. Now, he's a man with a mind that don't do anything but churn out dollars. And you just a spalpeen, a young Irisher. I'd like to have seen his face, that I would!'

'It wasn't very pleasant,' said Joseph. All his tensed muscles were relaxing. He felt dazed, feeble, but oddly exhilarated, as if delivered from devastating peril.

'I bet it wasn't,' said Mr Healey. 'So how is it now?'

'He will let you buy one-third of the shares at the inside price. And I will give Harry one quarter of my royalties.'

Mr Healey shook his head, as if marvelling, as if incredulous. He gazed at Joseph as though at a miracle he did not accept, and could not accept.

Joseph unrolled the blueprints and extracted a sheaf of papers from them. 'Here is the agreement I have with Mr Handell,' he said. 'We fought over every paragraph.'

Mr Healey accepted the sheaf of papers and read them slowly. Then he put them down. He said, 'Sometimes, Irish, I wonder if you got good sense. And then I read this, and I see the sly Irish hand in every line. Tied him up, proper, you have. Must be something to that patent of yours. When's he going to pay you anything on it? Got to be a binder, you know.'

Joseph let out a long breath. 'I said I wouldn't cash his cheque for five thousand dollars until you had looked over the contract and approved of it.'

'You've got the cheque?'

'Right here, sir,' and Joseph reached into the inside pocket of his coat and pulled out his pocket-book. He gave a slip of paper to Mr Healey, who pretended to scrutinise it. The warm spring sunlight flowed into the study and Joseph watched Mr Healey's face and could not read it. He was only conscious of relief, weakening and almost paralysing relief.

Mr Healey returned the cheque. He studied Joseph. 'What if I'd kicked you out, Joe, after what you told me?'

'I'd have been sorry, sir. But I wouldn't have starved. Mr Handell offered me a position with him in Pittsburgh.'

'At twice your present salary, eh?'

'Yes.'

'And you refused. Joe, you keep me off my feet. One minute I think you're bright and the next I think you're stupid. Can't make up my mind.'

'What would you have done, Mr Healey?' and Joseph smiled for the first time.

Mr Healey put up two fat defensive palms. Then he dropped them slowly. 'That ain't a question I'm going to answer, Irish,' he said.

He put a hand across his desk. 'But let's shake on it, Joe. And you cash that cheque and buy your options, and more. No, sir, I'm not going to answer that question of yours. No use thinking back in your life. You just got to go ahead.'

He stood up. 'Best you get to work.' He looked at his watch. 'Got to call on Jim Spaulding. All right, Irish. I don't say you're very smart, but sometimes there's better things than being smart. I reckon.'

As Joseph went to the door Mr Healey said, 'What do you mean, you'd have been sorry if I'd kicked you out?'

Joseph put his hand on the door, then looked over his shoulder. 'I don't know, sir,' he answered, and left. Mr Healey smiled as the door closed and began to hum under his breath.

Mr James Spaulding sat back in his office chair and regarded Mr Healey with a plastic face, full of emotional expression – for effect – combining consternation, stupefaction, and absolute stunned amazement. Not all of it was hypocritical.

'Ed,' he said, in a low and musical and shaking voice, 'you must have lost your wits. I refuse to execute this document until you have had time to consider, to reflect, to judge whether or not you have been under evil coercion and influence . . .'

'The only evil coercion and influence, Jim, that ever bothers me comes from politicians – and lawyers. Now, don't look as though I stuck a knife in you. You know we know each other too well for foolishness.'

'Forgive me!' sang Mr Spaulding, on the verge of tears. 'But his youth! His inexperience, his – his . . . I am not impressed!'

He glanced down at the document with loathing, as if it held smelly filth. He let his hands visibly tremble. Mr Healey was highly amused. 'Come on, Jim,' he said. 'This ain't the op'ry house or a minstrel show. Save the theatrics for the judges and the juries. I know you up and down, as you think you know me. Read that there paper over again, and see what's in it for you, too.'

Mr Spaulding re-read a portion. He seemed about to cry. Mr Healey chuckled. The two men looked at each other, cynical, without illusion, yet with sardonic affection. Mr Spaulding then put on an expression of solemn and almost religious dedication, and Mr Healey kindly refrained from laughing.

'Very well, Ed, if this is what you want I can only respect your wishes.' Mr Spaulding put his hand on the document as if about to swear an oath, and as if the document were the Bible. In truth, he respected it far more.

CHAPTER TWENTY-ONE

MR HEALEY's fondness for Miss Emmy had increased, for as the years had advanced so had his desire for variety in women decreased. Miss Emmy, to him, was simultaneously his wife and his daughter. She was a fond habit. He was weary of changes. He had had enough in his youth and early manhood. Now Miss Emmy was to him the favourite cushion for his head, the silent custodian for his shy secret thoughts, the breast of his comfort. He had mentioned her in his will.

Miss Emmy was shrewd and knowing. But her urgent desire for Joseph Armagh had not abated at all. His continued refusal to see her as a delectable and complaisant young woman enraged her. It also insulted her. Did that Irish nobody regard her as beneath him, he with all his pretensions? She would waylay him in the upper and lower halls, languishing, swinging her satin and embroidered hoops, letting him glimpse the expanse of her white breast, beguiling him with her tossed curls and ringlets, coming close to him so he could smell her perfumes – she wafted scented kerchiefs in his face – and dropping her long-lashed eyes at him and then opening them suddenly so that he could see their brilliance fixed upon him. She smiled; she sighed; she pined and grieved eloquently when they were alone. She fluttered fans at him and looked archly over their tops. Joseph treated her with cold courtesy, slipped by her, and left her. He would not engage in conversation with her except at the table and in the company of Mr Healey. He thought Miss Emmy a vulgar trollop, and her airs ridiculous, considering who and what she was.

He also could not forget Katherine Hennessey. Never deliberately did he remember her; but he could not forget her face, her entrancing eyes, her devotion and self-sacrifice, and her exhausted collapse at the concert probably after weeks of attending the war wounded. There had been something about her which remained stubbornly in his mind, resisting all his efforts to reject. Perhaps it had been her simplicity, her ardour, her shining-eyed courage, which had reminded him of his mother. He hated himself for remembering. He forced himself to work harder so as to forget. He hated Senator Hennessey for a number of reasons beyond his brutal sensuality, his cruel hypocrisy, his politician's shameless exigency, his greed and grossness. He hated him because he was Katherine Hennessey's husband, and because as a husband he had betrayed her again and again, and had contempt for her. Mr Healey had laughingly informed Joseph of the Senator's tireless exploits with women, and his reputation as a womaniser. He had used his wife's money, as well as his father's, to advance himself, yet, said Mr Healey with regret, he treated Katherine as if she were a slut and not truly worthy of his respect and consideration. However, he always called her to his side to be photographed with her, the very image of the adoring husband, the family man, the loving father. She always obeyed. She loved him.

Miss Emmy, the trollop and the drab, had no interest for Joseph. To him, she was a parody of Katherine Hennessey, even if he frequently visited the brothels from which she had come. Her airs and her graces made him loathe her, though they grimly amused him. Sometimes her fine eyes reminded him of Katherine, and he wanted to strike her for this blasphemy. Miss Emmy would see, then, his fierce concentrated look, and thought that it was only, after all, his shyness and his regard for his employer which restrained him. She watched for an opportunity to help him overcome such delicacies.

Haroun Zieff had become overseer in the oil-fields, so no longer slept over the stables but occupied the room he had originally occupied years ago as a waif. But his occupation was not regular. His work often compelled him to remain in or near the fields at night, when a well was ready for 'blowing'. For the danger and responsibility Mr Healey paid him thirty-five dollars a week, and a jocular bonus when a well 'came in'.

Joseph had to wait several impatient days before Harry returned from his tours to tell him that all was well, that their employer had not thrown him, Joseph, out, and that everything had been arranged amicably. The two young men sat in Harry's room – the green room – and congratulated each other. Joseph suddenly said, 'Now, I know why I thought Captain Oglethorpe looked a little familiar. You and he resemble each other. You're both brigands.'

Harry had listened to Joseph's account of the attack on

the wharf – though he had not disclosed exactly why he had been there at all with Mr Montrose. It had been vaguely referred to as a 'shipment', but Harry's eyes had sparkled with mirth though the rest of his face remained serious. 'You should have killed the bastard,' he said.

Joseph stood up. 'I suppose you're right,' he said.

He heard a faint rustling outside the door and smiled a little. Mrs Murray, the massive troll, was listening again outside the door for any morsel she could gather to be relayed to Mr Healey. Her malignance against Joseph had not decreased in these years, but had grown, and was as unrelenting and as sleepless as all evil. It gave him pleasure to see her furtiveness and hear her flustered mutter that she was 'just passing'. But she was more wary now. When he flung open the door he could see just the hurrying shadow of her down the hall. It was early spring evening and the lights had not been lit as yet upstairs, though they fluttered below. Mr Healey was in his study. Dinner was over. The new warmth of the year, and his growing burden of work, was tiring Joseph. He hesitated after he had closed Harry's door. Mr Healey, these days, liked him to visit him briefly in the evenings before bedtime, in the study. They talked business, but most of the time they merely sat in genial silence while Mr Healey studied Joseph and Joseph made a few notes for the next day.

He decided to visit the man who had made so much possible for him, and had given him the only lasting kindness of his life. Joseph disliked the gratitude he felt for what Mr Healey had done, reminding himself that he had given due service in kind. Gratitude involved a man with another man, and that weakened him. But lately it had come to him that Mr Healey was lonely, as all men are lonely. So he went towards the staircase, yawning a little.

Mr Healey's bedroom door opened and Miss Emmy appeared on the threshold. The two young people looked at each other, Joseph stepped back, instinctively, and Miss Emmy was obviously startled to see him so close to the door. She stared at him in the warm dusky light, which flowed upwards from below, and suddenly her face flushed and an overpowering emotion ran over it. Never had Joseph appeared to her so desirable, so strong, so virile, so young as she was young, and so full of health and vitality. She stepped impulsively across the threshold, her pale laces and ribbons and satin robe flowing about her, her mass of bright hair curiously agitated, and she flung her arms about his neck, and before he could even lift his hand she had kissed his lips and had then pressed her head against his chest, murmuring deeply and wantonly in her smooth throat.

She had not planned her seduction like this, with not only Mrs Murray in the house, but Bill Strickland in the kitchen, Harry in his room, and Mr Healey in his study. She had not given danger a single thought, though she was naturally cautious. Joseph's unexpected appearance, the strength of his face so suddenly close to her, the sleek russet gleaming of his thick hair, and his lean figure, had overcome her prudence.

He felt nothing but disgust and contempt. The heat of her young body, the smoothness of her flesh, her urgent lips, her scent, the brush of her loosened hair against his hands, revolted him. He did not want to hurt her and so stopped himself from hurling her backwards into the room, but more than anything else he was angered that she should want to betray the man who doted on her and had protected her for many years. But at last he knew that he had to do something. He dared not speak for fear of arousing Mr Healey below and having him open the study door to see what could clearly be seen at the head of the staircase. He could only thrust. He was amazed at her feverish strength, at the power of her desire, at the avidity of her clutching. He caught her wrists which were crossed behind his neck, and as he did so he felt an iron grasp on his shoulder.

Miss Emmy uttered a faint cry and fell back from Joseph, a hand against her mouth. For Bill Strickland, who had come up from the kitchen by way of the back staircase, had seized Joseph in a hating and gloating grasp, and was now whirling him about to face him, one gigantic fist raised to smash into his face. His own face, never completely human, was distorted with rage and satisfaction and his intention to kill or at least terribly maim. It was the face of a wild animal. The eyes glowed in the semi-darkness. A monstrous joy made them flicker, for now this young man, this usurper, this enemy of Master Healey, this contemptuous evader of glances, was in his hands and he meant to destroy him once and for all. Mrs Murray, over the years, had convinced the mindless creature that Joseph had 'his plots' against Mr Healey, and at the end, some day, he would rob and injure him. And

162

so he had. He was trying to steal Miss Emmy from the Master, and Miss Emmy was Mr Healey's property, and so Joseph, the hated and suspected, was a thief and a robber.

Joseph was younger but not nearly as strong as Bill Strickland. He was more lithe, and quicker. He averted his head just as the murderous fist lashed at his face, and the blow passed his ear with a whistling sound and the great clenched hand crashed loudly into the wall. At that instant Joseph freed himself and stepped back. None, not even the paralysed Miss Emmy, saw Mrs Murray's head rising from the back staircase, nor the opening of Harry's door.

Joseph's first thought, a prudent one, was either to run back to his room and try to lock the door against this madman, or race down the stairs to the study and the protection of Mr Healey, for he was not foolhardy and he knew he was no physical match for this enraged beast who had killed many times before, and who surely meant to kill him. But Bill was quicker now. He had whined softly in his throat as his fist had crashed into the wall. However, the pain made him wilder and more terrible. He was on Joseph in an instant, his hands reaching for the young man's throat. His thumbs sank into Joseph's flesh, and Joseph felt his breath stopped and the agony of his almost crushed windpipe.

I am murdered, thought Joseph, as flecks of bloody light and stars sparkled before him and he struggled to breathe. Darkness began to close in about him. He felt his body collapsing, sinking, his knees buckling. Then, just as he fell to the floor the dreadful pressure on his throat was released, and his head swam in mingled dusk and shadow. He knelt there, gasping, clawing at his throat, heaving great breaths of air, groaning. He did not see Miss Emmy, numb and stunned, standing in her doorway, nor the figure of Mrs Murray, elatedly watching from a distance. He was concerned only with living.

Then he heard muffled but violent movement. He could raise his head now and dimly see. And he saw an astonishing sight. He saw the huge figure of Bill Strickland staggering dangerously close to the stairway, and perched on his back and beating him like a savage monkey was Harry Zeff. He rode Bill Strickland like a jockey, his curly head was rising above the other man's, his sturdy fists rising and falling on face, nose, ear, forehead, his fingers sometimes clutching a feature and wrenching it, and sometimes tearing at handfuls of hair.

Joseph pushed himself to his feet, and leaned against the wall, and watched, incredulous. Strickland tried to free himself from his torturing and antic burden, whose legs were wrapped agilely around his trunklike waist. Blood streamed down Bill's face. He actually danced. Harry leaned down and bit him savagely in the side of his neck. That drove Bill to greater madness. He reached behind him, seized Harry's short legs, tore the youth from his body and hurled him to the floor. He then raised an immense boot to kick him in the side of the head.

Joseph forgot his own weakness, the gasping of his breath, his trembling legs and shaking body. He was on Bill in an instant. He caught him by the neck just as the foot came down and smashed harmlessly beside Harry's shrinking head. He had pulled the brute at the very instant before he could have brought his foot down on Harry, and so Bill was off balance, and stumbling, with Joseph facing him, and Joseph still holding him desperately.

Now Bill Strickland's back faced the long stairway and his heels teetered on the edge of the first step downwards. He rocked a little, tried to grasp Joseph not only to take him but to save himself. Then his arms began to describe great pinwheels in the empty air. He was fast losing all balance that remained to him.

Then he uttered a loud hoarse roar of terror. Joseph pressed him harder. He kicked again. The wheeling arms became frantic. And then the large heavy body tilted backwards and downwards, lifted into the air as if bouncing, then fell to the stairs, raised again, bounced, rolled down the final stairs and crashed with a thunderous sound to the floor below, the legs and arms sprawling, the head broken.

The study door was flung open, and light gushed into the hall, and Mr Healey appeared, a cigar in his hand. 'What the hell!' he shouted. 'What is going on here?' He paused, and saw Bill Strickland silent and bleeding not far from him on the floor. 'Bill!' he shouted. He came into the hall, walking slowly and carefully, disbelieving, and he stared down at the obviously dead man from whose lips there was trickling a thin red stream. 'By God,' he said, in a soft, hushed voice. 'Jaysus. Bill.' He stood there for several stunned seconds.

Then he looked up. He saw Joseph standing there, gasping,

and Harry Zeff, holding Joseph's arm like a younger brother. He saw Joseph clutching the banister, his head bent. But their eyes met in silence. A door softly closed. Miss Emmy had retreated.

'Did you push him, Joe?' asked Mr Healey, not loudly, not accusingly.

'Yes,' said Joseph, and his voice was hoarse and ragged.

It was at that moment that Mrs Murray appeared behind Joseph, and she screamed down at her employer. 'Mr Healey! This ragamuffin was ahugging and kissing Miss Emmy and trying to pull her into your own bedroom! Your own bedroom, Mister! And Bill here tried to stop him and he threw him down the stairs and murdered him!'

'Is that so?' said Mr Healey, still in that soft and half-wondering tone. He looked down at the dead man, studying him as if he had never seen him before. Then, ponderously, he began to walk up the stairs, looking again at Joseph's face, looking at him directly, never wavering. He mounted steadily, without haste, without a quickening of breath, and watched only Joseph, who stepped back a little to give him room at the top.

'Now, tell me,' he said. Then he glanced at the door and raised his voice a little. 'Miss Emmy! You come right out here, fast as you can! Hear me?'

The door opened very reluctantly, and Miss Emmy, white with fright and fear, stood on the threshold, quaking, her hands against her mouth, her eyes fixed on Mr Healey, dilated and wide. He gave her only a quick look, and turned to Joseph again and repeated: 'Now, tell me.'

'I told you, sir!' shrieked Mrs Murray, raising fists as if to pummel Joseph's bent back, for he was spent and had to cling to the banister, and his head had dropped. 'He tried to take Miss Emmy, there, back in your room, dragging her, kind of, and Bill . . .'

It was Harry who interrupted her frenzied cries. He said to Mr Healey, 'That's a lie, sir. Joe had just left me. Then I wanted to tell him something, and followed him into the hall. And we both saw that man of yours there, that Bill, attacking Miss Emmy and trying to drag her back into her bedroom. Joe jumped him. But Joe isn't that strong, so I jumped Bill, too, right on his back.' He held out his blood-stained fingers for Mr Healey to see. 'But he got me, though. He pulled me off his back and tried to stomp me while I lay on the floor, and Joe caught him again and pushed him away, and he went right for Joe's throat – you can see the marks for yourself – and Joe shoved him. And he fell down the stairs. All by himself.'

The elfish face was earnest and absolutely sincere, but Mr Healey was not quite deceived. He was still watching Joseph. 'Is it true, son?' he asked.

Joseph said, without lifting his head, 'It is true, sir.'

'Lies! Liars!' cried Mrs Murray. 'He had been after Miss Emmy for a long time! I saw it, myself. He thought he saw his chance tonight, and with you, sir, right down there, in your own house, and he not having any shame nor caring what you done for him, and trying to take your woman and robbing you, and when poor Bill tried to stop him he killed him! I saw it with my own eyes, my own eyes, my . . .'

'Shut up,' said Mr Healey, with gentleness. He looked at Miss Emmy. 'Honey,' he said, 'who is telling the truth?'

The girl wet her white lips. Her eyes looked hunted. Her glance fled to Mrs Murray, her gloating enemy, then to Joseph, and then to Harry, and finally back to Mr Healey who was waiting courteously for her answer. She was an astute girl. Let Mr Healey suspect for an instant that she had waylaid Joseph and that would be the end of her, for if she agreed with Mrs Murray the young men would tell the truth. She knew enough by this time of the affection Mr Healey had for Joseph, and his trust in him, and she did not doubt that he would take Joseph's word before hers, and Mrs Murray's. There was also Harry, and he was looking at her in a most peculiar and threatening way, his eyes glinting in the half-light, his teeth shining a little between his parted lips.

Miss Emmy shrank. She whimpered. She pushed back her disordered hair. She looked at Mr Healey. 'Mr Zeff told the truth,' she said. 'Bill – he's always been staring at me and I knew he . . . I always kept away from him. But I – I thought I'd go downstairs and talk to you. I was lonesome. And when I came into the hall, there Bill was, and he put his arms around me and tried to – he tried to drag me back into the room, and he kissed me . . .' She put her hands over her eyes and sobbed sincerely, and sincerely shuddered.

'Lies! You are all liars!' screamed Mrs Murray, beside herself with frustration and hate and rage. 'Miss Emmy, you stand

166

there and tell Mr Healey them lies, and you know they're lies, and you know it was this – this man here – who tried to take you, and not poor Bill, who tried to protect you and got killed for it!'

'Shut up,' said Mr Healey in an absent voice. 'Now, there's three against one, Miz Murray. Miss Emmy, Joe here, and Harry, and they all tell the same story. What do you think the law would say to that, ma'am? My woman, Joe, and Harry? Everybody knows what I thought about Bill, and how he kind of lived for me, and they'd know I wouldn't protect his murderer, now, would I?'

'I saw it, I saw it!' Mrs Murray screeched. 'They're all lying! They're all thieves and robbers and killers! And they'll kill you too, Mr Healey, one of these days!' She flung herself in the direction of Miss Emmy. 'Why don't you tell the truth, you little whore, you no-account little bitch!'

Miss Emmy was staring at Joseph. He was protecting her. He was saving her from what he guessed would probably happen to her if the truth was spoken. Tears gushed into her eyes. She exclaimed to Joseph, 'Oh, Mr Francis, thank you, thank you!'

Mr Healey made a humming sound. 'Well, I reckon that settles it. I got to thinking, lately, that Bill wasn't in a good mind. Kind of loco, as they say. Acted up some, sometimes. Well. He was like a brother to me, kind of like a good watchdog. Would've given his life for me. But probably not for anybody else. He must have gone off his head, not thinking, tonight. Poor Bill.' He sighed.

Then he swung suddenly to Miss Emmy, and she shrank back. 'I always said, and I say it now, that no man, 'cept he's crazy, makes up to a woman unless she's given him encouragement, one way or another, flirting maybe, just out of conceit, not meaning anything, but being just a female.' At that he lifted his fat hand and struck Miss Emmy calmly but heavily across the face. 'And Bill wasn't all that crazy. He'd been encouraged, and I hope that's all.'

But while he spoke he watched Joseph, who had lifted his head. He saw no emotion, no protest, on Joseph's face, but only a faint contemptuous indifference, and he knew all of the truth.

Miss Emmy had fallen against her half-shut door, and had staggered backwards into the room. Recovering herself, she

167

flung herself on the bed and wept. Mr Healey watched her through the open door, and he sighed. 'Damned little bitch,' he said. 'But reckon there's no real harm in her. Got to remember she's only a woman. Weak vessels, like it says in the Holy Book.'

He turned to Mrs Murray, who had dumbly watched the blow. 'Miz Murray,' he said, in the kindest voice, 'I reckon you'll have to tell the truth, and no prejudice, as the law says. I know you don't like Joe, here. Never did. But that's no call to slander him and try to get him arrested. Miz Murray, I sort of remember Pittsburgh. You remember, too?'

The woman looked at him with sudden stark terror, and she moved back a little. 'I got a real good memory, I'm thinking,' said Mr Healey. 'Never forget a thing. Now you, Harry, you go for Sheriff Blackwell. He's a real good true friend of mine, and he won't make no fuss. Tell him what happened, and come back with him, and we'll all talk quiet, like, with each other. Miss Emmy, too. And you, Miz Murray. Nice and quiet. Keep it in the family. And we'll give poor Bill, down there, a right nice funeral, no expense spared. Poor Bill. Must've lost his head, not thinking, not that he ever really thought. Let him rest in peace. I don't hold no grudge against him.'

He nodded to Joseph. 'Joe, the marks on your throat are right convincing. Show them to the Sheriff.'

Joseph's pale lips parted as if he would speak, but Mr Healey put his hand on his shoulder. 'Go lie down awhile, until the Sheriff comes. Joe, I don't hold anything against you. A man has to save his life. And I'll remember what you did for Miss Emmy, too.'

He looked at Harry. 'Better take Joe to his room before you go for the Sheriff. And if you've got some whisky, son, give him some, a lot. Looks like he needs it. Don't shake your stupid head, Joe. Do what I tell you.'

Harry took Joseph's arm and led him into his room. He went for his bottle of bourbon and poured a large amount in a glass and handed it to Joseph, who was sitting mutely on the bed. 'Come on, Joe, drink,' he said.

Joseph took the glass. He said, 'Do you realise I . . .?'

'Yes. So you did. But that isn't important. You're the one who's alive, aren't you? And who were you trying to save, anyway? Me. The second time.' Harry's dark face widened in a white grin. 'Come on, drink. Now, that's better.' He was relieved. For Joseph had looked like a dead man, with livid skin and glazed eyes and shaken mouth. Harry had poured a drink in another glass. He caught Joseph's eye and smiled again, and said, 'To life! For, by God that's all there is!'

He raised his glass and laughed, and watched Joseph sip from his own glass and watched the pallor retreat. But Joseph thought: It was his life or mine. The only thing is that I liked to do it. At the very last, I wouldn't have stopped it.

CHAPTER TWENTY-TWO

ONE day Mr Healey informed Joseph that he was no longer to supervise the contraband-running, which was now taking place at least five times a month and carrying heavier and heavier cargoes. Joseph was relieved, but also dismayed. 'You doubt my ability, Mr Healey, or you don't trust my judgment.'

'Boyo,' said Mr Healey, 'that's not the reason.' He smiled rosily. 'Got to protect my investment, that's all. No, you stay at home now. I've got enough other men.'

Joseph had induced Mr Healey to replace Bill Strickland with Harry Zeff. Mr Healey had shown surprise. 'You mean, you want him to drive me around everywhere and saddle and harness-up horses, like a stable-boy, and be my servant at my beck and call, for fifteen dollars a week, like Bill? And eat in the kitchen with Miz Murray and sleep over the stables again?'

'No,' said Joseph. 'I want him to be – what is the military term? – your man at arms, your bodyguard, your guide, your protection, in the fields and in town. You know how it is in Titusville now, overrun with criminals and thieves and adventurers. Harry isn't afraid of anything. He tackled Bill Strickland alone, you will remember – until I could help him. Harry's very bright. He knows the oil business better than you, Mr Healey. He knows it from well-blowing to refinery, to pipeline, to distribution. He has a nose for it. He knows how to save money. And you can trust him with your life, with absolute confidence.' Joseph smiled. 'For these invaluable services you will pay Harry seventy-five dollars a week, and board and room, and a bonus every five thousand barrels, say, of one hundred dollars.'

'You're a robber yourself, Irish,' said Mr Healey. 'You'll bankrupt me yet.'

'And you'll order Mrs Murray to stop persecuting and brutalising Liza, one of your maids, Mr Healey. She is nearly eighteen, and a very nice girl, though you may not have noticed, and an orphan, and shy and timid, and getting to be quite pretty. I am violating no confidences when I tell you that Harry intends to marry her – when he has five thousand dollars.'

Mr Healey shouted, 'I'll have no finagling among the help in my house, boyo! It's not a brothel, a bawdy house!'

'Liza, I have said, Mr Healey, is a very nice girl, and a good and dutiful one, never slovenly nor remiss, always polite and obliging. Harry would no more think of violating her than his own sister, if he had one. But he intends to marry her in time. I hope the time will come soon.'

'Maybe you'd like me to finance the wedding,' said Mr Healey, outraged. 'My oil-field manager and a kitchen drab!'

Joseph spoke quietly. 'Liza is no drab. She is a very sweet and innocent girl and how she endures Mrs Murray is something I don't know. She could work in other houses, at better pay, but she wants to be near Harry. Mrs Murray should be warned, and Liza should receive ten dollars a month, instead of four. Mrs Murray is getting old. The burden is falling heavier and heavier on Liza, now, who is practically in charge of the kitchen and the other hired girls. Mrs Murray doesn't hesitate to beat Liza occasionally.'

'I don't know why it is, maybe I'm senile,' said Mr Healey, 'but you got a tongue could wangle anybody. Maybe you kissed the Blarney Stone in Ireland?' He peered at Joseph. 'Going in for good works, Irish, as you mellow? Seems I remember the time you wanted to rid yourself of Harry, and told me he wasn't no concern of yours.'

'I owe my life to Harry,' said Joseph, his face stiff and cold, his sunken eyes almost disappearing as he looked at Mr Healey, who was smiling at him mockingly. 'He owes his life to me. That makes some sort of a – bond – if you want to call it that.'

'Thought it wasn't in your nature to accept bonds,' said Mr Healey.

'It isn't,' said Joseph. Mr Healey hummed, smiling.

Joseph, always indifferent to the war, felt neither relief nor joy when it neared its end, except that a large source of profits was about to be terminated, and abruptly. There were rumours, uttered in hope, that the war might continue in forays for many years, so that the factories could continue to spew out prosperity in the North and the workers in them flourish. To multitudes, the end of the war brought dismay and confusion. It had been exciting and rewarding.

Though the war continued in sporadic bursts here and there through the desperate South it was known that it had come to an end. Mr Lincoln said, 'We now have the task of the reconciliation of brothers, of binding wounds, of the hand of friendship extended from victor to foe, of lifting up the wounded of both North and South, and of a national mourning for our heroic dead wherever they were born. There shall be no vengeance, for none is needed. There shall be no riches nor plunder for evil men, who batten on the flesh and blood of the helpless. We are one nation, and one nation we will remain until we are destroyed by our Vandals from within.'

With that, he sealed his death warrant. The hand that pulled the trigger of the gun which killed him that balmy evening in Washington, in April, 1865, might have belonged to an obscure actor. But the power that controlled that hand was not suspected, nor did even the owner of the hand suspect. Political assassins, as Mr Montrose was to say, have many sponsors, all in accord, and none but they know their names.

Mr Healey had grown enormously fat through the years, loving his drink and his food with the passion only a full-blooded man can know. He had loved women as well, and still did to a limited extent. He had loved money, but not so much as his physical well-being and his joy in living.

His doctor was old-fashioned, and bled him when his head ached too violently and he became dizzy. His doctor also advised him to 'use judiciousness in viands'. Mr Healey had never been judicious, except when it came to money. 'If I die,' he would say, 'let me die with my boots on, after a good meal with lots to drink. Hell, is life worth watching everything you put in your mouth, and being what they call

171

"moderate"? A life of moderation, Joe, is for near-corpses and those who hate living.'

Mr Healey did not die with his boots on. He died almost immediately after an ecstatic romp, naked, in his bed, with Miss Emmy. He had recently concluded a gigantic meal of his favourite food and drink. He died as he had wanted to die, with delicious tastes in his mouth and his body on the soft body of a woman, and happiness in his heart and aware of his own interpretation of the splendour of life. He died without illness and dwindling and fear, without a doctor at his elbow, without a nurse holding his hand, without pain or agony. He died in the scent of Miss Emmy's perfume, his lips fastened on hers. An artery had burst voluptuously in his brain or his heart, and he never knew it.

It was Miss Emmy's shrieks, as she ran naked into the hall, that aroused Joseph and Harry Zeff and Mrs Murray, and the maids. Joseph was the first in the bedroom. There lay Mr Healey, fat and bloated and still rosy, with a smile of total bliss on his mouth, as if he had encountered angels as full-blooded as himself, and as masculine, and had joined their roistering company with shouts of laughter.

'He was a man,' said Harry Zeff, as he decently covered Mr Healey's body with a sheet. Mr Healey received no more pungent accolade nor more true.

CHAPTER TWENTY-THREE

JOSEPH, who had believed that he could never again experience the anguish of human emotion, and that he was removed from the common torments of men, was appalled and distraught over the grief he felt for Mr Healey. No matter how his disciplined mind fought with sorrow the sorrow kept emerging, to darken and distort his thought, to drown out rationality, to flood over plans and conjectures. He tried to think over his now-threatened future, but it faded before he could consider it in new torrents of grief. He was incredulous to discover how deeply Mr Healey had intruded into his cold and isolated spirit. He found himself listening for the roaring laughter, the spill of genial obscenities, the robust slamming of doors, the pound of heavy boots. The house appeared to darken, and even the golden warmth of April days became dun. As for the horror that gripped the nation over the assassination of President Lincoln – Joseph never knew it, nor cared.

It was Harry Zeff who arranged for the funeral, and sent for the priest of the little Catholic church. The priest had heard of Mr Healey. He had not thought of him as a Catholic man, he, the owner of brothels and gambling houses and saloons and the runner of bootleg whisky. He had never seen Mr Healey in his church. But Mr Healey, though he had died unshriven, was given Christian burial, even if the old priest sincerely doubted that he had died in a state of grace, and certainly he had not received Extreme Unction and was probably laden with sins which would take him an eternity to expiate. 'He was a good man,' Harry told the priest. 'He had never turned a sufferer away from his door.' The priest sighed again. 'That's more than many professed Christians can say,' he admitted.

Mr Healey was buried in the little Catholic graveyard near the church, in a fine plot. The undertaker had come from Philadelphia with an entourage. He ordered – after consultation with Mr Spaulding – a giant cross of marble fully fourteen feet high. Mr Healey may not have lived as a Catholic Christian, but, as Harry Zeff contentedly remarked, 'He was buried as one, and never was there a kinder man.' The old priest, whom doubt had begun to plague, was stupefied when Mr Spaulding gave him a sheaf of money totalling fifteen hundred dollars. 'Mr Healey would like that,' he said, with a grandiloquent gesture. The priest had visions of roast beef and a statue of the Blessed Mother which would truly honour her, and the Poor Box, not to mention two more pews and a new cassock for himself and a month of good meals for the two Sisters of Charity who taught in the tiny church school on the outskirts of Titusville, and something for the Missions. 'He never came to see me,' the priest mentioned, to which Harry replied, 'He was a very modest and humble man. A Christian.'

Two days after the funeral Joseph received a note by hand from Mr James Spaulding:

'The honour of your presence is requested at the office of Mr Spaulding of Titusville at 2 a.m., Thursday, of this week, in connection with various bequests in the matter of the concern of the last Will and Testament of Mr Edward Cullen Healey, late and lamented citizen of this fair city.'

The summoned beneficiaries met at Mr Spaulding's office on the designated day and time.

'I have here, before me,' said Mr Spaulding, touching the papers with a reverent hand, 'the last Will and Testament of my beloved friend, Edward Cullen Healey, who died on the day our even more beloved President died – and perhaps there – there is a portent, a meaning we of feeble intellect and dark understanding cannot penetrate. We can only bow our heads in wonder. We can only meditate, reflect, seeking humility, overcome by awe.'

The gathering said not a word. But Joseph thought he heard a ghostly echo of Mr Healey's boisterous laughter and even, perhaps, a ribald word. Mr Spaulding took out his scented kerchief and elaborately and slowly wiped brow, then eyes, then blew his nose sonorously. He replaced the kerchief. He began to read again, and every word was like an invocation.

Each man employed in Mr Healey's offices was to receive a year's full salary in addition to his regular salary, and a bonus of five hundred dollars extra at Christmas, provided he remain for that period at least 'in the employ of my major legatee, who inherits my residuary estate'. He was also to receive an immediate lump sum of three thousand dollars, 'in gratitude for loyal services'. Each Christmas he remained in the employ of the 'major legatee' he would receive an additional five hundred dollars.

Mr Montrose received twenty thousand dollars outright, and 'a prayer that he serve my major legatee for a period of one year at least'. He also received sundry little treasures he had admired in Mr Healey's house, 'notably a Sanger portrait of George Washington'. In addition, he received one hundred shares in the Pennsylvania Railroad and 'three of the producing wells next to the Parker Farm'. 'There are no words,' Mr Healey had dictated, 'which can convey my affection for Mr Montrose, who has served me well for over a decade from the date of this Will.'

Mr Healey prayed that Mr Montrose would find it in his heart to remain with 'my major legatee' until his conscience is satisfied that said Major Legatee was fully qualified to continue without that supreme wisdom, delicacy of tact, perfection of judgment, of which my dear friend, Mr Montrose, is the Proud Possessor.

Joseph glanced at Mr Montrose who seemed greatly moved. His fine catlike face became very serious, and he looked aside.

Harry Zeff was left the sum of five thousand dollars, and at this Harry let out a loud and involuntary whistle which made everyone jump in his chair. A slight ripple of laughter ran through the room, shaken, unintended, and Mr Spaulding looked as horrified as a priest might look if the Host were desecrated. He hid the will with his spread hands. He gulped. He implored the ceiling for mercy with uplifted eyes. His jaw trembled; his mouth shook. The sun-ray quivered in his hair which, all at once, appeared to rise on his head in a holy breeze.

Harry was immediately thrown into immense embarrassment and confusion, though everyone eyed him with sympathy as well as with smothered mirth. His dusky face was crimson. He cowered in his chair. Even Joseph was amused, and he thought of young Liza.

The unpardonable interruption was ignored by Mr Spaulding and after a prolonged delay he began to read again. There were small sums to the girls who worked in his house, a sum of money for a madam he particularly appreciated, ten thousand dollars to St Francis's Working Boys' Home in Philadelphia, gifts to a seminary, an orphanage in Pittsburgh and – to Joseph's dark amazement – the sum of two thousand dollars for Masses for his unregenerate soul. Mrs Murray received the sum of one thousand dollars 'provided she quits my house and Titusville within ten days' of Mr Healey's death.

There were other small but pleasant remembrances to friends in various cities. Miss Emmy received an income for life of five thousand dollars a year, an incredible sum, riches.

Joseph had never heard a will read before. When Mr Spaulding stopped reading he felt a slight sadness, for there had been no mention of his name, no remembrance. It is not the money, he thought, but I believed that we were friends, that he had some regard for me. If he had left me but his watch, a trinket from his chain, a book, a picture . . .

Now Mr Spaulding's voice rose on a radiant crest. 'We now come to the Major Legatee mentioned in this last Will

175

and Testament of my beloved friend, Edward Cullen Healey.'

Long breaths were taken in the room, except for Joseph, who felt nothing but impatience now, nothing but a desire to leave, to feel his hurt alone, and, he thought vaguely, to run back to the house and steal the daguerreotype. (Surely no one wanted it but himself, and Mr Spaulding's natural malice would be delighted to refuse any offer from him and cut him with any disappointment and frustration.)

Mr Spaulding leaned forward in his chair. He had the attention of all, except Joseph. Then Joseph heard his name . . . 'my dear young friend, my son in all but birth, my countryman, who has so often shown me his affection and loyalty – though he did not know this himself – Joseph Francis Xavier Armagh . . .'

A deep murmur ran through the office, and every head turned and every eye stared at Joseph, whose mouth opened in a muttered, 'What? What?'

Mr Spaulding rose slowly and majestically and came from behind his desk. He went weightily down the rows of chairs. He paused beside Joseph. He held out his hand, and bowed. 'My felicitations, Mr Francis,' he said, 'or, I should say, Mr Armagh.'

Joseph was stunned. He had heard nothing but his name and a few other words. He did not want to touch Mr Spaulding's hand but thinking of that portrait on the desk in Mr Healey's study he forced himself to take the warm damp fingers. He said, 'All I want is that daguerreotype, on his desk, in the gilt frame. I will pay for it . . .'

At that everyone in the room burst into loud and affectionate laughter. Harry leaned towards Joseph and slapped him heartily on the back, recovering from his own stunned disbelief. Even Mr Spaulding smiled tenderly, leaned down to place his hand gently on Joseph's thin shoulder. Great grins spread from face to face, and Joseph's words were repeated over and over, to renewed laughter.

'All that, and all else too, my dear boy,' he said. 'An Empire. A mountain of gold.'

It was indeed. Joseph Francis Xavier Armagh was the Major Legatee of Edward Cullen Healey. Mr Healey's vast 'interests' now belonged to him, 'without let or hindrance'. Brothels. Refineries. Saloons. Newspaper mortgages. Property in Pittsburgh, Titusville, Boston, New York, Philadelphia.

Wells. Endless investments. Enormous sums of money in various banks. A hotel, flourishing, in Philadelphia. Mines. Investments in several lavish hotels in New York, stocks, bonds in countless industries, including munitions and railroads. He was the sole executor, though the assistance of Mr Spaulding – at a large annual fee – was designated.

'I don't believe it,' said Joseph, and he looked about him and the room swam in a shifting mist and the sunlight seemed to dance in the confines of the windows and the blue sky beyond tilted dizzily. He had brilliantly enlarged visions of his brother and sister, of Sister Elizabeth, of Green Hills, and he thought that he had lost his mind. Someone was pressing a glass of whisky against his mouth. He drank it, dumbly. He saw Mr Montrose's face floating in front of him. He felt the hard clasp of Harry's hand. His own was cold and sweating. Then he had an awful impulse to burst into tears.

'I don't believe it,' he repeated, helplessly, again and again. His hand was shaken by others. He heard voices. He closed his eyes and hid in the darkness for a while.

CHAPTER TWENTY-FOUR

MARY REGINA ARMAGH stood in a thick scattering of blood-red oak leaves and surveyed the great white house before her. She said, 'But, Joe, it's very big, isn't it, for just three people, and Sean will be going to Harvard. Then only two will be there.'

'Now, Regina,' said Joseph in the special voice which was only for her, gentle and firm and paternal, 'there will be servants. You know the Hennessey house yonder, with the maids and the butler and the stable-boys, and it is only for two, for the Senator is rarely there.'

The girl lifted her shining regard to her brother. 'Can you afford it, Joe? It must be very expensive.'

He kept his face grave. 'I can afford it, my love. You mustn't trouble yourself. I am no spendthrift.'

Regina said, looking down at the autumn-littered earth, 'You've worked so hard for us, Joe. You've sacrificed for us and given us all you could, even when it meant depriving yourself. I should hate myself if I thought you built this house for us and it meant worry and more work for you.'

'I think,' said Sean, 'that Joe knows what he's doing. He always did.' The lilting voice was touched, in its music, with a faint note of malice. He was as tall as his brother, at nearly nineteen, but sinuous and gracefully swaying in all his motions, and, to Joseph, disgustingly poetic in appearance.

Regina knew that Sister Elizabeth had often written to Joseph about Sean, with tactful pleadings, though Sister Elizabeth had too much common sense to countenance parasitism or those she called 'perpetual whining Poor Souls'. But Sister Elizabeth knew the realities of life, and Sean was one of those realities, and so had to be dealt with. She therefore had written letters to Joseph pleading for Sean – not that she approved of the youth – but in truth to make the lives of the brothers a little easier for both. Sean was Sean, and so he had been born, and not even the direst circumstances would ever be able to change him from a lissome young man to a stern man of business and the dealer with the iron truth. 'Perhaps,' Sister Elizabeth had once said to the young girl, 'he will marry a rich woman who will adore him, and not expect anything from him but love, pleasing attentions, tenderness and laughter. If Joseph fails to be tolerant of him it will be tragic for both of them.'

Regina, then, as subtly and as tactfully as she could, stood between the two brothers, the grim and resolute Joseph and the bewildered butterfly who could not understand his brother, and so had to take refuge, in defence, in a light malice, little laughs – and avoidance. Of the two, Regina pitied Joseph the most, a sentiment which would not have pleased the sentimental but of which Sister Elizabeth would have approved. She also pitied Sean, so easily wounded, so easily baffled when others failed to laugh with him or appreciate his jokes or his beautiful singing voice and his ardent involvement with beauty.

The three stood near the large white-brick and pillared house which Joseph had built for his family near the larger and more ostentatious house of Senator Hennessey. It had taken nearly two years to build, and it stood on a slight rise on ten acres of immaculately landscaped grounds, all groups of trees on plushy grass and gardens and conservatories and summer houses and gazebos. A little brook flowed on the property, and it, too, had been brought into order, with primroses planted on its banks, and summer lilies, and iris and young willows.

The house was ready for its occupants. Much time had gone into the ordering and choosing of furniture, rugs and draperies and pictures. Joseph knew that he had no taste for such things, and so, at the urging of Regina – he could never deny her anything – had permitted his sister to ask the aid of the ailing Katherine Hennessey, who loved her. Katherine, during those months, had come to life with this new interest, and asked Joseph only how much he desired to spend, and when he said, 'Anything at all, so long as it is appropriate and the best of its kind,' she was delighted and invigorated. Her taste was marvellous, yet not exclusively feminine, except when it came to Regina's rooms. There was not a vista which did not entrance and invite, and this was evident even to Joseph's eyes. He loved to walk about his house, when it was being decorated and furnished, and never interfered, but his own rooms were austere, almost bare, containing only essentials even if those were rich and choice. 'Monks' cells,' Sean had remarked to Regina. His own quarters' furnishings had been of his choosing, and were airy and beautiful and excelled the taste even of Katherine Hennessey, who admired him and, looking at her young daughter, shyly thought of him as her daughter Bernadette's husband. He was so lovable, so kind. Katherine would sigh, remembering a husband who was neither, but whom she could only helplessly love.

She thought Joseph the kindest and most masculine and most admirable of men, for with her he was all consideration and he had a way of looking at her which warmed and made her feel a faint stirring of happiness. She did not know that it was because she was cherished and loved by this ironic and gloomy-faced young man, and that her every word, her every gesture, the way she walked, the soft sweetness of her laugh, her glance and her smile, was an occasion for his terrible and brooding adoration, and his even more terrible despair. He had bought the land for his house for the one reason that it was near her own, and that at least he would see her occasionally if only at a distance. He knew that if Katherine ever guessed what he thought of her she would never see him again, and so he was careful. This was not too hard. He had had to be careful all his life.

But he determined to avenge her. It sometimes seemed

179

incredible to him that she could endure her husband.

Once Joseph asked Regina with his cold abruptness, 'What's wrong with Sean?'

She had thought for a moment, and then she had said, 'He is afraid that you think he is foolish, or something, and not serious. He has never told me. It is just something I have felt, Joe. He is truly grateful to you; he knows what you have done for us, but you, in some way, will not let him tell you. He is not strong as you are strong, Joe. You have a very sharp way of speaking. Sean is now a man, not a little boy. You are not his father. Treat him as a respected brother and not one you believe has no wits at all.'

'But he has no wits,' said Joseph, and then he smiled.

Today, they went back to the Hospice, where they were staying for a few days. Very shortly they would move into the house on Willoughby Road. Sean and Regina would not see Titusville again. For some reason which Joseph was never to understand Sean had found it exciting, in spite of his delicate airs and elegance. He had taken a great fancy to Mr Montrose, and Mr Montrose appeared to have affection for him, something else which vexed and confused Joseph. (Mr Montrose had left for Virginia a year ago.) Sean, in Titusville, was alert and glowing and interested. He even went out to the oil-fields. He would walk the crowded and noisy streets with an air of delight. He had attached himself to Harry Zeff and his young wife, Liza, with happy devotion. (Harry was now to Joseph what Mr Montrose had been to Mr Healey.) Harry seemed to like him and enjoy his company. He would listen to Sean when he sang Irish ballads, and applaud with enthusiasm.

'Why don't you teach him to be a man in the raw business of life, Harry?' Joseph once asked.

'There are many ways of being a man, Joe,' said Harry.

'He's feckless and a milksop.'

Harry and Liza had built a house for themselves in Titusville which decorously followed the fashion of old and established residences. They had urged Joseph to stay with them when he was in Titusville, but he preferred the solitude of his hotel. Besides, the distant cries of Harry's infant twin sons annoyed Joseph. Liza had the delusion of the common born: she believed everyone was interested in her offspring and would interrupt Joseph and Harry, when they were in her house, by triumphantly bringing the squalling little boys into Harry's 'study'. Even Harry, the perpetually good-natured, would have to order her to leave, which made her cry. Joseph liked Liza and remembered her days of brutality in Mr Healey's house. But she was now comparatively rich, and had nursemaids, and the intrusion was unpardonable.

'Why don't you get married?' Harry Zeff asked his friend.

The very thought was repugnant to Joseph. His old habit of considering his sister and his brother intruded on him. 'I have seen no woman as yet,' he said, 'that I would want to marry.' He thought of Katherine Hennessey.

Then Harry said, watching him, 'You are a multi-million-aire now, Joe. Who is going to get your money? Your sister? She will probably marry. Your brother . . .' and Harry paused, more keenly watching him.

Sean.

Sean would go to Harvard. Then what would he do? Would Harvard make a responsible man of him, serious, determined to succeed? Would it change his character, make it resolute and strong? Joseph thought, and he was appalled. He knew that men never changed their nature.

CHAPTER TWENTY-FIVE

KATHERINE HENNESSEY walked slowly and with considerable feebleness across the vast and whitely shining hall of her house.

A profound hope had come to Katherine Hennessey recently, for her husband would run for Governor of the Commonwealth in November, and he would be at home more often, perhaps every week-end and at every holiday, and several consecutive weeks in the year. She had hated Washington and its mud and its teeming people and its predatory politicians, and its dank streets ugly to her, for all their width, and the blank Circles and the ostentatiously large government building.

She was quite convinced that Washington had put its own disgusting mark on her husband – poor Tom – and had wearied him to death, and had separated him from his family because of endless and devoted duties. Even in summer, that most awful and impossible summer of Washington, he had had to remain in Washington, toiling for the welfare of the Commonwealth of Pennsylvania and the whole nation, enduring the sodden heat, the stinks, the almost tropical rains and storms, and the pervading mud. She had frequently, when the pain was too great, gently upbraided her husband, and had wept, and had forgotten that gentlemen detested tears and fled from them, and that they deserved more consideration from their wives.

Since Senator Hennessey had announced that he was the candidate of his party for the office of Governor in the autumn – explaining in luscious tones and with trembling inflections that he wished to be more with his beloved family – Katherine had bewitched herself with the delusion that all she had ever suspected, all she had ever known of her husband had been the fantasies of her own hard and obdurate heart, her own abominable hallucinations, her own narrow soul. Why else would dear Tom have given up his labours in Washington as a prominent and popular Senator, if not for the desire to return more frequently to the bosom of his family?

Tonight, thought Katherine Hennessey as she walked slowly and with a slight panting difficulty across the marble to the bronze doors, dearest Tom would be home for his darling daughter's seventeenth birthday celebration. She smiled fondly as she put her thin white hand on the handle of the door. Seventeen. She herself had been a wife and mother just before her seventeenth birthday, but young ladies these days were more independent and saucy and had strong minds. Darling Bernadette! She was wilful and not always respectful to her elders, but she had such a spirit, such a liveliness, such a way of tossing her long sleek brown curls, such a sparkle of brilliant defiance in her eyes, that one forgave her on the spot. No wonder dear Tom loved his daughter so much. At her age he must have been her masculine replica, and Katherine pondered, with love, on the young Tom she had never known but whom she cherished in Bernadette. I am, thought Katherine, as she pantingly pulled open the bronze doors, unworthily blessed. She was amused at her weakness. I am an old woman, she thought. I am going on thirty-four. That is young no longer. I am beginning to feel the infirmities of age.

I must be careful of my health and strength, for my darlings sakes.

She was going to stroll on the lawns and among the gardens, as her doctor had recommended. She had dutifully taken her iron pills this morning. Neither she nor her doctor ever once suspected that her suppressed knowledge of the shame, brutality, betrayal, rejection, contempt and humiliation she had endured since her marriage, and the endless exploitation, had destroyed her health and endurance for all time.

She was at last able to open the heavy door far enough to let her go out. She did not know that young Bernadette had come half-way down the stairs to the hall while she had been feebly making her way across it, and had been watching her mother with a mixture of disdain and cynicism and wondering and contemptuous pity. Mama was such a fool, such an old-fashioned elderly woman, such, really, an imbecile. She knew nothing at all about Papa, whom Bernadette loved very much.

Bernadette went to one of the windows beside the doors and watched her mother's piteously thin and fragile figure moving with slow difficulty across the lawns. The girl shook her head with amused exasperation. Now the silly thing was talking to a stable-boy, with that deep seriousness and that deep kind smile she always wore when speaking to anybody. Couldn't she ever see how absurd she was, gazing at people like an illuminated saint? No wonder Papa had 'associated' with brighter and gayer women! After all, a man can stand so much of a fool, and then he must console himself. Bernadette had not been appalled at the giggling revelations of her schoolmates at St Amelia's Female Academy in Philadelphia which concerned her father. In many ways, secretly, she was proud of her father's virility and manifest masculinity. At least he was a man, and not a caricature of a woman as her mother was. Bernadette was not deceived that her father was seeking the Governorship to be 'with my beloved family more often'. She knew very well, from reading hints in the newspapers, that Papa was about finished in Washington, and that the State legislature was no longer in a mood to re-appoint him once again. Papa had been entirely too zestful in Washington, though Bernadette never condemned him. She thought him delightful, and justified.

The man Bernadette really desperately loved and desired

183

was Joseph Francis Xavier Armagh, the brother of a girl she tolerated and cultivated assiduously only for one reason. Mary Regina was almost as silly as Mama – and Bernadette resented and envied the other girl's beauty. Regina was sent to no Female Academy. Her brother kept her at home with a governess, Miss Faulk, to teach her graces and manners, and a tutor, Timothy Dineen, to educate her and Sean. Bernadette had long ago discerned Joseph's deep attachment to his sister, and so Bernadette had pursued that sister relentlessly, with sweetness, sometimes even with fawnings, and always with loudly expressed affection and devotion.

It was not Joseph's wealth alone which had early attracted the nubile Bernadette, but his very appearance, his air of assurance and power and distinction, his look of ruthlessness, of cold dominance. Sean was like a waving blossom compared with an oak, and Bernadette despised Sean, who was now in Harvard and not doing excellently.

Bernadette had hinted of her attachment to Joseph a year ago, and her father had laughed. 'You could do worse, my pet,' he had said. 'He has even more money than I have, and is a director and a power in many companies. He is no fool, and has a ·lot of pride, and will go very far, and is deeply involved in politics – I am relying on his support, I must confess, in his newspaper, *The Philadelphia Messenger,* which has great influence. He will never run for anything, himself – one must remember his – er – his . . .' Tom had paused. One didn't mention brothels to one's daughter. He continued, 'With his connections. Some of them not quite gentlemanly. Well, we'll see, later.'

It was now 'later', in Bernadette's opinion. Mama had been a wife and mother at seventeen. Why, thought Bernadette, I am almost an old maid! I'm not even remotely bespoken. Who wants callow boys, anyway, instead of a man like Joe, who is just like Papa?

She knew that she amused Joseph with her pertness and her witticisms, which sometimes bordered on his own irony, and that he believed she loved his sister devotedly. She had guessed that at times her effrontery amused him even more, and her liveliness and vitality. She had no doubt but that she need only lift a finger and Joseph would fall at her feet. She intended to lift that finger tomorrow. She knew that her father would have preferred that Bernadette had desired Sean, nearer her own age, and very Anglo-Saxon in appearance. But to that preference she was indifferent.

She would advance an idea to her father tonight: she wanted to be tutored by Timothy Dineen, too. 'He has taught Regina twice as much as I have learned in Philadelphia. It is only a step for me to the Armaghs' house, and you know how dearly I love Regina, and I would be among my closest friends in Green Hills.' She would then encounter Joseph more often in his own house, if her little gambit failed tomorrow. But how could it fail? Who was he, compared with Bernadette Hennessey, in establishment? She loved him, she told herself with virtue, despite what he was. Such pure love must surely be returned. Besides, her house was far more grand, and she had a lady for a mother.

Bernadette, watching her mother through the window, had her attention caught by something moving briskly through the gates on the gravelled road and towards the house. In a moment she saw that it was one of the better hacks of the depot, and that it contained a young lady. Bernadette thought that the woman was probably the mother or the chaperon of one of her own guests due tonight. But where was the guest? Bernadette opened the bronze doors and walked out upon the white steps of the pillared portico.

The lady, assisted by the driver, alighted on the path and Bernadette saw that she was very beautiful and young, and not more than twenty-one, and arrayed lavishly in lavender silk and lace, and that she had marvellously slender ankles and a mass of pale hair under her little tilted hat. Though she had a controlled air, and was apparently of excellent breeding, there was something agitated about her, and the inquisitive Bernadette was surprised.

Katherine, equally surprised, left the flower-bed and went to the stranger, making a soft, self-deprecating gesture with her thin hands. She then motioned towards the house, but the lady – who was regarding Katherine with earnest attention – shook her head slightly. Katherine paused, as if a little baffled. Bernadette could hear their voices, though not their words. Then Katherine was no longer speaking; the wind caught her blue dress and it was as if it had touched the shroud of a dead woman. Bernadette wanted to run to join them but manners had been literally beaten into her by the

Sisters, and so she cautiously advanced only to the steps of the portico and strained to hear.

The strange young lady continued to speak, and Bernadette saw that her mother was very still, only her blue dress and her hair blowing a little, and that she was, suddenly, dwindled and shrunken in appearance. The young lady's voice rose desperately. 'I implore you, Mrs Hennessey, to be merciful and kind! To understand, to remember that I am a sister-woman in a terrible situation. Not to judge me, or your husband, but only to be kind and compassionate. It was probably most wrong of us – I know it was, and we are guilty, and from my heart I ask your pardon, and even your pity, for one so much younger than yourself. You have a daughter. Consider me as a daughter, too, who comes to you in wretchedness not only pleading for forgiveness, but asking your help.'

Then Katherine spoke in a dry and almost inaudible voice: 'But – what did he tell you, about me, about himself?' She put her hand to her slight breast in a pathetic gesture.

The young lady's face was running with tears as she leaned towards Katherine. 'Only what you know yourself, Mrs Hennessey, that he intends to leave you when he is elected Governor, and that he has asked you for a divorce and you have refused, in spite of my helpless position. Is it possible that you will continue to deny our child his father's name, you who are a mother yourself? Could any human being be so cruel? I don't believe it, your face is so gentle, so – tender. Tom must have been mistaken. He has told me that you will not let him go, because you want his money, and that you never loved each other, and it was a marriage of convenience, which he has always regretted. But surely you know this! He prefers, as he has told you, that you sue for the divorce, but, if not, he will be forced to do so, even at the expense of his career, for he has our unborn child to consider. Mrs Hennessey, I appeal to your womanly heart, your pity, to let him go at once! He does not know I have come to you, but I was driven – I wanted to appeal . . .'

Katherine rocked vaguely on her heels. She put her hand to her face, as if in bemused wonder, a dream, in incredulity. Her fragile body swayed. Bernadette started down the stairs, only half comprehending. Then Katherine turned, very, very slowly, her hands fumbling helplessly in the air, and she faced the house and took two uncertain steps towards it, her

186

white face blank and without any expression at all. She staggered. She threw up her arms as if drowning, and then she dropped to the shining green grass and lay there, tossed and thrown, a bundle of bodiless blue. Bernadette began to run. She reached her mother and stood beside her but did not bend or touch her. She looked only at the beautiful young lady who was staring at Katherine, aghast, her hand to her lips.

'Who are you?' she asked of the stranger, and the woman, still looking only at Katherine, said faintly, 'I – I am a friend of the Senator's – a friend. He wants to leave his wife but she will not let him go.' She became aware of the young girl. She looked at Bernadette with stretched green eyes. 'Who are you?' she whispered.

'I am the Senator's daughter,' said Bernadette. 'And you are a liar.'

When Joseph Armagh entered the great hall of the Hennessey house he saw that Bernadette, dishevelled and weeping and swollen of face, was the only one there. The hall had been partially decorated, and then deserted. There was utter silence in the enormous mansion, a sensation that death was already present.

Bernadette, crying wildly, ran to Joseph and flung herself on his chest. His arms rose automatically and held her, and he listened to her incoherent cries with a stunned expression. He listened to her words, finally, with suddenly sharp attention.

'She lied, she lied!' Bernadette half-screamed. 'She is an adventuress – my father – she lied. She killed my mother. I heard it all . . .'

'Your mother sent for me,' said Joseph, still holding the girl, whose morning dress was crumpled and stained.

Bernadette shrieked, 'She won't see him! He doesn't dare go into her room! The priest is here – Extreme Unction – and the doctor's with her! To say such things about my father! To think my mother believed them – Oh, my poor mother!' The long tube-like curls had long ago lost their roundness. Bernadette's fine lank hair swathed her like a brown veil, and numerous tendrils on her cheeks and forehead were wet with sweat and tears.

Joseph took his own handkerchief and wiped the girl's streaming face and eyes and she sobbed brokenly and clutched

187

him again and convulsively clung to him. He looked about for servants, for someone who would take this weeping child away and comfort her, but every door was shut.

She seized Joseph again, looking up at him, frantic and distraught. 'Don't leave me, Joe, don't leave me!'

Where was that bastard of a father of hers, that he was not with her to comfort and help her?

'I won't leave you,' he said. 'But your mother sent for me, an hour ago. Where is your father?'

'In his room. I don't know – in his room. He can't stand it – he doesn't know what to do . . .'

I bet, thought Joseph. And he felt again that powerful urge to kill.

He took Bernadette to a sofa and forced her to sit upon it. He looked at a staring maid who had suddenly appeared. 'Stay with Miss Bernadette,' he said. 'Don't leave her for a moment.' He paused. 'Which is Mrs Hennessey's bedroom?' With pity he looked down at Bernadette, so agonised, so broken, her arms swinging close to the floor, her long hair hanging about her, her face hidden, her voice keening lamentations and despair.

'Second door to your left, on the floor above,' said the maid.

Joseph went to the wide marble staircase with its gilded banister and it wound above him. He reached another wide long hall, the white floor partially covered with an Oriental runner; landscapes, excellently painted, hung on the walls. Sofas lined one side. Heavy carved doors of polished wood stood shut before Joseph. At first he did not see Tom Hennessey sitting with his head in his hands on a love-seat, the very portrait of despair, nor the priest beside him who looked only ahead as if the other man was not there at all. Here the light of the chandelier was not so vivid, and the hall wavered in half-shadow. When he finally saw the two men Joseph stopped and he looked at Tom Hennessey and a ball of fire and acid stuck in his throat and his vision jerked with the intensity of his hatred.

The priest saw him and rose. 'Father Scanlon,' he said briefly. 'And you are Mr Armagh for whom Mrs Hennessey is asking?'

'Yes,' said Joseph and shook hands with the priest. 'How is Mrs Hennessey?'

The priest glanced at the Senator who cowered lower on his

seat, and he said, 'She has received the Last Rites.' His grave calm eyes studied Joseph. 'It is not expected that she will — live.'

He went before Joseph and opened a door and then stood aside. In the centre of the room stood a richly canopied bed, and in that bed lay Katherine Hennessey gazing at nothing. Her doctor sat beside her and held his hand on her pulse.

Her tawny hair was spread out on her white silken pillows like a glowing wave, and her white face was absolutely still, and she appeared already dead to Joseph as he slowly approached her. But she felt his presence. Her eyes, dulled now and empty, faintly brightened, and she whispered his name. He bent over her in silence with a sick and ferocious sorrow, and she moved her free hand and he took it. It was as cold as death. He said, 'I came, Katherine.' It was the first time he had ever used her name. The faint brightness in her eyes increased. She turned her head to the doctor and whispered, 'Alone, please.' The satin coverlet covered her to her throat, but she shivered in the warm air, her slight body hardly lifting the quilt.

The doctor stood up, shaking his head dolefully at Joseph, and he murmured, 'Only a minute or two.' When the doctor had gone Joseph knelt beside the bed, and Katherine held his hand as if only he could keep her alive, and the iciness of her fingers recalled the touch of his dying mother.

Katherine's dying face was the face of a girl, a suffering and tortured girl, and her lips were grey and her nose was pinched and the nostrils moved in and out as she tried for her last breaths. She did not look away from Joseph, whose head was so near hers, but her eyes probed into his earnestly, hopefully, pleadingly.

'Yes?' said Joseph. 'Yes, dear. What is it?'

'Bernadette,' she whispered. 'My little girl, my child. She loves you, Joseph, and I know you love her and that you have just been waiting to speak . . .' Her throat almost closed, and she panted and struggled, her chin jutting out.

Joseph knelt very still beside the bed and looked at her and his hand tightened about hers to give her strength, to keep her for a while. Her words entered his mind slowly, and with only a dull astonishment.

'Take her, keep her,' said the expiring woman. 'She will be — safe — with you, my dear. Take her away — so innocent — so young . . . Joseph? Promise me?'

'Yes, Katherine,' he said, with all the power of his love for her. 'I promise.'

She sighed deeply. Her eyes still held his in that pathetic hope and certitude, and she tried to smile. Then she sighed again, and closed her eyes.

He knelt there, watching her, holding her hand, and he did not see the doctor return with the priest and did not hear the beginning of the Litany for the Dying. He did not see Tom Hennessey standing in the doorway, shrinking, not daring to enter. He saw only Katherine's face, becoming smaller and smaller, but quiet now and with growing peace. He did not see the great golden Crucifix that stood over the bed. Nothing existed, had being, but Katherine Hennessey.

Only he heard her final faint breath. He still knelt, not moving. Her hand was flaccid in his. Then he dropped his head so it lay beside Katherine's and he closed his eyes and the awful ripping of grief tore him apart, and he felt that he, too, had died. His cheek touched hers and slowly he turned his head and touched her fallen flesh with his lips.

'Go forth, Christian soul,' the priest intoned, and Joseph was again on the ship beside his mother, and there was nothing at all anywhere but anguish and darkness and pain.

Later, when he went slowly down the stairs to the hall, feeling his way with his feet like an old man, he found Tom Hennessey sitting beside his daughter and holding her in his arms and comforting her, and Bernadette had clenched her young arms about her father's neck and she was sobbing against his chest.

'It isn't true, my darling,' said the Senator. 'It was all lies. The woman tried to make me leave your mother – she was mad and infatuated – I tried to drive her away – I wrote her a foolish letter because I pitied her – I confess I was a little drunk – My darling, your blessed mother had always been delicate, her heart, but she understood – she understood. You mustn't grieve. It is for the best – an end to her suffering . . .' His voice had never been so deep and so resonant and so rich, and Bernadette's sobs lessened.

Then the Senator saw Joseph near him, silent and watching, and the eyes of the men met and neither spoke. For a long time their eyes held each other. At last Joseph, hardly making a sound, left the hall, opened the door and went out into the warm summer night and closed the door after him. But the Senator stared at the door for a considerable space, for never had a man looked at him like that before.

CHAPTER TWENTY-SIX

JOSEPH arrived at Mr Spaulding's office with Timothy Dineen one August day before noon, for he had been out in the oil-fields since early morning accompanied by his manager, Harry Zeff. (The Armagh Enterprises now had impressive offices in Philadelphia, and that city was Harry's headquarters, and his assistants were the younger men who had been Mr Healey's 'associates', plus clerks and lawyers to the number of over two hundred.)

Mr Spaulding was all love and heartiness on greeting the young man, and full of solicitude and little tender cries of congratulations. He patted and plucked, though he knew very well that Joseph detested intimacies or even the touch of others.

'Sit down, dear boy, do!' exclaimed Mr Spaulding. He ignored Timothy who abhorred him. Joseph sat down in a deep red leather chair and Timothy stood near him as though guarding him, his black eyes studying Mr Spaulding as if he expected him to produce a knife or another lethal instrument. 'Brandy, Joe? Whisky? Wine? I have them all!'

'Nothing,' said Joseph. He looked worn yet more potent than ever, and his leanness had increased rather than diminished with his prosperity.

Mr Spaulding cleared his throat and glanced at Timothy. 'Mr Dineen?'

'Whisky,' said Timothy. His short strong body was broad now with good living, but his muscles were firm and active and his black hair was abundant and carefully waved.

'Whisky it is!' cried Mr Spaulding in delight, as if Timothy had given him extraordinary pleasure. 'What a warm day it is, to be sure. Yes, indeed. We expect cooler days at this time in August.' He smiled expansively and lovingly as he poured whisky and soda into a tall glass for Timothy, and extended it to him.

Mr Spaulding sat down and beamed at Joseph. 'I have been reading all about you in the papers, dear boy! "Amazing entrepreneur! Associate of the great New York Wall Street Financier, Mr Jay Regan – the Goulds – the Fisks! Proud that he is a citizen of this mighty Commonwealth! Railroads, mining, oil, milling, building, financial baron!"'

'Not to mention my brothels,' said Joseph, 'nor my rum-running from the South into my Northern distilleries.'

Mr Spaulding held up tender palms. 'They are services deeply appreciated if not publicly approved,' he chuckled. 'Do you not serve humanity intimately as well as industrially and financially? This is not to be deplored, no matter the blue noses.'

'Nor my gun-running here and there, in Mexico and abroad,' said Joseph, as if Mr Spaulding had not spoken. The older man chuckled again, but now his eyes were wary. Joseph was baiting him. He said, 'We must make a living at anything that comes to our hands.'

Joseph said, 'Harry Zeff tells me your recent reports to him are well in order. I haven't much time. I am taking the two o'clock to Winfield. I have a mission for you.' He paused. He did not move even a finger, yet he gave the appearance of ruthless quickening. 'I want you to send me, post haste, a full report on Governor Tom Hennessey. Everything you have, know of accurately, and from your files, which Mr Healey began and enlarged. No matter how small – I want it. I should like a brief sketch of his father, too.'

A hot and brilliant silence fell in the large offices, which smelled of warm leather and wax and lemon-oil. Mr Spaulding had folded his hands on his desk. He regarded Joseph intently. His smile had disappeared but his eyes were brighter and the heavy lids lower.

Then Mr Spaulding said – Joseph's eyes had suddenly frightened him: 'Your father-in-law.' His voice, usually so fruity and full of tremolos, was flat and expressionless.

'My father-in-law.'

'The grandfather of your two children.'

'The grandfather of my two children.'

Timothy shifted on his neat feet and drank deeply of his whisky. There was a sudden shrill singing of cicadas soaring through the open windows. The hills beyond, though still green, showed a tarnishing here and there where hot yellow dust had settled on them, and all at once the traffic on the street was very imminent in the room.

'The Governor is running again for office this autumn,' said Mr Spaulding, who was becoming unnerved. 'Has what you desire anything to do with that?'

'Yes,' said Joseph. His quiet hands, clasped on his knee – long and thin and well-shaped – did not stir.

'But,' suggested Mr Spaulding, and now he licked a corner of his lips with a wet and darting tongue, 'more than that?'

'More than that.' Then the laconic Joseph said, 'I want him absolutely ruined. Stripped. Dishonoured. Prison, if possible, though I doubt we can arrange that. He's been too sly and has had too much help to cover up.'

Mr Spaulding leaned back in his chair. He was never shocked at anything, and even this did not startle him. But he was curious.

'It might rebound on you, Joe,' he said. 'Your father-in-law.'

'How can it?' said Joseph. 'I control quite a number of newspapers, especially those in Pennsylvania. I have influence in New York, too. But even if some muck-raking sheet blares it out, how can it hurt me?' He gave a faint smile. 'I am not running for public office. I am not a politician who can be hurt by public opinion, or votes. There is nothing anyone can do to me, either the people or the government. I am entirely too rich. My affairs are – respectable. I am a director of the big Handell Oil Company, and director of many other companies. I am invulnerable. A word or two to influential politicians . . .' He raised one hand briefly. 'I think we could even keep it out of the newspapers entirely. We will give him a chance to submit or be publicly crucified. He has only to renounce any desire to be Governor again – and accede to the loss of his fortune, to the extent we can manage. I will be the one to give him that advice.'

'He will never know who did it,' said Mr Spaulding.

'I intend to inform him, when it is done,' said Joseph.

Mr Spaulding caught his breath. He had guessed long ago that Joseph hated his father-in-law, but he had thought it a conflict of temperament. Governor Hennessey had been over-whelmingly pleased by his daughter's choice of a husband.

Her wedding had drawn dignitaries from all over the Commonwealth, and Washington, and two foreign ambassadors had been present. The wedding had taken place in Philadelphia in the Governor's house and it was still mentioned frequently among society, and even in New York. It had been so lavish, so ostentatious, that one or two small newspapers had protested 'this extragavance in the midst of a Panic – people starving – strikers being murdered by the railroaders – miners being shot down in their own little shacks before their wives and children – the display must invite the anger of Providence.'

'You will inform him,' said Mr Spaulding in a thoughtful tone, remembering everything. 'Of course, Joseph, it is not my affair, but we have been friends since you were a youth and I first taught you law at our dear Ed Healey's behest. May I ask why?'

'No,' said Joseph, and saw Katherine Hennessey's face.

Mr Spaulding sighed. He stirred some papers on his desk. His eyelids blinked rapidly. He said, in a subdued voice, 'Mrs Armagh – Bernadette, your wife – even if she never guesses the – the – *diablo ex machina,* as it were – will be very hurt, for she was always devoted to her father, and he to her.'

Joseph smiled with grimness. 'Mr Spaulding,' he said, 'you feel no commiseration for Mrs Armagh, though you have known her from childhood. You are merely curious. I don't intend to satisfy your curiosity. As for Mrs Armagh being distressed, I doubt it. She has never been pleased that her father saw fit to marry a girl not much older than herself, a few months after we were married. A girl, I might recall to you, who already had an ambiguous child less than a year old.'

'There was no scandal, Joseph.'

'Of course not. I saw to that, and so did Hennessey. He adopted the boy. Very kind of him, was it not?' He thought of the day Katherine Hennessey had died, and the young woman who had come to her with her pleas. The young lady, it was later discovered – but not publicly – had been the daughter of a Congressman, and a powerful one also. On her marriage to Tom Hennessey the newspapers had declared that she was 'a young widow, relict of one of our heroic officers who later died as a result of his wounds and left her with an afflicted little boy.' (The affliction was the fact that he 'had never seen his young father'.)

Joseph felt no hatred for Elizabeth Hennessey, the new young wife. She, too, had been a victim of the Senator's lies, cruelties, seductions and betrayal. Her father must have had considerable power in the White House, Joseph had thought when the marriage had taken place. He later discovered that the Congressman had been a relative of the President, and one much favoured by him.

A silence had again fallen in Mr Spaulding's office. He was still avid with curiosity. He felt no commiseration for Governor Hennessey and what this would all mean to him. Joseph Armagh was stronger than the Governor. Joseph Armagh would destroy the Governor, for his own reasons, which were not known to Mr Spaulding. The weaker, as usual, would go down. That was the law of nature and why should man quarrel with it? It was not even a matter of morality, or, coming down to it, legality.

'Time is money,' said Joseph. 'The more time the less money. Paradox, isn't it?'

Mr Spaulding understood. 'Say, about six weeks before the elections?'

'No. He must withdraw his candidacy as soon as possible. That is the first step.' He made a motion as if to rise, and Mr Spaulding said with haste, 'I will attend to it as soon as possible. The information goes, as usual, to your house in Green Hills, and not your office?'

'Yes,' said Joseph, and stood up and Timothy put down his empty glass.

Mr Spaulding rose and the two men looked at each other over the desk. 'Jim,' said Joseph, 'you have been loyal and most helpful to me through these years since Mr Healey died. In appreciation – your birthday is next week, isn't it? – you will receive a small token from me. This will not be part of the payment upon receipt of the evidence I have requested.' His voice was a rich parody of Mr Spaulding's but the latter did not notice.

'Joseph,' said Mr Spaulding, with real emotion, 'you are too kind.'

The astute and intellectual Timothy Dineen never deceived himself that he had Joseph Armagh's full and unrestrained confidence. In the matter of business, it was true, Joseph trusted him and never questioned him. But he never spoke of his own feelings or his own reasons for doing anything, nor approached Timothy beyond the ordinary hedges of friendship and mutual respect. Timothy often guessed a number of things, intuitive as all the Irish, but he was never really positive. Joseph came as close as possible to regarding any other human being as a confidant when with Harry Zeff, but even here there was some reservation of self, some refusal of commitment, some detachment, some restraint.

'I often wonder why he married Mrs Armagh,' Timothy had once said to Harry. 'He certainly has no sound attachment to her. That's obvious to anybody.'

'I've wondered, too,' said Harry. 'It was a big surprise to me. Joe isn't the marrying kind. I don't think he ever cared about a woman in his life, except as a frequent necessity. Yes, there is his sister, of course, but she's hardly a woman to him.' Harry had given Timothy a quick and covert glance, but Timothy had only nodded.

'Sometimes I'm sorry for Mrs Armagh,' said Timothy, 'though she's a lady hard to be sorry for, with that temper and that cynicism of hers, and her sceptical outlook and her — well, real malice for people. Yet she loves him to distraction. In comparison, her children are nothing to her.'

'Well,' said Harry, 'he's rich and strong, and women love that, and he's handsome in a hard sort of way. Must appeal to women. I'm sorry for Mrs Joe, too.'

Timothy, this hot August afternoon, after leaving Mr Spaulding, was riding back to Winfield in Joseph's private railroad coach, which had once belonged to Mr Healey. He sat at a table going over his papers. Joseph sat in a chair near the large windows and looked out through them, but Timothy knew he was not seeing anything of the hot landscape, all gold and green and russet and purple and blue, which was moving rapidly beyond them. What did men like Joseph Armagh think, when they were alone, or when they forgot their companions? Did Joseph think of his brother, Sean? Timothy remembered the day when Joseph had received a letter from Sean, the last letter he was to receive from the laughing and heedless and finally rebellious young man. Sean had left Harvard without even a farewell to his teachers or fellow-students. Sean had not cared in the least for them, or for dull disciplined learning, or the law Joseph had insisted he study. Sean wanted to sing, to laugh with joyous companions, to drink until he fell unconscious – but still singing – to play happy music, and beautiful music, and, as he had told Joseph, to live. Timothy had once heard them raging at each other.

'You are a grey stone!' Sean had shouted. 'You aren't a man, a human being at all! What do you know of life and loving, of pain – lovely deep pain down in your heart – of turmoil in your soul, if you have one? What do you know of deprivation and grief and hunger and anguish? You know nothing, nothing, but your damned money, and making more of it, no matter how, and the hell with everything and everybody else!'

Sean, in his wild passion and his sense of personal injury, had not noticed the sudden terribleness of Joseph's face, and the clenching of his lips. He had cried on: 'What do you know of loneliness, and loss of hope? You rarely if ever came to see me in the orphanage! Yes, I was told you were "working", for God's sake, and had no money to visit me! That's a lie! You could have spared some of your money to come, and tell me that you thought about me and cared about me. But you didn't. There I was, stuck in the mud of that damned orphanage, among snivelling nuns and dirty brats, with no beauty and no pleasure and no anticipations – and there you were off, forgetting me, and Regina, and not giving us a thought – just making your damned money! And what has it done for you, pray? Nothing. You can't even enjoy it!'

Joseph had not answered. His face became even more terrible, and Sean became even more frantic about his 'wrongs'.

'You must have hated us! Yes, you've provided for us, and it must have killed you, almost. You deserted us when we needed you most, as little children. And for what? Just for money. Once, when I was nine I had the pneumonia. You never came. It was nothing to you. You probably hoped I'd die.'

Joseph had stood up then, and Timothy had seen a long and awful trembling along his body. Joseph had lifted his hand and had struck Sean wordlessly but savagely across the face, and then had left the room. Sean had whimpered. Then, holding his flaming cheek, he had collapsed into a chair and had wailed aloud in self-pity, and then noticing the quiet

197

Timothy, had pleaded with him for compassion. Timothy listened, and then he had said almost gently, 'You are a dog. a selfish swine, and you don't deserve one more thought from your brother. Go on and play. That is about all you are worth, and at your age, too, for Christ's sake!'

That was the last time Timothy saw Sean Armagh. Sean returned to Harvard the next day, after the Christmas holidays. It was the final year at Harvard, and Sean had left the university in the spring, and had disappeared. Only Timothy, sent there to investigate, noticed that Sean had been careful to take with him everything of value in his handsome room. which Joseph had bought for him, and his best clothing and his fine luggage.

It took several months to find Sean, and Timothy led the search. He was finally discovered, gloriously dishevelled, golden-haired, drunk and soiled, laughing and drinking and joking and singing in the saloons of Boston. Sometimes he was accompanied by a fiddler. Sometimes there was an ancient piano which he could make thunder and ring and clamour and dance at will. He played and he sang for a handful of pennies, for beer and whisky, for free lunch, for applause. for camaraderie, the spurious friendship of the saloons, the spurious warmth and companionship and admiration. In a few months he was penniless and ragged.

'We can't let him starve,' said Joseph, with that terrible look on his face when his brother was mentioned. 'We can't give him any money in any amount, either. He would just throw it away on his fellow-ruffians, and drunkards and ne'er-do-wells.'

'Let him starve,' Timothy had said with unusual feeling and Joseph had glanced up at him sharply, had studied him, and then had slightly smiled.

'No,' he said. 'We can't let him starve. I don't know why, but we can't. Perhaps it is because his sister wouldn't like it. Does he have a rooming-house? Well, see that he gets ten dollars a week. Tell one of my boys in Boston to give it to him, Tim.

But two years ago Sean had disappeared. He had not been found since. No one knew, or professed not to know. He might have been murdered, been injured or died and buried in Potter's Field. The hospitals were canvassed, the poor houses, the refuges for such as Sean. He was not there.

Joseph never spoke now of his brother. He never searched for him. Had Sean come to him, begging for forgiveness, Joseph would have helped him. But he would never forgive Sean. Sean was as dead to him as if he had seen him in his grave. He would never forget. Regina must have guessed this for she did not speak of Sean to Joseph, but only to Timothy, and sometimes she would put her hands over her face and cry.

Was Joseph, today, as the train roared in its passage, thinking of any of this? Timothy asked himself. He did not know. Joseph's harsh profile was illuminated by the falling sun. He neither smoked nor drank. He rarely attended social events in Green Hills or Philadelphia or New York or Boston, or in other cities, unless they were connected with business. He had a wife he did not love but who occasionally amused or beguiled him a little, and sometimes even made him laugh when she teased or cajoled him. Perhaps he had some fondness for her. She was not pretty, but she was charming in a lively and hoydenish way, and she had a sharp and diverting tongue. She filled the house with her loud Irish voice, her laughter and her gusto, and her admonitions o ervants and to children.

Rory and Ann, the twins, were nearly five years old. Did Joseph love his children? He was sedulous about them and often spoke to his wife about her carelessness concerning them. They were denied nothing, and Timothy thought this unfortunate. The young should be deprived frequently, as a matter of discipline. Perhaps Joseph was fond of them, but would give them nothing more than fondness. He was, perhaps, as Harry Zeff had said, afraid to love, suspicious of love, and cynical above all things. And, thought Timothy, who can blame him, remembering Sean? Love betrayed, if it did not descend into hatred, became wariness and indifference and doubt, fearful of fresh hurt. Except for his sister, Joseph Armagh was joyless.

CHAPTER TWENTY-SEVEN

GOVERNOR HENNESSEY had given half his interest in his house to his daughter as a wedding gift when she married Joseph Armagh. ('It was his wife's, not his, anyway.' Joseph had remarked.) When she was twenty-one she inherited half her mother's estate. The other half had gone to Tom, who was already married to the Congressman's daughter.

So Joseph now lived in the great and beautiful mansion at which he had once stared, on an early April evening, many years ago. The Governor rarely visited that house. He and Joseph had nothing to say to each other, though Tom chatted heartily in the presence of his son-in-law, to cover Joseph's silences. He told his daughter that he 'adored' his grand-children, though they somewhat subdued his picture of himself – in their presence – as an ageless gallant. He was now in his sixties, and as vain and sensual and ambitious as always. His young wife Elizabeth came with him on his visits to Green Hills, but it was most evident that she and Bernadette would never be friends and would only tolerate each other. Elizabeth was, intrinsically, a kind and composed young woman, and very intelligent, and she had long forgiven – though not forgotten – her husband's betrayal of her. But more than anything else he loved his little son, Courtney, whom he had 'adopted' as the orphaned child of a dead hero. This further inflamed Bernadette's jealousy, and when the child was present she either ignored him or shouted at him pettishly and ordered him to behave himself. She was not so stringent with her own children, and forgave them their selfishness and their tendency to quarrel loudly with each other, and to answer her insolently.

She was endlessly giving parties to introduce Regina to eligible young men, who became infatuated with her at first sight – and with her brother's money. But Regina smilingly rejected all ardent overtures, though with kindness. Her dark beauty was a radiance which attracted both men and women, young and old. She had but to put on a gown and it was a glowing robe on her lovely figure. Joseph had given her a magnificent sapphire necklace, bracelets and ring, and pins for her black hair, but they were no more brilliant and shining than her blue eyes between those odd golden lashes.

'Why don't you help me to get Regina married?' Bernadette asked Joseph. 'Have you no affection for your sister? Do you want to see her dry up in old-maidhood, and sit by the chimney corner?'

'Regina prefers her life as it is, perhaps,' said Joseph.

Bernadette, who was as cynical about religion as she was about everything else with the exception of Joseph, made Novenas earnestly for the marriage of Regina. If Regina would marry, she would pray, she would learn to love her. Surely the Blessed Mother did not like it that she hated Regina, though it was not, of course, 'my fault'. So Bernadette wheedled the saints and God and His Blessed Mother, to get Regina out of her house.

'What have you got against marriage?' she once asked Regina.

'Why, nothing at all, dear Bernadette,' said Regina, surprised, her sweet clear voice amused. 'I think it is a holy estate, as the Church teaches.'

'Why don't you enter it then?' demanded Bernadette. 'Everybody thinks it so odd that you are still unmarried, at your age. Why can't you fall in love?'

But I am in love, thought Regina, and tears filled her eyes. My heart is dying with love. My spirit is filled with love. I think of nothing – but my love.

She said, and her voice was low and searching, 'You do love Joseph, don't you, Bernadette? Truly and eternally love him?'

'Can you ask that? Dare you ask that!' cried Bernadette, and those round full eyes glittered with emotion and anger. 'I love him more than anything in the world. Everything else in the world is nothing to me, compared with Joseph.'

'I know,' said Regina, and knew that the time had finally come and she could go in peace. 'Always remember that, dear Bernadette. Hold fast to my brother. He needs love more than anything in this world, and he has had so little. Help him. Comfort him.'

Two days after Joseph had returned to Green Hills from Titusville, Regina went to her brother's rooms in the great and echoing mansion, the rooms which had once been Governor Hennessey's.

I have always been a stranger in this house, thought Regina, as she climbed the stairs to her brother's rooms. I have never had a home except in the orphanage. She was whitely resolute tonight, but her throat and breast hurt with almost incredible pain, and she prayed under her breath, and it seemed to her that her lungs were locked and she could not breathe. A cool sweat had broken out over her face and her body, and she could feel the dampness in her armpits and over her neck and back and in her palms. Her heart was beating with tremendous force, and she gasped as she climbed those wide marble stairs and the lighted chandelier burned her eyes. She prayed, 'Oh, dear Lord, help me. Help me to make Joe understand, dear Blessed Mother,' Regina prayed. 'Help him to know that I must go to my Love, to the only marriage I desire and have ever desired, since I was a child.'

Joseph knew her knock and so he was putting aside his book when she entered and his saturnine face showed a lightening and a pleasure no other person ever evoked. It was almost a lover's smile, with a far blue glinting under his auburn brows. He stood up to greet his sister, tall and concave of body, and severely dressed even in the privacy of his own rooms. No one had ever seen him dishevelled, not even his wife, and he was always compact and brittle in appearance, with the wiry strength of his countrymen. 'Regina,' he said, and took her by the hand and sat her down in a dark leather chair near his. He turned down his reading lamp a little so it would not shine in her eyes.

Regina dreaded to begin what she must say, so she said, instead, 'What are you reading, Joe?'

'Law,' he said. 'I'm always reading law.' He thought of what Cicero had said: 'Politicians are not born. They are excreted.' It was hardly a quotation to mention to a young lady, but he smiled again. 'I find it invaluable in politics. How do you know what law it is profitable to break unless you know there is such a law?'

She did not smile, as he had expected. He sat down opposite her. 'Joe,' she said, 'I wish you were not always trying to give the impression of being a villain. You know you are not.'

He liked to joke with Regina. However, he saw that she was serious and distressed. 'I'm glad you have a good opinion of me. Regina.' She looked down at the hands she had folded in her lap.

'Joe, dear, to the end of my life I will always have a good opinion of you, no matter . . .'

He was instantly alert. 'No matter – what?'

He suddenly thought of Tom Hennessey, and he stared at Regina sharply and repeated, 'No matter . . . what?'

'I meant to say,' the girl answered very quietly, 'even if you stopped loving me, as your sister.'

He was relieved, yet he had the feeling that she had been evasive. Now she looked up at him straightly and he saw that there were tears in her eyes.

'For God's sake, Regina!' he said. 'Why should I ever stop loving you?'

'Promise?' she said, like a child, and tried to smile.

'I promise.' But his uneasiness increased.

'Even if I leave you, Joe?'

He did not answer her immediately. His eyes fixed themselves upon her intently and for the first time she saw something in them that frightened her. But he spoke calmly enough. 'Why should you leave me? Are you thinking of marrying, Regina?'

'In a way,' she replied, and he could hardly hear her, for she had averted her head again. 'The only marriage I ever wanted.'

He stood up as if goaded to his feet, but he said nothing, and only watched her. She put out her hand to him but he would not see it.

'Oh, Joe,' she said, and it was a cry of pain. 'I have tried, Joe, I have tried with all my strength, to put it – aside. But it has grown stronger and more demanding all through these years, and now I can't resist it any longer. I must go. To the Carmelite Order, in Maryland. I must go at once. Oh Joe, don't look at me like that! I can't bear it. You must know that I've wanted this all my life, ever since I could remember, even as a very young child in the orphanage. When I first spoke of it to you, you said I was too young to know my own mind, and that I must see the world, and, Joe – ' the tears were heavier in her eyes than before – 'I can't bear this world. I can't bear it. Once you said to me. "A sane and intelligent man finds this world horrifying, mad," and it's quite true. I don't want to be part of it, Joe. I can't be part of it any longer.'

She stood up in agitation and stood before him and he looked down at her with an expression that terrified her. But she swallowed her rising fear, and clasped her hands tightly before her and her face implored him to understand.

'What do you know of living?' he asked in a voice of such immense disgust that she took a step backwards. 'A convent girl. You may be twenty-three, but you are like a schoolgirl still. I've taken you to Europe, and to dozens of cities here, but they made no impression on you. You never saw them, did you?'

'Yes, I saw them, Joe.'

'If you had seen them you'd have wanted them. But the nuns blinded you, made a fool and a dolt out of you, deceived you, seduced you into nonsense and superstition and medieval fantasies, filled your mind with idiotic dreams and visions and myths. Destroyed you, my sister.'

But she was shaking her beautiful head slowly. 'No, that is not true. No one even suggested to me that I had a vocation . . .'

But Joseph had burst into harsh and raucous laughter. 'A vocation, by God! A vocation for what? Prison? Isolation? Endless witless prayers? Sacrifices? For what? For whom? To what end? What purpose?'

He went on in the most cruel voice she had ever heard: 'It was all wasted on you, all that I . . . You know nothing at all. You never had to struggle for anything, or work for anything. You've lived in luxury since you were thirteen years old, the luxury I provided for you. It probably has palled on you, so you turn to mysteries and occult imaginings, out of sheer idleness! What have I denied you? I gave you and . . .' he stopped a moment and his gasping was louder than ever. 'I gave you my life, and all there was in it. I thought I also gave you reality, the enlightenment, the education, which a sensible woman should have. I gave you the world I fought for, and now you come to me with vapourings and girlish simperings and little coynesses and tell me that it was all for nothing, that you don't want what I have given you. You want, you say, stone cold floors on which to kneel and pray your stupid vain prayers, and confess sins that you never committed, and hide behind screens so that no one will ever see you. You want to hide. Yes, you want to hide!'

'Joe,' she said, but he waved her fiercely into silence again.

'From what are you hiding, Regina? The world, you will say. But the world has never abused you as it abused me. It never showed you its real face, as it showed me. You know nothing, you fool, you know nothing! And in your stupidity you indulge yourself in romantic illusions of a cloistered life, where all is white lilies and incense, and pretty statues and imbecile serenity and pious music – and those doltish prayers! You are bored. Why don't you marry, as all women marry, and have children and live the life other women live with contentment?'

She heard the torment in his voice, the despair, the frantic suffering, and she looked up and her face was full of compassion and love as well as fear.

'Joe, you don't understand. I love . . . I want to serve, if only with prayers. I love . . . Joe.'

'Love what?' he exclaimed, with another ruthless gesture. 'What God? What witlessness is that? There is no God, you damned fool of a maudlin woman! There is nothing to serve, nothing to pray to, nothing that hears, nothing that has mercy. I know. My father lies in Potter's Field, in an unmarked grave, and my mother's bones lie in the sea – for all their prayers and all their faith and all their charity. I saw hundreds die of the Famine, men, women, children, infants, old grandmothers – lying in the ditches of the roadways, biting their hands in their last convulsions of hunger. Did your God hear, or care, or send His angels to feed those innocents? Those of us who survived were turned away from the ports of this country, either to return to Ireland to starve to death or wander like vagabonds on vagabond ships hoping for harbour, for a crust of bread – literally, a crust of bread.'

Then Regina said, 'It is for such a world that I must pray, and serve with my prayers. Why do you execrate God for the wickedness of man? Man has his choices. If he chooses evil that is free will and not even God will, or can, interefere. I know you have no faith, dear Joe. It would be useless to me to try to convince you – for who can speak of the knowledge of the heart and the soul? It is only there. I have pity for this world. You think I know nothing.' Her mouth trembled but her eyes held his resolutely. 'But I know too much, Joe. Who am I to reproach you, who did all things for your family? I don't think even God reproaches you – too much. In a way, Joe, your whole life has been a prayer – for those who did not deserve such a sacrifice – Sean and me. No, no. We did not deserve it. I doubt anyone deserves such selflessness.'

Joseph was taken aback, even in his fury and contempt and rage. He forced himself to stop panting. He could not stop the hard roar of his heart, but he spoke with reasonable quiet, 'If you think and believe that, how can you bring yourself to want to leave me, desert me, betray me, for a nothingness, for a lie, for emptiness?'

'I'm not really leaving you, Joe, nor deserting nor betraying you. You will never be outside my prayers, my love. I will only love you more deeply, and be even more grateful to you. You will always be in my thoughts, for, in this world, you are the only dear thing to me.'

She stood before him. He felt an almost voluptuous sense of horror and revulsion, and it showed in his expression and again Regina took a step backward with renewed fear.

'I will not let you go. I won't let you destroy yourself,' he said.

'I will not be destroying myself. I will be saving myself, Joe.'

But now she could only helplessly shake her head, as if she had no control of her own movements. He watched her and he wanted to take her in his arms and hold her savagely and he also wanted to kill her.

She finally said, 'I wanted you to understand how I feel, dear Joe. I knew it would cause you grief and make you angry. But I thought you'd understand, a little, about my own happiness, for there is no happiness for me in this world and never will be. I must go where there is peace and prayer and penance. It is all I want; there is nothing else. If you understood, even that little, you would say, "Go, my sister. Everyone must find happiness, or at least peace, in his own way."'

'Happiness!' he exclaimed, with new and overpowering disgust. 'What fool talks of happiness? There never was such a thing except for hypocrites and liars and the mad. There never was any peace, and never will there be in this world, and this world is all we know and all we'll ever know. We must make our own compromises with it, and accept it. But you want to run from it! If that isn't weakness and cowardice I'd like to know what it is.'

Again she shook her head hopelessly. She could not speak of the great love in her soul, her great and humble acceptance and joy in that acceptance, for it would only infuriate her brother more. She said at last, 'I must go, dearest Joe. I have already made the arrangements. I leave tomorrow night. I did not tell you before, because I was afraid – afraid of my own vacillation – that you would persuade me . . . But nothing can turn me aside, now. Nothing. Not even you, Joe.'

She looked at him but he only stared at her with raw hate, a man betrayed and, he thought, betrayed with malice and smug satisfaction. He thought of Sean who had accused him with a cruelty surpassing his own, and had deserted him. So he said in so quiet a voice that Regina could hardly hear him, 'Go, and go to hell, you slut. Go, the both of you. You weren't worth a year of my life. You weren't worth even one hour – either of you.'

'I know. Only I know, Joe,' said Regina, and walked silently from the room. He watched her go. He had thought he had known all the desolation it was possible for a man to endure, but this was the worst of all. Now he would not put out his hand to stop his sister, even if he could have stopped her. She had become as dead to him as his brother, and as hateful.

Regina went to her own room and knelt on her *prie-dieu* before the crucifix on the wall, and she cried silently and tried to pray but there was only pain in her now and a last remembrance of her brother's face.

Bernadette had been aroused in her room by the loud exclamations and shouts of her husband and had tiptoed into the long warm hall to listen. She had heard most of the conversation between Joseph and Regina, and she had felt a huge leap of exultation. Now she would be rid of that simpleton, Regina, and Joseph would finally realise that he had no one in the world but his wife, faithful, devoted, endlessly loving.

Joseph did not appear the next day at all. When Regina, weeping, confided in Bernadette that she must go, and why, Bernadette made large dry eyes of sympathy and uttered the most tender words of encouragement, and gave Regina the warmest embraces. 'Of course I understand, love!' she cried. 'I never knew anyone who had a vocation before, but I understand! You can't resist it. It would be a sin to resist. Don't

207

worry about Joe. I will console him, and he'll come to accept it all, himself.'

So Regina was comforted and never knew she had been comforted by a young woman who despised her and was glad to see the last of her, and that her consolations had been false and hypocritical. The girl left in more peace than she had believed possible, clinging for a last moment to Bernadette, who accompanied her to the depot with her meagre luggage. She already looks like a nun, the dunce, thought Bernadette, as she murmured against Regina's cheek and uttered the most extravagant promises, with elation in her heart and the deepest relief.

When Joseph finally appeared the day after Regina had left Bernadette was all indignation against Regina, and sympathy, but he looked at her and said, 'We will not speak of her again, if you please.'

CHAPTER TWENTY-EIGHT

J O S E P H received an interesting letter from Mr Spaulding one cool September day, addressed to the house in Green Hills. After its effusions of friendship and attachment, it said, with the utmost delicacy:

'Our friends accepted the contribution to the Party with grateful astonishment for your unequalled generosity, which, they declared, demonstrates your concern for the Commonwealth and her weal. They will at once attend to the other matters which I earnestly brought to their attention, and trust you will be gratified at the result.'

After loving inquiries concerning Joseph's family, Mr Spaulding added the following: 'I should not be surprised if a mutual friend visited you almost immediately. If so, extend to him my obedient regard.'

Governor Tom Hennessey sent a brief telegram to his son-in-law. 'Expect me in Green Hills on Thursday inst for business consultation.' On reading this telegram Joseph smiled a little in exultation. He informed Bernadette who was aroused out of her own doldrums since that last conversation with her husband. 'We shall have a party!' she exclaimed. But Joseph said, 'My love, let us first find out how long your father can remain with us. He may have to leave for Philadelphia almost at once.'

A carriage was sent to the depot for the Governor, and Bernadette was in it. But the Governor was unusually taciturn with his daughter. He seemed pale and preoccupied, and there were deep clefts in his usually robust and florid face, and his eyes appeared turned inwards and haunted. He mumbled, 'My darling, your husband is not a leisurely gallant nor a dilettante nor idler. He has problems, like myself. Like myself,' he added, and looked at Bernadette impatiently, willing her to stop her chatter. 'Did you think he has nothing to do but dance attendance on you and play with your children? A man's life is apart from these, and greater than these, though this may offend you and your vanity.'

He went immediately to Joseph's rooms, and into the large room which Joseph now used as a study and which had once been the Governor's flamboyant bedroom. Joseph met him there with a quiet word and an offer of an immediate drink, which the Governor accepted with gratitude. 'A large whisky,' he said. 'Perhaps you'd better have one, too. I have bad news.'

Joseph had never been an accomplished actor at any time. How did a man arrange his face so that it expressed apprehension – even if no apprehension was felt – and what did he put in his voice? Joseph saw Mr Montrose's expressive countenance, and so made his own a passable facsimile of concern and attentive solicitude. He tried for Mr Montrose's flexibility of voice, and said, 'Have you, then? Then we must talk about it.'

'I'll make it brief,' Tom said, and his voice was rough with renewed agitation and now with open anger and despair. 'I was informed, yesterday, by our Party that I would not receive the nomination this year. Yet only a month ago I was assured of it by the State Chairman, himself. Who else?'

Joseph had seated himself nearby in the growing dusk of the room. Here it was becoming dim and shadowy, for great trees loomed outside and their tops brushed against the windows. Joseph, unusual for him, had mixed himself a whisky and soda, and he carefully sipped at it and looked at the floor, as if pondering.

He said, 'Now why should they do that? What do they have against you?'

Tom put down his glass with a thump on a nearby table. 'Nothing!' he shouted. 'Haven't I done everything they suggested? Haven't I followed all their directives? I've served the Party well, by God! Now they turn on me.' He breathed heavily. 'I've even done some things – well, they were profitable for all concerned, but I took on the possible danger, myself. They profited more than I did.'

Joseph shook his head. 'I'm not a politician, Tom. I don't know the ways and the reasons of politicians.'

Tom laughed cynically. 'Oh Joe, don't be so humble. You know damned well you are one of the big political powers in this Commonwealth. Just tell those bastards to change their minds at once or they'll hear from you. It is as simple as that. They wouldn't dare cross you.'

'I have heard hints,' said Joseph, 'that they'd prefer a younger man. Hancock, for one. After all, you aren't young any longer, Tom. And you've made your fortune. They take all that into consideration.'

Tom studied him. Joseph's air was entirely too disinterested: he had never been one to shilly-shally like this. It was not in character.

'Joe,' said the Governor, quietly.

He's an astute bastard, thought Joseph, and I am no actor. I am not even a good liar. He looked at Tom with an expression he hoped was concerned and disarming. 'All right, Tom. What do you want me to do?'

'I've told you. Tell them to change their minds – or no more funds, no more bribery.'

'I don't bribe,' said Joseph. 'I send only small gifts of appreciation. No one has any evidence of my bribing anyone.'

'You took care of that, you and your Philadelphia lawyers,' said Tom, with mounting anger. He saw Joseph shrug his thin shoulders. He saw Joseph smile at him faintly.

'Very well,' said Joseph. 'I will write to them tonight. I hope it will help to change their minds.'

'Telegraph,' said Tom Hennessey. 'I hear they intend to nominate Hancock on Monday. There's no time for writing.'

'Very well,' Joseph repeated. He went to his desk and wrote for a few moments in his angular tight script. He brought the paper to Tom, who put on spectacles to read it.

210

'All contributions recently made are to be used as previously designated in behalf of the candidate heretofore chosen. Joseph Armagh.'

Tom Hennessey scrutinised it. He wished it could have been warmer, more explicit, and that it had mentioned his name or referred directly to him. Then he saw that this might not be prudent. He said, with some surprise, 'I see you have already made a large contribution.'

'Yes, very large. In August. After all, are you not the perennial candidate?'

'When you made that contribution you had no idea about — Hancock?'

Joseph stood up. He looked at Tom with glittering blue eyes full of cold umbrage, and Tom was so frightened that he sat up in his chair and stared. Joseph said, 'When did they mention Hancock to you?'

Tom's full face, so sensual and brutal, trembled. 'Monday, Joe.' When Joseph did not speak he cried, 'Joe, I'm sorry! I am almost out of my mind. I see bogies everywhere. When will you send that telegram?' His hands had become wet and cold.

'At once,' said Joseph, and went to the bell-rope. His whole attitude expressed rigid offence, and Tom was alarmed again. It would be fatal to antagonise Joseph Armagh, to whom he greatly owed his past elections. Tom said, with an attempt at a placating smile, rueful and affectionate, 'Yes, I see bogies everywhere. Probably in Bernadette and your children, too, and Elizabeth!' He tried to laugh. Then as relief flowed through him he laughed again, with real heartiness, and took up his drink.

'That telegram will settle it,' he said.

'I hope so,' said Joseph. A maid came into the room and Joseph directed that she give the telegraph message to a groom, who was to take it to the depot at once. When the maid had left Tom said, his voice breaking, 'I can't tell you what this means to me, Joe, and how grateful I am. I tell you, I've been on the verge of apoplexy since Monday. I have scarcely slept or eaten.'

Joseph considered him with those small hidden eyes which were so inexplicable. 'Then you must make up for it tonight,' he said. 'In the bosom of your family.'

Joseph was unusually pleasant and amiable to Tom Hen-

211

nessey at the dinner table that night, and Bernadette marvelled, for she had never seen her husband so kind to her father before, nor so – almost – intimate. There had always been a reserve in Joseph towards Tom Hennessey, but now it appeared to have disappeared. She begged her father to remain 'for a little festivity'.

Joseph thought, let the swine enjoy himself now and in the next days. It will be the last time. The condemned man's final meal. He smiled at Tom and directed a maid to give his father-in-law more wine. Tom's light eyes sparkled with satisfaction.

Joseph waited. One week. Two weeks. As he waited he inwardly grew colder, and felt his own impatient exultation. He was not surprised that on the morning of the fifteenth day he received a telegram from his father-in-law: 'Will arrive tonight at five must see you alone at once.'

Joseph waited in his rooms. Never had time crept so slowly on sluggish feet. He kept glancing at his watch. Twenty past five. Twenty-five past. Five-thirty. He heard hooves and wheels and he stood up and looked through the window and saw the glittering black family Victoria moving through the gates, drawn by two absolutely white horses. Joseph opened a cabinet, then, and laid out whisky and soda and glasses then rang the bell for the butler. 'Governor Hennessey's luggage should be taken to his room but I should like to confer with him as soon as possible, in my study.'

He rearranged the neatness of his plain white cuffs, and then his cravat, and rubbed his hands over his thick hair. He looked tall and black and deadly in the quiet room. There was an ice-cold exultation in him. He had destroyed worthier men than Governor Hennessey in his surge to power and money, but he had done it with no animosity at all, no feeling of vengeance or triumph. It was only business. But this was vengeance indeed, a personal vendetta, a focusing of loathing and enmity and hate long in the gestation, long in the gathering. The arrogant and swaggering Governor, seemingly invulnerable, had become vulnerable and had been destroyed.

Joseph made himself sit down and open a book. He heard the butler greeting the Governor, heard Tom Hennessey's mumbled reply – he who never mumbled – and then heard the

212

quick but stumbling footsteps up the stairs and down the long hall to Joseph's rooms. The Governor appeared on the threshold and Joseph rose, his face shut and without expression.

Tom Hennessey, large, over-fleshed, flamboyant and impressive, now appeared dishevelled and soiled, hasty and sweaty. All his colour was gone. His face was like cracked plaster, quivering, his sensual mouth hanging loose, his chin uncertain, his forehead glazed and wet. Always immaculate, 'the glass of fashion', he seemed unbuttoned and roughened now. There was a wild agitation about him, a trembling uncertainty, a desperate upheaval. His light eyes, always cynical and domineering, now had a distraught and leaping shine. His longish brown and grey hair, usually carefully combed and cajoled into waves, hung over his cheeks and neck and forehead, tangled and ungroomed.

Joseph said, 'How are you, Tom? Was your train late?'

The Governor walked unsteadily into the room. He looked about him, as if he had never seen this room or this man before, and did not know where he was. He took an aimless step or two, towards the windows, back again, then to one side. He stood at last behind a chair and gripped its back and looked at Joseph, and his breath was grating and noisy in the sunlit room.

'They have ruined me,' he said, and his voice was thick and unsure.

'Who?' said Joseph and came closer to his father-in-law.

The Governor raised one formidable forefinger, and then it wobbled and drooped and his hand fell to his side. 'I will find out, and I will cut their throats,' he said with the utmost malignancy. His eyes jumped. 'They haven't finished with me yet.'

'Please sit down, Tom,' said Joseph and hoped that he was conveying solicitude. He took his father-in-law's shivering big arm and forced him into the chair he had been clutching. 'Let me get you a drink. Then you must tell me about it.'

Joseph put a glass half full of whisky into the large white hand with its rings and its polished nails. Tom drank deeply, gluttonously, as if the glass held the elixir of life and strength. He inhaled raucously. His heavy shoulders visibly shook. He looked at the glass. Then he glanced up at Joseph with his reddened eyes, like the eyes of a tormented bull, and he said, 'You haven't heard?'

'No,' said Joseph. 'I haven't even seen any newspapers this past week. I've had too much work here in Green Hills. But what is wrong? Who has ruined you?'

The Governor became still. He looked up at Joseph and those eyes fixed themselves on the younger man as if he had suddenly sensed something direful. He watched Joseph as he said, 'You must know that though the Party gave out the idea they were going to nominate me after all, they didn't. Day before yesterday they told me finally it was going to be Hancock.'

Joseph frowned. He sat on the edge of his desk and considered his boots. He compressed his lips, slightly shook his head. He said, 'They did not tell me.'

'Not you? Not the biggest contributor to the Party? Not you who named the five State Senators last year, and got them elected? They never told you, wrote you, telegraphed you?' The Governor sat upright in his chair, and panted, but did not look away.

'No,' said Joseph, 'they never told me.'

Now he turned his face to Tom and Tom saw his fierce concentrated eyes, his implacable face, the blade of his mouth and the white tension of his nose, and he misinterpreted them. He said, 'I don't understand it. You, of all people.' His voice was broken and rusty. 'My son-in-law.' He drank again, took the glass from his thick mouth and groaned. 'But you can do something, even now.'

'What do you suggest, Tom?'

'Threaten them. It isn't too late.' Then his face sagged. 'Yes, it is too late.' He put down his glass with a crash on the desk and rubbed his hands over and over his shaken face as if he were washing it. 'It's too late. I forgot. There's worse.'

His shoulders heaved under his creased fawn coat. He bent his face in his rubbing hands and Joseph thought he was weeping. All the strong muscles and the fat of the great body visibly shrank, as though disintegrating. Now he was no longer the buoyant and commanding Governor of the Commonwealth, the former colourful Senator of the United States of America, the owner of enormous wealth and power. He was a shattered old man, wrecked, thrown down, dismantled, full of bewilderment and despair and an agony he had never known before in his life, and a sense of demented incredulity.

He felt another glass being pressed against the back of one

of the massaging and aimless hands. He started. Then he reached for the glass and fumbled it to his lips and the liquid went partly into his mouth and partly down his chin, dribbling. Joseph watched him and the quiet ferocity of his face deepened. He said, 'You haven't told me. What is "worse"?'

The awful eyes, robbed of all humanity by anguish, disbelief and torture, glared at Joseph. The large features were convulsed, misshapen. 'Worse!' he said. 'They – know everything. It isn't just Washington, though that's bad enough in their hypocritical eyes. Oh, God help me, God help me! Since I was Governor – Joe, you know yourself. You profited. The State contracts, roads, bridges, right of ways, government buildings. All of it. Yes, I profited, too. But they did, more than I. More than even you. I did what they told me to. I obeyed every suggestion. I never objected. I was their man, wasn't I?' His eyes enlarged on Joseph, blood-flecked, mad. 'Do you know what they told me yesterday? That I was, in my way, the head of a Tweed Ring, here in this Commonwealth! They dared to tell me that! Who profited most? They did! Do you hear me, they did!'

'Yes,' said Joseph. 'But can you prove it?'

'Prove it!' shouted the Governor in a roaring voice. 'Of course I can . . .'

He stared at Joseph.

'Can you? How?'

'The contractors . . .'

'The contractors are men making a living, and they can be intimidated by politicians as you know only too well, Tom. Do you think they will confess to the influence and the threats and the promises that were brought to bear on them? And so hang themselves, or at least be forced into bankruptcy and litigation and prosecution? And perhaps even be murdered? We all know what politicians are, don't we, Tom?'

He regarded the Governor with gravity. 'But I'm sure our friends told you that, yesterday, didn't they?'

Tom's big fingers smoothed themselves over and over the empty glass. He licked the drops of whisky on his mouth. He was shaking as if struck by a powerful wind. 'Yes,' he whispered, 'they did. But I thought you would help me.'

Joseph sighed. 'I'm no Samson, Tom, and neither are you. We can make an effort to show who really profited. I have a battery of lawyers in Philadelphia and they are ferrets. They could find out – though they'd put themselves into physical peril, as they'd know. We can appeal to the Attorney General. We can appeal to muck-rakers and zealous reformers in the Commonwealth. I can print accusations in my newspapers, and screaming editorials. And what will it amount to? If your – friends – are indicted, so will you be, Tom. So will I. We're all in it together, robbing the people. That's what they'd call it, wouldn't they? And it would be the truth.'

He smiled a little. 'The other Party would be out of its mind with delight – if we told them. We could testify under promised immunity. State's evidence. Corruption, malfeasance, theft, graft, spoils, intimidation of contractors to the State, looting, exploitation of labour, inferior materials at the highest prices, subornation, perjury. Everything. Of course, we could plead that we were intimidated, threatened. Do you think the people would believe it? You, the rich Governor, I, the financier and what not? Come, Tom.'

The hazed eyes did not leave him. But a maddened speculation had begun to gleam in them. Tom said in a clearer voice, 'You do not know it all, Joe. They have told me I have to make "recompense". That I must return "the money" to the Commonwealth. With interest, with "judicial and righteous penalties". They told me. It will take almost all the money I have, all my investments. Everything. They have even shown me documents from Washington . . . They have even – forged – documents showing the source of the Hennessey money. Blackbirding. Things like that. Only part of the money, they told me, will be returned to the Commonwealth. The rest . . .'

'Is for them?'

'Yes.'

'They were that bold?'

But Tom Hennessey did not reply. He was studying Joseph as he had never studied friend or enemy before, with all the concentration and power of his intellect, which was not small, and all his intuition, all his Irish subtlety. Still watching with the complete focusing of his mind he said, 'Yes, Joe. That bold. Something, somebody, is behind it. They wouldn't be that bold without orders.'

Joseph looked deeply into the eyes below him. He said, 'They can't take everything. They won't take everything. You still have Katherine's money. You still have your wife's money.

It is enough to keep you in modest circumstances, in your house in Philadelphia. Anything is preferable to scandal, exposure, indictment, prosecution, gaol. Isn't it? Anything is preferable to living in fear, isn't it? In the end you'd be better off financially by not fighting these – atrocious – demands. Do you realise how much lawyers would demand? They'd reduce you to poverty, Tom. I know lawyers.'

'You are asking me to do nothing at all?' Tom was slowly rising from his chair, clutching the arms and back. 'You are asking me to do that?'

'I am advising you,' said Joseph.

'And – you will do nothing – to help me?'

Neither of the two men saw Bernadette, all black velvet and lace and bangles and veiled hat and gloves on the threshold. She had just appeared. She had run happily up the stairs to greet her father, and her face still held the fading remnants of a smile, the mouth half open and upturned, the eyes flashing, the hand outheld. But she had come upon her husband and her father, confronting each other, and the sharp Bernadette had suddenly known that here was not a friendly family discussion but two adversaries. She felt the hatred in the room, the feral smell of deadly enmity. She had known instantly that one of these men was maddened beyond endurance, and the other was the maddener, ruthless and terrible. She had heard their last words. Her hand slowly fell to her side and she had a sensation of giddiness and terror.

She could hardly recognise her father in this broken man, whose potency was dwindling before her eyes, whose hair was dishevelled, whose clothes were untidy, whose head was bent like the head of a dying bull stopped in his charge. She could not recognise her husband in this lean stiff man with the vindictive smile, the narrowed eyes, the contracted muscles held as if about to strike. She put her hand to her mouth, an unusually feeble gesture for Bernadette.

'I will do nothing to help you,' said Joseph in the softest voice. 'Not even if your life depended on it.'

Tom Hennessey pondered on that. He looked about him vaguely, and now Bernadette could see his inflamed and bloody eyes which did not see her at all. Tom put his hand to his head. He licked his lips.

'What did you say?' he muttered.

'Nothing to help you. Not to save your life, Tom.'

Tom put his hands to his throat and moved his big head. He gasped. He did not look away from Joseph. There was now a deep crimson flush on his forehead, a rising of thickened veins in his neck.

'Why?' he asked.

'Katherine,' said Joseph.

'Katherine,' Tom repeated, in a dull low tone. 'Katherine. What had she to do with you?'

'Nothing. It was what you did to Katherine.'

Tom's gaze fixed itself with renewed intensity on Joseph. The crimson flush was deepening. He slowly raised his right hand and pointed at Joseph.

'Now I remember,' he said, and his voice was very choked. 'You were a lad. You – you had been looking at this house. I knew I'd remember some time. A dirty shanty Irisher. That's all you were, all you are. You wanted this house. Shanty Irish. A beggar. You plotted it all. From the beginning. You – took my daughter. It was all part of it. All part of it. Dirty shanty Irish.' He stopped and groaned and panted. He said, 'Katherine. Yes, I remember. You were always . . . It was Katherine. You waited a long time, Irish.'

'I waited a long time,' said Joseph. 'But Katherine never knew. On the night she died she asked me to marry your daughter. It was her wish. And so I did.'

Tom saw his face and for the first time in his life he shuddered before another man. He lifted his arms and clenched his fists. He staggered towards Joseph beating his hands impotently, blindly, in the air. He fell forward, stumbling, reeling. Bernadette uttered a thin shriek. Tom fell upon Joseph, still flailing. Then, instinctively, for he felt the older man sagging and collapsing, Joseph caught him in his arms, staggered himself a moment, then held Tom Hennessey, fallen against his chest, arms hanging.

It was then that Joseph saw Bernadette. He did not care what she had heard or what she had seen. He said to her, 'Help me to put your father in a chair.'

But Tom was unconscious now. He slipped out of the chair in which they put him, Bernadette all the while crying and half-screaming and slapping her gloved hands together in distraction. Tom lay on the floor between them with a suffused face, breathing stertorously, his eyes half open.

'You've killed my father!' Bernadette shrieked. 'What did

you do to my father?'

'Ring for someone,' said Joseph. 'Send for a doctor, and some of the grooms and we'll put your father to bed.'

His voice was cold and neutral. Bernadette stopped her crying. She stared at her husband, blinking, big tears on her smooth golden cheeks.

'I heard,' she said. 'You never cared anything about me, did you?'

'No,' said Joseph, though he again felt a dim pity for her, 'I never did. But there is nothing we can do about it now, is there?'

The doctor, and other doctors summoned from Philadelphia and even Pittsburgh, said that the Governor had had a stroke, that his whole left side was paralysed, that he would probably never speak again nor leave his bed. It was possible that he would not be fully aware or conscious of his surroundings from this time on, and must have constant nursing. He could not be moved. His life depended on it.

Bernadette, pale and quiet, said, 'This is my father's house. He will stay in it as long as he lives, and I will never leave him. Send for his wife – and her child.'

So Tom Hennessey had returned to his house and would remain there until he died. Joseph found a profound irony in this. He could even laugh quietly to himself at the irony. He was all courtesy to the grief-stricken Elizabeth, whom Bernadette hated. Elizabeth's little boy, Courtney, joined Rory and Ann in the nursery.

Bernadette wanted to say to Elizabeth, to wound her, 'My husband killed your husband,' but her helpless and now devastated love for Joseph prevented her. No matter what Joseph did, to her, to anyone else, her besottedness was not shaken though she now feared him. Her mother: had Joseph really loved her mother? Yes, it was so. She, Bernadette, must live with that all her life.

Joseph's newspaper in Philadelphia expressed its sorrow for 'the stricken Governor', and prayed for his recovery.

When Tom Hennessey died two years later – after an existence which had held no awareness of love or hatred or money or influence or power or even living – he was eulogised in the press as 'the greatest and most humane Governor this Commonwealth has ever known. The defender of the weak, the

219

upholder of the working man, the staunch fighter for the Right, for Progress, the hater of corruption and exploitation, the patriot, the far-sighted politician who had dreams of a nobler America – this was Governor Thomas Hennessey, who was stricken down at the height of his struggle for the Nation. We grieve with his family. We pray for his soul.'

Tom was buried beside his wife, who had loved him.

CHAPTER TWENTY-NINE

JOSEPH ARMAGH said to his son, Rory: 'You are not doing exceptionally well in mathematics at your school. But I notice that you excel in history and English and German and French, Latin and literature.' He smiled at the boy. 'So, I am pleased with you. However, you will have to be more proficient in mathematics to get into Harvard.' He laughed. 'For an intellectual you are singularly healthy and sane and pragmatic.'

'I know enough about mathematics to think I should get an increase in my allowance,' said Rory with his beguiling and impudent smile. 'I get only two dollars more than Kevin.'

'A dollar is a dollar, and it is a lot of money. Three dollars a week for a lad of fifteen is sufficient. Kevin buys his own pets out of his one dollar a week, and is very serious for a spalpeen only nine years old.'

Rory was tall and slender and moved lithely and quickly but with his father's strength and economy of movement. He was exceedingly handsome, with a buoyant and energetic air, which he had inherited from his mother. He was also courtly and gallant, even at his young age, and was always ready with a pungent joke. He had Joseph's once-russet hair, but his curled over his forehead, about his ears and almost down to his nape. But the russet was brighter than Joseph's had ever been, with a more pronounced reddish tinge, and was vital and coarse. He had a big well-shaped nose with a slight tilt at the tip, and a smiling mouth, also well-shaped, and large white teeth. His eyes, under red-gold brows, were light blue and mocking and usually mirthful, though frequently touched with good-humoured cynicism. Like Joseph's, his cheek-bones were broad, his chin determined. He gave off an almost visible aura of gusto and health and joy in life, and exceptional intelligence. His pink lower lip had a sensual thickness to it.

He was also exigent, in a charming and coaxing way, though he could also be brutal when necessary. He appeared more mature than his age. Unlike other very handsome youths he was always curious, always searching for new knowledge, new insights, and he found humanity uproariously funny. Except for his father. He knew, even at fifteen, almost all there was to know about Joseph and had acquired his knowledge in many avid and devious ways and from scores of other men and from the newspapers, and from his mother, and he found his father endlessly fascinating. Joseph was the only creature Rory feared, and perhaps loved. Young as he was, he was not a virgin, nor had been since he was fourteen. Girls, and even older women, were as attracted to him as he was attracted to them, and even from his earliest youth he was gaily licentious and did not care who knew it. He was as brave as his father, but unlike Joseph he loved danger and the excitement of it. He would be, many said with conviction, an extraordinary man, not only because of his appearance and his ability to fascinate men as well as women, but because of his intellectual qualities, his eloquent and manly speaking voice, and his flair for smiling sarcasm.

He was already a politician in the small world he still occupied. Though he was sometimes suspected by his school-fellows to be 'bookish', he led them. He rode a horse like a centaur, played tennis magnificently, and could climb like a monkey, for he was fearless. At times he was even rowdy.

His twin sister, Ann Marie, did not resemble him in the slightest. She was a slender, rather thin and quiet girl, some-what tall and of so flat a figure that her mother constantly wailed over it. Once as noisy as her brother, she was now inclined to silence, probably, Joseph thought, because her mother 'never stopped talking'. She had fine straight, light brown hair, which she dressed simply as befitting a schoolgirl of fifteen, an oval face with a clear pale complexion, large sherry-brown eyes, a small nose and a controlled mouth resem-bling her father's. Her mother had convinced her, when she had been still very young, that she possessed no beauty but was 'very plain', so the girl wore clothes without distinction. But Joseph, once becoming aware of her, saw that she had the austere elegance so much admired by the Irish, and it startled him, for his children were fourteen years old before he was actually conscious of their being and their identities.

For, to him, Rory and Ann Marie had been 'Bernadette's children', or the grandchildren of the loathed Tom Hennessey. As such, he had little interest in them and less affection, beyond an indulgent vague fondness when he saw them playing or listened to their arguments. He had often forgotten their existence, and sometimes, hearing their distant voices, he had wondered who possessed them. He paid their bills at preparatory (boarding) schools in Boston and Philadelphia, but as Timothy Dineen wrote out the cheques for all expenses and Joseph merely signed them, he was hardly aware even of this. To Joseph Armagh, his 'family' had meant his parents, and then his brother and sister. Bernadette's 'family' was something else again and not part of himself as Sean and Regina had been. On more than one occasion, when someone asked about the welfare of his family, he had absently but sincerely seemed surprised and had replied, 'I have no family.' He finally discovered that others looked at him, then, in a sidelong and speculative fashion, which was more than a little unpleasant, and so he was careful now in his answers and, while he never demonstrated enthusiasm, he would say, 'My family is well, thank you,' and change the subject impatiently.

He never visited his children at their schools, nor had he shown any interest in their progress. As he was not very often in Green Hills it would sometimes be months before he saw his children. He did see them at Christmas and Easter, and found their presence boring and avoided them. It was as if his profound devotion to his brother and sister, his total engrossment with them, had depleted the vital reserves of love in himself and had drained him dusty. There was nothing left to give to others, and since Sean and Regina had 'deserted' him he was more than ever detached from other human beings, and absolutely indifferent. The spring of his affections was filled with stones.

Bernadette's adoration and love for him had become fanatically obsessive since she had learned that he cared nothing for her and had married her only at her dying mother's deluded request. She had her father's tenacity of purpose: she would win Joseph's love no matter how long it would take, and she dedicated herself to his interest and his well-being and served him with a slavishness that everyone knew, and even pitied, because Joseph was not conscious of it at all. He only knew that Bernadette was no longer insistent with him or demanding. He was not grateful for this blessing, nor did he care. The less he saw of his wife the more contented he was. He appreciated her as a fine housekeeper and an excellent hostess, and that was all he desired of her. He had not approached her sexually since his younger son, Kevin, had been born. He had not wanted another child; he held Bernadette to blame for Kevin, and so he had avoided her since that time.

He was not cruel or harsh with her. She simply was absent from his mind, and when he was away from Green Hills he never thought of her at all. Had she died he would have felt no regret. He rarely conversed with her, and since Kevin's birth she could no longer amuse him or make him give his grudging laugh. Sometimes he appeared startled, as if wondering who she was, when she entered a room.

Bernadette, though not a stupid woman, still did not know the extent of his disinterest in her. She had the romantic notion that selfless and passionate love would eventually reach him, and as she was optimistic by nature she was infrequently discouraged. On those rare occasions she would ask herself in despair: what do I see in him? Why do I love him with all my heart and soul? He is not handsome in the accepted fashion. His voice is cold and short. He is not suave nor considerate. He shows me no tenderness. He looks at me blankly, Yet, how I love him, how I adore him! I would die for him.

His indifference to her children did not disturb her as once it had done in a faint fashion. The fewer those whom Joseph cared about, the more she was pleased. She was jealous of Timothy Dineen, and was elated when James Spaulding died and Timothy had been dispatched to take his place in Titusville and Joseph's interests in the north-west section of the Commonwealth and in Ohio and in Chicago. (There were eight lawyers working under Timothy in Titusville, and a very large office force.) Joseph had a new and handsome secretary, one Charles Devereaux, a brilliant lawyer, a man of his own age who, Bernadette dimly knew, was from 'somewhere in Virginia'. Charles had enormous responsibilities, of which Bernadette did not even try to guess. She was passionately jealous of him, for he accompanied Joseph everywhere and lived in this house when Joseph was in Green Hills, and there seemed, to Bernadette, too much affection between them and too much attachment. It was only when Charles was present that Joseph really laughed or exhibited the slightest animation. Sometimes she complained petulantly to Joseph about this, saying that he preferred the company of his secretary-associate to the presence of his wife and children, but Joseph never answered, and so Bernadette came to hate Charles. His exceptional and almost beautiful appearance would have attracted her under other circumstances, but now she thought of him as an enemy who had 'stolen' affection rightfully belonging to 'the family'. As for Harry Zeff and his Liza, they never came to Green Hills. Bernadette had made it very obvious that she despised the presence of 'that Arab' and 'his servant girl', and found them offensive and an insult to herself. 'One of these days,' she said significantly to Joseph, nodding her head wisely as if she had secret information, 'that Harry will betray you. But you never listen to me.'

She had made herself so cutting and vicious to Elizabeth Hennessey that Elizabeth had bought the house that Joseph had built for his family and had removed herself and her son. Sometimes Bernadette wondered why Elizabeth remained in Green Hills at all. Of course, Joseph 'managed' Mrs Hennessey's affairs, as a kindness to the widow whose husband he had destroyed, Bernadette conceded. But he could have done that as well if she had gone back to her native Philadelphia. Elizabeth was rarely invited to the Hennessey house except at Christmas and New Year's Day, and Courtney, her son, attended the same school in Boston as did Rory. Bernadette did not see her half-brother more than once a year and had no interest in him. He was, in her opinion, a 'poor thing' contrasted with the resplendent Rory.

Bernadette had lost the charm of youth, and was now a very plump matron heavily encased in restraining whale-bone, with a large bosom and larger hips, but always extremely fashionable and overdressed. Never very pretty, her round flattish face had acquired a double chin and her original golden tint of complexion had become engorged. She had nothing left now but her fine and sparkling hazel eyes. She wore her thin brown hair, which was modishly cut short in the latest fashion, elaborately and painfully curled all over her blunt head. She also dipped into the paint pots and not always

224

discreetly. But her vivacity and energy, if sometimes a little forced now, still pleased her many friends if her growing overbearing manner and autocratic and malicious judgments did not. She was the leader of society in Green Hills, as due the wife of so powerful and distinguished and dangerous a husband, and was also feared in Philadelphia and other cities. Now, as she would contentedly and proudly assert, she could 'mingle' at ease with the Belmonts, the Goulds, the Fisks, the Regans and Morgans and others in New York, and there was none who could belittle or snub her. Her jewels rivalled the jewels of any other woman. She favoured Worth as her dressmaker, and her millinery was superb. When, once a year or so, she insisted on accompanying Joseph to Europe – her only insistence these days – she had a French maid with her and so many trunks and bags that an extra state-room had to be engaged besides the one she occupied and the one Joseph used. Joseph became reconciled to her presence. As always, she was a perfect hostess to his colleagues.

Once she had said to Joseph, 'No one now ever seems to care we are Irish.' She had said this with smugness and with a triumphant toss of her curled head. She did not understand why Joseph had given her his fierce and concentrated look which lasted several minutes, and why she had felt so abashed and so bewildered. She had not detected the rage and contempt in his eyes, nor the hatred that had caused a blue fire under his brows. She only knew that in some fashion she had offended him, and so had fawned humbly upon him. He had not spoken to her for several days after that.

Then, when her children were fifteen years old, she received the most wounding and most crushing experience of her life.

In 1875 Joseph had visited Mr Montrose – whom he now knew as Clair Devereaux – in Virginia. The beautiful new plantation house had impressed Joseph and so had the flourishing fields of cotton and the herds of cattle and the fine horses. 'Without your help in the purchase of the adjoining property I'd now be the usual bankrupt Southern plantation owner – thanks to Yankee carpet-baggers and sundry other scallawags,' Clair had said, shaking Joseph's hand warmly and with deep affection. Then he had added, 'This is my dear wife, Luane, whom I married in Pittsburgh two years ago.'

Joseph thought that Luane Devereaux was one of the

most beautiful women he had ever met. He saw her wonderful grey eyes, her masses of black hair, her full rosy mouth and her lovely body. He knew, now, the history of the Devereaux. Ostensibly, in Virginia, she was Clair's concubine and servant. Later he met their son, Charles, who had been wounded in the war which had killed his grandfather. Joseph was astonished at his resemblance to his father, for he had Clair's curling yellow hair and subtle face and height, though he had inherited his mother's eyes. Charles, at that time, had been graduated from Harvard Law School and was practising in Boston. He had married a Boston girl of good family.

Charles had given Joseph a challenging look on the first meeting, but Joseph had ignored it and had thought Charles somewhat of a fool. Later, he changed his opinion. He met Charles three times after that, and slowly Charles came to trust him and no longer challenged him with his cold grey eyes. Charles became very successful, and a partner in his firm in Boston. When Mr Spaulding had died of old age and infirmities Joseph had offered Charles his place, at a very large salary. Charles had hesitated, and then had said to Joseph bluntly, 'I assume my – history – won't be broadcast in Titusville?'

Joseph said, 'Don't be a damned idiot. I am not offering you this because I have had long association with your father, and admire him. I am offering it because I think you are competent. If I've been mistaken I'll boot you out without any ceremony at all.'

Charles had understood that Joseph had deliberately misunderstood him. He also knew that his 'history' was meaningless to Joseph, though he did not discount the fact that Joseph could be very dangerous indeed if necessary. So Charles, who had inherited his own father's intrepid love for danger, and knew all about Joseph, had accepted the offer. He had an impressive house in Titusville where he lived with his wife and consulted with Timothy Dineen, but he travelled with Joseph and was his 'confidential legal adviser' and associate. He was a fanatical Southerner and often amused Joseph with his derision for Northerners and 'Yankee expediency'. He was exigent, himself, and lacked all scruples when it came to Joseph's interests.

In 1880 Clair and Luane Devereaux had died of the flux and Joseph had attended their funeral. He had said nothing when Clair had been buried in the Devereaux's family plot and Luane had been buried among former slaves. But he saw Charles's face. He said to Charles, 'What does it matter where a man's bones are buried? My father's grave is unknown. My mother's bones lie in the sea. At least your mother has a resting place and a tombstone. Who is more fortunate, you or I?' From that time on Charles gave Joseph his unrestrained loyalty.

It was a never-ending source of cynical and inner hilarity to Joseph that Charles had a slight aversion to Harry Zeff, and sometimes, like Bernadette, referred to him as 'the Arab', though he truly admired Harry's genius for organisation and management, and learned from him and was politely deferential to him. To Joseph, the spectacle of humanity was absurd and its pretensions laughable. When Harry said of Charles, with some admiration, 'That's a mean Southern bastard,' Harry did not understand why Joseph's small eyes glittered with merriment. 'You'd think,' Harry said, 'that no one born north of the Mason-Dixon line had any right to call himself human. Or claim to be an intelligent gentleman.'

It was on one warm June day, brilliant with sun and suffused with the fragrance of roses, that Joseph became really aware of his children.

He and Charles were in Green Hills for a few days. Joseph was at his desk in his rooms and Charles was standing by a window looking over the glistening green grass and the flowers and the long lawns and trees. He suddenly said, 'They are fine young people. I wish I had children of my own.'

Joseph had looked up impatiently. 'What?' he said.

'Your children,' said Charles. 'Rory looks like one of those Greek gods we hear about, and the girl is delicate and graceful. A lady.'

Joseph stood up and went to the window and looked out. Anything that caught the attention of Charles Devereaux must be remarkable, for Charles, like himself, was usually uninterested in others and considered few worthy enough to deserve a remark.

Rory and Ann Marie were walking side by side over the long lawns in the sun. There was a deep affection between them. They were holding hands like very young lovers, and their heads were bent and they were evidently talking seriously. Rory's reddish head was bright in the sunlight, and seemed haloed with colour, and he walked like a dancer with poise and economy and ease. His handsome boy's face was absorbed and. attentive. He was somewhat of a dandy and wore the latest fashions, which became him. Ann Marie walked beside him, with a faintly timid air and lightness, her blue dress clinging to her slight but proud figure, her brown hair shining, her pale face gentle and quiet. She kept glancing at her brother very soberly, and occasionally she nodded.

For the first time Joseph was thoroughly and completely aware of them, and that they were his children, and were personable and human with a poignant air of youth and identity. They were also beautiful and in some way moving. Joseph leaned on the marble window-sill and stared at his children and then said to himself, in reluctant and even angry wonder: 'My children!'

At some distance behind them Kevin ambled, his stocky child's body, broad and strong, possessed of the awkwardness of childhood. He had a dark square face with hard facial bones, very resolute and grave. It was the gravity that redeemed it from pugnacity. His deep brown hair was a mass of curls. His dark brown eyes were examining something he held in his hands, and he was intent upon it.

Joseph, at the window today, did not know he was smiling as he looked down at his children. He did not know, until somewhat later, that love for them had come to him on that June day and that finally they were his own and part of himself, and that he had acquired another family.

On Rory's fifteenth birthday Joseph said to him, trying to smile, 'I am going to make you President of the United States of America.' Rory looked at his father with impudent thoughtfulness and said, 'You'll try damned hard anyway, Pa. And I'll try with you.' Then Joseph knew that his son would do anything to please him, and he had felt sharp pain and a sudden blank confusion.

Rory asked, 'Why should that be important to you, Pa?'

Joseph had considered, and Rory watched him and saw the darkening of his face and the tightening of his mouth. Joseph said, 'I could never explain it to you, I am afraid. I have too many memories.' Rory had nodded, as if he understood in entirety.

For Ann Marie Joseph had acquired a special tenderness. She had a simplicity of character which both frightened and touched him. It was not Regina's simplicity, which had been full of knowledge, but a limpid simplicity that knew nothing of evil and so denied it. For Kevin Joseph now had a rough and rollicking affection, and he sometimes called Kevin 'you old man. I think you were born with a beard.' Rory acquired learning with ease and insouciance, but Kevin laboured earnestly and grubbily.

When Joseph learned that his children had always loved him he was both ashamed and remorseful, and was sometimes incredulous. But there it was. He had done nothing to gain their love, and yet they had given it to him as they had not given it to their mother who had indulged them. It finally came to Bernadette that they thought their mother somewhat silly, and as Bernadette was not silly in the least she had been outraged.

She had always been glad when they were absent, so that she could think of no one but Joseph. A year after the day Joseph had secretly acknowledged his children as his own she had learned that he loved them. For that she never forgave them. Her jealousy crushed and almost demolished her. It wounded her in her deepest places. Without an effort they had gained Joseph's love, and she, who gave her life to him, was rejected. She became distraught. She regretted that she had ever given birth to them. They were her rivals, her enemies. To please Joseph she pretended solicitude and affection for them. They had stolen from her, she believed, what was rightfully hers.

To Bernadette the most grievous day of her life occurred when she had complained to Joseph of Ann Marie's 'ugliness', and had said, 'I doubt the girl will ever make a good marriage with her lack of beauty and presence. Dear me, she is not in the least charming. She has no style at all.'

Joseph had turned on her with so vindictive a face and with such a savage look that she had recoiled.

He said, 'Let my children alone. I warn you, let my children alone.'

Bernadette, abandoned, felt the first profound prostration she had ever experienced. She had been forced to take to her bed, she who was never ill. For days she lay in her darkened room, unable to weep, and could only stare dry-eyed at the painted ceiling. She could not even speak. She felt that she was dying, and actually longed for death.

When she recovered a little from her grief she had aged. It is just a matter of time, she would tell herself. They will soon be married and gone, and I will be alone with Joseph, and he will finally know that he has no one but me. We are not getting younger. Some day he will understand and love me, and I can only wait for that.

She knew, by now, his many infidelities. She knew of the woman he loved. But she was his wife, and a wife's position was impregnable, upheld by God and society and all legal sanctions. Even Joseph Armagh could not forever ignore these. Now there remained to her, in her clutching despair, only her husband and herself.

CHAPTER THIRTY

ONE of his classmates said to Rory Armagh, 'Your father is only an Irish whore-master.'

Rory replied, 'And your grandfather was a pious Puritan blackbirder, who baptised miserable savages and blessed them then spirited them into slavery, though it was against the law. Nothing like a few prayers on the way to the bank!'

'Hah!' said the other youth. 'At least my father doesn't bed with his mother-in-law.'

Rory, the good-tempered and genial, had then almost beaten his opponent to death with a wild savagery he had never displayed before in all his vigorous life. He was immediately expelled, and returned to Green Hills, and his father, in Philadelphia, received a formal letter from the headmaster, one Geoffrey Armstead.

'I regret to inform you, sir, that your son, Rory Daniel Armagh, has been expelled from this school because of a violent and unprovoked attack he made on young Mr Anthony Masters during recess on April 21st inst., in the Yard. Mr Masters has been confined to the infirmary with sundry lacerations and bruises and a broken arm and a concussion, and his condition is serious. It is not believed he will be able to return to his classes for several weeks. Mr Burney Masters, of Boston, who is a revered and distinguished member of Boston Society, is much incensed over this brutal punishment inflicted on his son and is considering legal action. I have the good repute of Our School to consider, and this dastardly attack will hardly enhance the Reputation of our Institution, and there will be Discussions among parents which will rebound upon the School. This is sad because so many of our graduates have gone on to careers of distinction in Public Affairs and business, and never before has there been such an Incident.'

Joseph returned at once to Green Hills with Charles Devereaux in a cold fury both against his son and Mr Armstead, who was no favourite of his. Joseph said, on the train, 'That damned supercilious old bastard! Prim-lipped Puritan and peck-sniffer! I had to pay twice the fee to get that damned Rory enrolled at that school, among the Genteel Scions of Boston and New York and Philadelphia, to quote Armstead, and now see what he does! Ruins and disgraces himself, and humiliates me.'

Charles said, 'Let us hear Rory's story from himself. I know of Armstead. He would appear at Harvard when I was there, at teas and such, with his wife, who is a mean little brown hen of a woman, though of such Noble Ancestry, as she would confess, herself. They make a fine pair.'

'Of course, I know that Rory is a favourite of yours,' said Joseph, with an angry glance at his secretary. 'If he had murdered young Masters you'd find some excuse for him.' He ran his lean fingers through his hair, and the implacable expression which everyone feared settled on his face. 'What can we do to ruin Armstead?'

Charles gave this long consideration. 'He is not a businessman. Inherited wealth, old family, sound investments, married into a rich family of the same calibre. No political background, and doesn't mingle with politicians. Of course, there is always something, as we've found out in the past. But that would take time, and Rory is only seven weeks away from graduation, so we must get to work at once to have him reinstated. The only thing we can do – if it is at all possible – is to put pressure on Mr Burney Masters, the father, to force his son to apologise publicly to Rory and withdraw his charges, and get Rory re-instated at once. Armstead could never refuse Mr Masters. Masters is an alumnus of that school and has a large scholarship running.'

'Burney Masters,' said Joseph, frowning. 'Didn't he run

against the Irish Mayor of Boston and lose?'

Charles smiled. He took out his notebook and pencil. 'So he did. And isn't the Mayor a friend of yours? Didn't you contribute to his campaign? It seems, if I remember correctly, that Mr Masters ran on a Reform Platform and said some unkind things about the Boston Irish during the campaign. Not that that will do us any good, however. It was a miracle that the present Mayor was elected under the circumstances. The Mayor is hardly one who can put pressure on Mr Armstead, who despises him. I believe the feeling is mutual.'

Charles leaned back in his comfortable chair in Joseph's private coach and thought for a considerable time. Joseph waited. Then Charles said 'Ah!' in a deep and contented voice.

'Mr Armagh, I do believe there is something. You will remember that all odds were with Mr Masters for his election over the present Mayor. Mr Masters conducted a strong and determined campaign, and is an eloquent speaker, and put a lot of money of his own into that campaign, and had the backing of all the Beacon Street elegants and gentry. The present Mayor was too florid – and too Irish – to be very effective, except among his own, and his way of dancing a little jig and singing an Irish ballad or two on the platform did not enhance his repute among the Proper Bostonians, though his own enthusiastically applauded him. Mr Masters not only led, according to the Boston newspapers, but his dignity and Presence, as they called it, "boded well for an administration which would not be soiled and corrupt as the previous one was, but one of which Bostonians could be Proud and vindicated as citizens of an honourable city".

'Then,' concluded Charles, 'something happened during the last three weeks of the campaign. Mr Masters made fewer and fewer public appearances. His speeches were weaker and more restrained, and less pejorative. He seemed to have lost steam. He made no appearance at all during the last week, and refused newspaper interviews except for one mild plea for his election. His posters disappeared. His people made no more house-to-house calls. There were no more bulletins on Major Issues. Now that is very interesting. I wonder what happened to Mr Masters?'

'I wondered at the time, myself,' said Joseph, sitting up and looking at Charles with interest. 'I asked Old Syrup, as we

232

called him, and he only smiled that peculiar Sphinx-like smile the Irish can assume when they have "something under their nose" which they prefer not to make public. So, he had something on Masters, something lethal. It must have been very good. Charles, send him a telegram in my name tonight and take a letter from me to him tomorrow.'

'He's a wily character,' said Charles. 'He wants to be governor, and he won't do anything, even for you, which will jeopardise that.'

'But I know something very lethal, myself, about Old Syrup,' said Joseph, with great satisfaction. 'If he wants to be governor he had better not antagonise me. I think we have concluded the problem. In the meantime I will deal with Rory.'

'With fairness and restraint, I hope,' said Charles. This time Joseph smiled a little.

The two men were met by a wailing Bernadette who exclaimed at once, 'Your son! He has disgraced us for ever! And I was such friends with Emma Masters, who leads Boston society, and we were received almost everywhere in Boston! The Armsteads were gracious to us, too, on more than one occasion, and were most civil. Now we will be outcasts in Boston, humiliated and ignored and snubbed, all due to your son's extravagant temper and viciousness and violence – attacking a refined young gentleman like young Masters!'

Only Charles saw that she felt considerable secret elation over this episode, for she believed that Rory would no longer be so loved by his father, and therefore would no longer be her rival. Joseph glared at her and said, 'Refined young gentlemen do not provoke attacks. I will be in my study. Send Rory to me at once.'

'If you do not punish him severely you will be lacking in your duty, Joe,' said Bernadette, a little dismayed at Joseph's reception of her complaint. 'To think he would have been graduated from that distinguished school in June, with honours, and now he will not graduate, he will be accepted only in the lowest establishments and will not be admitted to Harvard, and he has ruined his future!'

'Send Rory to me,' said Joseph, and left her abruptly. Charles accompanied him. By the time they had reached Joseph's room Joseph was again in an icy rage against his son, for he had had to leave important business in Philadelphia.

Joseph did not like intrigues for intrigue's sake, and only indulged in them when absolutely necessary.

Rory, immaculately dressed as always, and resplendently handsome in spite of an impressive black eye, came at once to the study.

Joseph let him stand before him like a penitent. 'So,' he said, 'my son is a boisterous and murderous hooligan, is he? Without any thought at all he tries to destroy his own future, which has already cost his father a pretty penny, sir. What have you to say for yourself?'

Rory said, and his cynical blue eyes were averted, 'He insulted – you – Pa.'

Charles stood behind Joseph's chair, and he tried to catch the seventeen-year-old youth's eye, but failed. There was a heavy sullenness on Rory's usually merry mouth, and a secretiveness.

'Now,' said Joseph, 'that's a very fine sentiment, I am thinking, protecting your father's honour. Look here, Rory, I have never concealed my activities from you. I have told you many times that businessmen are not concerned with legal or illegal activities, so long as they don't engage the attention – too keenly – of the law, and even then that can be surmounted.'

He paused and looked at Rory. But Rory, with rare stubbornness, was staring at his feet. He did not look defiant in an immature way, or rebellious as many youths appear when castigated by a father. He had the appearance of someone who is protecting something, or someone. However, only Charles noticed this, and not Joseph, who was growing coldly angry again.

Rory said, 'He called you – names.'

Joseph's thin mouth tightened even more. 'Rory, I have been called every name you can imagine, and many more. Some I have deserved; some I have not. It is of no importance to me and should not be of importance to you. I thought you understood that. You will be called names, too, in the future. If you are sensitive to name-calling then you had better settle for a clerkship in one of my offices, or teach in some obscure little school, or open a shop. Now, Rory, let us put this nonsense aside. I will do what I can to get you re-instated. I think it is possible.'

'My marks,' said Rory, without looking at his father, 'are

high enough so that I don't need to return to that school. I excelled in all the curriculum. I didn't even have to take the last examination; my record stood for itself. Old Armstead knows that. He is only being malicious, because he hates you, Pa, and me – because we are Irish. He'd do anything to frustrate you. You will remember how he opposed my entry into his damned stupid school.' Now the boy flushed and he looked at his father with an anger equalling Joseph's own. 'I resent it that you had to pay double to get me enrolled there!'

'Who told you that?' asked Joseph, sharply.

'Old Armstead, himself, with that spittle-satisfaction of his, four days ago.'

Joseph and Charles exchanged a glance.

'If I can't make my way with my own endowments in any damned school or college I don't want it!' exclaimed Rory, his face deepening in colour. 'I won't be mortified any longer.'

Charles said, 'Every man has to endure belittlement for one thing or another, Rory. He has to make his compromises, though without weakness. If he can conceal something about himself which is injurious, then he should do so. If he has nothing really deadly to be ashamed of, but it is said that he has, then he should fight.'

Rory was extremely fond of Charles, but now he said to him with bitterness, 'That is all very well for you, Charles, but you are a Devereaux of Virginia and no one could ever unjustly point a finger at your parents, or yourself.'

There was a sudden long silence. Charles looked again at Joseph who shook his head peremptorily. But Charles drew a deep breath and said, 'You are wrong, Rory. I am a Negro.'

Rory flung up his head and gaped at Charles, his mouth opening. 'What!' he cried, incredulously.

Charles nodded, with a beautiful and amiable smile. 'My mother was also a Devereaux, by blood, but she was born a slave, and she bore me, an illegitimate darkie, to my father.'

Rory stared wide-eyed at Charles's yellow hair, sharp features and grey eyes. He looked stunned.

'Rory,' said Charles, 'if someone asked me if I were a Negro I would say yes. I feel no disgrace, no inferiority. But it is my affair, my secret if you will have it so. It is no business of anyone else's. Before, say – Divinity – there is no colour, no race. There are only men. But the world doesn't know that and so a man often has to protect himself from undeserved malice and cruelty. He keeps any harmful secret to himself.'

Joseph was moved as he had rarely been moved before. That the proud Charles Devereaux should risk telling a seventeen-year-old youth such a dangerous secret told Joseph more than anything else of Charles's loyalty to him and his attachment to his famliy. Joseph was not a man for gestures, but he put his hand briefly on Charles's arm.

Rory was still staring at Charles, and now the stony hardness of his young and vital face softened. 'By golly,' he said, almost in a whisper. He thought. Then he said, 'I guess I'm not the man you are, Charles.' However, the secretiveness had returned to his eyes, and Charles saw it.

'I reckon,' he said, 'that young Masters didn't only call your father an Irish something-or-other, but said something else about him.'

'Yes,' said Rory, after a long pause.

'It can't be very important,' said Joseph, still touched. 'What was it, Rory?'

Rory was silent. He was staring at his boots again and the heavy flush had come back to his face.

'Well?' demanded Joseph with impatience.

'I can't tell you, Pa.'

'Is it that disgraceful?' Joseph was smiling again.

'To me, it is,' said Rory.

'My God, lad, don't be a fool. You know what I am. I've never pretended to be anything different from what I am. I never hide anything, though I don't shout it to the skies. I'm not concerned with people's opinion of me, nor should you be.'

'Suppose, Mr Armagh,' Charles intervened, 'that we let Rory have his own little secret. Later, he'll laugh at it. Every man is entitled to one little secret of his own, isn't that so, Rory?'

'Maybe Pa doesn't want this to be known, or talked about,' said Rory and he looked at his father with such poignant love that Charles was shaken. But Joseph was curious and did not notice the emotion in his son's eyes.

'If young Masters knew it, then everybody knows it,' said Joseph.

'But it is a lie!' Rory cried out. 'A dirty lie! I couldn't let a lie like that pass before the whole school!'

Something dangerous flickered between Joseph's eyelashes. He considered his son. The truth did not occur to him. He had been most careful, most discreet, in one single area of his life, more completely secretive than ever before, and he did not think of that one area now for he believed that only he and one other knew about it.

He said, 'I hope you aren't turning into a dainty milksop, Rory. Lies are told by the thousands about me. It doesn't matter; I don't care. But what was this particular lie that so inflames you? We can settle it between ourselves.'

A look of complete despair, but of increased stubbornness, fell over Rory's face. He shook his head. 'I can't, I won't, tell you, Pa.'

Joseph stood up so suddenly, and with so ferocious a face, that even Charles fell back. Joseph said in a quiet but terrible voice, 'Don't defy me, you young jackanapes. Don't tell me you "can't", or "won't". I'll not have that impudence from you, that lack of respect, that insult. Out with it!'

Charles had recovered himself. He said, 'Mr Armagh, suppose you let Rory tell me what it is, between us two, and let me be the judge? Would that satisfy you, Rory?'

But Rory was shaking his head. 'I'd never repeat it to anyone!'

Joseph hit his son fiercely across the face, the way he had hit his brother, Sean. But, unlike Sean, Rory did not collapse, did not burst into tears, did not turn away. He rocked on his heels for a moment, then straightened himself, and looked at his father steadily, almost expressionless. The mark of Joseph's hand flared out on his cheek.

Regret was not a common emotion for Joseph, but all at once, as he stared at his son he felt regret and a kind of deep shame. The boy was fearlessly confronting him in silence. He would endure any punishment to protect his father, and Joseph suddenly understood that and his regret deepened to remorse. Charles stood in silence, a little aghast.

But Joseph said, in his grudging tone, 'All right, then, you wretched young spalpeen, you can keep your damned silly secret, and be damned to you, if your secret is so precious. Who cares about it? I thought you had more sense, and more manhood, than to be affected by lies. I never was. I have accepted humiliations you haven't heard of yet – and bided my time. There was only one thing I could never have accepted, and that would have been a filthiness against my parents, my father or my mother.'

Rory looked aside. He did not speak. Charles saw that his cheek was quivering. Joseph tried to smile. 'There is very little, my son, that would be a real calumny against me. So take it with more ease than you did this time. Very well. You may go.'

Rory bowed shortly to his father and then to Charles. It was at Charles that he looked directly, and it was with great respect and a glint of admiration. Then he left the room, walking stiffly, his head held high, his shoulders squared. When he had gone Joseph shook his head and laughed his grating laugh.

'It seems that no matter what I've told him, and let him know, about myself, he still is squeamish. I don't like that, Charles.'

'He has courage, and that is a rare virtue,' said Charles. 'He is like a rock. He won't give way; he won't crumble. It's not so much a matter of rectitude, but of honour.'

Joseph was pleased. But he shrugged. 'There's no place for honour in this world,' he said. 'My father never understood that, and so he perished. Well, then. Let us get on with the matter of the Honourable Mr Masters.' He looked at Charles. 'Yes, the lad has courage, hasn't he? I hope it is the right kind. What do you think young Masters said about me, Charles?'

But Charles did not know. However, he wondered how Anthony Masters had come by his knowledge. Someone had been indiscreet. Charles did not know that it was Bernadette who had babbled to her 'dear friend, Emma Masters', in a moment of wine-induced lachrymose confidence, and the meek pious Emma, always avid for titbits which could injure others, had told her husband, and her son had overheard. Like all well-kept secrets, it had been simple to discover. Bernadette did not even remember that hazy evening and the false sympathy of which she had been the victim. Had she remembered she would have been terrified of Joseph's knowing, but that was the only thing that was important about the matter. Besides, she would have thought, Joseph's infidelities were well known. One more was insignificant, though this was the

most unbearable of all. She had discovered it when she was
the least aware of discovering anything.

The affair of Mr Burney Masters was absurdly easy for
Charles to conclude, far easier than many others he had
concluded. He did it with almost immediate dispatch.

'Old Syrup', the Mayor of Boston, was happy to receive a
communication from his dear friend, Joseph Armagh which
implied that if it was his Honour's desire to be governor Mr
Armagh would oblige him with a breathtaking campaign
contribution, or, better still, if he desired to be a Senator Mr
Armagh was on the most amiable terms with many of the
Massachusetts members of the legislature. In fact, Mr Armagh's influence in Washington, itself, was stupendous.

'Old Syrup' enthusiastically hated the Brahmins of Boston
who had tried to defeat him, had humiliated him and despised
him during his struggling and desperate political career, and
had exploited him and starved him in their manufactories
and mills in his earliest youth. He gave Charles Devereaux
a quick and friendly vignette of those days, as they sat together drinking brandy and smoking cigars in the Mayor's
lavish offices in City Hall. His first young wife had died of
'the consumption' for lack of food and warmth and adequate
shelter. During her funeral Mass the church had been invaded
by street vandals and her poor wooden coffin had been
befouled, as well as the Host. The priest had been beaten
unconscious, and the mourners scattered with blows. 'Even
the little colleens.'

'I tell you, sir,' said the Mayor to Charles Devereaux, 'not
even the darkies in the South was ever treated the way us
Irish was treated in this country, I am thinking. You're a
Southerner, sir? I heard it in your voice. Slave-owners, eh?
But you took care of them. You've got to be oppressed, Mr
Devereaux, sir, or your people oppressed, to know what it's
like.' He looked at Charles's patrician face and fine clothing
with a sort of belligerence. 'But, you don't know, do you?'

'I have some imagination, your Honour,' said Charles, with
a smile.

'Well, so Joe wants to put a hard hand on Burney Masters,
does he?'

Charles had laid a thick sheaf of banknotes on the desk

at the very beginning, and in some admirable fashion they had disappeared as if into blank air. Nothing was said about them, out of respect, not even a word of thanks.

Mr Burney Masters, about four years ago, had been caught in *flagrante delicto* with a pretty young shoeshine lad only twelve years old. 'Right there, in his own garden, on Beacon Hill,' said the fat Mayor, with glowing satisfaction and many chuckles. 'I'd bin having him watched for a long time. He had that sweet pursy look that men like him have, that lovin' look. I'd met his kind before. You wouldn't think it now, sir, but I was a good-looking lad, meself, and was approached by Masters, many the time. Right in the mills. They got the certain look: anxious. Tender. Looking out for your interests. Always talking concern and the like, and helpin' a lad out, advance himself. Soft gentle hands. Writin' letters to the newspapers, deploring-like "exploited labour". Gettin' themselves a reputation for Good Deeds. Sufferin' for The People. Good causes. Whigs. Busy like bees, protestin'. Now, I don't say every man like that is what Masters is, but a hell of a lot of them are. They don't care much for the wimmin, and the girls. Just lads.' The Mayor shook his huge head deploringly. 'Scholars, a lot of them. Some of them write books, exposin' one thing or another. Gives me pleasure, sometimes, to expose 'em, too.'

It seemed that the shoeshine lad was not the only one. There was also a very young handyman in the Masters' household who, with a little urging, revealed considerable data concerning himself and other boys and Mr Burney Masters. 'So,' said the Mayor, leaning back in his chair, 'we had him A word or two. And that's how he lost the election. Well. Glad to mention it to Mr Masters, on Joe's behalf, and that Rory of his. Consider it settled.'

It was. Within a few days Rory was back at his school. Young Anthony Masters, from his infirmary bed, confessed he had 'unbearably provoked' Rory by 'defaming his father'. 'Something,' Mr Armstead said virtuously, 'no manly youth could endure, and certainly no gentleman. We are sad that it led to bad temper and violence, but One can Understand. The Age of Chivalry and Honour has not yet departed.'

Rory, resentful inwardly but smiling outwardly, was graduated with honours in June. He did not know how it had all come about but he knew his father was potent. He would have preferred to have beaten young Anthony Masters all over again, but, because of Joseph, Rory restrained himself and kept his eyes fixed ahead, though Anthony stood beside him.

CHAPTER THIRTY-ONE

JOSEPH ARMAGH never knew exactly when he had become conscious of Elizabeth Hennessey as a desirable woman. He did not ask himself, for he was no tyro at physical attraction, nor did women as people ever occur to him, except for his mother and Regina, and, perhaps, Sister Elizabeth, long since dead. When he became aware of Elizabeth his own daughter, Ann Marie, was only six years old and Kevin had just been born.

Elizabeth, four years older than Bernadette, had come to live in the Hennessey house with her son, Courtney, after the Senator had been stricken with a stroke. Though Bernadette had constantly maligned her and her 'poor thing' of a son, and had resented her presence, Joseph was indifferently aware that Elizabeth was a reserved woman with beautiful manners. She was also very pretty in a cool aristocratic way which did not particularly appeal to him. He preferred stupid romping women of zest and laughter and animal ebullience who made no demands on him and who were easily forgotten. In any event he would not have, deliberately, noticed the widow of Tom Hennessey. Anyone connected with the Senator held only aversion for him, including Bernadette, and, at that time, his own children. He had offered to manage Elizabeth's affairs from his own office. That had been a matter of courtesy. He had expected her to refuse. But she had accepted. She looked at the world with unruffled interest and accepted, and apparently had no attachment to anyone except her son, Courtney, and even with him she was aloof.

Her son was very like her in appearance, manner and silent movement. It was not for many years that Joseph learned that Courtney and Rory were deeply fond of each other, and that there was between them a sort of David and Jonathan affection. Certainly no two youths were ever so dissimilar in temperament, outlook and ambitions, for Courtney, though intelligent according to Rory, was a poor scholar and rather languid and inactive. Rory, himself, often tutored Courtney and would sometimes mockingly call him 'Uncle Courtney', which, for some peculiar reason, was a source of mild hilarity to the boys. It was the only time Joseph ever heard the older boy laugh outright, and the only time he would show some animation such as striking Rory affectionately on the shoulder with his bony fist, and calling Rory 'you fat Irish hooligan'. Courtney, himself, was thin almost to emaciation, and Bernadette scornfully reported him as 'playing with his food, and we have the best cooks in town'. The presence of Elizabeth and her son in this house finally hotly infuriated Bernadette, who found Elizabeth's calm and lack of responsiveness 'unnatural.' Though Courtney was her half-brother she could not endure him. When she learned that he wrote 'poems', she nodded her head and said sagely, 'Well, that's to be expected, isn't it?' as if the writing of poems was somehow unmanly and depraved. She never learned that Rory also wrote poetry, though not with the fineness and delicacy of Courtney's.

It was when Courtney was about seven years old that Joseph became aware of Elizabeth Hennessey for the first time, beyond the mere fact of her quiet presence at the dining table or in passing her in the wide marble halls of the Hennessey mansion. Sometimes she would nod to him in her passage, but she rarely spoke. She was apparently as indifferent to him as he was to her and noticed him about as much.

One day before the Christmas holidays Joseph strolled into the conservatories. It was a gloomy day of thick grey snow falling outside. The conservatories were particularly fragrant just now with the scent of roses and lilies in forced bloom, and there was also a fugitive scent of almond from somewhere and a breathing of warm fecund earth. Gaslights flickered and illuminated the broad glass windows against which the snow hissed and the wind battered.

Joseph thought himself alone, for this was the dinner hour of the gardeners and their day's work was done. He saw before him the long aisle between the plants and the rainbow colours of flowers, and prepared to wander among them. Then he heard another door open from another section of the house; a rapid tattoo of footsteps, and then Bernadette's loud, and

242

now somewhat shrill voice railing in outraged anger. 'Elizabeth! How dare you cut my white rosebuds! You know very well that they are for our Christmas Day dinner! Such effrontery, not even to ask me! Such – impudence!' It was the voice she used to servants. Joseph stopped, half hidden behind a huge tubbed plant which stood on the floor.

Joseph heard a rustle of silk and then he saw Elizabeth's pale blonde head rising between two aisles at his left, and at some distance. She said in a voice without real intonation, and certainly without emotion, 'I am sorry, Bernadette. I wanted to ask you but you were upstairs with a headache and I didn't want to disturb you. I've only cut half a dozen, and there are so many dozens left. Courtney is in bed with that awful cold of his, and he does like white roses so, and I thought I'd cut these few for him.'

'Oh, you wanted them for that sickly, miserable son of yours, did you?' Bernadette shouted with coarse derision. Now Joseph could see her, in her scarlet velvet dress which was too small for her slightly obese figure, her curled head bobbing with hateful emphasis, her plump flat face distorted with contempt and ridicule. 'He's always abed like a consumptive girl in a decline! Now, let me tell you something, Elizabeth Hennessey! This is *my* house, and *I* am mistress here, and you and your son are here only by my sufferance and good nature and regard for my father, and from this time hence you are to *ask* me for any favour, for any flowers, for any decisions, and not have the impertinence to do what you will without regard for my station!' She snorted. 'And yours. If you have any, which you do not.'

Elizabeth stood there in silence before this virago whose dislike and hatred and resentment had suddenly broken forth from any controls she had heretofore kept over them for the sake of vague decency in the presence of others.

'I want to tell you something else too, my woman!' Bernadette continued to shout. 'I've wanted to tell you this for a long time and only refrained out of respect for my father. He never could endure you.' Her face was gloating with elation and joy that she could finally vent her stifled loathing on Elizabeth. 'He was forced to marry you and adopt your brat, because your father had more political power than he did! But no one really believed you were the widow of a war hero, and that Courtney is his son, Miss! You were probably

243

a wanton woman and don't even know the paternity of your son. You, with your namby-pamby ways and graces and pretensions of being a lady – you who co-habited with a man to whom you were not married and God knows how many other men! Don't you know you are the laughing-stock of half a dozen cities, not to mention Green Hills? You are absolutely shameless. You go among respectable people of propriety and reputation as if you deserved to be in their company, and not on the streets where you really belong, and only the fact that you are my father's widow prevents my friends from drawing aside their skirts when you appear. You are hardly more than a strumpet, and everybody knows it!'

Elizabeth's face had changed. It had become rigid and immobile. She said, in her chilly voice, 'You have forgotten. Your father left me his share in this house, and your mother left you her share. I pay my portion here, and my son's expenses.' She fixed the panting Bernadette with her great green eyes. 'I will not reply to your filthy insinuations, which are worthy of you, Bernadette, for you are a vulgar and cruel woman. You are without sensibilities or ordinary decency, and if you are avoided by your family it is your own fault.'

'What!' screamed Bernadette, advancing a few more paces towards Elizabeth.

'Don't come any nearer me,' said Elizabeth, and now her face and voice were charged with passion. 'I warn you. Don't come nearer.'

Joseph, to his amused amazement, saw the desire to kill on Elizabeth's face, and with it her desperate fight for control.

'I want you out of this house, my house, tomorrow!' shrieked Bernadette. 'Bag and baggage, out of my house!'

'This is my house, too, and I will leave it when I desire, and not before.' Elizabeth's voice was louder but still under control. She held the roses tightly. 'These, too, are my flowers, as well as yours, and I will cut them when I will, and not defer to you at any time, from this day forward.'

Bernadette raised her arm, her fist clenched, and advanced directly in front of Elizabeth, her face was evil with rage. But Elizabeth caught that arm in mid-air, as the fist was descending on her, and with a gesture of full loathing and disgust she flung Bernadette from her with such strength that Bernadette staggered, tried to get her balance, fell against the plants near her, then fell heavily to the floor. Instantly she yelled like a banshee, and she uttered imprecations that Joseph had not believed she knew. They were full of foul words and gaspings.

Elizabeth looked down at her, then turned with dignity and scorn and moved up the aisles towards Joseph. She saw him for the first time, and stopped abruptly, and scarlet waves ran over her white face. Her green eyes were blazing with an ardour and anger he never guessed she was capable of, and her mouth was parted.

Bernadette was still howling threats on the floor, and struggling to rise. Joseph smiled at Elizabeth. 'I am glad you said that, and did that,' he said. 'I've been wanting to do the same for a long time. But after all, I am a man, and that would be improper, wouldn't it?'

She stared at him. Bernadette was on her feet now, and she too stared down the aisle at her husband, tears on her cheeks. But she had stopped her shrieks. There was something here that terrified her, though she had not heard Joseph's remark which had been almost inaudible except to Elizabeth.

Joseph stood aside for Elizabeth to pass. She still held her roses. She began to move past him, then, without volition halted when they were only inches apart. Her eyes did not drop or falter, but now there was a film of tears over their greenness. For the first time, looking down at her, she became a desirable woman to him, and not only a desirable woman but a woman of mind and high pride and spirit and self-respect – a truly womanly woman, such as his mother had been, and his sister, and Sister Elizabeth.

'Don't leave,' said Joseph to her.

She gave him the very shadow of a smile. 'I don't intend to,' she replied, and he laughed a little and bowed to her as she went on her way.

Now Bernadette was at his side, clutching him, weeping, crying out her fury at Elizabeth. He pushed her away, and she stood and looked at him with fear and suffering.

'You spoke and acted like a slut, with no self-discipline at all, and no shame,' he said, and his voice was harsh and brutal. 'I heard it all, so don't lie as usual. Until you mend your manners, and treat Elizabeth with consideration you must not speak to me. I don't like fishwives.' He added, 'You owe Elizabeth an apology. I suppose it is useless to ask you for that, but you can show it in some fashion if that is possible for you.'

He left her then as if she had been an abominably bumptious servant, and Bernadette was left alone to cry in a lonely desolation that had nothing to do with Elizabeth. From that night on she held her tongue in the presence of the other woman, never again spoke to her directly but only obliquely, and was expansively polite to her when Joseph was in Green Hills.

Six months later Elizabeth bought Joseph's first house from him and left the Hennessey mansion with her son. A month after that they became lovers.

Three months later he said to her in the small but expensive hotel where they often met in New York, 'I will divorce Bernadette, and we will be married.'

Elizabeth said, 'You have three children, one only a toddler, and we are Catholics, and I have a son also, and we have duties.'

For the first time Joseph was angry with her. He said roughly, 'You don't mind committing adultery with me, and I believe that is against the Church, too.'

Elizabeth looked at him seriously and said, 'In some way, I don't think either of us is committing adultery. Our marriages were adulterous, and that is the worst kind.'

He said, still roughly, 'What about Tom Hennessey? You wanted him, didn't you?'

She smiled a smile he had never seen before, full of mischief and light. 'I was young, and he seduced me. But I seduced you. In some fashion that is quite different!'

'That may be logical,' said Joseph, 'but it is hardly theological.'

The months and the years that followed seemed to him incredible in their wonder and strange ease and lightness. He had always felt old, cramped, constricted, and now he knew what it was to feel young, released and almost free. It was an ambiguous feeling, touched with vulnerability and even with a little fear at times, as if he were no longer his own man, his own fortress, his own invincibility, sufficient unto himself.

He had never known what it was to trust fully in all his life, but he trusted Elizabeth and this often disturbed him. After all, she was a woman, he would think for the first years; she was another human being and mankind was capricious, changeable, inclined to treachery. Then as time passed he felt less apprehensive in trusting Elizabeth, and came to trust her fully and without any reserve at all. She was that paradox to him: an intelligent woman. He found himself not only talking humorously to her and even with a little heavy banter – which surprised him as a new language – but confiding some of the aspects of his enterprises with her, though hardly all.

He was also surprised by her subtlety, by her quickness of perception, her common sense, her sudden insights, her shrewd grasp of intricate matters, and her comments. She never pretended to be revolted by some of the things he told her, nor did she appear to believe that she should be revolted. She would listen with gravity, and if she had reservations she would voice them, and, to his delight, he sometimes found them practical.

Once he said to her, 'There are times when I can hardly believe you are a woman!' To which Elizabeth would reply wryly, 'I never believed that intelligence was a matter of sex, though that is the delusion of many.'

On one occasion he said to her, 'Elizabeth, you are a great gentleman,' and she smiled. She thought to herself, 'My darling, you are the man I have been waiting for all my life. How fortunate it is that we both know at last.'

Elizabeth was an endless and fascinating discovery to Joseph. She had, he would tell her, a thousand faces. She was a thousand different women. She shared his love for music. Her own knowledge of the art was necessarily more formal, for she had been taught at her schools, but she too discovered different men in Joseph. His perception, his engrossment with it when she accompanied him to the Academy of Music in New York, touched her almost to tears, and she marvelled. His library, filled with the books he was constantly buying, and reading, commanded her respect and admiration. He had had little formal education, as he had often told her, but he was in all ways an extremely educated man and not the 'money-grabbing brute' her father had called him. He had, she discovered, a sensitivity that he carefully kept within the core of him, as though it were a shameful secret and an entry for enemies. Bernadette had once jeeringly told her of Sean and Regina, and Elizabeth guessed that Joseph would never forgive nor forget nor recover from his sorrow.

She gave him, once more, a motivation for living. He found

himself enjoying life, reluctantly, and finding pleasure where he had never known it lived. His entry into her world of the mind and the spirit was cautious, half-retreating, dubious, sometimes sardonic, but he entered just the same and found it absorbing. Finally his impulses to suicide became fewer and fewer, and at last he felt the urge but once or twice a year, when he was away from Elizabeth for longer than he desired. He was still gloomy and distant with others, still suspicious and contemptuous and reserved, but he was less apt to be so as the years passed, and his first impression of strangers was less automatically condemning.

It was probably Elizabeth – unknown to both of them – who had made him see his children for the first time, or rather her influence over him. She had often told him of her affection for them, particularly Ann Marie who was very like her, but he had dismissed this as womanish sentimentality. However unconscious it was, however, Elizabeth had succeeded in gentling him to some extent. He only knew that he loved her and that without her life would blacken for him again.

Bernadette, who had long suspected her husband of infidelities – she had received many arch hints from her friends in Philadelphia and New York – did not discover Joseph's liaison with Elizabeth until five years after it began.

Bernadette had known hatred before for Elizabeth. Now she hated her with so powerful a hatred that it was like a fire in her, never extinguished. For her husband she could only helplessly feel an enlargement of her love, and her continued determination to have him love her in return. At last she persuaded herself that as Elizabeth was a 'light woman' Joseph would eventually grow tired of her. Strumpets did not engage the affections of gentlemen for an excessive period of time.

To the end of her life she would say, 'My husband never even glanced at another woman but me. He was most devoted, always. As for myself, I lived for no one else. We were all the world to each other. Our life together was an idyll.'

CHAPTER THIRTY-TWO

ONE day when Joseph and Charles Devereaux had finished a long conference with Harry Zeff in Philadelphia Harry slipped a note into Charles's hand, with a wink. It asked Charles to come back into Harry's office as soon as possible, confidentially. It took Charles an hour to arrange this, and Harry smiled with relief and nodded. Though he was hardly fifty, his hair was a glossy riot of white curls which made the swarthiness of his face much more striking, but he had not lost his cherubic look of mischief and humour. He had grown stout with good living, satisfaction with life, the love and adoration of Liza and the affection of his children. Nor did the fact that he was now twice a millionaire distress him.

'How you stay so young,' he said to Charles. 'You're almost Joe's age but you don't look more than thirty-five. Not dyeing your hair, are you, Charlie?'

'Hardly,' said Charles, seating his elegant body into the chair opposite Harry. Harry's offices were lavish with leather, fine pictures on the panelled walls, rich carpets, and a fire chuckling on the black marble hearth this cold and snowy winter day. Harry leaned back in his chair and puffed on his big cigar and put his thumbs in the armholes of his vest. 'It seems we have a problem,' he said to Charles, and now he looked as serious as it was possible for him to be. 'You've heard of Sean, Joe's brother, who disappeared somewhere in the slums of Boston a long time ago?'

'Yes,' said Charles. 'It is also my job to destroy, unread, the twice-yearly letters Joe receives from his sister. He won't even give the poor woman the satisfaction of knowing that at least he saw them, by returning them to her.'

Harry frowned at the tip of his cigar. 'Well, you know Joe, Charles.'

'Indeed I do,' said Charles. 'He never forgives or forgets. Look what he did to Handell of the Handell Oil Company a few years ago. Cornered all the stock and threw Handell out, almost a bankrupt.'

'Um,' said Harry. 'I know. But you've got to remember

that Handell tried a little fast trickery on Joe, in the matter of Joe's invention of the kerosene fuelling for industrial machinery. Well, we aren't discussing Handell, who's dead now anyway. It's Sean Paul Armagh, Joe's brother.'

'Dead, too?'

Harry scratched his fat chin. 'No. But I have yesterday's Boston paper here and you can read it for yourself.' He grumbled, 'Damn it, why didn't the fool keep his mouth shut?'

Charles took the newspaper. Prominently featured on the second page under the headline, 'Great Success for Tenor, Singer of Irish Ballads!' was a photograph of a slight, rather pretty middle-aged man with a charming deprecatory smile and thin fair hair, alleged to be Sean Paul. The lively story then went on to explain that Mr Paul had sung for many years' in various of our public establishments which cater to the working men who drink beer and liquors – a somewhat deplorable habit of those of that class' and then had come to the attention of a kindly gentleman whom Mr Paul designated only as 'Mr Harry,' who had, to quote Mr Paul, 'rescued me from penury and failure and encouraged me, with money and consolations beyond a mere expression of gratitude.' It was 'Mr Harry' who had had him taught formal music and voice, 'in various musical establishments and under the best of teachers, two of operatic fame,' and had then 'launched me on the road to success.'

Charles laid down the paper and looked at Harry with suppressed amusement. 'I gather,' he said, 'that you are the enigmatic benefactor of Sean Armagh, the modest gentleman who avoids the limelight.'

'How could you have possibly guessed?' said Harry, with more gloom than Charles had ever seen before. 'Well, damn it, I was in Boston, and I like beer and I went to a pub, as Joe calls saloons, and there was Sean singing like an angel – and not drinking. Like a damned angel. He looks like one, too. That's a bad photograph. He reeks with charm and softness and ingratiation, and all of it's sincere. Every man jack there was crying in his beer, and I cried too. Voice like a soaring sweet horn, or maybe it's a flute. Never could tell the difference between instruments. But it rang back from the walls and the ceiling, and no one moved except to wipe his eyes and sob a little.' Harry paused. 'I knew I had to help him.'

Charles spoke with unusual gentleness. 'And you are afraid that Joe will blow up when he finds out about his brother, as he will very soon?'

'Look,' said Harry, 'I've known Joe since we were boys together. He saved my life. I saved his. I'd give my life for him, and he knows it. But he can't stand deceit. He can't stand treachery. He won't stand underhandedness. That's not his way. He's got his own code of honour. He'll think I deceived him, diddled him, had a joke at his expense, betrayed him.'

'I understand,' said Charles. 'You're in a good hot pickle, Harry.' He scrutinised the unhappy man. 'If you know his fancy lady, why not confide in her, very fast? You think she has a lot of influence over him.'

Harry's dusky face sharpened and came alive with anger. 'Don't call her a "fancy lady"!' he shouted. 'I know her. I saw him with her several times. She is a great lady!'

'Well, ask her advice. And you'd better be quick about it, Harry. He sometimes looks at the Boston papers when he has time.'

'You've given me an idea,' said Harry, and tore up the newspaper and put it into his wastepaper basket.

Elizabeth, when Harry called upon her, knew at once from his manner that he had more than guessed at the liaison between her and Joseph Armagh. She knew Harry well, liked his Liza and himself, and had admiration for both and the utmost courtesy. Still, his almost boyish awkwardness at approaching her now made her colour a little, then she resumed her dignity and listened with her special attentiveness. At last she said, 'Yes, I understand, Harry. I also understand Joseph, and your predicament. I will do my very best.' She paused. 'I am to be in New York next Tuesday. I will do my best.' She smiled at the stout, relieved man. 'It was so kind, so good of you, Harry, so compassionate. Compassion is a rare thing in this world. I am sure we can bring Joseph to respect it and not condemn it. He isn't quite as formidable as – as he once was. At least I like to believe that.'

There was a blizzard in New York the next Tuesday, and Elizabeth's rooms in the quiet small hotel were warm with lamplight and firelight. She had dressed carefully in Joseph's favourite colour which matched the pale green of her eyes, and the long gown, with its tight bodice and draped bustle, twinkled with brilliant buttons. She had perfumed herself with a violet scent, his favourite, though she never guessed why he preferred it.

'You never grow older, my darling,' he said to her, after he had removed his snowy greatcoat and hat and gloves and had kissed her with that curious reticence of his.

'Yes, I do very well for an old lady of forty-four,' said Elizabeth in her tranquil voice. 'But then, when one is in love, and loves, one never grows old.'

Joseph watched Elizabeth arrange the round table for their dining near the fire. A hotel servant could do that but she liked to preside and prepare for Joseph and he watched her with a love that had not diminished with the years but had grown more solid and rooted. In her turn, as she worked Elizabeth gave him glances full of tenderness. He said, 'Elizabeth, I have to go again to Geneva in April. Come with me.

'But doesn't Bernadette – usually go with you?'

'Yes. I am ending that. Come with me.'

Elizabeth hesitated. She thought of Sean. She did not want to annoy Joseph just now so she said, 'Please let me think about it, Joseph. I always liked Geneva.'

He was very pleased. 'Then,' he said, 'it is decided.' He had the sharp eyes of love. 'Have you been to see your doctor? Your colour has not improved and you seem thinner.'

'He says it is my age,' replied Elizabeth. She knew her hands were almost transparent now and that an unusual weariness had been her almost constant companion during the past six months. 'No consumption, if that is worrying you, Joseph. After all, years do tell, you know. He could find nothing wrong, my doctor.'

'Forty-four is not a great age,' said Joseph, and an intense sick alarm came to him such as he had not felt since his mother had become moribund on the ship, and it dried his mouth and throat and made him cough and reach for his glass of wine. 'Anaemia, perhaps? All you ladies are always having anaemia.'

'I have had three chills this winter,' said Elizabeth, 'and I am not young any longer. That is probably the trouble. Perhaps I need a change, such as Geneva,' and she smiled at him over her wine glass. 'How wonderful it would be to travel in Europe with you, Joseph,' and now she gave the matter sincere thought. He reached over the table and touched her hand and his small blue eyes were the eyes of a shy youth.

Then she spoke with much animation. 'I have just received notice that Sean Paul, the glorious Irish tenor, is coming to New York in three weeks, for a recital at the Academy of Music. I do hope, dear Joseph, that you will be able to take me.'

Her smile was still serene but her heart began to beat quickly. Joseph's austere face changed, darkened. 'Sean Paul?' he said, lingering over the name. 'I never heard of him.'

'He isn't young. Possibly near my own age. But he is quite celebrated in Boston, I hear. He sings Irish ballads, and operatic selections, and people are quite mad about him. He has always preferred quite private recitals but has now been induced to give pleasure to wider audiences. I do believe I have the leaflet announcing his New York recital with me!' She rose with a rustle of green silk and disappeared into her bedroom and Joseph waited with a slowly gathering heavy anger. Nonsense, he said to himself. It couldn't be the – same. Sean had probably died of intoxication, in some nameless gutter, and good riddance to him. Then with the anger came pain and the old sense of loss and despair.

Elizabeth returned with the leaflet which featured Sean's photograph, and she gave it to Joseph. He did not at first read the lyrical announcements, the quotations from music critics. He looked at the shy, smiling photograph and knew that this was his brother. Feeling giddy and unreal, he then read the quotations. Again he stared at the photograph. Sean. It was truly Sean. He could not understand his emotions now, but there was a weak slackening in him, a faintness, and his eyes blurred. He put the leaflet on the table but he still stared at it and Elizabeth watched him with trepidation.

He became aware that a long silence had come between him and Elizabeth. He looked at her now and saw her waiting and anticipatory smile. He said, 'You never saw my brother, Sean?'

'No.' Now she assumed an expression of perplexity. 'I only saw Regina once or twice, but not Sean.' She put her hand suddenly over her mouth and pretended astonished delight and incredulousness. 'Oh, Joseph! Is this wonderful singer, this marvellous Irish tenor, your brother, Sean? Oh, I can't bear it! How proud you must be! How elated!' She leaned across the table and took his hand and her face shone with genuine pleasure.

He made the preliminary motion of discarding her hand. so immeasurable was his enigmatic and complicated rage. But she clung to it, and he looked into her eyes and he knew he could not reject Elizabeth even with the slightest gesture.

'Yes,' he said. 'He is my brother. But it is a long story.'

'Tell me about it,' she said.

When he had finished, Elizabeth said, 'But, don't you see, Joseph? You have succeeded with Sean after all. Without the education he had received he wouldn't have known anything, really. Education, though often despised in youth, makes its importance emphatic in maturity. It makes for discrimination. Had Sean been uneducated, ignorant, he would never have understood more than saloon singing, or had any aspirations beyond that. But he knew there was something else: excellence. That you gave to him. That should be your pride and your comfort.'

'Why the hell hasn't he written to me?' asked Joseph, and Elizabeth knew she was succeeding and closed her eyes for a moment.

'Perhaps he was ashamed, remembering all you had done for him. You are quite an inexorable character, you know, my dear, and I have a feeling you always frightened your family.'

'Hah,' said Joseph. He took up the leaflet again and studied it. He turned it over. 'My dear benefactor, one whom I shall call Mr Harry, came to my assistance when I most needed it. To him, then, and to a relative I do not care to name at this time, I owe my success and the adulations I have received. I dedicate my New York recital to them, as I do all my prayers.'

Joseph rose suddenly. He said in a terrible voice, 'Harry Zeff. He did this behind my back. He never came to me and said, "Your brother has been found and needs your help." No. He preferred to wait to mortify me with my brother's – success. Gloating. Throwing it into my face that he could do more for Sean than I could! Laughing at me – behind my back. Why? Why? I made his fortune for him. But what could I ever expect but ingratitude and slyness and treachery? And a murderous envy?'

Elizabeth stood up also, trembling. She put her hand on his

254

arm and for the first time he pushed that hand aside. He was aglow with rage and humiliation.

'This is the end – for Harry,' he said in that frightening voice.

Elizabeth said, 'Will you listen to me for one moment, Joseph? If you do not, then we must not meet again, even if I die of it. I could not bear to see you.'

Even in his monstrous rage he heard her, and knew that she meant it, and he stood still and waited, his hands clenched.

'Do you honestly believe,' said Elizabeth, in a marvelling voice, 'that Harry Zeff would ever do anything to mortify or injure you, or gloat over you? Gloat over you! My God, Joseph! I don't believe it, that you should think so. Why, you must be out of your mind! But Harry knows you, and fears you. He knows what you had planned for Sean. He knows how Sean – deserted – you. He knows what you must have suffered. Please try to understand, though I doubt you ever understood anyone in your life, even me, who loves you.

'Yes, he helped Sean. He believed in Sean. He encouraged Sean to make the most of his voice, and paid for it himself. Did you ever ask yourself why? It is because Harry loves you, Joseph. He didn't want that part of your life to be defeated, to have come to nothing. Sean has made a wonderful success. He owes that mostly to you. Harry only helped him to achieve it and enhance what you had already given.'

Joseph heard her. Then, when she had finished he glowered so that his eyes disappeared. 'Now then,' he said, 'how do you know all this, Elizabeth, about Harry and my brother? Have I been led up the garden path?'

Elizabeth put her hands tightly over her face for a moment. When she dropped her hands she looked thinner and more exhausted than before and Joseph saw it and the awful alarm returned to him. 'Please sit down, Joseph,' she said, and her tone was so quiet he could hardly hear her. He sat down, rigidly, perched on his chair and Elizabeth sat down also.

She knew that Joseph could bear only the truth, and that even if the truth destroyed him he must have it. There was nothing else to do and so she told him the complete story, with candour and in that newly exhausted voice full of pleading and love. When she had finished she lay back in her chair with closed eyes as if she were asleep or had fainted.

Joseph looked at her face and it was for her that he felt

255

compassion. He knelt down beside her and took her in his arms and kissed her forehead and her cheek, and then she was clinging to him, crying. 'Why is it,' she wept, 'that you reject love and tenderness so? Oh, I know, my dearest. Your life has been so dreadful, so barren, and you have known betrayal and misery. You are wary now, and who can blame you? Harry would have told you, but he was afraid, for you are no gentle character, my darling. You struck fear in your brother, too, and in Regina, though you perhaps never knew it. Do you know how frightful it is to have others fear you?'

He said, 'Elizabeth, are you afraid of me?'

She put her wet cheek against his, and her arms about his neck. 'No, my love. I do not have any fear of you. You see, I know all about you and with love and understanding everything else is nothing. Isn't that what St Paul said? Yes.'

A few days later Joseph walked into Harry Zeff's offices and said with what for him passed as a genial smile, 'By the way, my brother, Sean, is singing in New York on Friday and Saturday. I know you don't like music very much, you heathen, but I should like to have you and Liza join me in New York, at the Fifth Avenue Hotel, as my guests. I have a box at the Academy of Music, and I insist you be there. After all, it isn't every day that a man has a famous Irish tenor as a brother, is it? After the recital we'll have a gala.'

Harry slowly stood up, his black eyes fixed on Joseph. He could not speak. He could only extend his hand and Joseph took it. Joseph said, in a very soft voice, 'You son of a bitch. You sentimental son of a bitch, Harry.'

CHAPTER THIRTY-THREE

RORY and Courtney walked in Harvard Yard together in the gold and gilt of the April sun and the flowering of forsythia. Rory was all placid youthfulness as he and Courtney sat on the wall and swung their legs and smoked and idly contemplated their fellows walking in the Yard. There was nothing on Rory's vivid face which revealed his capacity for thought and reflection. He seemed a rather colourful and beefy young man with nothing on his mind but girls and whisky and athletics and adventures, and spending unearned money. Then he said, 'I thought you and Ann Marie would be openly engaged by this time. Or has she changed her mind?'

'She's afraid to speak to her mother about it,' said Courtney, and he frowned. 'She knows how your mother hates my mother, and me. Ann Marie is a very timid girl, you know.'

'I never noticed it,' said Rory, remembering the vigorous way Ann Marie would pull his hair when they were in the nursery. He smiled. 'I thought it would be announced on our twenty-first birthday, but it wasn't. I've talked to her, as you suggested, but she actually quails at the idea of speaking to Ma.'

Then he scowled and looked down at the grass. He had never been unaware of the liaison between his father and 'Aunt' Elizabeth. But he loved both, and approved of the affair which had gone on over the years. Ma was impossible. Rory did not blame his father. However, he understood his twin sister's fear of approaching their mother on the subject of an engagement to Courtney Hennessey.

'I talked to my mother about six months ago,' said Courtney. Rory stared at him, surprised, raising his bronze eyebrows. 'I thought she'd faint,' Courtney continued. 'She was very agitated. She said it was "impossible", and she wouldn't tell me why. Do you have an idea?'

Rory considered this. 'No, I don't. There is no impediment to the marriage that I can conceive of. You are the son of Everett Wickersham, your mother's first husband, and you were only adopted by my grandfather. No consanguinity to the least degree. So that can't be it. Your mother – likes – my father. There shouldn't be any objection there. And Ann Marie and I love your mother. So why should Aunt Elizabeth be "faint" at the very suggestion?'

'I don't know,' said Courtney, feeling miserable in the fresh sunshine.

'Suppose I speak to Pa?' said Rory. 'He has no patience with foolishness. He likes you, too.'

'I should not like any disagreements in the family,' said Courtney. 'I am not exactly "family" in the meaning of the word, though I was adopted by Tom Hennessey. I am not really your "uncle", or Bernadette's brother, except by courtesy of adoption, which means nothing. I do know, though, that my

257

mother was very disturbed at the idea and turned very white and became upset. She told me I must put it out of my mind.' Courtney grimaced. 'I've wanted to marry Ann Marie since I was ten years old!' He thought again, despondently. 'Since I spoke to Ma she seems to have failed in health. She is growing thin and nervous. She keeps looking at me, as if she is about to burst out crying. I just don't understand. She loves Ann Marie like a daughter – which is more than you can say for your own mother.' He looked bitterly at Rory.

Rory shrugged, tranquilly. 'Oh, I know Ma. Maybe Aunt Elizabeth is afraid of my mother and doesn't want her to come down on Ann Marie too hard. Hatred is a very stupid thing, unless you can make it work for you,' added Rory, the politician.

'How can we make the hatred between your mother and mine "work" for us?' asked Courtney.

'Let me think about it,' said Rory. 'Maybe I can get Pa on your side. He doesn't give a hoot for Ma's feelings or opinions.' He said it without rancour.

'I only know this,' said Courtney. 'I love your sister, and I am going to marry her even if we have to elope. But she cries at the thought. But I think I've just about persuaded her. She talks of the "family". So long as we have you on our side, Rory, and eventually my mother, why should we care?'

To his surprise Rory did not answer for a moment. Then Rory said, 'There must be something. I'll find out.'

'Good,' said Courtney. 'How are you and Maggie Chisholm getting along?'

'Her Dad won't have her marry a Catholic,' said Rory, smiling with humour. 'Nor an Irisher. I'm beyond the pale. Her Dad has a nose like a fox, and sniffs. When I go to see her he acts as if she had dragged something smelly from the gutter into the house. Old Boston. But we're going to be married.'

'You can't be married in the Church,' said Courtney, 'unless Maggie agrees to it and brings up your children as Catholics.'

'Who says anything about the Church?' said Rory, with a magnificent gesture. 'I'd marry Maggie before a Muslim priest, if it came to that. Or a justice of the peace.'

'Heretic,' said Courtney. They heard the bells ring for dinner and slid from the wall and made their way towards Memorial

Hall in the last warm rays of the sun. They locked their arms together, both aware of the deep affection between them and the trust.

After dinner, and whistling happily, Rory went to call on Miss Marjorie Chisholm on Beacon Hill. Her mother was dead and the female head of the small family was a romantic and loving aunt who favoured Rory and would be discreet about his forbidden visits. Marjorie's father dined at this time every week with his grim mother some distance away.

Maggie was tiny. Her head scarcely reached Rory's shoulder, and she had a dainty figure, delightfully doll-like. She was dark and vivacious, with great black eyes full of laughter, long black lashes and thick black brows, and black hair from which glistening ringlets were always escaping and framing her olive-tinted small and pointed face. She dressed exquisitely but demurely, and she could dance as expertly as Rory and played tennis almost as competently as did Rory himself. She was quite the belle of Boston, and she was nineteen years old, and intelligent and sprightly and extremely witty as well as kind. She had fallen in love with Rory Armagh the moment she had met him, and as she had an iron will under all that gay and effervescent exterior she had decided, within five minutes, that she would marry him. It took Rory a month to decide that for himself.

Mr Albert Chisholm had felt contempt for Rory on the very first meeting, for he knew all about Joseph Armagh. He was an upright man because he had never been tempted to be anything else, and had never known poverty or anxiety. To Mr Chisholm Rory was not only an undesirable suitor for his only daughter because of his, Rory's, father and his 'nefarious enterprises and engagement in Despicable Politics', but because of Rory himself. He thought Rory too 'light-minded', too 'undependable', too careless, too brash. But then, he would say to his daughter with disdain, he was Irish and everyone knew what the Irish 'were'. No man of propriety or position had anything to do with them, or admitted them to his house. They were born without conscience or compunction or morals or firmness of character. They 'pushed' themselves, even worse than did the Jews, and tried to invade decent society which had a Duty to morality and to the country.

'Yet, Daddy, your trusted secretary is a Jew,' said Marjorie. 'My dear girl, Bernard is *entirely* different from the average

Jew! Surely you must have seen that for yourself. But this young Armagh – he is typical of the Irish. No, he must never enter this house again. I forbid you to see him.'

Naturally, Marjorie saw Rory at least twice and sometimes even three times a week. They were now at the stage where they were seriously discussing an elopement.

'You think your Pa is against us,' said Rory, 'but it would be nothing compared to what my own Pa would say, my sweetheart. He'd look once at your Pa, with his white sideburns and moustache and his air of smelling something foul all the time, and he'd laugh at him. Now, Pa has no religion, but let someone say anything about the "Papists" and he'll have that man's lights and livers. And Pa mistrusts men like your father. He calls them hypocrites and names I wouldn't repeat to your darling innocent ears – he's met too many of them in his lifetime. And demolished too many of them. Not out of resentment for the superior way they've acted towards him, but just because he knew what they were and despised them.'

Marjorie had a temper, and loyalty. She flared up and bridled and her pretty dark face flushed. 'Sir, just *what* is my Daddy?'

'Oh, come on, Maggie. I'm not trying to offend you. I'm just saying what my Pa would think of yours. Pa eats men like your progenitor alive, for breakfast. Pa's no easy boy. He's got a back stiffer than your father's. In fact, your Pa is a willow branch compared with Pa. Besides, Pa wants me to marry an heiress, rich in her own right, someone whose father is powerful internationally, like himself, who is known, to quote him.'

'Somebody flamboyant and vulgar!' cried young Marjorie.

'Well, not exactly,' said Rory, admiring the fire in the big black eyes. 'A lady, too. And my Pa would think your father's money mere wooden nickels.'

'Indeed!' exclaimed Marjorie, her little rounded breast heaving. 'Perhaps you had better, sir, start searching for that American princess of yours and leave this insignificant Bostonian chit alone!'

'I happen to love "this insignificant Bostonian chit",' said Rory, and took her in his long strong arms and kissed her soundly, and she became weak and trembling. 'Ah, love,' said Rory, 'what does it matter what they think?'

She nestled her head against his shoulder and clung to him, her ringlets brushing his mouth. But she was also practical.

'You have your law school to go through,' she said, in a shaking voice. 'Years! I'll be old, old, and so will you.'

'We'll elope, quietly, to some other state, and no one will know and when I've been graduated we'll tell them all to go to hell.'

'But we wouldn't be able to – to . . .' and Marjorie blushed furiously.

'Sleep together?' said Rory, kindly, kissing her again. 'Of course we will! I have it all figured out. I will get a small apartment in Cambridge and we can meet there without anyone knowing. And you needn't worry about any – consequences. I know how to protect you.' His mouth parted hers and sought, and she thought she would faint. She pulled her lips from his.

Marjorie was very red now. But she pressed her head against the region where she imagined his heart to be and murmured, 'Ah, Rory, Rory.' Her little body was wincing with inexplicable thrills, and she was at once ashamed and hungry.

Tonight they had decided to take Aunt Emma into their confidence. After kissing Rory with enthusiasm Marjorie led him into the 'back room', as Aunt Emma called it, though it was a small sitting-room for the family. No one, of course, ever used the dark chill double parlours except when guests were present. Marjorie's aunt was knitting placidly, an endless pile of grey wool which was never completed. She looked at Rory and her face became rosy and pretty and she accepted his kiss like a loving mother and told him, as always, that he was 'the handsomest young spark I have ever seen'. He had brought her a bouquet of daffodils and narcissi – none of which would grow in Albert's wet dank garden – and had delicately refrained from bringing Marjorie the same. This was a politician's deft gesture, and Marjorie grinned wickedly. 'Oh, my dear,' said Aunt Emma, sniffing the bouquet and then lifting damp eyes to Rory, 'how did you know they are my favourites, the bright blossoms of spring?'

He leaned towards the lady, all earnestness, gravity and boyish sincerity. The light blue eyes were the eyes of a very young boy and his somewhat fleshy and highly coloured face was very serious. This caught Aunt Emma's attention immediately. She had never seen him look so beguiling, so trustful, so pleading.

'You know, Aunt Emma,' he said, 'that Maggie and I love

each other, don't you?'

'Indeed, my dear, I do know.' Miss Chisholm sighed again, deeply, reverberatingly. It was the sort of romantic tragedy on which she doted. She thought her niece and Rory another Juliet and Romeo.

'But,' she added, her kind voice trembling, 'Albert will never permit you to marry.'

'However,' said Rory, watching her, and now taking her short fat hand, 'we do intend to marry. Almost immediately. We are going to elope.'

'Oh, oh!' cried Miss Chisholm, seeing Romeo and Juliet marrying surreptitiously in some dark, candle-lighted cave with only monks for witnesses, 'Albert will simply never countenance that!'

Rory gave Marjorie a look and she bit her lip. 'Countenance that or not, that is what we are going to do, Aunt Emma.' He patted her hand. Reluctantly, she removed it. Her eyes were full of tears. 'But, Rory, I have heard from Marjorie that your own father would be so opposed, too!'

'There comes a time when children must think for themselves – if they love each other,' said Rory. 'For what is more than love?'

As this was Miss Chisholm's own sentiment, she hesitated and for an instant girlish delight shone on her face. But she was not a New Englander for nothing. She said, 'But Marjorie will have no money until she is twenty-one, and even then she will not get it if she insists on marrying someone to whom her father objects. Then she will have to wait until she is thirty.'

'I know,' said Rory. As he had never known poverty he said, 'We don't mind being poor, Aunt Emma, for a little while, until I am graduated from law school . . .'

'Three years,' said Miss Chisholm, the New Englander dominant in her now. 'And, Rory, do you have anything but your allowance from your father?'

Rory had always thought his father unduly penurious and suspicious of students' profligacy, and so his allowance was only fifty dollars a month. 'It's enough for skylarking,' Joseph had said.

'I have an allowance of thirty dollars a month, just for pin-money,' said Marjorie. She looked at Rory with a look he could not fully interpret. 'Aunt Emma, we don't intend to tell

262

anyone, but you. I will go on living here at home, and Rory . . .'

Miss Chisholm was excessively shocked. She looked from Marjorie to Rory, and then back to Marjorie again. Her face was quite white. 'But, my dears! You intend to *deceive* your poor parents, not tell them . . .'

'What else can we do?' asked Marjorie now, blinking her eyes at her aunt. 'We don't like it, but we have no choice.' Her aunt had fallen back in her chair, horrified.

'So – so deceiving, my dear children! So disrespectful! So disobedient! It would be best to tell them, keep your consciences in good order, live together openly in the sight of God and man . . .'

'On eighty dollars a month?' asked Rory. 'We might not even have that, if we tell the old gentlemen. We might be cut off with nothing, and I wouldn't put it past my Pa to haul me out of law school, either, and set me to work at slave-labour, for nothing, in one of his damned offices. As a lesson. Then Maggie and I would be parted – ' he paused and looked at Miss Chisholm, weighing her – 'for eternity.'

Miss Chisholm quivered inwardly, shuddered deliciously, closed her eyes and let her head fall back in grief. 'Like myself,' she whispered.

'Oh God,' Marjorie's mouth formed the words soundlessly.

'So,' said Rory, 'we can only necessarily – deceive our Pas until I am graduated from law school. Then we can be bold, and tell all the world.'

Miss Chisholm recovered and became Bostonian again. 'Still,' she said, opening her eyes and they were a little sharp now, 'your father, Rory, might never forgive you, and then you'd have to wait until Marjorie is thirty for her money. Your father is a very rich man, Rory. A prudent young man thinks of – inheritances. He does not lightly reject them.' Romeo and Juliet wistfully faded into limbo. 'I do love you, Rory, but I'd feel very sad if Marjorie married a penniless . . .'

'I'd inherit from my mother,' said Rory, speaking with outward assurance but with no assurance within. He knew how besotted his mother was. She would do as Joseph told her, not out of fear for him but only to please him.

'She is very rich, Rory, in her own right?'

'Rolling in it,' said Rory. 'She inherited gobs from her

263

mother, and her father. She owns our – mansion – in Green Hills, in Pennsylvania. You must have seen photographs of it. It frequently appears in the newspapers when Mama gives a soirée or something, for personages. Presidents have been our guests. My grandfather was a Senator, you know, and then Governor of Pennsylvania for several terms.' He knew his Miss Chisholms.

'Yes, yes, dear, I know. And you are your Mama's favourite child?'

'Absolutely,' said Rory with never a droop of his eyelids. 'Denies me nothing.'

'Then,' said Miss Chisholm, 'you must tell your Mama at once. No doubt she will come to your rescue.' She spoke briskly and smiled with happiness.

The sharpness of the remark caught Rory without an immediate response. Then he sighed, dropped his head, looked mournful. 'Mama,' he said, 'is absolutely terrified of my father. She is in very poor health. An annoyed word from him would crush her, perhaps destroy her.' He saw Bernadette's short obese body and engorged complexion and snapping eyes, and visualised her as a drooping flower. It almost made him laugh out loud. 'But she has told me secretly of her will. I – I receive – though I pray that her health will improve and that God will spare her for many years to her devoted family – three-quarters of her fortune. Some – ' and now Rory let his wide blue eyes wander to a musing distance – 'fifteen million dollars.'

'Fifteen million dollars,' whispered Miss Chisholm. She calculated interest. 'It is invested, secure?'

'Good as gold,' said Rory. He resolutely would not look at Marjorie and the black mischief in her eyes. 'Mama doesn't believe in using even the interest on interest, not to speak of capital, which is sacred.'

'She is in poor health, you say?' said Miss Chisholm in a sad voice.

'Very poor. Heart, I believe.'

'You damned liar,' mouthed Marjorie at Rory, for she had finally cornered his eye.

'But if she discovers you deceived her – three years from now?'

Rory gave a sigh that was almost a dry sob. 'I doubt she will ever know,' he said in the politician's rich and unctuous voice. He partly covered his eyes with his hand. 'The doctors

264

give us little hope. For her long survival.'

Miss Chisholm moistened her lips and considered, though her face was full of maternal sympathy for the rascally young man. Fifteen million dollars, at four per cent, in a short time . . . Possibly more, with the investments. Mr Chisholm's fortune was much less than that, much less. And dear Rory was so intelligent. Any law firm would be overjoyed to have him grace its staff. One had only to be discreet . . . How unfortunate that he was Irish, and a Papist! Were he not dear Albert would approve the match instantly. He would strut like a peacock, and boast in his genteel way.

Rory's face was still partly hidden by his hand and Miss Chisholm wanted to comfort him. She did touch his strong broad knee with the tips of her fingers, gently. How sad to know one's dear Mama was on the edge of her grave and none could save her! Fifteen million dollars. The lamplight made the scoundrel's head glow in red-gold. Marjorie sat primly in her chair, her eyes downcast, but the dimples rioting in her cheeks.

'What can I do for you, dear children?' asked Miss Chisholm. (Albert, later, would 'come around'. Fifteen million dollars, with interest at four per cent, was not to be despised.)

Marjorie said, 'We are going to elope, perhaps the day after tomorrow, dearest Aunt Emma. Then we are going . . .' She paused. It would be indelicate to mention that Rory had already rented three furnished rooms in Cambridge. 'We will be – away, for perhaps three days. It is Rory's spring vacation. Then he must visit his parents, of course. I should like you, dearest Aunt, to tell Papa that I am visiting Annabelle Towers, in Philadelphia.'

'Can't you tell him yourself, my cherub?'

'I intend to. But you could mention to Papa that I received an invitation this morning, and then later I will speak to him.'

'But Marjorie, that would be a fib!'

Miss Chisholm was shocked, she who was always equivocating, in fear, before her redoubtable brother. Marjorie sighed, as if dejected. 'What else can we do?' she murmured. 'We love each other.'

'I see,' said Miss Chisholm, already formulating the 'fib' in her mind. 'And then you will return home, Marjorie, and Rory will go to his parents. You will live apart – oh, my dear children! – for three long years! How will you bear it, married

265

in the sight of God but not in the sight of men?'

Then she thought again of the fifteen million dollars and the poor Mama in a dying condition, poor sweet lady. It might be only a few short months.

'We will bear it,' said Rory, with a very noble expression, which constituents would later learn to trust and admire. 'After all, everything can be borne for Love. Didn't St Paul say it was the greatest of all, more than faith and hope?'

This appeal to Miss Chisholm's favourite saint quite undid her. She put her handkerchief to her eyes and cried a little. Never once did it occur to her that these plotters would hold any assignation before it was safe to do so. They would be married, but they would live in chastity, pure and untouched, bearing all things for love's sake, trusting in their Heavenly Father – and in fifteen million dollars, something intractable remarked in Miss Chisholm's really pragmatic mind.

She said with sorrow, 'I did so plan, all Marjorie's life, on a beautiful wedding, in the church in which she was baptised. Rory, you are a Roman – forgive me, dear, I did not intend to offend you – but will your Church approve? I understand that . . .'

Rory said, 'We will find a minister. Aunt Emma, what are trappings where love is concerned?'

But Miss Chisholm was about to suggest that the young lovers wait until poor dear Mama – but ah, that would be most uncouth and cruel. She said, 'You don't mind being married by a Protestant minister, Rory?'

Rory almost said, 'I'd be happy to be married before Satan, if it was to Maggie,' but he had the thought that this would be too much for Miss Chisholm, who had weakened. He said, with a grand gesture, 'Is not even a minister a Man of God? Who can deny that?'

Miss Chisholm was not quite certain that she liked the 'even', but did not comment. 'But I will not see my dearest niece married!'

'I will bring you my bouquet,' said Marjorie, kissing her.

They were married before a Presbyterian minister two days later, in Connecticut, in a small obscure village where the name of Armagh meant nothing, but the fifty dollars Rory gave the astounded minister quite shook the threadbare poor old man and made tears come into his eyes. This young couple were dressed so modestly and plainly. It was obvious this was

266

a great sacrifice, and he said so to Rory, with a timid smile.

'Think nothing of it,' said Rory, and then when Marjorie pinched his arm warningly he added, 'It is the happiest occasion of my life, and I have been saving my money for a long time for it.'

They returned to Cambridge discreetly and hid themselves in the dingy three rooms Rory had rented for twenty dollars a month. They had few if any amenities, but they were ecstatic. Then Marjorie said, 'Are we really married, Rory? I mean, in the eyes of your Church?'

Rory hesitated but only for an instant, then he said, 'Married? Of course we are married! Don't be an idiot, Maggie. Here, let me unbutton your dress. How beautiful your little shoulders are – and what is this I see? Now, now, aren't we married?'

Never again was Rory to know such happiness as he knew in those three rooms in a poor section of Cambridge. He was to remember that to the day he died, and his last conscious thought was, 'Maggie, oh dear little Maggie! My God, my darling Maggie!'

CHAPTER THIRTY-FOUR

JOSEPH went to Boston to see his son, Rory.

'Now,' he said, 'I am all for hard work and ambition, and that you have, boyo. But why elect to attend summer classes and rush through law school like a fire engine?'

Rory's amiable blue eyes had a little secrecy about them. But then he made himself look frankly at his father as they sat together in his humid room. Joseph was not deceived. 'Why should I waste three years?' asked Rory. 'I can do it in two. Isn't life for living? If I want to start to live a little sooner, what's wrong with that, Pa?'

'I thought you were going to spend the summer on Long Island with those friends of yours, sailing and boating and what not, as you've been doing the past two years. They're important to cultivate, too.'

'I'd rather go on,' said Rory.

'Giving up all those sports you're mad about? Come on,

Rory, out with it.'

'I'm going on twenty-two,' said the young man. 'I can't see myself in school until I am twenty-five or so. I told you, Pa: I want to start living as soon as possible.'

'And you think being one of my stable of lawyers will be "living"?'

Rory's eyes shifted. 'If you want me, Pa.'

Joseph frowned. 'You're being evasive. I never had time to live. I don't want that to happen to you.' He was astonished at his own words. He looked at the signet ring on his finger which Elizabeth had given him, but he was not thinking of his mistress. 'I would be the last to advise you to trifle with time and waste it, for I know how valuable it is. But on the way I'd like to know that you have been . . .'

'Enjoying myself?' Rory was deeply touched. He drew his chair closer to his father's, and they smiled at each other. 'Pa, you've made life easy for your family. Don't think we are ungrateful, Ann Marie and me, and even that black bear of a Kevin. Black Irish. You deserve having us off your hands as soon as possible.' He thought of his sister, and hesitated. Joseph said quickly, 'Well, what is it? Don't try to hide things from me, Rory. I always find out, you know. You've tried it in the past.'

'Ann Marie,' said Rory. He stood up and put his big hands in his pockets and started to walk up and down the room, not slouching, but with a fast loping stride that was at once strong and graceful.

'The hell,' said Joseph. 'What about Ann Marie?' He loved his sons dearly, and in particular Rory, but Ann Marie was his darling. 'She's been looking languid lately and I've thought about it, but her mother says she is well and just moons about. Is there something wrong?'

Rory stood at the window and looked out. Well, he had promised Courtney and now if ever was the time, seeing Pa was in a soft mood, very rare with him. He said, 'She wants to get married.'

'What's wrong with that?' asked Joseph. 'Does her mother know? Who's the man? Somebody impossible, perhaps?' He sat up in his chair.

'Somebody I'd consider very eligible,' said Rory. He could feel the heat and colour in his fresh face, and he waited for it to subside for he would rather have been drawn and quar-

tered than to let his father know that he knew about him and
Elizabeth.

'One of your Harvard jackanapes with no money, and no
family? Come on, Rory, speak up.'

'He has money, and comes of a good family,' said Rory, and
had to smile. Now he turned from the window. 'Perhaps you
wouldn't think so, but I do.' He looked at his father and he
tensed. 'It's Courtney. Courtney Hennessey. Our adopted
uncle,' and he laughed a little.

He was prepared for his father to frown, to consider, perhaps
even to object for a moment or two, for men really did not
want their daughters to marry. But he was not prepared for the
fierce change on Joseph's face, and he could not read it, and
was aghast. Did the old man consider that his mistress's son
was no match for Ann Marie? Yet, he had always shown
Courtney an offhand kindness and even some distant consideration and affection.

Then Joseph said in so soft a voice – though his eyes were
appalling – that Rory could hardly hear him. 'You are out of
your mind! Courtney Hennessey?'

Oh God, thought Rory. What's the matter with him? What's
wrong with Courtney? He said, 'Pa, what's wrong with
Courtney? I know that – I know that Ma hates his mother and
him, and I don't know why, but then Ma hates practically
everybody. You wouldn't let her objections stand in the way of
Ann Marie and Courtney, would you? Ann Marie's no kid
any longer, Pa. She has a right to her life.'

But Joseph hardly heard him. He began to speak, then
gasped. He thought of Elizabeth. It came to him with stunning power that Rory, of course, believed the general story
that Courtney was the son of a deceased military hero, and not,
in fact, his real uncle. What in God's name can I say? thought
the stricken man. Elizabeth. Why hasn't the truth been told
long before this? Ann Marie, my child, my little girl. Bernadette. I know her. This will be a fine rich and vindictive joke
to her, a final triumph over Elizabeth. He began to speak again
and was forced to cough. 'Has – anyone told your mother
yet?'

'No, Pa. She doesn't know – yet. Courtney has been pressing
her to tell Ma, but she's afraid. Ann Marie's such a mouse.
We call girls like her "mice", here in Harvard. You know.
Soft and gentle and retiring, with nothing much to say for

themselves, and always avoiding unpleasantnesses, and you know how unpleasant Ma can be.'

But Joseph merely stared at him blindly, desperately looking for a way out of this dilemma, a way that would be no shame to Elizabeth and no cruelty to Ann Marie. But what was the way but the truth? He said, 'I can only say this: it is impossible. There is an – impediment. Go to any priest and ask him.'

'Courtney did,' said Rory. 'The priest had to look it up. He had his doubts for a while, but then he said that as Courtney was no in-law, really, but only the adopted son of my grandfather, the real son of a stranger . . . ' Rory stopped, for his father even in his fixed silence was more formidable than the young man had ever seen him. Something took Rory by the throat.

'I said,' Joseph repeated, 'that there is an impediment.'

'But what? If there is, Ann Marie and Courtney ought to know. If some Church authorities object – well, there are always other resources, and we aren't all that pious, either, are we?' He thought of Maggie, waiting for him in those three wonderful shabby rooms.

Joseph stood up. He was only in his early fifties but all at once, to Rory, he appeared old, even broken, and weakened, and this alarmed the young man more than ever. A raging Joseph was to be greatly feared, but he could be faced, as Rory had discovered before, and he could even be reasonable when his cold rage subsided. At least, sometimes. But this man was not raging. He was turning now and Rory saw his face, almost pleading and completely devastated.

'I should have been told before,' he said, and Rory knew that he was speaking only to himself. 'I might have stopped it in the beginning.' He looked at Rory with an expression in his eyes which Rory had never seen. 'Believe me, Rory, there is truly an impediment. I can't tell you, but there is. You must tell Courtney . . .'

'What?' said Rory. 'What shall I tell Courtney – and Ann Marie?'

When Joseph did not immediately reply Rory went on, 'I promised Courtney I would try for him. I promised to find out – if there was something. But I can't go to him with a foolish vagueness. I have to have facts – or something.'

Joseph still did not speak. Then Rory's mind began to

whirl. How long had Pa known 'Aunt' Elizabeth? How long
had the liaison been in existence? Before he married Bernadette? No. He would have married Elizabeth. Courtney was
no brother, thank God. But what was he? Then Rory's
thoughts came to a black dead halt and he and his father
looked at each other without words.

Joseph saw his son's widening shocked eyes. He nodded,
and turned away. Rory stood up and said quietly, 'My God.
So that's it. All that cover-up, all those years. Why?'

'Don't be a fool,' said Joseph. 'There were too many to
consider. Mrs Hennessey. Courtney, himself. Your grandfather's – position. But your mother and I – we always knew.
Women, before you were born, were not automatically ab-
solved even when they married the man . . . It may be different
in these days. It wasn't, then. Mrs Hennessey was not a strumpet, but she would have been branded so, marriage later or
not. She had been seduced and deceived by a scoundrel, God
damn his soul.'

Rory went and stood beside his father. He had the queerest
desire to console Joseph, though why he should console him
he did not know. Certainly Courtney and Ann Marie were the
miserable ones, the wronged ones, and not Joseph Armagh.

'What in hell am I going to tell Courtney?' Rory said in a
wretched voice. He added, 'I need a drink.' He looked over
his shoulder at Joseph and said, 'I think you need one too,
Pa.'

'That I do,' said Joseph, and now his old almost obliterated
brogue came back in his voice. 'Several, I am thinking.' He
almost fell into his chair. Rory put a fine engraved glass into
his hand, then stood before his father. They both drank
deeply, as if dying of thirst. Rory looked down into the glass.
He said, 'There were the old Pharaohs – they married their
sisters. It went on for centuries, dynasty after dynasty. It was
accepted. It was even the law. Courtney – he's only half an
uncle,' and Rory tried for a small and dismal laugh. 'He
needn't know. Ann Marie needn't know. There aren't any
inherited diseases in the family that I heard of. Pa, I don't
find the idea repulsive. No one would ever know.'

'You've forgotten your mother,' said Joseph. 'She knows.
She's denied Courtney's blood tie often to me, because she
hates Elizabeth and would have her a trollop if she could. But

271

– she knows well enough. And, she'd tell Ann Marie at once, with pleasure, to hurt Elizabeth. And Courtney. And me.'

'I don't think . . .' Rory began, and then actually blushed and seeing this Joseph was faintly and ironically amused. He thought of the day he had struck Rory, only a few years ago, and he knew now, with a sudden enlightenment, that Rory had not wanted to 'shame' his father by letting him know that he knew of him and Elizabeth, and that others knew, also. He reached out and awkwardly touched his son's hanging hand, then withdrew it in embarrassment. He was a stranger to such gestures.

'How she found out I don't know,' said Joseph. 'But she did. I can see it in her face when she speaks of Elizabeth. She would kill her if she dared. It doesn't concern me. Your mother knows that I married her, not for money, not after seduction, but for a reason I prefer to keep to myself. It happened a long time ago. I am entirely indifferent to what your mother wants, and I was always indifferent to her. I never deceived her about my feelings, so I am not guilty of anything but marrying her. Perhaps I should not have done so. But I did. I don't regret it now. I have my children.'

'Pa,' Rory began. Then he saw that his father was merely being factual and not sentimental. Joseph continued, 'It was to protect Elizabeth that I took as many precautions as I could, and not to protect your mother. Perhaps I should feel sorry for your mother, and sometimes I think I do, but that is of no importance either. The important thing is the impediment which stands in the way of Courtney and Ann Marie. It is not only an impediment, it is highly illegal, and punishable by law, and be sure your mother would see to that! You and your Pharaohs. I can see that you are a born lawyer.'

But Rory did not smile. Not asking, he refilled their glasses and they drank again. Even little Marjorie was temporarily forgotten in this extremity. 'What shall I tell Courtney?' Rory asked, wincing inside.

'Suppose his mother could be persuaded to tell him the truth? I'd rather he wouldn't tell Ann Marie though.'

'He'd hate his mother, and his father. His father! My grandfather! Isn't that the damnedest thing?'

'I doubt he'd hate his mother,' but Joseph thought, with a sick wrench, of Elizabeth, and the deep love between her and her son. 'Perhaps she can explain it so that he will understand. Don't you tell him, though, for God's sake. The fewer people he thinks know about this the better he will eventually feel.'

'Courtney's already told her about Ann Marie, and wanting to marry her, Pa,' said Rory. Joseph looked up, freshly shocked. 'And Aunt Elizabeth, he said, got damned agitated and became sick, and thin, and told him it was "impossible". She wouldn't talk about it any longer to him.'

So, that is what has been hurting my love, thought Joseph.

'I'll suggest to Elizabeth that she tell Courtney,' said Joseph. 'You had better tell him to visit her in a few days. Give me a week. I hear he is staying the summer with you at law school. I never thought he'd be an extraordinary lawyer, but I suppose you two can't be separated.'

For the first time Rory showed bitterness. 'It seems there is something more between Courtney and me than mere "friendship",' he said. 'Well, nothing can be changed now. It's a terrible mess.' He suddenly remembered Marjorie and swore under his breath. 'I have to write a note to somebody, and send it, if you'll excuse me. I'm breaking an engagement. I want to be with you for a little longer, Pa. Let's go out to dinner together.'

Joseph had frequently suggested dinner with his son in the past but sometimes Rory had not been very enthusiastic, and never had he invited his father before. Joseph looked at his son again and Rory returned the look, then all at once they simultaneously extended their hands to each other and shook them.

'And for an encore, let us go hear your Uncle Sean on his last recital of the season,' said Joseph. 'I haven't seen him since he returned from Europe two months ago. Why doesn't he get married, or something?'

But Rory knew, if Joseph did not, and Rory went to write his note to Marjorie. His young mind was full of misery.

CHAPTER THIRTY-FIVE

COURTNEY HENNESSEY arrived home in Green Hills very early in the morning, after his mother had written him briefly that she had 'something of grave importance to impart to you, my dear'.

The breakfast room, octagon in shape, was serene in pale yellow and green, and the table was already laid and the gold silk of the curtains was moving in the light warm wind. His mother sat at her place, palely beautiful as always, in her green morning dress, her hair hanging down her back and caught at the nape by a green ribbon. She looks like a girl, thought Courtney, cheered, as he bent to kiss her. She patted his cheek, and then saw his hands and said, 'Oh, you are all soot, my dear. Do wash, and I will wait and just drink a little coffee before you come back.'

'I was worried about you,' said Courtney, 'so didn't stop to wash.'

Now for the first time he saw the violet shadows under her eyes, her unusual pallor, the tight little lines about her mouth. She glanced away. 'I am quite well, Courtney. Do come back soon.' Her voice was low and yet, it was 'troubled'. Her proud shoulders sagged as if she were very tired and had spent some sleepless nights. Courtney rushed up to his rooms and washed, took off his heavy brown suit and replaced it with a light grey one, smoothed his hair, and ran downstairs again. He sat down, and his mother started, for she had not heard him enter.

'News of any kind,' she said, 'can always wait for a contented digestion, can't it?'

'It depends,' said Courtney. 'If it is bad news, yes. Good news, no.' He watched her intently from under his yellow lashes.

'I don't know,' said Elizabeth, in a subdued voice, 'whether the news is "bad" or not. It may be – for you, my dear. I don't know. You are young, and the young can rebound.' She helped him to creamed eggs and hot toast and poured coffee for him, and he saw how translucent her fine hands were. He also noticed, for the first time, that she was not wearing her wedding ring. There was no line indicating that it had ever been there. When had she removed it? Then he breathed deeply, with passionate relief. She was going to be married! He smiled. Dear Mama. He was happy for her, knowing her loneliness. He only hoped the man was worthy, and not some mountebank or blackguard looking for her money.

He ate a hearty breakfast, and urged his mother to eat also. She attempted to, and failed. She kept watching her son, and he saw this, and smiled to himself again. She was hesitating to speak. She said, 'I miss you so much this summer, dear, since you decided to rush through law school with Rory.' Ah, thought Courtney, she is delicately leading up to the revelation, and paving the way.

'I can't leave him there alone in Boston,' said Courtney. 'God knows what he'd be up to without my supervision. The girls are mad for him, and Boston is full of unmarried girls, and he would most likely get into mischief.'

'Rory may seem impulsive,' said Elizabeth, 'but he really isn't. He's a very calculating young man. I don't mean that unkindly, for I am very fond of Rory, and he amuses me. I mean that whatever he does is well thought out beforehand. He studies all the advantages, all the risks, before he makes a move, and never speaks of it first. That is what makes people think he is impetuous – it just seems sudden to them, though it is not.'

'You make him sound cold-blooded,' said Courtney to his mother. 'Or mistrustful.'

They both thought of Rory's twin sister, Ann Marie. Courtney drank a little coffee. His heart had begun to beat fast. It was time that he should again speak to his mother, and when Elizabeth saw his face she became weak and frightened. But at least he would be the one to open the subject and not herself, and perhaps she could avert the final revelation.

'Mother,' he said, putting down his cup and turning his face resolutely to her, 'I talked to you about Ann Marie quite a long time ago, but you became so agitated and repeated so often that it was "impossible", that I let the matter drop temporarily. After all, I was still in school. And I was afraid that I would make you ill, you were so disturbed. Mother, what have you against Ann Marie?'

Elizabeth clenched her hands together in her lap and her green eyes fixed themselves bravely on her son. 'Courtney, I do have a reason – to object. I told you it was a most important reason. My dear, you are the only child I have. I would not have you make a mistake. There is bad blood in the Hennesseys.'

'You married one,' said Courtney. 'He wasn't so bad. In fact, he was a kind old codger, treated me like a son. Couldn't have been a better father, and I only adopted. I think he cared more about me than he did about his real child, Bernadette. If you felt that way about the Hennesseys – and you once told me you had known the Senator for a long time before you married him in Washington – why did you marry him?'

'I loved him,' said Elizabeth and bent her head.

'Did I hear past tense? Don't you still care about him, even if he is dead?'

'No. I see now it was only infatuation. Courtney, he was indeed kind and loving to you, better than most – real – fathers. But he was a bad man, Courtney, and I must confess that to you. A very bad man. In fact, he was really – criminal. It is too long a story to tell you. Bernadette is no better than her father was. She is even an evil woman, in many respects. Yes, the Hennesseys have bad blood. I don't want you even to think . . .'

'In short,' said Courtney, after a moment or two, 'you are telling me that it would be too much for you if I married Ann Marie.'

'Yes,' she whispered. She looked up at him and saw the determined pallor on his face. 'There is also the impediment.'

'Mother,' he said, holding to patience, 'there is no consanguinity, and that you know. I have discussed this matter with priests. One was doubtful. The other was sure it would be perfectly all right. Bernadette and I have no blood relationship. I am not really Ann Marie's "uncle". I am the son of Everett Wickersham, and though I am grateful that the Senator thought enough of me to adopt me and give me his name I now wish to God that you had let it be, and let me retain my real name.'

Elizabeth squeezed her white, paper-thin eyelids together in extreme pain.

'Even if there is a technical impediment, and the Church

objected, I should still marry Ann Marie,' said Courtney, with firm gentleness.

'But would Ann Marie?' asked his mother, opening her exhausted eyes again.

'I've discussed it with her. Mother, we are very much in love. She says she will marry me. And nothing is going to stop us. I don't care if her parents throw her out. I doubt Uncle Joseph would, though. Still, it doesn't matter. You can throw me out, too, if you want to. I have money of my own, which the Senator was kind enough to leave me. But, I am going to marry that girl and as soon as possible, even if the sky falls in.'

'Have you thought of the legal side of it?' asked Elizabeth, feeling that it was no use at all, and there would be no last-minute mercy for her.

'Of course, Mother! I am studying law, you know, and am taught by lawyers, and I asked about it, and they thought even the question was absurd. There is no legal impediment to our marriage.'

Elizabeth pushed herself to her feet and moved feebly to one of the windows and looked out. She said, 'You can't marry Ann Marie, Courtney. I can't bear . . . the very thought . . .'

'I thought you loved her,' said Courtney, with bitterness.

'I do,' said Elizabeth, so faintly that he hardly could hear her. She put her hand against the side of the window to support her, for she felt she would fall. 'But, there is her mother – the Hennesseys.'

'She also has another inheritance,' said Courtney. 'You once told me that her mother was a lady, a beautiful person, though you only saw her once.'

Elizabeth remembered that disastrous day, twenty-three years ago. 'So she was, Katherine,' she said. 'A very wronged woman, who was destroyed by her husband. But all the Hennessey blood has come out in Bernadette, and it is in her children, too. Rory has much of it. Would you care for children like Bernadette, Courtney?'

'No. But there is the Wickersham side, too, have you forgotten? And your side, Mother. I think we will be too much for the "Hennessey blood".'

His mother was silent. Was she really so thin and he had not noticed before, and so delicate in appearance? She still

277

had not turned to him. She was clutching the side of the window. Then she was speaking again. 'Joseph Armagh would not permit it. I know.'

Courtney stood up. 'You are mistaken, Mother. Rory and I have discussed all this. He knows his father has some affection for me. He believes there will be no objection from that quarter. And even if there is, it doesn't matter. Mother, I am soon leaving to meet Ann Marie, and we are going at once to her mother and tell her.'

Elizabeth turned so swiftly from the window that she tottered, and had to catch a curtain to support her, and her face and eyes were so filled with horror and fear that Courtney was shocked. She cried, 'You must stop her! She mustn't tell Bernadette! I know Bernadette! I know what she will say to that poor girl, and it will kill her!' She pressed her hands to her breast like one pleading for her own life. 'Courtney, in God's name, just tell Ann Marie that for several reasons – reasons – you cannot marry her. Tell her as gently as possible, and then leave her and never see her again. You are both young. You will both forget.' Her eyes were stretched and full of agonised tears.

He stood and looked at her in silence, and now the dread premonition he had felt months ago returned to him, confusing and torturing him. But he also saw his mother's frantic despair, her overwhelming suffering, her fear.

He said, 'Is that what you wanted to tell me, Mother, that I can't marry Ann Marie? Is that why you called me home?'

She nodded, unable to speak, but her eyes were imploring, begging him to agree and not ask anything else. Finally she could say in a broken voice, 'I – I felt – that you hadn't given up, that you were still determined to marry that child. So I sent for you. I knew it had to be stopped at once . . .'

'Give me one sound reason why I should not marry her, and what I should tell her. That is all I ask, Mother. A sound reason, and not an emotional or superstitious one. If I consider it sound, then I promise you I will give it full consideration, and perhaps act on it. But if it is not sound, then . . .' He spread out his hands eloquently.

'Believe me, dear Courtney, it is sound.'

'Then, tell me!' he cried, overcome with wild impatience. 'I am not a child! I am a man!'

'I can't tell you,' she said, and her lips twisted in suffering.

'If I could, I would. But you must believe me.'

He shook his head in an equal despair. 'Mother, you aren't making sense. There is no "sound" reason. The only one would be if I were really Ann Marie's uncle.'

Elizabeth fumbled for her chair, blindly, and fell into it. She leaned her elbows on the table and covered her face with her hands. Courtney stood and looked down at her. He felt suddenly paralysed. The paralysis was making his lips thick and without feeling, his throat dry and parched. He could hardly breathe. He tried to move his head, to throw off this choking, this vomitous feeling in his stomach, this melting of his body. He could not look away from his mother. He heard her weeping. It seemed the most desolate sound he had ever heard, and yet he was filled with a madness of anger and torment.

Gardeners were mowing the lawn outside and the breeze brought in the fragrance of fresh cut grass, and a boy was whistling, and the trees were rustling, and a distant dog barked and someone called, laughing, outside. But in this room was a deadly silence, the silence that follows a murder, an ugly pent silence, and it was enhanced by the light and the scent from beyond the windows.

'You should have told me, long ago,' he said, and thought he would vomit right there. 'You shouldn't have let it go so long. You should have told me, before it reached this point.'

His mother groaned from behind her sheltering hands, 'How was I to know it would come to this? I hoped you would forget, after I spoke to you before.'

'So the Senator was really my father?'

'Yes.' He could hardly hear her.

'And I was born before he married you?'

She could only bow her head. He hated her now, yet he both loved and pitied her as he had never done before. He wanted to denounce her, and he wanted to comfort her. He strangled a little and coughed, and the black desolation rose to his face, his lips and his eyes like deathly water, and he was drowning.

'And Bernadette is really my sister? God, if that isn't a frightful joke! Bernadette, Mother, she knows, too?'

'Yes,' Elizabeth murmured. 'She does.'

'Who else?'

'Joseph Armagh.'

'They are the only ones?'

279

She nodded again, her face still covered. She could speak a little more clearly, though her voice was still muffled and faint. 'Bernadette was told – what everyone else believes – but she knew right from the first that you are the son of her father. She has denied this to me, repeatedly, trying to humiliate me. But she knows the truth. And she would like to throw it into Ann Marie's face, that poor child, to hurt her, and us.'

'You should have told me, years ago.'

Elizabeth said, 'Why should I have? To brand you, to make you feel ashamed, as a child? To make you despise your mother? What purpose would that have served? If you had not wanted to marry Ann Marie you would never have known, Courtney. Can you tell me one reason why I should have told you "years ago"?' A dim astonishment stood in her eyes.

'No,' he said after a moment, 'there was no reason to tell me, until now.' He looked at his watch. 'I must go soon to meet Ann Marie. Somehow, I must tell her – something. I can't tell her the truth.' He now looked as broken and exhausted as his mother.

Elizabeth came to distraught life. 'You must tell Ann Marie not to speak to her mother – about any of this! For the girl's sake. I know Bernadette!'

'Yes,' he said. He began to turn away, but compassion took him, and he went to his mother and bent and kissed her wet cheek. She clung to him and groaned. 'I wish I had never been born,' she said. 'I wish I were dead. I would have died to save you from this, my son.'

Ann Marie had been blissful when she received Courtney's letter that he would arrive on a certain day and that he would speak to his mother, but that he would accompany her when Ann Marie 'spoke' to hers. Before that, he would meet Ann Marie in the woods and they would 'take our usual ride' in the open country. The 'usual ride' consisted of a bridle path some half mile distant from Willoughby Road, away from low-hanging limbs and up and down a moderate hill. The time of meeting was to be half past ten.

Ann Marie glanced at her boudoir clock at her bedside. It was nearly half past seven, this bright July day. Eagerly, she looked through her window. The Hennessey carriage was rolling up the driveway to the *porte-cochère*, and there was Courtney, getting out of the carriage. The girl strained at the window, her heart beating with joy and ecstasy at the distant view of her lover, his head shining palely in the sun. She could hardly bear her rapture. She wanted to run from the house, even in her nightgown, and go to Courtney and throw her arms about his neck and kiss him, and let him hold her tightly as he had done before. She closed her eyes, quickening with delight, with longing, with abysmal passion. When she opened her eyes Courtney was no longer there, and the carriage was going back to the stables.

She did not deserve Courtney, she, only a mouse. She must have courage. What a disgrace she would be to Courtney in his professional life, and his social meetings, if she shrank from everyone and hid herself as was her custom! He would be mortified for ever and come to despise her. He had told her it was not hard to be courageous, and that she must cultivate some assertion or she would suffer lifelong wretchedness. Today, she would not wait for Courtney to be beside her when she told Mama. She would begin to lose her cowardice today. When she met Courtney, as arranged, she would tell him, with superb serenity, that she had already told her mother, and he would be proud of her. She stood up, in her thin silken nightgown and looked at herself resolutely in the mirror, and she thought she saw a certain firmness there, a certain maturity, in spite of the shadowy morning image of a girl seeming much younger than her actual years, with abashed eyes and a way of averting her head, letting her hair veil her from open revelation.

Her mother breakfasted in bed at nine, luxuriously and with petulant sounds. No one ever intruded upon her there, except Papa, who rarely intruded. Ann Marie, with her new resolution, decided to intrude. Let her heart beat furiously as it did now, and her breath become painful, and her flesh weak. It did not matter. She must begin to be brave.

She bathed, brushed her long hair carefully, braided it and tied it severely with a ribbon at her nape, then put on her brown riding habit and boots. She knew she looked best in this plain and austere garb, with the jaunty brown derby on her head, and her gloves on her hands. Her awkwardness became elegance, and she was not unaware of this. She took off her hat and gloves and went down to the ornate breakfast room with its tiled floor and centre fountain with goldfish swimming in the bubbling bowl, and its rounded ceiling depict-

281

ing nymphs and satyrs and secret leafy bowers and little pools of water. The big windows were open on the hot gardens, all scarlet and rose and yellow, and long lawns. The heat of the day was rising.

The maid informed her that Kevin had already had his breakfast and was out riding. Ann Marie, who had given a thought to having Kevin present when she went to her mother, was at first disappointed, and then resolute. Yes, the time had come for her to be brave. She put her hat and gloves on an empty chair. There was a shaking in her middle but she forced herself to eat and to drink coffee. She glanced very often at the watch pinned to her lapel. Nine o'clock. She would wait until Mama had finished her breakfast. That would be at least half past nine. The maid said, 'Mrs Armagh had a telegram this morning, Miss Ann Marie. Mr Armagh will be home tonight at eight.'

'Oh, how wonderful, Alice,' said Ann Marie. She was blissful again. It would be a family gala, in spite of Mama. Fortified by Courtney, Kevin and her father, what could harm or frighten her? Once one had courage nothing could terrify. In two hours she would be in Courtney's arms, laughing happily and incoherently, her lips against his neck, safe with him, for ever rescued and secure. They would ride together in the hot day, talking of their future together as they always did. They would live in a little town house in Boston while Courtney completed his studies. Ann Marie closed her eyes, unable to endure the bright gold of her happiness. She said a little prayer of gratitude within herself. When she opened her eyes the morning, the furnishings of the room, the shine at the windows, were almost too much to bear, so brilliant were they, so tender, so promising. Mama, of course, would not suffer a small wedding. After the Nuptial Mass crowds would gather here on the lawns, and there would be lanterns and dancing and music and laughter, and she, Ann Marie, in white silk and lace and with a bridal veil, would dance with Courtney and there would be no one else in the world at all. Perhaps August the tenth. That would give Mama plenty of time. No doubt she would manage a Papal Blessing, too. Ann Marie smiled, and the maid who served her thought: Why, she is really a very pretty young lady!

Ann Marie's favourite dog, a white setter, stole into the breakfast room, which was forbidden to him, and the girl slyly fed him bits of buttered toast and a strip of bacon, while the maid frowned, disapproving. Ann Marie said, 'How did he get into the house, this monstrous creature?' She patted him affectionately and he put a paw on her knee and begged for more titbits. 'Alice, do bring him some more toast.' Her voice shook with her joy, and her throat trembled with it. She bent and hugged the dog, and kissed his snowy head and she laughed, and the maid thought: 'What's come over her this morning? She looks all shiny.'

Ann Marie said, 'Alice, would you ask Mrs Armagh's maid if I may see my mother? It is very important.'

While she waited Ann Marie paled and the trembling returned and she sat up rigidly in her chair and told herself again and again that she must be brave. For one cowardly moment she hoped that her mother would refuse to see her 'at this hour'. Then she castigated herself. There was no time like the present. If her mother did not want to see her now she would go to her anyway, and demand to talk to her. The maid returned and said that Mrs Armagh would see her daughter, though she felt unwell today. No wonder, thought Ann Marie. She eats too much at dinner. Mama ate enormously, voluptuously, passionately, as if there were some hunger in herself that could not be appeased, and drank quantities of wine so that her face became glazed and her temper vicious. Ann Marie sighed. She did not understand her mother at all.

It was time. Ann Marie stood up, put on her hat and gloves and grasped her crop. She said to the maid, 'Alice, will you ask the stable-boys to put on Missy's saddle for me, as I want to ride in half an hour?'

She went into the great white marble hall, trying to control the sudden pounding of her heart, and she ran up the white stairs admonishing herself. When she reached the top to catch her breath she felt a sudden hard chill, a darkening of everything. Then she went firmly down the upper hall to her mother's rooms, and there was a cold sweat on her forehead and between her shoulder-blades, and fear had returned to her. It was as if a ghost was walking beside her, whose face was invisible.

CHAPTER THIRTY-SIX

BERNADETTE was still in bed, a mounded figure in pink silk and lace, her hair in curlers, her flat round face reddened with food, her eyes hostile and vindictive as she looked at her daughter. But she smiled, the flesh heavily moving on its bones. As usual the coverlet was sprinkled with the crumbs of her breakfast, and a few coffee stains. She was still chewing a small creamy pastry and her lips were richly smeared, glossy with fat.

'What on earth is so important, at this hour?' she asked, and reached for her coffee cup, at which she drank thirstily. She licked her fingers and wiped them on the satin brocade cover. 'Annie, I wish you wouldn't wear a riding habit so often. It looks so mannish.' She called Ann Marie 'Annie' because it humiliated the girl and derided her, as if she were an inconsequential servant impudently climbing up from the kitchen. She sighed gustily. 'Of course, with your figure all prettiness is wasted, unless the bosom is padded with handkerchiefs.'

'Mama, I must talk to you,' said Ann Marie. There was a white line on her upper lip and Bernadette, who never missed anything, saw it.

'Talk, then,' said Bernadette, and yawned vastly.

'I've wanted to talk to you about this for a long time,' said Ann Marie, beginning to sweat in her habit yet feeling cold. Her voice trembled.

'About what?' said Bernadette. She laboriously lifted herself on the pillows and squinted at her daughter. 'What is the matter with you? You seem about to faint. Is your news so terrible?' She laughed derisively. 'What could happen to you here in Green Hills, you moping about the house and riding and gardening, like a withered spinster? At your age. I was a married woman at that age, with children. Of course, we can't expect that of you. Perhaps you want to go into a nunnery, like your addle-headed Aunt Regina?'

She looked at Ann Marie's hands. She said, 'Hasn't anyone told you that you do not wear riding gloves in the house? Take them off.'

The big gaudy room was full of hot sun and a hotter breeze. Ann Marie looked at the hovering maid, avid for gossip. 'I'd like to be alone with you, Mama,' said the girl.

Bernadette was immediately interested. She waved her fat arm at the maid and dismissed her, and the woman left reluctantly. Bernadette reached for another pastry, examined it, frowned, bit it tentatively, then devoured it, making smacking noises almost sexual in the hot quiet. 'Go on,' she said to her daughter, who was looking down at her hands, now bare.

Ann Marie said in a low voice, 'I am going to be engaged, Mama. Today.'

Bernadette sat up in a flurry. 'No,' she exclaimed. 'Is it possible? Who, for heaven's sake? Robert Lindley, who has been haunting this house, or Gerald Simpson, or Samuel Herbert or Gordon Hamilton?' Her eyes were elated, glinting, opened. 'Robert Lindley!' she cried. 'When did he propose and why didn't you tell me? He is a great catch – for someone like you, Annie, a great catch!'

Oh God, thought Ann Marie. Please help me. Her lips felt cold and damp. She said, 'None of them, Mama. It is someone else.'

'Well, tell me!' shouted Bernadette. 'Must I drag it from you? Or is it someone impossible, someone without a penny or family, who will disgrace us?' Her face darkened to crimson, and animosity danced in her eyes.

'Ma, it is someone of family, and money,' said Ann Marie. Had the sun been clouded? Why was it so chilly in here, this hot day?

'Good! Excellent! What is his name? For God's sake, girl, speak up.'

'Someone I have loved all my life,' said Ann Marie, and heard herself stammering. She looked at her mother now, imploring, hoping for kindness and mercy and affection. 'Mama, it is someone you do not like. But we love each other. No matter what happens, we are going to be married. We have talked of this for three years.'

Bernadette was angry. 'I can't imagine myself disliking any young man of family and money! What's wrong with you? I am just amazed that such a gentleman would want you – if he does – and it not all your vapourish imagination, Annie. You've talked of it for three years, and never told me? Is that respectful to your mother? Or does his mother object to the match?'

Her anger deepened. 'If he is independent, what does it matter if his mother objects? Your father is a match for anybody.'

'I know,' said Ann Marie. 'And I feel that Papa will not object. He likes the young man. But you don't, Mama. That is why I am here now, to tell you.'

Bernadette swore, as roughly as her father had sworn. 'If you don't tell me at once, my girl, I will lose my mind. Why are you so secretive? I hate secretive people, but you were always sly. Speak up!'

A thick numbness rose in Ann Marie's throat, and she was terrified. Her mother looked so – imminent. So fat, so gross, so threatening. Be brave, she said in herself. What can happen to me, except her rage? She can't kill me. Don't be such a mouse, Ann Marie, such a quaking fool.

She tried to meet Bernadette's eyes.

The room dimmed all about her. Her lips were cracking, her bones felt as if they were breaking, one by one. 'It's Courtney,' she whispered.

'Who?' said Bernadette. She craned forward, as though suddenly deafened, her big breasts spilling over her belly.

'Courtney, Mama.'

Bernadette could only stare at her daughter. The dark blood began to recede from her face, leaving it like wet dough. Her eyes sank in her fat so that they were hardly visible. Her lips turned livid. She began to heave as if smothering, her fat body shaking. Heavy clefts appeared about her mouth, and in her forehead. Her nose became very white, sunken between her cheeks.

'Are you out of your mind?' she asked, and her voice was hoarse. 'Your uncle! You must be demented.' She looked sick.

'Mama,' said Ann Marie, and then stopped. Her mother's aspect of shock, of incredulity, frightened her even more. She at last could say, 'I know you don't like him, or Aunt Elizabeth. But we love each other. We are going to be married.' It was out now, and she tried to look at her mother but Bernadette's appearance was growing more dreadful every moment. 'It doesn't matter what anyone can say,' the girl continued through her parched throat. 'We are going to be married.'

Bernadette let herself sink slowly back on to her pillows, but her eyes never left her daughter's face. She studied her. She said, 'I think the law will have something to say about that.' She was incredulous again, and now her easy rage was loosed within her. 'What are you talking about, you idiot! He is your uncle!'

'Not really, Mama.' Why was her own voice so weak, so placating, like a child's? 'Just my adoptive uncle. There is no impediment to our marriage. He is only the adopted son of my grandfather. I know you've resented him all these years, because your father adopted him. It – it was not kind. He had nothing to do with it.'

But Bernadette was still staring at her as at something that could not be believed. She seemed to have lost speech, she who was usually so voluble.

Then an evil spark began to grow in the depths of her eyes, and she sucked her lips in and out and watched her daughter, and the glazed look she wore after dinner at night spread over her face, but it was cracked now, webbed, like old china.

'Does Elizabeth Hennessey know about this?' she asked, and Ann Marie did not recognise that voice for a hideous elation lay under it, a breathless excitement, a secret and almost uncontrollable jubilation. It fascinated Ann Marie, even while her fear grew.

'No, Mama. But Courtney is here this morning, and he is going to tell her.' She hesitated. 'He wanted to come here with me, later, to tell you, too.'

Bernadette spoke softly and viciously, and looked at a distance. 'He will never dare to come here again. So he is going to tell his mother, is he? I should like to be there when he does!'

Ann Marie felt herself draining, withering away. 'Mama,' she said, 'we don't care what others will say. We are going to be married.' (If she could only stop that dreadful vibration in her legs and arms!)

'Oh, I don't think you are, I really don't think so,' said Bernadette and now she turned her jumping eyes on her daughter again. 'I don't think the law would like it.'

'Mama, you said that before. What has the law got to do with it? There is no legal impediment, and Courtney now thinks there is no religious one, either.'

'Oh, he does, does he?' Again Bernadette was smiling and exultant. 'So he doesn't know, does he? I hope his mother is telling him right at this minute. I've waited a long time for revenge on that trollop, and now it has come. That trollop, who seduced my father into marriage to give her brat his name,

287

and mine! Let her suffer now as she has made me suffer, she and that precious son of hers.'

Ann Marie stood up, and held to the back of her chair. 'Mama, I am meeting Courtney soon.'

Bernadette, again staring at her, licked the corner of her lips and a speculative and gloating look filled her eyes so that they sparkled as they had done in her youth. She seemed, for all her stare, to be coming to a decision. Then she said, 'How far has this gone, my girl? How far beyond kissing and hand-holding?'

Ann Marie's pale face turned scarlet and her face quivered. 'Mama,' she said. Watching her closely for a moment Bernadette began to nod her big head.

'Very well. You are not a strumpet like his mother.' What shall I do? she asked herself. Let her go and have him tell her, himself, ashamed and degraded? She tasted the thought and smiled. But she could not wait for later developments, and to hear it from the mouth of this silly chit. She studied Ann Marie. The maternal instinct was not entirely stifled in her though she disliked the girl and was jealous of Joseph's love for her. Well, she would have a little revenge on Joseph, too, when he saw his daughter's grief. It was a mother's place to warn and enlighten her daughter, she thought with sudden virtue, and made her face grieved and even a little sympathetic.

'Sit down, Annie,' she said. 'You will need support when I tell you what you must know. Sit down, I say. Don't stand there gaping like a dying fish. There, that's better.' The girl sat again on the edge of the chair, her feet planted firmly as if preparing for flight.

Bernadette folded her hands together like one about to pray and rested them on one fat knee. 'We all thought to spare that Hennessey woman, for the sake of her child, and her own good name. We were wrong. We should have blazoned out the truth from the very beginning, so my daughter would not have come to this pass.'

'What, Mama?' the girl whispered. She leaned forward.

'That Courtney Hennessey is indeed your uncle, my brother, my half-brother, if you will. His father was your grandfather – my father. Now, what have you to say to that, Miss?'

She waited, brutal eyes fixed on her daughter. Ann Marie did not move for a full minute, but her young face grew grey. Then she put her hand to her cheek as if it had been struck violently. Her tawny eyes had widened, dimmed.

'I – I don't . . .' She began, then coughed.

Bernadette waited until the strangling sound stopped. Pity was not completely dead in her. After all, this was her daughter, and now her old smouldering anger against Elizabeth deepened into fury.

'You mean you don't believe it, Ann Marie?' She reached out and put her hand on the habit of the girl. 'Yes, I agree it is frightful, but it is true. Your father knows. I think that is why he is coming home tonight – to help you. Courtney Hennessey had no name before my father gave him his, and he was born a year before my father married his mother. She had political influence. She forced him. We held our peace for the sake of our father's reputation. After all, he was a Senator, and scandal would have ruined him.' Now her fury blazed out. 'She seduced him while my poor mother was still alive! She tried to make my father leave my mother! She came to this house, this very house, and broke my mother's heart so that she died that night. I was there. I heard it all. She was already in a delicate condition, the drab.'

She began to cry, snuffling, and the tears were sincere and acid with hatred. 'Will there be no end to the misery that woman has caused this family? First my father, then my mother, then me, and now my daughter.' She thought of Joseph, and her tears came faster, but of Joseph and Elizabeth she dared not, even now, speak. 'I wish she were dead.'

Bernadette lifted her streaming face and gazed at her daughter and there was genuine sorrow on it, if only a little, as well as fury. 'Ann Marie, my dear child, you have been as wronged as your grandparents were wronged, and I, and I was only seventeen when it happened – when she killed my mother. She took my mother from me, and then my father, and all she had to offer was a brat born out of wedlock!'

Ann Marie stood up, that stunned grey look deepening on her face. Then, very slowly, horror brimmed her eyes and she shuddered and she held her cheeks with her hands as if mortally stricken.

'We almost eloped – last Easter,' she muttered, and shuddered again.

'And that would have been incest,' said Bernadette. 'Thank God you were spared that, and this family, and all the shame and notoriety. No decent man would have married you after

289

an incestuous marriage had been annulled. You would be worse in his eyes than a doxy. A doxy like Elizabeth Hennessey.'

Ann Marie's face now expressed nothing at all but a dazed absent-mindedness. She put on her gloves and took up her crop. She looked about her at the room, and she could smell coffee and toast and bacon and heavy scent and heat and hot wool and hot silk, and her stomach turned over. She went quickly towards the door. 'Where are you going?' Bernadette cried after her.

'I don't know,' the girl said, in a dim voice. 'I really don't know.' She stopped at the door like one bemused in a strange place, and uncertain where to go next. Her profile was as sharp as white stone. Then she had gone. Bernadette called after her and got out of bed in a sweltering flurry of lace and silk, but Ann Marie had disappeared.

Kevin was in the stables when his sister approached at a stumbling run, her habit skirt dragging unheeded in the dust, her hat askew on her head, her face agape and blank. Kevin had just returned from his ride. 'Hey!' he called to his sister, 'What is all the hurry?'

But Ann Marie, as if she did not see or hear him, was stammering to a stable-boy. 'Is my horse – Missy – is my horse ready?' She had begun to pant. Her nostrils were dilated and her eyes had a crazed expression. Kevin was suddenly frightened. He had never seen Ann Marie like this before, so distracted, so quietly frantic, so ghastly of colour. He put his hand on her arm. She appeared not to be conscious of his presence. Her slight breast was rising and falling rapidly, as if she had been running for miles.

'Ann Marie!' he almost shouted in her ear. She started away from him then, and cringed, but she did not look at him. The stable-boy was bringing her horse and offering his hand to assist her. She sprang up into the saddle and Kevin was aghast at her face. He watched her wheel the horse and race off, her skirt billowing in the breeze she created.

He said to the stable-boy, 'Quick! Bring out my horse again.'

Ann Marie was only a distant little cloud of dust now. Kevin leaped into his saddle and galloped after his sister, and he knew the first real fear of his somewhat stolid young life. Something had happened to his sister, and she had seemed out of her mind.

Courtney Hennessey, riding to meet Ann Marie, had given long and wretched thought to what he must tell the girl. He held back his own pain, which would devour him if he let it, so that he could concentrate on the alleviation of pain in Ann Marie. He could only tell her the oldest story, or lie, of all, that he was interested in another girl now, whom he had met in Boston, and that he knew, at last, that his love for Ann Marie had been the love of a brother for a sister, and not real attachment. Banal, banal, he cursed to himself. Perhaps he could say that it would be 'years' before they could marry, and that she must not wait for him, and then he would quit law school and go abroad for a year, thus putting him behind Rory and extending his studies. Then, abroad, he would not write to Ann Marie. He might even stay longer, until his acute grief and despair subsided. He might try to convince her he was a scoundrel, unfit to touch her hand. Very melodramatic, he told himself with contempt.

The woods were deep and meshed and filled with old dead leaves and moss and vines, and some of the trees were virgin timber with low boughs tangled together. No sound came from the woods, and nothing except a scent of fecund decay and a cool aromatic breath of dampness. The trail Courtney and Ann Marie took by-passed the woods and wound about them, and then descended again to the land below. Sometimes Ann Marie would bring a basket for mushrooms growing in the woods, or arbutus in the spring, or glossy chestnuts in the autumn. Courtney bent his head almost to his horse's neck as if the weight of pain was too heavy for him. Nothing that his mother had told him had lessened his love for Ann Marie. In fact, it was heightened, for now it was forbidden, and he knew that never again would he come up this hill and never know again what he had known before.

He heard the swift pounding of hoofs rising from the other trail which led up the hill and his heart pounded with torment in answer. He thought he heard following hooves, but dismissed the idea as an echo. Then all at once Ann Marie and her young mare burst up before him, as if jumping from the ground, and Courtney tried to smile and he lifted his hand.

But Ann Marie reined in her horse so suddenly that the mare half reared then fell back, whinnying in indignation. Ann Marie sat straight and high in her saddle, and her habit was lifted by a light wind, but she had lost her hat. She sat there and looked at Courtney and then he said to himself with a kind of terror, 'She knows!' He saw her face, convulsed, frightfully white and sunken, and he saw the horror in her eyes and the leaping despair and the agony. She looked down upon him and seemed to recognise him as something not of her world, not of her life, but threatening and indescribably catastrophic. It was a disastrous face that confronted Courtney.

'Ann Marie!' he cried, and spurred his horse to approach her. But she swung her mare about and in an instant she had plunged wildly into the woods, the terrified mare crashing and stumbling, rising and falling in the uneven terrain. Before Courtney could even reach the edge of the woods the girl and the horse had disappeared, leaving only echoes behind them, and smashing sounds.

She will be hurt in there, she will die in there, thought Courtney, and got off his horse and his legs shook under him. He could feel the blood driving to his heart, and cold sweat rushed out over him, and everything took on the sharp brightness and sharp shadows of nightmare and dread. He heard a shout; he hardly heard it as he ran for the woods, and then he heard his name called, and he halted. Kevin, on his own horse, had arrived. Kevin swung down and flung aside his reins.

'Where the hell is she? Where's Ann Marie?' he shouted. 'I followed her up here. She was riding like mad!'

Even then Courtney could take thought. He said, 'She just rode up, and then – then her mare bolted into the woods. She didn't say a word. Nothing.'

'Jesus,' said Kevin, and they both listened for a moment to the distant breaking and tearing sounds. Kevin's face was horrified and desperately alarmed. Big though he was, and somewhat clumsy when in a house, he ran with Courtney to the woods and they pounded into them, and were immediately drenched with dank coolness and dimness. Kevin lurched like a great black bear, native to this element, apparently lumbering but moving with sure speed, dodging tree trunks and low hanging limbs, sometimes sinking into small natural pits, jumping over stones, wading through old pungent leaves, pushing aside brush, leaping over fallen trunks, and arousing, in his passage, cries of dismay and panic from the hidden creatures who had been stricken into voice and movement by this impetuous intrusion. Courtney, who had considered himself more agile than this bulky youth, found himself panting behind him, falling once in a while, tearing his clothing on brambles and thorns, bruising and ripping his flesh, staggering against an unseen trunk in the dimness, spraining muscles in his ankles and legs, and panting and sobbing aloud.

Kevin wasted no breath on shouts and calls. His eye followed the crushed path of his sister's horse, and the branches which still swayed after her flight. He heard Courtney behind him but did not look back. He was like a battering ram in that green and sullen dimness, that twilight of entwined trees. He splattered through a little rill, and then ran faster, as if gaining new strength, and Courtney almost lost him.

Something was shrilling and screaming at a distance, and Kevin stopped a moment to listen, and then ran in that direction, with Courtney fast upon him. Now Kevin's strength and speed increased. He plunged into thickets instead of pulling them aside with his hands, which were now bleeding. He stopped only once to call, 'Ann Marie! Where are you!' Only the awful shrilling answered him, a disembodied plea, and Courtney came abreast of him and he saw the young man's broad and deadly white face like a ghost in the duskiness and the fear in his dark brown and starting eyes. 'It's her horse,' he said to Courtney. And he ran on again, with Courtney at his heels.

Then Kevin stopped so suddenly that Courtney fell against that big brown back, started to fall and had to catch the heavy muscular arm of the youth. There was a hot anguish in his right ankle, as if it were broken and his shoes were filled with water. He looked over Kevin's shoulder, and then it was as if everything deafened about him, and died.

Missy, the mare, lay sprawled near a tree, which she had struck, her legs threshing the air, her long neck outstretched, her teeth glimmering in torture, her eyes rolled up. And near her lay the broken body of Ann Marie, almost lost in that obscurity, for her habit was nearly the colour of it, and she did not move nor utter the slightest cry. Kevin saw all this. He saw that the writhing mare's hooves would soon strike his sister and he ran to her and huddled down and pulled her free and safe. She was like a flaccid doll in his hands, her hair tumbled about her in a brown veil, her arms hanging loosely. Her habit was shredded and ripped.

'Oh God, no,' said Courtney aloud, and ran to Kevin, who was gently lowering his sister to the ground again. The fearful shrilling of the mare was louder; her screams sent wing-echoes through the woods, and answering cries. The two young men bent over Ann Marie and Courtney brushed her hair from her face and for the first time he saw that the hair on her skull was matted and black and streaming with blood.

They knelt on their hands and knees above the girl, their breath loud and raucous in the cool dusk. They could see her girl's face, still and closed and shut, the tawny lashes on her white cheeks, the blood beginning to darken her forehead and temples. Courtney fumbled for her pulse, and then he burst out into the first tears he had shed since he had been a child. 'She is alive,' he said. 'We can't move her. Kevin, run down to the house and bring people up here to help us.' His voice was so quiet in contrast with his tears and his expression that Kevin looked quickly at him. 'We'll need a carriage and a door and blankets, and send someone for a doctor so he'll be there when we bring her down.'

'Tell me again,' said Kevin, and he looked at Courtney with such a face that the other man flinched. 'What happened to my sister?'

'I don't know. We always met there. We were to meet this morning. She had arrived just before you. She said nothing at all to me, though I spoke to her.' Courtney caught his breath, let it out slowly. 'Then the mare turned – she must have been frightened by something, and she ran into the woods with Ann Marie. That is all. You came right at once.'

'I saw her in the stables,' said Kevin, and he spoke precisely through his big white clenched teeth. 'Something was wrong with her. It was as if she had seen or heard something – in the house, or had been told something. Do you know?'

Courtney cursed furiously. 'Damn you, go for help, for doctors! Why are you just kneeling there and staring at me? I know nothing, except that her horse bolted. Get along now, or she'll die here. I'll stay. For Christ's sake, can't you see she's badly hurt, you glowering idiot? Do you want her to die while you jabber away?'

'I'll find out,' said Kevin, in an ominous voice, 'I don't

believe that horse bolted. I believe Ann Marie deliberately spurred her into these woods, for just this very thing.' He jumped to his feet and ran off the way he had gone and Courtney could hear the noisy slogging of his running feet.

Now Courtney was alone with the unconscious girl, whose head was bedded in a head of moss. She did not move. She lay as if already dead, so small, so rumpled, so silent and so still, so battered and torn and bleeding. The horse shrilled and screamed nearby and Courtney cried out in total anguish, 'For God's sake, be quiet, Missy! For God's sake!' But the horse threshed and shrieked and rolled in her own agony, her burnished brown hide streaming with blood.

'Who did this to you, Ann Marie?' said Courtney. 'Who could have driven you to this? For you knew, didn't you? Someone told you. Who, my love, who, my dearest love?'

Then he knew. There was no one else who could have told the girl the truth but her mother, Bernadette. Her father was not due until tonight. There was no one else but Bernadette. Ann Marie had 'spoken' to her mother after all, in spite of warnings.

She was like a child lying there in the woods, stricken and alone, thrown down, abandoned, mortally hurt, seeming to sink deeper, moment by moment, into the black leaves which were her bed. Courtney bent his head and touched her cheek with his own and he cried as he had never cried before, and something burned and shifted and lusted in him and he knew the deepest and most murderous hatred he would ever know.

His incoherent words mingled with the screaming of the dying mare, and the flutter and chatter in the trees. His voice rose, senselessly, frenzied. 'Ann Marie! Where are you? Come back, come back to me! Don't leave me.'

He did not know the precise moment when she opened her eyes and looked at him clearly, knowing him, but when he finally realised through the red haze of his grief that she was conscious he thought he would collapse with joy. He saw that she was even smiling a little, her white lips curving in the sweet smile he had always loved.

'Courtney?' she said.

He held her hands tighter. He bent over her more closely. He looked into her eyes. 'Ann Marie?' he whispered.

She looked at him trustfully. Her hands were a little warmer. He bent over her again and he kissed her softly on her mouth, and her chill lips moved in response, and her fingers tightened on his own. Her eyes were so clear, so unharmed, and even in that duskiness he could see himself reflected in the amber of them as he had so seen himself many times before. 'Dear Courtney,' she said. 'I love you, Courtney.'

Then he saw a strange thing happen. He saw his reflection retreating, moving backwards, becoming smaller and smaller in the iris of those steady eyes. Now he was but the tiniest of faces in that iris, and that face dwindled and wavered and then became a shapeless speck, and then was gone.

'Ann Marie!' he said.

But she was looking at him starkly now and with full knowledge, and without a movement or a change of expression she uttered the most awful groan, and it seemed to rise not from her lips or throat but from some vital part in her body. She closed her eyes and murmured, 'Mama told me.' She was silent.

He called her name frantically over and over, but she did not respond and he did not know if she heard him or had fallen unconscious again. There was nothing now but the screams of the tormented horse and the frightened response from the trees and the effluvia of decay and the fungus smell and a faint creaking among the trees and a growing dimness in which all things were dissolving.

Courtney lay down beside the girl and held her hand and he wished he could die there with her or that neither of them need ever again know what they had learned this day, but would awaken as if from a nightmare they had dreamed together.

PART TWO

Rory Daniel Armagh

'For they eat the bread of wickedness, and drink the wine of violence.'

—Proverbs 4:17

CHAPTER THIRTY-SEVEN

THE nightmare would never end. Courtney and Kevin and Elizabeth sat in a small parlour at the rear of the drawing-rooms in the Armagh house, in a silence too heavy to break even by a sigh or a murmur. It was nearly midnight and three physicians were upstairs in Ann Marie's room, and her father was with them, and Bernadette was under sedation in her gaudy bedroom, and the hours passed one by one. Occasionally a maid came in with fresh tea and cinnamon toast and to remove cups which had not been touched. Famous physicians had been summoned from Philadelphia, Boston and New York, by telegram, and would be arriving tomorrow. In the meanwhile Ann Marie was almost moribund. Everyone in the little parlour started and trembled at any nearby sound or distant voice, terrified to receive fatal news, hoping that Ann Marie still lived, that there was a chance for her life.

The climb down the hill had been part of the continuing nightmare, with Ann Marie laid on a door covered by blankets and herself wrapped in them, and with Kevin and Courtney riding behind. Courtney remembered, with a shudder, how Kevin had returned to him with a rifle in his hand and had efficiently and mercifully put an end to the suffering of Ann Marie's horse. He had done it without a glance of regret or sadness; it was a task to be done and so must be done. The shot had clamoured through the surly green gloom of the woods, but Ann Marie had not heard it. Then had begun the descent down the hill to the waiting victoria with a covered door hastily removed from the house, and men ready to lay the unconscious girl upon it, the men who had carefully carried her from the stubborn forest.

Courtney knew that Kevin must be told, and Kevin turned his bleak square face to the other man and his dark eyes were cold and hostile. 'Are you ready to tell me?' he asked.

So Courtney told him as tersely and as emotionlessly as possible, and in very few words. 'There is no doubt your mother told Ann Marie, though I had warned her to wait until I was with her. I didn't know then anything about the truth; I just wanted to be beside Ann Marie when your mother was told that we – that we – were going to be – married.'

Kevin had listened without any expression on his broad face. When Courtney had revealed his own blood relationship to Kevin the younger man's eyes had flickered and widened and he had stared at Courtney intently, but said nothing. If he thought anything at all about Courtney's reddened and mortified look he did not show it. They rode on slowly, when Courtney had finished, and Kevin had looked straight ahead.

'We must learn our own story, that no one said anything to Ann Marie, and that her horse had been frightened by something – a rabbit, a squirrel, a distant hunter's shot – whatever – and had bolted into the woods. We both saw it. That is our story.'

Kevin had nodded briefly and the strong hard jaw became harder and his somewhat heavy lips had tightened. He had said, at last, 'But what if Ann Marie becomes conscious, and tells him?'

'I don't think she will,' said Courtney, and he bent his head. 'She is too kind, too gentle, too understanding. She would not hurt either of her parents, not even if she died for it.'

The great gilt and teakwood clock in the hall chimed half past twelve. No one in that room had eaten a dinner, and none had been offered by the housekeeper or cook. It was as if everything had withdrawn, in that house, to one room on the second floor. The huge glittering chandelier in the hall looked down on desertion.

Then they all heard slow steps on the marble stairs and Courtney and Kevin stood up and the two young men clenched their hands and stared at the door, afraid to go into the corridor that led to the hall, and afraid not to. Then Joseph appeared in the doorway and they saw his face, grown old with anxiety and fear and dread. But his eyes were more alive than any of those present had seen them before. It was as if a fire burned behind their bitter and startling blue, and his wide thin mouth curved inwards.

It was at Elizabeth that he looked first, and she slowly rose and said, 'Joseph? How is Ann Marie?' Her own eyes were strained and brilliantly green in the lamplight, and her mouth shook.

He said to her in a rusty voice, 'She is alive, but that is all. She has not regained consciousness. They are afraid her skull is fractured and that she is bleeding internally. No bones were

300

broken, except for her left arm. One doctor has left; the others will remain until the specialists arrive tomorrow. She will have nurses then, too. They have been sent for.' He paused. 'We can only hope that she will survive the first shock.'

When they had all gone Joseph sat by his daughter, watching the faces of the physicians who ministered to her, seeing the long brown braids on her pillow, the hollow remoteness of her young profile, the arm in its sling, the bandage on her head where her hair had been shaved. He listened for her breathing. Occasionally she moaned.

It was almost dawn when – as if in a vision that stood before him in unwavering light – he saw the face of Senator Bassett, one of many men he had brought to ruin in his search for what he thought of as 'justice'. The Senator was a man of integrity who had committed suicide rather than waver from a principle and he had sent a last note to Joseph, which Joseph remembered now with the same sick feeling he had when he opened the letter. 'With my dying breath I can only say this to you', the Senator had written. 'I have laid a curse on you and none of those you cherish will ever prosper or fulfil your dreams and your hopes.'

It was ridiculous, even to remember that curse. It was, this superstition, fit only for old wives in chimney corners, cackling of banshees and the little people and omens and visitations and mouldy curses. But Joseph sat by his daughter and he thought of Senator Bassett whom he had murdered as surely as any assassin.

CHAPTER THIRTY-EIGHT

THERE was not a night that Elizabeth Hennessey did not sit upstairs at her bedroom window and watch the Armagh house. It was January now, and the lawns and the trees were covered with snow and there was a wide desolation on the sky near sunset, when a lavender shadow ran over the whiteness of the earth and the steepled spruces and the pines stood black against a coldly sparkling orange west. Not even at Christmas had lights been lit in that house, except for the upper servants' quarters, and no movement could be seen at black windows, and no coming or going. No sleigh-bells scattered thin music in the silence, chimneys smoked but desultorily; the roofs were marble under the moon. The New Year came and went, and there were no yellow opened doors, no laughter, no guests, no ball as usual.

For Joseph and Bernadette had taken their daughter, Ann Marie, to Europe in September for a hopeless round of celebrated neurologists in Geneva, Paris, Rome and London, and brain specialists. Kevin and Rory were at their university, and did not come home for the holidays. Courtney had accompanied Joseph and Bernadette during their desperate hegira until Bernadette had more than made it plain that he was unwanted and unwelcome. He was now in Amalfi and gave his mother no indication of when he would return. Elizabeth guessed that he knew of her liaison with Joseph Armagh, and that in some way, in his grief-stricken misery and confusion, he blamed her for his birth, Ann Marie's condition, and the final humiliation of her affair. Some day, she knew, when his grief was less, he would see more clearly. In the meantime she had to be satisfied with his brief cold notes to which she replied with maternal warmth and love.

It was Rory who kept her informed of the family, from letters from his mother. Joseph's letters to her were abrupt with sorrow and despair, and she knew she must not reply to them. Ann Marie could walk now, feed herself, help a nurse to dress and bathe her, but beyond that she had been reduced to the intelligence of a child of less than three, and had no memory of her past life, no memory of Elizabeth and Courtney Hennessey, and did not remember her brothers from visit to visit. She had lost the years of her education and her experience. The only clue that sometimes heartened the family was an awful and unremitting fear of horses and terror of even a small copse of trees. But as the months passed these fears began to abate so that the parents were able to take her, without a blindfold, into a carriage. So, the last hope was dwindling out, and Joseph was trying to reconcile himself to the fact that his shy and timid young daughter would remain an infant for the rest of her life. Once only he wrote to Elizabeth: 'It were better if she had died, for though her bodily health has been restored and she is becoming quite plump, her mental faculties do not increase. The only consolation I have is that she is seemingly contented, as she was

302

as a very young child, and laughs and plays as that child, and is docile and affectionate, and, above all, happy with the innocence of childhood. Her lineaments and colour are those of a young child. Who knows but what this is kinder to her than maturity, and growing old and bitter and disillusioned and sad, and full of the fears of maturity? At least she will never know these, never know loss or discontent or wretchedness. She is in the Limbo about which we were taught by the priests, that is, in a state of "natural" happiness where there is no darkness, no fright, no longing, but only affection and kind words and care.'

Rory wrote Elizabeth that the family expected to return in the spring with Ann Marie. Doctors had strongly urged that the girl be placed in 'a comfortable retreat with those other unfortunates who had been born in that condition, where she will receive professional solicitude and be taught simple tasks and be among her own kind'. Bernadette had eagerly agreed, thinking of the melancholy presence of her daughter in her house, with attendant nurses and constant comings and goings of physicians, and 'disruptions', as Rory quoted his mother. But Joseph had refused. His daughter would live and die in her home.

In early January Joseph cabled his son Rory: 'Meet me in London on the 17th this month.'

Damn, thought Rory. Has some doctor given him some new hope? No, that is not like the Old Man. It is something else. Pa is one of the kind that doesn't 'hope', and I'll give him credit for that. He's too realistic.

He said to his wife, Marjorie: 'I have to leave you for a while, my love, for my father is asking me to go to him in London.' Marjorie said, with spirit, 'Take me with you. I'd like to meet your father. Yes, dear, I know. You still have your education to complete and you are Papa's puppet and are afraid to let him know that you are married to a descendant – lateral – of Paul Revere. It would lower the tone of your family.' She added, pensively, 'I wonder what Daddy would think of all this. I really do.'

'Maggie, don't be a shrew.'

Marjorie smiled sweetly. 'That is always the crushing answer of a man, isn't it? It's supposed to make a wife grovel.' She threw herself into his arms and cried, 'Rory, Rory! Just don't stop loving me! Just go to your father and remember I am here, waiting. Rory, I'd die for you. And isn't that something I should be ashamed of? Never mind. Kiss me.'

Rory knew that nothing could be so dank, dark, cold and miserable than England in winter, so wet and depressing, so foggy and smoky, with every chimney-pot thickly and turgidly spewing out black soot and the stench of coal gas, and with a sky hardly lighter. However, he liked sea journeys and the ship was comfortable and luxurious – Rory had hounded 'old' Charlie Devereaux for first-class fare, something which Joseph did not approve of for 'profligates'. So Rory had a fine state-room all to himself, his breakfast in bed, a place at the Captain's table, and a chair on the sheltered portion of the promenade deck.

Rory hardly liked the captain better than the captain liked him, but Rory was not a man who cultivated dislike and grudges and prejudices as a matter of course. It was too time-consuming, when there were more interesting things to notice and enjoy, particularly the company of a very young lady who sat at his left hand and who was accompanied by a strict middle-aged lady with an enormous bosom glittering with jet, a face like a partly domesticated harpy with a suspicious mind and a dark little eye 'like a snake's', the jovial Rory remarked to himself. Rory learned almost at once that the interesting young girl was Miss Claudia Worthington, and that she was the daughter of the Ambassador from the United States of America to the Court of Her Majesty, Queen Victoria – the Court of St James. She had had a bad 'chill' in the winter and had just recovered, but was not returning to her finishing school in New York, where she was in her last term, but was going to 'Papa and Mama' in London 'for the summer, and journeys to Devon and Paris'. Miss Lucy Kirby, the formidable harpy, was her chaperon and had been her governess, and was also her personal attendant.

Claudia was only sixteen, but a knowledgeable and sophisticated sixteen, for she knew the value of position and money. Rory thought her affected at first, or even not very well-bred, for there was a certain exaggeration of gentility and ceremony about her. She wore gloves at all times, and took them off only at the table, to reveal hands which were not at all elegant or even pretty, and had large knuckles and hard angles.

But Rory saw almost at once that she was not conscious of the imperfections of her hands, and that she wore gloves all the time as the mark of a lady who also had a Position.

His first impression of Claudia Worthington was that she was not in the least pretty or enticing, but 'foreign' in appearance, and he was not sure that he liked 'foreignness' in women. She had an angular face with broad cheekbones and deep hollows under them, a straight, somewhat arrogant nose, a very broad, pink mouth, and tilted eyes which made him think of them as 'Oriental'. They were of an unusual colour, dark greenish brown. Her eyebrows were abnormally thick and black and almost met at the bridge of her nose, and were tilted also. She had a strong and obstinate chin with a dimple. She is a sullen piece, Rory had thought the first day, and had decided to ignore her.

Then, at dinner, he was startled. It was not that she wore anything unusual. The mauve silk gown with its pearl-beaded bodice decorated with a jewelled watch was stylish enough and enhanced her figure. It was something else. He found he could hardly look away from this unpretty girl, with the pouting pink underlip and the very unprovocative profile. Just when he had decided that she was quite ordinary in appearance, he found himself thinking, 'Why, she is exotic, captivating, unusual!' The next instant she was only a schoolgirl on holiday again, chattering about something inconsequential in her rather light and immature voice, a voice quite infantile. She had a mannerism of hurrying too fast in her speech so that her words ran together, then catching her breath in a rush. Sometimes her voice was inaudible, though her lips continued to move rapidly.

It was this quality of hers – to appear commonplace at one moment then inordinately esoteric the next – without a feature changing – which was entrancing.

In the days that followed Rory tried to fathom the secret of bona fide charm, but it was not to be known, nor analysed. But Rory noticed that she never failed to mention the financial position of anyone she spoke of, or quoted, or their social eminence.

Claudia and Miss Kirby were met at Southampton by two of the Ambassador's attachés. Claudia graciously introduced them to Rory, and mentioned that his dear Papa was the famous Joseph Armagh, and Rory was invited to accompany the party in their special coach to London. But Rory had had, for the present, quite enough of Miss Worthington, for all her charm, and hastily excused himself and disappeared.

He avoided Claudia and her party at the great and thunderous and smoky station in London, and found himself a hack and was on his way to the sombre if luxurious hotel at which Joseph usually stayed in the city. As Rory feared, it was dank and rainy and dark in London, and a foggy mist brooded over it, and black umbrellas glistened everywhere on the milling streets and the omnibuses splashed through puddles and there was the pervading stink of coal gas. Even the shop lights looked dim and dreary.

The hotel was huge and old, ponderous and comfortable, and, thank God, there was a large fire in the fireplace in the lobby and so the interior was just a little warmer than it was outside. The suite was enormous, and thank God again, filled with firelight and lamplight and blessedly warm. Rory knew that his father could not bear the cold, but he did not know why. He could only be grateful. He saw at once that Joseph had grown much older, and was thinner than ever, though controlled as usual. The broad stripes of whitish-grey in his thick russet hair had widened. He greeted his son as though he had seen him but the day before. But Rory said, 'How is Ann Marie? Is she, and Ma, with you?'

'They are in a sanatorium in Paris,' said Joseph. 'Ann Marie? She is the same. Rosy and healthy, flourishing.' He paused. He looked down. 'She will never recover her mind. We are reconciled to that now.' His closed face did not change but there was a sinking about his mouth. 'I am here for only a few days, Rory. On business. It is time that you were introduced to – the men who matter.'

'The ones I met in New York?'

'No. You saw only the Americans. Now you will meet the international . . .' He stopped. Then repeated, 'The men who matter.' He explained no further. They had a sumptuous dinner in their private dining-room but Rory noticed that his father ate very little. But then, he never did. He hardly touched the wine, which Rory drank with gusto, his ruddy face becoming even more ruddy. From time to time his father studied him acutely if not openly. The fires crackled; the scent of roast beef and Yorkshire pudding and kidney pie was comforting.

Rory liked to make his father smile and forget his sombreness. So in his lively and amusing way he told him about

Claudia. 'The Ambassador's daughter?' said Joseph, show-ing some interest. 'A chit, you say? The Ambassador. That sod.'

It was rare for Joseph to utter obscenities, and Rory was immediately interested. 'I thought he was an old friend of yours, Pa.'

'Friend? I have no friends,' said Joseph. He studied his still-filled wine glass. 'Except, perhaps, for Harry Zeff and Charles Devereaux. I have – acquaintances. I recommended Steve to certain people, and the President. He owes me a lot.'

'If you have such a low opinion of him why did you recom-mend him?' asked the inquisitive Rory.

Joseph looked at him with pent impatience. 'Haven't you learned yet, from all that I have already told you, that politics is entirely removed from personalities, boyo? Do you think I, and the men I know, go about recommending good men of character and integrity? Don't be a fool, Rory, and disappoint me. Such men would not serve our purposes in the least. We pick the men who will serve us. The Ambassador has power in the other party, too, for he is a rich man though not a man I'd want to see in the company of my daughter.' The darkness deepened on his face as he thought of Ann Marie. 'Nor with a young son of mine, either. He can help, when you run for Congressman, a few years from now.'

Surfeited, drowsy, comfortable, Rory leaned back in his chair and his pale blue eyes were apparently candid. 'Pa,' he said, 'why do you want me to be a Congressman, then a Senator, perhaps a Governor, or, as you used to say, President of the United States of America?' He smiled as at some happy jest, but his father gave him one of his fierce glances and Rory no longer smiled.

'I thought I told you,' said Joseph, in slow but emphatic words. 'The country that would not accept me and my family, the country which rejected me, the country which despised me – it will accept my sons as Representatives, Senators, or what-ever. That will be my . . .' He stopped, sipped a little wine.

Rory was uneasy. 'But you are accepted now, Pa. It was a long time ago.'

'It will never be "a long time ago",' said Joseph, and his long thin fingers clenched into a fist on the table. 'We Irish have long memories.'

And black ones, too, thought Rory, who had no black

memories and no memory of pain at all.

'Tell me again about that girl, Claudia,' said Joseph, and Rory was startled. But he talked merrily of Claudia Worthington, and did not notice that Joseph was watching him closely and that occasionally he drew in his mouth as if deeply thinking. Sometimes he smiled, and always he watched as Rory, a little drunk now, gave a very colourful picture of the young lady, and tried to describe her fascinating and elusive quality.

'You were impressed with her then, I am thinking,' said Joseph.

Rory considered. 'She is not pretty, and then she is suddenly beautiful,' he said. 'But she isn't quite seventeen. One of these days she may be a remarkable woman, though she hasn't the brains of a gnat.'

'Brains aren't necessary in a woman,' said Joseph. 'In fact, they are detrimental. You should have accepted their offer of the private coach.'

'Why?'

'Damn it!' said Joseph. 'Do I have to spell every word out for you, you young idiot?'

The dining-room was hot now and full of the scent of food and wine and spring flowers. But all at once Rory was cold, even shivering, with a sick premonition.

Joseph stood and Rory stared up at him. Joseph said, 'I thought I taught you that you must never let a single opportunity go by, but always make use of the smallest. The Ambassador's daughter is not a small opportunity. Remember that.'

CHAPTER THIRTY-NINE

'T H I S,' said Joseph, 'is where the Committee for Foreign Studies meets regularly, in London.'

Rory knew all about the international Committee for Foreign Studies, for he had seen its discreet American quarters from the outside, on Fifth Avenue in New York. Nothing proclaimed its presence. His father had shown him one day. 'Here,' he had said, 'and in their quarters in other capitals, lives the real power of the world, and here it is decided what the world will do.'

Rory knew that the Committee for Foreign Studies had some three hundred members in nearly every country in the world, all bankers or industrialists, politicians and financiers, and that they had meeting places in every capital and that those meetings were discreet and unostentatious and that the general public was unaware of them. The meeting place in London was an old and decorous mansion of grey stone and ostensibly owned by a British banker who lived alone and was reputed to be a bachelor by his neighbours.

They controlled interests in almost all the important newspapers in the world, appointed writers for those newspapers, and editors, directed editorial policy. They were the real owners of publishing houses, of magazines, of all the media that guided public information. They were the ones who really appointed the Cabinets of Presidents, and the Ministers to government in nearly all other countries. They controlled elections, built up their candidates, financed them, everywhere in the world. Any presumptuous or intrepid man who did not meet with their approval was lampooned in the press, discreetly libelled, or 'exposed'. The politicians, themselves, were often quite unaware of who had advanced or destroyed them. Even Presidents did not always know. Kings and emperors sometimes were vaguely aware of the momentous shadow that hung over their thrones and decided the destinies of their nations, and many were quite convinced that should they denounce that shadow they would be exiled, or perhaps even assassinated. The grip on events was not iron, but it was equally pervasive and persuasive, as soft and silent as mist which concealed invincible armies. They were never quoted in the press concerning politics or wars or other policies. There was never any public opinion except through their mannikins, who were excellently chosen for their popularity with the people. It was possible that only Popes knew who and what they were, for the Vatican, too, had listening posts in every capital, but by a peculiar coincidence if a Pope hinted of what he knew, an anti-clerical movement began in chosen countries and the Pope found himself in quite a desperate situation. The gentlemen had many weapons and never hesitated to use them, on kings, emperors, princes, Popes and Presidents. Sometimes it needed but one emphatic event. Sometimes it needed *coups d'état*. But whatever was needed was ruthlessly and invincibly employed, not only as a punishment but as a warning to others. Revolution was one of their weapons, and 'popular uprisings', and incendiarisms and attacks on the forces of law and order.

The Invisible Government controlled public opinion over assassinations. They sometimes made the murdered man a hero – and attributed to him opinions which only confirmed their own powers. All that he had wished to warn his people against was obliterated in a rose-shower of sentimentality, or was perverted against those who had stood with him in fighting the enemies of his country.

This Rory learned on the January day he met the dangerous men in London and began to understand them. They did not speak of 'assassinations', for they were delicate gentlemen, and decorous. But the implications were there. They did not speak of controlling governments. They spoke of 'information' and 'guidance' to rulers.

'They are all bastards,' Joseph had told his son. 'They are, without doubt, the wickedest men on earth, though I am sure they would be astonished to hear they were wicked. They might even be outraged. Many, I am sure, even believe in God and support churches, and this is no hypocrisy on their part. I remember what Disraeli, the Prime Minister of England, said about them, with some surprise, "The world is governed by very different personages from what is imagined by those who are *not* behind the scenes!" I believe he had a little success, for a time, in opposing them, but it was no use. It is like opposing Mount Everest.'

'But they didn't assassinate him,' Rory had said.

'No. Perhaps, being a brilliant and astute man, he discovered too much about them, which his heirs, and his Monarch, might have made public. I believe I heard something about that, years ago. I also heard he was an enormous cynic – and who can blame him? Had he exposed them, do you think the people would have listened?'

Rory had thought. Then he had said, 'You are one of the richest men in America, Pa. Perhaps those bastards served your purpose once, but now you don't need them. Why not get out?'

'You don't resign from a club like that,' Joseph had said, with a twitch of his mouth. 'To use another metaphor, I have a tiger by the tail, and you know what happens to a man who lets go of the tail.'

'But you want me to know them, and for them to know me?'

Joseph had considered him a few moments. 'Yes. They can make you, Rory. They can make you President of the United States of America, though you'd never see a hand of them anywhere, or hear one of their voices, or catch a glimpse of them. And – they could destroy you, too, and no one would ever know who did it.' He really smiled then. 'Don't be afraid of that, though. I, like Disraeli, know too much about them.'

'And all I'd have to do is serve them like a good little valet? Is that it, Pa? An obedient little servant. Never questioning. Running about with a silver salver.'

Then Joseph's face had become bleak. 'Aren't we all servants in one way or another? Don't be a fool, Rory.' There were those who were always silenced by Joseph's ambiguous remarks, or confused by them, but Rory was not among them, a fact which Joseph did not as yet know. 'You should never have joined them in the first place, Pa.'

'Idiot,' Joseph had replied, and he was smiling again. 'Without them I'd really not be what I am. And what I am is what I have lived for, all the days of my life.'

When they were in their carriage returning to the hotel after meeting the Committee, Joseph said – for Rory, the voluble, was uncharacteristically quiet: 'What do you think of all that, my bucko?'

'You've told me a lot about them before, Pa. But now I've seen them. A couple are not much older than I am, yet they all look old. Is it the portrait of Dorian Gray in reverse? Are they young somewhere else?'

'Don't be frivolous,' said Joseph, who knew his son was not. 'I've told you: the majority of them are good Christian gentlemen, with quiet secluded homes and devoted families. If you asked them just what they are they would answer that they are a fraternal organisation engaged in the business of consolidating the world under one government in the name of peace and tranquillity and orderly society. Call – us – a mutual aid organisation, too.'

'You are quite right, Pa,' said Rory, after a moment. 'They are, in fact, sons of bitches.' He looked genial again. 'I don't think they liked some of your remarks, and I don't think they entirely trust you, which is regrettable, isn't it?'

'Just don't talk so much,' said Joseph, and frowned. 'Men's

lives have hung on their tongues. Make no mistake: these men are the real rulers of the world, as I've told you before. They didn't give you their names today, but eventually they will. Yes, they will.'

CHAPTER FORTY

JOSEPH and Rory went to the Ambassador's ball, in the American Embassy, a huge grey and gloomy building which was, however, adequately heated – for which Rory was grateful. There was no man present, he thought, who looked as distinguished as his father in his formal clothing, and he noticed that the gorgeously clad ladies noticed that fact also. Was it his detached and impassive look, his air of restrained strength, his dispassionate conversation, his cold courtesy? Rory had no answer, but his eyes followed Joseph with admiration.

The American Ambassador, his Excellency, Mr. Stephen Worthington, was the gayest and most vivacious of all, and he had, Rory observed, his daughter's magnetism. He was always surrounded by swirling groups, sparkling and flattering. His lady was a dun little person in a dim grey gown, and had a way of seeking corners.

Claudia, of course, was there, in girlish gauze and white silk with a slim diamond necklace and a diamond bracelet, all in the best of taste and not ostentatious. Rory danced with her, and tried to avoid looking at her directly, for then he was disarmed and fascinated, again and again attempting to fathom her elusive charm. She chattered breathlessly, as she danced, pointing out 'distinguished persons', and hardly uttering a sentence when she did not mention 'dear Papa', and what this noted gentleman had said of Papa and what Papa had said to him, and how Papa was so graciously received by all the European monarchs, and how attached Her Majesty, Queen Victoria, was to him, she who did not particularly care for Americans. Why, only a year ago she had come out of her widowed seclusion to be present here at a ball, and she stayed all of fifteen minutes! 'Remarkable,' said Rory, trying not to look at her, and trying to concentrate only on that silly infantile voice which was sometimes inaudible in its breathlessness. She smelled of jasmine, and for ever after Rory hated that scent. He thought of Marjorie, and her naughty bantering, and her telling little jokes, and ached.

He danced with a multitude of ladies, young and old, even his shy and frightened hostess. He was gallant, dashing, handsome. Younger feminine eyes followed him, and so did older eyes, lovingly. He was witty, bright, courtly. He hardly seemed American, thought many, forgiving him. Gentlemen found him surprisingly adroit and informed and intelligent. He had surreptitiously visited the one small table which held 'vulgar' whisky, and he had visited it several times. He felt the need for it, though Joseph had often warned him that 'the creature' was direful for Irishmen.

Joseph, who never missed anything, was quite aware that his son was visiting, too often, that secluded and a little shameful table with the whisky. He also noticed that Miss Claudia was pursuing him with girlish ardour. He also saw that Rory was dexterously trying to avoid her, and he frowned.

He waited until the next morning when Rory was painfully sober before he made any comment. 'Distasteful as reality often is,' Joseph said then, 'we have to face it.'

Now he is going to suggest something really disagreeable and appalling, thought Rory and blinked at his father rosily.

'The Ambassador and I had a few minutes of conversation last night, before you almost disgraced yourself and had to be helped to our carriage by two footmen,' said Joseph. 'A very interesting conversation.'

I bet, thought Rory, but he looked at Joseph with genuine affection.

'We came to the conclusion – after observing a few incidents – that a marriage will be arranged between you and Miss Worthington, say a year or so from now.'

Rory became very still. The fork lay in his hand without moving. The heavy eyes were fixed. Rory felt sick again. 'I don't like her,' he said. 'She's foolish and silly and without brains, and she bores me to death. I wouldn't marry her if she was the last woman on earth.'

Joseph leaned back in his chair, but he was tense. 'I knew you'd say that, bucko. What does all that matter? Are you looking for hearts and flowers, for God's sake? Are you romantic?' and he looked as if he wished to spit. 'Romance, and love, are for children and imbecile young girls, not for

313

intelligent adults. Do you think I loved your mother, or found her intelligent and full of witty conversation? Men don't consider these things when they are planning on an advantageous marriage. Only adolescent Americans want what they call "love". No wonder marriage is in such a bad state in America, with all that moonlight and roses and summer breezes! They're a bad foundation for a judicious marriage, with advantages.'

'You can't marry a woman who revolts you,' said Rory.

'Does she that? I saw you staring at her as if she were a basilisk,' said Joseph. 'When she danced with someone else you still stared after her.'

'I couldn't help it,' said Rory. 'She's got that damned something or other – I don't know. But I can't stand the girl, honestly. To be honest again, it wouldn't be fair to her, either.'

The sleet hissed against the windows, the air darkened, the wind rose, and the fire rose also. Joseph considered his son. Then he said, 'But you are going to marry her just the same, Rory. That does not mean you have to be faithful to her. There are other women.'

'Suppose I wanted to marry one of them?' asked Rory.

For the first time that Rory could recall Joseph looked away from a direct confrontation. He stared at the windows. 'You don't,' he said. 'Not unless you want to throw your career away. Or the lady is unwilling. Or there are – impediments.'

So Aunt Elizabeth was 'unwilling', thought Rory, and felt compassion for his father.

'It is settled, then,' said Joseph. 'You will marry Miss Claudia within two years.'

Rory's facial muscles bulged about his full-lipped mouth. He played with his fork. He said, 'I want to marry someone else. We – we are practically engaged.'

Joseph stood up abruptly. 'Who, for Christ's sake, you idiot?'

'A girl I met in Boston. A wonderful girl, intelligent, dear, beautiful, kind, and generally adorable,' said Rory. 'A girl of a rich Boston family, who'd grace our name, to use an old-fashioned expression.'

'Who?' repeated Joseph, and his voice was pouncing.

'You don't know her, Pa,' said Rory, and now he was

314

frightened. That damned whisky. It could surely betray a man. 'It really isn't official. I–I am just playing with the thought. A lovely girl. You'd like her.' He had an idea. 'Her father opposes the alliance.'

Joseph's face blackened. 'He does that, does he? One of those Boston Brahmins who despises the Irish, and Papists?'

'I think I'm bringing him around,' said Rory.

'You mean you are humiliating yourself – you, the son of Joseph Armagh?' Joseph's look was dangerous. 'A Boston chit, a miss with dainty little manners! Money, you say? How much?'

'Not as much as we have. Her father is a member of an old Boston law firm. His father, and grandfather, established it. He is quite wealthy. No money problems there.'

Joseph slowly sat down. His voice was too quiet. 'Have you spoken for the lady already?'

'No.'

'Have I met her father?'

Rory hesitated. 'I don't know. Perhaps.'

'I know them all. I must have met him, if he's a lawyer – and rich. Now, listen to me, boyo. The day you become engaged to Miss Claudia Worthington I will give you two million dollars. The day you marry her you will receive ten million. Can your Boston chit match that?'

Rory was silent.

'If you reject Miss Claudia,' said Joseph – 'and listen to me carefully – you will not be my son any longer. You will receive nothing more from me, living or dead. Is that perfectly clear?'

Oh God, thought Rory, thinking of his fifty dollars a month and Marjorie's thirty and of the dreary little flat in Cambridge which was his heaven. He said, trying to smile, 'Claudia is only sixteen. Well, nearly seventeen. We'll have a year or so to consider, won't we?'

'True. In the meantime you will not see the Boston lady any longer – unless she is willing to oblige you, outside of marriage. Some of these Boston ladies are quite – ardent – let us say, for all their hoity-toity manners and "family".' Joseph smiled unpleasantly.

Rory said, 'I still have to complete law school.'

'Who says you do not? In fact, I insist on it. When you pass the bar the marriage will take place.' Joseph slapped the table with an air of finality. 'It is settled, then, though it was settled last night between Steve and me. A most suitable marriage, and the girl is obviously infatuated with you, though I cannot tell why.' Joseph invited Rory to smile with him, and Rory finally succeeded in doing so. His back, or something, was aching like a fever in him, or as if broken. Just let me finish law school, he thought. That's all I want. Then the hell with everything else, and I'll have my Maggie.

I'll find out, thought Joseph. I'll set Charles on this at once, and a few other of my men. We've got to stop it before it becomes serious.

Maggie, thought Rory. He also thought of the ominous men he had met, and he remembered how he had planned, in the future, to circumvent them. He dropped his aching head in his hands and was nauseated again. But he was by nature optimistic. He had a year, perhaps two years, and who knew what would happen in that time?

What would his father say, and do, when he discovered that his son was already married? Rory did not underestimate Joseph. He knew his father would stop at nothing. The only solution, then, was not to let him even be suspicious, and to wait until he, Rory, had passed his bar examinations. Rory saw the men of the Committee for Foreign Studies, and he felt that he had committed an act of absolute betrayal, though he could not understand why at this agitated moment.

CHAPTER FORTY-ONE

FOR the first time in his life, as he crossed the tumultuous and angry grey Atlantic on his way home, Rory Armagh felt the need of a confidant. It was not so much the thought of the bankers and giant financiers – including some noblemen – whom he had met in Europe, which so disturbed him, but the implications and ramifications of their growing power. He remembered that the Committee for Foreign Studies was mainly an American establishment, with a branch in England, and that the Committee was only part of a whole, under different names in different nations and with different nationalities. In America, there were at least five generals who were members of the Committee. The vast interlocking organisations, with their one aim and their one mind, was what was so appalling to Rory, and their brotherhood control of politicians.

Rory's only confidant now was his father, who was also his teacher, however wry and derisive in his remarks concerning his colleagues. Rory no longer asked Joseph why he belonged to the Committee for Foreign Studies, and the infamous Scardo Society in America, composed of intellectual radicals. For he knew that in a distorted way this was Joseph's revenge on a world which had so frightfully abused him as a child and youth, and, worst of all, had forced him to deny his very intrinsic identity. This had been an assault not only on his physical survival but on his spirit. Was this true also of the other men? Rory did not know.

Sometimes Rory asked himself: Doesn't our own government know? If they do not, then they are fools. If they do know, they are traitors. Which is worse?

His other confidant, besides his father, who had warned him not to speak to anyone of what he had superficially learned in London, was Courtney Hennessey, in whom he had usually confided more than in anyone else, even Marjorie. But Courtney was immured in Amalfi, damn him! and even if he were not he must never know what Rory already knew. However, he would have been a 'comfort'. His normality, his cool common sense, his lack of hysteria and impulsiveness, would have been soothing to Rory, might even have given him some assurance that the normal people far outnumbered the villains – which Rory frequently doubted anyway.

He began to drink, not only at the table in the great dining-room on the ship, but in his state-room. He began to brood, and all the deep melancholy of the Irish mysticism invaded him. But when he appeared on the decks and in the public rooms there was none gayer, more voluble, more full of jokes and twinklings and laughter, than Rory Armagh. None of this was simulated, but was genuine as of the moment. Yet his character became more and more firmly knitted, and much of the amiable embroidery of it was slowly but steadily discarded from the fabric. He felt this change in himself, and was not certain he liked it. He knew the potentialities for this change had always been in him, but he had kept them under control until now.

He discovered a complaisant and fairly well-known young actress on board, accompanied by an enormous amount of trunks and a personal maid, and within four days he had found himself happily admitted to her bed. They drank champagne together, and laughed, and romped, and for hours, sometimes, Rory could forget the 'deadly quiet men', as his father had called them, and what he was nebulously deciding to do about them in the future. Never once, as he lay entangled with the pretty young actress, did he feel that he was unfaithful to Marjorie. Marjorie lived on a different plateau in his life. In New York, he said a loving and joyful farewell to the actress and proceeded to Boston and to Marjorie.

His mind had been taken up with its unique glooms and dismays and horrors on the ship, with the exception of the hours of interlude with the actress, and so he had not given too much thought to his predicament concerning Marjorie. Indeed, the predicament was really his father. He never once considered giving up his young wife, whom he adored. Now, as he entered the miserable little flat in Cambridge this new problem asserted itself with black anxiety.

Marjorie was waiting for him, for he had sent her a telegram from New York. She had lit fires and filled the dun rooms with hot-house flowers, from her father's own conservatory. She had arranged a fine dinner. When Rory saw her he felt a blaze of emotion in himself, delight, joy, peace, and wholeness. Her neat little figure, so trim and without a sign of fussiness, was clad in a white silk shirt-waist, very severe, even with cuff-links, and buttoned down the front with little pearls, and a black silk skirt. Her dark pompadour kept breaking out into tendrils about her saucy little face, with the smooth olive cheeks just touched with apricot, and her black eyes were huge and dancing. She threw herself into his arms and he caught the scent of lemon verbena, and the fragrance of her young body. He swung her up in his arms and danced about the rooms with her and she kissed him and laughed and protested, and clung to him.

Immediately he forgot everything, or at least all he feared stood at a sombre distance in his mind, not permitted to invade this beatitude of being with Marjorie. He must tell her all about his journey, whom he met, what he said and did – and, after a pause – how was his father?

He evaded the answers for a while during which he triumphantly waved a long blue velvet box under Marjorie's little

318

nose. While she jumped and struggled for it, and her mass of curls fell down her back, and she shouted, he laughed and settled the answers to her questions in his mind.

It seemed that Joseph, to give his son an idea of the comforting feeling of wealth, had presented him with a cheque for two thousand pounds. Stunned by all these riches, Rory had gone shopping for a trinket for Marjorie on Bond Street. His first impulse was to spend it all on the trinket, but his natural prudence, hidden under all that generous outpouring of humour and *laissez-faire*, advised him that he might need some of that money in Boston, too. So he had spent one thousand juicy pounds on a beautiful opal and diamond necklace for Marjorie, with a pair of ear-rings to match. Capturing the box at last Marjorie opened it eagerly and screamed with delighted shock at the magnificence, and her little fingers trembled and her eyes glowed as she fastened the jewellery at neck and ears. Rory watched her with such an inner bulging of his heart that his eyes filled with moisture.

'Where on earth did you get the money?' cried Marjorie. 'You must have stolen it!'

'Hard though it may be to believe, Papa gave it to me,' said Rory. Marjorie's face went blank. She looked at him slowly. 'Oh, Rory, you told him then?' Her own eyes became moist with relief.

'Yes, I told him – in a way,' said Rory. 'I had to break it easy to the old boy. I told him that I was practically engaged to a chit of a Bostonian girl, of fairly good family, and of some mediocre intelligence, and sometimes pretty.'

'Rory, behave yourself. You must tell me. What did he say?'

'Well, my love, he reminded me I have to finish law school. I didn't tell him we were already married.' Rory paused. 'That would have been a little too much at that time for him to digest. So I let it rest there.'

Marjorie's black eyes sharpened on him. 'Just what does that mean, rascal?'

'It means that we get him used to the idea that we have – plans.'

'Fiddlesticks! I know you, Rory. You are hiding something.'

Rory spread out his hands disarmingly and nothing could have been more candid and boyish than those light blue eyes. 'You wrong me, sweetheart, you really do. I have told you all there is. I did tell Pa that your father was a distinguished lawyer in Boston, and he asked if he knew him and I said I didn't know. I didn't mention names. I thought it best; let him mull over what I'd already told him.'

Marjorie stood on tiptoe to kiss his mouth warmly. 'Rory, you never exactly lie, but often you don't exactly not lie, either. You are a very wily Irishman. You tell people only what you want them to know, and not a word more or less, and let them make of it what they will. Even me.'

'You don't trust me,' said Rory, with an air of injury.

'Of course I don't! Do you think I am a fool? Never mind, my pet. Do let me see what I look like in the crown jewels.' She ran to a dusty mirror and preened in the low lamplight and firelight, and the gems glistened and sparkled in a very satisfactory fashion. 'But how shall I explain them to Papa?' she asked.

'Hide them. Wear them just for me,' said Rory, and took her hand and led her into the tiny bedroom, while she protested very mildly and mentioned roasting beef.

Marjorie completely forgot to ask Rory what the business had entailed in London, which was just as well because Rory could never have told her.

When he returned to his rooms at Harvard he found a telegram waiting for him, which had been delivered just that day. He read it over and over, disbelievingly, aghast. He actually trembled. Then he sent his father a cable: 'Uncle Sean died this morning cable funeral arrangements.'

Sean Armagh, who had continued his 'professional name' of Sean Paul during his concerts and recitals, kept a suite of rooms in a Boston hotel for when he was present there, which was often. 'For here it was, in this Athens of the West, where I was discovered,' he would say, with a soft theatrical gesture of his thin white hand. It was not hard for him to fill his eyes with tears at will, for he was by nature emotional, and people in Boston were always touched. It was a large suite of several rooms in an old but grand hotel full of gilt and rose damask and marble stairways, and he occupied it with his business manager, Mr Herbert Hayes, a large portly man of much presence and much brown hair and much jewellery, about forty-four years old, also a bachelor. Though considerably younger than Sean he treated Sean as if he were a child, and a not very intelligent child, and bullied him, was proud of him, and loved him. He arranged everything for his client, and Sean had nothing to do but practise and sing and enrapture audiences, and read *billets-doux* from ladies.

Joseph, not having had the advantage of an academic education, not having ever resided in a college dormitory, nor having ever been a member of a fraternity, did not know what was 'wrong' with Sean. Rory and Kevin, his sons, did and without any doubt and with such sly chucklings and lewd winks. 'It was being brought up by all those nuns,' said Kevin, 'and never seeing any other men but priests who were cowed by the Sisters anyway.'

'I think,' Rory had once remarked, 'that Pa's character was such that a character like Sean's sort of got crushed in any encounter. Not that Uncle Sean had a character of much strength, anyway, or much resolution or manliness. Rice pudding with custard could describe Uncle Sean's spirit, to be charitable. Pa once did remark that our sweet singing uncle was "womanish", and it upset him, but he made excuses that his brother was an "artist". Uncle's petulant little ways were excused under the same copybook heading. "At least," Pa would say, "he made something of himself with his singing and talent, which is more than could have been said about our father, whom he much resembles." Pa must have loved his Dada once; he wouldn't have been so bitter about him if he hadn't. When Uncle Sean succeeded, that made Pa forgive both his Dada and our nightingale uncle. But he has never found out about him, which is just as well. I doubt that Pa would have known what it meant, anyway.'

Joseph would have known. He had read too widely and too largely not to have understood if it had been put before him in plain words. But his natural Irish prudity in part insulated him from recognising what was 'wrong' with his brother. Moreover, he thought such activities not only unmentionable even when among men, but esoteric and inexplicable, and probably engaged in 'only by foreigners'. He never once suspected homo-sexualism among any of his colleagues or acquaintances, not even when it was blatant, and he certainly would not have believed it existed in his own family. He might tell Sean to 'be a man', as he did whenever he encountered him, and did not know that it was impossible for Sean to 'be a man'.

Sean had tried to attach himself to Harry Zeff, out of both

gratitude and love, but Harry had soon suspected and had abruptly removed himself as benefactor and friend. Thereafter had followed several 'love affairs' between Sean and the new friends he made among the camp-followers of the arts. He had finally settled on one love, his manager, for a number of years, Herbert Hayes, who was also of his persuasion. It was Herbert who had taught Sean to be discreet, and not to throw his arms affectionately about other men in public – even when the gesture was comparatively innocent – and not to mention his aversion to the ladies but, on the contrary, to pretend to be a gallant and a womaniser, 'like your brother'. Herbert, too, had taught him to hint of an unrequited or deceased love, whom he could never forget and to whose memory he was still devoted and loyal. This was not hard for Sean to do, for he was an actor as well as a singer by birth. Herbert let him wear exotic clothing, for that was more or less expected of an artist, but he never let it get effeminate.

It had been Herbert Hayes who, from prison, had sent Rory the telegram announcing Sean's death. For Herbert had murdered him. Sean had fallen wildly in love with a new young accompanist, and had told Herbert of his passion, and had asked Herbert to remain as his business manager but to cut 'all ties of affection with me'. Herbert, betrayed, desperate, crushed and then made nearly insane, had simply strangled the man to whom he had given so much and with such devotion and dedication, and then had called the police.

All this Rory discovered from the police, when he went to his uncle's suite. They were callously locking up all the dainty treasures with which Sean travelled, and they were not deferential to the stunned young man but cynically, and half laughing, gave him full information. 'Yes, yes, I know what my uncle was,' said Rory, looking about him dazedly. 'Poor Herbert. I suppose he will be hanged. I wonder what the hell I am going to tell my father.'

The newspapers solved his problem in large black headlines, in Boston and New York and Philadelphia and Washington, and other large cities. They were most discreet, and coyly so, but a knowledgeable person could guess at once the import of their insinuations. Rory kept the newspapers for his father, who had cabled he would return to America at once to take charge of matters, and the funeral.

Rory met Joseph in New York, alone. The young man

thought this best. When Joseph immediately demanded of him the cause of Sean's death Rory replied, 'Let us get out of this hack and into the hotel. I have the newspapers for you.'

When Rory and Joseph reached Delmonico's Rory said, 'It's very cold and you are tired, Pa. You need a drink.' Joseph scowled at him. 'I seem to remember that on every gloomy occasion you reach for the bottle, Rory. Well, then, let's have it.'

The steam pipes clanked desolately but Rory had ordered a fire, remembering how cold affected his father. He mixed a hot toddy for Joseph and Joseph drank gingerly, and then with a sudden thirst Rory had never seen him exhibit before. When he appeared to be relaxing, and warming, Rory said, 'I won't beat about the bush. I thought you ought to see some of the newspapers from Boston, and some from the yellow press in New York, before you go to Boston to arrange for the funeral and bring Uncle Sean to the family plot in Green Hills.'

'Why should I see the newspapers?' demanded Joseph. 'What is all this mystery? Well, let me have the damned things.'

So Rory gave his father a sheaf of headlines and shouting print, and made himself another drink and prudently absented himself for a while in the next room. He heard no sound but the turning of pages, except for one exclamation, 'Oh, my God!' Rory winced, and wished he had brought the whisky bottle with him into this room. The hell with you, Uncle Jenny Lind, he addressed the dead man, grimly. It wasn't enough that you once kicked him in the teeth, but you had to do this thing to him, too.

Rory saw the sudden welling of the fire as Joseph savagely thrust the papers into it. But Joseph did not call him immediately. For Joseph was thinking again of Senator Bassett. He was not thinking of the explicit scandal which had fallen upon his family. He could only see the face of the man he had destroyed, and he saw that face in the bright coals on the hearth, and he heard, again, the dead voice and re-read the last letter the unfortunate man had ever written, in which he had laid the curse.

After a long time Joseph called his son and Rory went back into the darkening room. 'I think,' said Joseph, 'I need another of your infernal drinks.' But when the silent Rory gave it to him he only held it in his hand and stared at the fire, and his face had become stark and pallid, and occasionally he shivered.

Sean was buried in the family plot with its huge obelisk, and he was buried quietly, and the innocent priest said, '. . . this sad and famous victim of an insensate act on the part of a madman. We can only mourn the loss of so magnificent a treasure . . . We can only condole with those who grieve, and remind them . . .'

The snow fell on the bronze casket and into the black and waiting grave, and those who had been invited to accompany the father and the two sons exchanged looks which were meekly malicious, except for Harry Zeff and Charles Devereaux and Timothy Dineen, who stood with Joseph like a bodyguard and let the snow fall on their uncovered heads. The handful of earth and the holy water also fell, and Joseph did not turn away but looked at his brother's coffin and nothing at all showed on his ravaged face.

Two days later, without even seeing Elizabeth, he returned to Europe. Before his trial, Herbert Hayes hanged himself in his cell.

CHAPTER FORTY-TWO

ON the night of February 15th the battleship *Maine* was blown up in Havana Harbour. Over two hundred American officers and crew were killed. No one ever discovered who or what had caused this disaster, but it was enough for the enthusiastic war-mongers throughout the country, and their bought press, to demand war. No one was quite certain who was the 'enemy', but after a little thought it was decided it was Spain. Later it was decided that a submarine mine, applied outside the ship, might be the cause, or again, it was argued, its munitions magazine had been exploded inside. Who was guilty? No one ever knew. Assistant Secretary of the Navy, Theodore Roosevelt, vehemently shouted that he was 'convinced' that the disaster in Havana Harbour was not an accident, but the rescued captain of the ship, Mr Charles D. Sigsbee, urged patience and calm until an investigation was concluded. Mr Roosevelt almost lost his mind with rage. In the meantime the Spanish Government expressed its horror, and went into mourning for the American dead. The government in Madrid made conciliation offers again and again, in despair, in an attempt to avoid a war, but Assistant Secretary of the Navy, Roosevelt, screamed for 'vengeance'.

President McKinley was a prudent man, and not a warmonger. He begged the country to wait for the official investigation. 'It is possible,' he said, 'that *agents provocateurs* are responsible for this, and not the Spanish Government. I have heard whispers, and I have heard rumours . . .' By these words he signed his death warrant.

Mr Roosevelt was beside himself. He said of the President, 'He has no more backbone than a chocolate éclair. Do you know what that white-livered cur up in the White House has done? He has prepared *two* messages, one for war and one for peace, and he doesn't know which one to send in!'

So they have moved, thought Rory Armagh, reading all this in the newspapers. It was not a nightmare after all. I was not frightening myself in the dark. What I heard in London was no gibberish of little plotters. It is the beginning of their Plan.

In the meantime the President, despite Mr Roosevelt and his friend, Captain Mahan, asked the American people to retain their senses and not be misled 'by those who would lead us into a war which I have heard – though it may be only a rumour, a rumour – is the overture to a series of wars to entangle our country in foreign adventures. What the purpose is I do not entirely know; I can only surmise. Let us remember what George Washington implored us to do, to have peaceful relations with all countries but foreign entanglements with none.'

'White-livered cur!' shouted Mr Roosevelt.

The pressure on the President via the press and Mr Roosevelt became insupportable. He pleaded over and over again that as America was only just emerging into new prosperity she should mind her own business and be judicious and balanced. But it was hopeless. The hysterical and enthusiastic masses, led by vociferous editorials in the yellow press, demanded war against Spain, though none was quite certain why there should be such a war. So, despairing, faintly aware of the powerful forces against him from a watching Europe and New York, he succumbed. On April 11th, 1898, the President, broken-hearted, frightened, sent in his war message.

On May 1st Commodore George Dewey steamed into Manila Bay, in command of America's Asiatic Squadron, and sank all the Spanish warships that were there – eight thousand miles away.

The Spanish Government in Cuba, and the insurrectos themselves, were dumb with astonishment and incredulity. They heard that Mr Roosevelt had joyously declared that the war was 'in behalf of American interests'. What those interests were no one was quite sure – except for the men in Washington and New York, in London and Berlin and Paris and Rome and Vienna and St Petersburg. They called a quiet and exultant meeting, and shook hands, and said little or nothing at all.

In June the American forces, singing, though they knew not why they sang, landed at Daiquiri, Cuba, with a loss of two men who had drowned. In July the miserable Spanish forces at San Juan Hill, Santiago, and at El Caney, were overwhelmed. On July 3rd Admiral Cervera's Spanish fleet, commanded by disbelieving officers, tried to escape from Santiago and were destroyed by American warships, ordered there days before. The invading Americans, on July 17th, captured Santiago, and the Spaniards surrendered.

On July 26th the Spanish Government in Madrid asked for the terms of surrender, and an armistice was signed in Paris on August 12th. It was no sooner signed than the news arrived that American forces had taken Manila, the Philippines, and Puerto Rico in the Caribbean Sea – there had been no resistance at all.

'How do you like *The Journal*'s War?' cried the New York *Journal* with exultant delight, and the American people roared happily in answer. From London the American Ambassador congratulated his friend, Theodore Roosevelt, in an exuberant letter. 'It has been a splendid little war!' he declared.

America had acquired many overseas bases now. President McKinley was not pleased. He thought of Theodore Roosevelt and his friend, Captain Mahan, and he had many other thoughts. It was unfortunate that he put some of them on paper and sent them to alleged friends he had considered sympathetic. They found thoughtful resting places on faraway desks in various cities in Europe.

Rory Armagh had lost interest long before the signing of the peace treaty in Paris. For his brother, Kevin, had died in the 'splendid little war', killed in Santiago on board the American battleship, *Texas*, on July 28th.

At the beginning of the spring vacation Kevin had said to his brother, 'I'm not going back to Green Hills this summer. I'm not going to do my usual stint in Philadelphia in Pa's offices, either. I've got a job for the *Boston Gazette*, doing feature articles on the war.'

'You?' said Rory, disbelieving. Kevin had smiled. 'You may think I'm just a plodder, and I am. But I can write factually. I may not be inspired or hysterical, but I can write objectively. So the paper hired me, and I'm off to the wars to report. I think it'll be over soon.'

'You are looking for excitement,' Rory had accused him, dismayed, thinking of their father. Kevin laughed. 'Know anybody less excitable than me? No, I'm looking for something'.

'What?' But Kevin had shrugged his big heavy shoulders, which were so effective on the football field. Kevin was 'deep', as Joseph would say. He never revealed anything he did not want to reveal, about himself or anyone else, so Rory knew there was no use pressing him. But Rory thought of what the faceless men had said in London: 'We cannot have nationalism and sovereign states, which divide and disperse our interests. We must work for a world Socialistic empire, which we will be able to control without tedious distractions of independent political entities and their internal and external quarrels.'

'In short,' Joseph had ironically told his son, 'they will plunder the people of the world through heavy taxation in every country, then "benevolently" return to the subdued masses part of that revenue in "gifts", "aids", "social justice", "sharing", all the people's money anyway – for which the cowed populace will be humbly grateful and become obedient and conforming. No, I won't tell you anything more. But you will learn as we go along, and accept it all.' He had stared a moment, thoughtfully, at Rory. 'We will have to see if you are reliable.'

'Pa,' Rory had said, 'you are not really one of them.'

Joseph had looked away. 'That may be your opinion, Rory. I am as interested as they are in power.'

When Joseph and Bernadette and Ann Marie returned in early April it was Rory's miserable and unwanted task – undertaken with some wincing and resentment – to inform his parents that Kevin had already left America as a correspondent for the *Boston Gazette*. Joseph was predictably angered, and Bernadette threw up her fat arms and cried, 'How ungrateful, how stupid, how like Kevin, to do this to his father! In the middle of term, too.'

Kevin's articles began to appear in the newspaper almost weekly. To his family's surprise there was a kind of surly jocularity in them, a cold underlying cynicism, as well as practical reporting. They contained no ebullient patriotism, no hero-singing, no excitement or jubilation about 'our war of liberation'. They were totally dispassionate which did not entirely please the sponsor. Then the articles stopped the latter part of June. Joseph, frowning, put inquiries in motion. He discovered that Kevin was no longer in the vicinity of Cuba. The newspaper asserted that, at his own desire, he had gone to the Philippines, 'somewhere', and had written that he wished to be an 'observer' on a battleship. The *Gazette* believed that the battleship's name was *Texas,* and expressed its hope that it would soon be in possession of 'dispatches'.

The next dispatch was a telegram from the Admiral of the American Fleet at Santiago that Mr Kevin Armagh had died as the result of a 'random wild shot, coming from the enemy', which had reached Kevin 'by a freak or ordinance of God', for it had not been directed at anyone or anything in particular. Standing in the great marble hall of his house, with the telegram in his hand, Joseph felt the atavistic Celt stirring in himself, a Celt who did not believe in the random or coincidental, but who believed in Fate. He stood in that hall, silent, motionless, for a long time before he went upstairs to inform his wife of the death of their son, for as much as it was possible for her to love any of her children she loved Kevin.

It was late on a very hot thirtieth of July, and Bernadette, whose corpulence was a heavy burden in the heat, had been napping before her lonely interlude with a bottle and a glass, and then dinner. She sat up in her bed in her darkened room as Joseph came in, sweating in her pink silk and lace nightgown, her greying hair wet about her face and straggling on her mountainous shoulders. Her face, round and puffed with fat, was crimson and steamy, her once-fine eyes sunken in flesh and dazed with sleep, her nose and chins oily. Her huge breasts pushed against the fragile silk like udders, and she smelled of expensive perfume and perspiration and talcum powder, and hot obesity. 'What, what?' she mumbled.

Joseph knew where she kept her secret bottles, for a vengeful maid, discharged by Bernadette, had told him of her mistress's generous tipples in the evening. Joseph knew that his wife was now frequently drunk before dinner, but he cared no more for that than he did for anything else concerning the desperate Bernadette. Still without speaking and while Bernadette stared after him, slowly coming to full consciousness and blinking rapidly, he went to the little French cabinet near a far wall, lifted the lid and took out a bottle of Irish whiskey and a sticky glass. She watched, and the crimson on her cheeks deepened and a fresh burst of sweat poured out upon her and stained the nightgown darkly. She watched him, numbly, as he poured a good measure of the whiskey into the glass. Only her eyes moved when he came to the bed and put the glass in her hand. 'Drink it,' he said. 'I think you are going to need it.'

How did he find out? Bernadette asked herself, mortified and heart-broken. It must have been that damned Charlotte, with the sly mouth. 'I don't think I want it,' she mumbled, dropping her eyes with mingled shame and wretchedness. 'It's too warm.'

'Drink it,' Joseph repeated.

For the first time she became aware of what he had done. Startled fully awake now, she looked up at him, her eyes as wide as possible in all that flesh. She knew at once that he had not done this in mockery and contempt, as he had done other things when he had discovered certain secrets of hers, and had exposed them. Then, to her stunned amazement, as she held the glass reluctantly in her bloated hand, he actually drew a white and gold chair near to the bed and sat down in it, and she saw his face completely for the first time and she saw that it was the colour of the whitish-grey in the russet of his hair and that his wide thin lips were as blue as huckleberries, and that every muscle in his face was as flat and stiff as ivory.

A horrible feeling of impending disaster hit Bernadette. He was going to leave her. He was going to divorce her so that he could marry that shameless Elizabeth Hennessey. He had given her the whiskey because as a last kindness to her he was softening the effects of his assault upon her very soul. 'No, no,' she groaned, her lips feeling thick and lifeless. 'Oh, no.'

'Drink it,' he said, and he was looking at her now not with his usual distant aversion, his murderous indifference, his open loathing, but with an expression she had seen but once before, when she had been little more than a child on the night her mother had died, and he had held her in the hall below and had tried to comfort her. She burst into tears, then afraid that he might newly despise her, she drank hurriedly, gasped, choked, drank again. He took the glass from her and put it on her bedside table, which was cluttered with lace handkerchiefs, bottles of perfume, a little dish of lozenges, a porcelain figure or two, and two or three rings. The heat of the room, with its closed draperies, was like the core of a burning coal and sickening with scent and the odour of a large wet body.

She panted, looking at him with eyes like a mortally stricken and humble animal lying before a hunter, and said, 'You are going away. Tell me.'

'I am not going away, Bernadette,' he said, almost gently. He could not look at her eyes, so tortured, so pleading, so despairing – no, he could not look at them now. 'It's just – I have bad news. It just arrived. Kevin . . .'

'Kevin? What about Kevin?' The glow was in her heart, too. He was not going to leave her. He would still be her husband. 'Kevin?' she repeated.

He had seen the glow and had accurately guessed its origin, but he could not detest her now or repulse her. 'I've had a telegram,' he said, and he felt the hoarseness and dryness in his throat. 'Kevin – he was on a battleship, *Texas*, at Santiago, as an observer for his newspaper. He was – shot. On July twenty-eighth. I've had a telegram, from the Admiral.' He felt her heavy hand slowly grow cold in his and saw her stupefied face, her thick dropped mouth, her empty eyes. She was trying to speak, coughed, mumbled, but did not look away from him. 'He,' she could say at last in a voice so faint he could hardly hear her, 'he wasn't a soldier. And isn't the war over?'

'Yes,' said Joseph. There was still no real feeling in him, no real awareness of the news he was telling, only a shocked stillness such as a soldier might feel when the steel entered him and the pain had not yet begun. The pain would inevitably begin, he knew, for pain was an old familiar and he knew all its nuances, its stealthy approaches, its sudden overwhelming anguishes, its sudden incredulity and savage rebellion. But as yet it was only creeping in the darkness towards him on silent feet, letting its victim try to gather resisting but hopeless strength. 'But he was killed,' said Joseph to his wife.

'Kevin,' whispered Bernadette, stunned, incredulous as he was. 'But he is only eighteen years old! It can't have happened to Kevin – he is only eighteen years old.'

Joseph could not speak. He had expected conventional weeping from the dramatic Bernadette, and he had expected to be forced to console her. But the stunned and awful shock in her eyes stunned him also, for now he knew that she loved her son, and he squeezed his own parched eyelids together and heard the first crackling of the enemy's approach to him.

Then Bernadette screamed, tore her hand from Joseph's and clapped both her hands with a frightening noise to her cheeks. She screamed over and over again, and her maid, in the next room, came running, aghast. 'Send for the doctor,' Joseph told her. 'Mr Kevin has been killed – in the war. Send for the doctor immediately.' He was barely heard above that tearing sound Bernadette was helplessly making, her eyes wild and bulging, vivid as fire with pain.

The doctor came – Joseph had not left his wife and had tried to calm her – and Bernadette was given a generous sedative. Only when it began to affect her did she cease her broken shrieking, her animal-like cries, her threshings on the bed, her calls upon God and her favourite Saints, her pleas to her husband that it must be a mistake, the war was over, it was some other mother's son, who would shoot Kevin, and why? and it was a nightmare, an error, the prank of an enemy, a wrong dispatch. Joseph must – must . . . He had held her back on her pillows, had tried to give her more whiskey, but she had struck the glass fiercely from his hand and then had clutched him like a drowning woman, rolling her head on his shoulder, pushing him away for a moment as if he had attacked her and she was defending herself, then clutching him again and rolling her head on his shoulder and writhing against him.

The doctor, the maid and Joseph waited beside her bed and slowly the screaming, that fearful screaming – hoarse and broken – had finally stopped. Bernadette lay on her pillows, drenched in her own sweat, a dishevelled but pathetic lump of flesh in her stained pink silk, panting and muttering. Then, for the first time, she had begun to cry, and the doctor nodded with sympathetic satisfaction. Joseph held her hand, and it was quiet at last, though trembling. She saw only her husband.

'There is a curse on us,' she whimpered, and her eyes widened with horror. 'Ann Marie. Your brother. Sean. Kevin. In one year, Joe, in one year. Who will be next? There is a curse on us, A curse on this family.'

Then her eyes closed and she fell asleep and instantly snored under the drug. The doctor said, with pity, 'She should sleep for several hours. I am leaving these pills, for later, when she wakes up. It is best to keep her under sedation for a few days. I will return tonight.'

There were things to be done before the pain took over entirely. There was a telegram to Rory, to Charles Devereaux, to Timothy Dineen, to Harry Zeff. There were telegrams to Washington requesting the return of the body of Kevin Armagh, to be buried in the family plot. There were telegrams to Senators, and other politicians. There were orders to the domestic staff in the house that no newspaper reporters were to be admitted. There was a message to the priest to come later to console Mrs Joseph Armagh. There were so many arrangements to be made – before the relentless and terrible enemy pounced, bringing with it an absolute helplessness. The dire panoply of death began.

After he had completed what he must do Joseph went to his daughter's rooms, the once pretty girlish rooms she had decorated herself, so sunlit and fresh in colour, so simple and charming. They were none of these now. They had been converted into a hospital centre, plain, functional, cleared of all but absolute necessities. One room held the three beds of the three constant nurses, and their paraphernalia. What had been the nursery but which had later been converted into a sitting-room for Ann Marie, was a nursery again, filled with childish toys and other playthings, bright with nursery pictures on the walls and a table at which Ann Marie now ate all her meals, for no longer would the rooms downstairs know her and no longer would she run down those marble stairs. She would be assisted down them in the mornings for a short ride with a nurse or two, and then would be taken upstairs again for her babyish naps, her bland meals. She would be tucked into bed at night, a nurse singing lullabies beside her, and she would sleep.

The sun was still blazing, but low in the sky and reddening it, when Joseph went into those rooms which Bernadette rarely entered. Ann Marie had eaten her bread and milk and fruit pudding and had drunk her mug of cocoa, and was now sitting where she always sat, near the window, in a white-padded hospital chair. For she was frequently and serenely incontinent, like a young child, and with as little shame, and as naturally. She was dressed for the night in a white plain dimity nightgown and a flowered wrapper, and her long soft brown hair had been braided into tight silky braids on her shoulders and her face was the face of a pampered, loved and contented child. Her slim body had reverted to the outlines of babyhood, also, so that she was plump and rosy and dimpled as she had been at the age of three. Her legs and arms and hands and feet were immature again, her face was flushed and round, her lips full and pink, her flesh shining, her eyes innocently questing and shyly smiling – those lovely sherry-coloured eyes with their long aureate lashes. She had never had what Bernadette had called 'a proper bust', and now what she had had was merged in the general softness of her child's body.

Now Joseph sat beside her and took one of her soft little hands and said to her, as he always said, 'Who am I, Ann Marie?'

'Papa,' she said with triumph, and smiled that radiant smile of hers, affectionate and confiding. It was a nightly game.

He looked into her eyes, and saw the healthily glistening whites of them, the lashes, the bright irises. He always looked deeply into them, hoping hopelessly for some sign of the soul of Ann Marie in them, some shadowy hint that the spirit had not left for ever. But it was the infant Ann Marie who looked back at him trustfully, the child in her cradle, the child in her nursery bed. So much for the theory of growing and maturing souls, he thought, as he had thought a thousand bitter times before. So much for immortal souls, gaining knowledge and wisdom and awareness. What Ann Marie had learned in twenty-three years was gone, eradicated, blotted out, as if it had never been at all.

There was a cloth doll in her lap, and now she took it in her arms and hugged it and uttered a gleeful little sound.

'Kiss Pudgy,' she told her father, and he dutifully kissed it, and closed his eyes against both the endless pain of his daughter's spiritual death and the pain that was threatening him. He said, 'Ann Marie, do you remember Kevin?'

She looked at him obediently. Only her voice was the voice of the woman she had been, clear, hesitant, hoping to please. 'Kevin? Kevin?' She shook her head and pouted as if she had been rebuked.

'Never mind, dear,' said her father, and passed his dry hands over his drier face, which felt scorched. He took up the doll again and shook it at her playfully and she laughed and snatched it from him, and hugged it again. 'My Pudgy,' she said. 'You can't have her, Papa.' The nurse, the younger one, was sitting nearby in her white clothing, knitting, and she smiled as if at the prattlings of a child and said, 'We are very good tonight, Mr Armagh.' She had heard the news of Kevin's death, but as Mr Armagh, who terrified everyone, had not spoken of it she did not speak of it or offer her condolences. 'We took our bath nicely, and tomorrow we'll go for a little walk, won't we, Ann Marie?'

'And see the flowers,' said Ann Marie, nodding. 'The flowers. And the trees.'

Joseph went into his wife's rooms again, and the sun was setting in scarlet majesty and the grounds about the house were peaceful and filled with shifting shadows of hot gilt and purple, and the tops of the trees were dancing in liquid gold. Joseph paused to look at all that which he owned, and the enemy crept nearer. 'A curse on the family,' Bernadette had wept. 'There is a curse on us. Ann Marie, Sean and now Kevin. A curse on us.'

Bernadette slept, stupefied, mouth open and drooling, and Joseph sat beside her and did not hear the muted dinner bell and did not go downstairs. He watched his wife until the room was dark and her maids began to light a lamp here and there. Then the pain came. Later, for the first time in his life he deliberately got drunk.

CHAPTER FORTY-THREE

JOSEPH had enough powerful influence to have Kevin's body shipped back to Green Hills as speedily as possible, in the sealed bronze casket he had ordered. Accompanying it were two captains of the American Fleet off Santiago, and a company of sailors in full dress. There was a note of condolence from the Admiral: 'It was indeed a random shot from one of the retreating Spanish men-of-war, though all had surrendered. The bullet, which was extracted, was of the manufacture of Barbour & Bouchard, the American munitions makers. Of course, we know that munitions makers sell to all customers – my deepest condolences and regrets. Young Mr Armagh endeared himself to us with his honesty, courage, intelligence and consideration – '

The Celt, the ancient Celt, stirred in Joseph again, the Celt of occult mysteries, of bloody vengeance, of Fate, of elves and fairies and screams in the night. Of banshees wailing under the moon, and misty bogs and green lakes as still as glass and hills of vapour. Kevin was part of that also. Joseph said to himself, over and over, 'Nonsense. It was an accident – as Ann Marie's was an accident.'

As Kevin had not been a soldier or a sailor there could be no military funeral in late August, but the captains and the sailors were there, and one of the sailors rendered Taps in the Armagh family plot in Green Hills with the tall marble obelisk looking down enigmatically. There would be a small marble cross on Kevin's grave, as there was on Sean's grave. The black earth waited, and the funeral – private – took place during a hot dark August day full of thunderous threat. Joseph stood with Bernadette, who was swathed in black veiling, and his son Rory whose full jovial face was set and sombre, and his henchmen, Charles and Timothy and Harry, and watched his younger son's coffin lowered into the ground to the murmurous prayers of the priest. A crowd of reporters, kept back by police, stood at a distance snapping photographs. Kevin was a hero. Though only a civilian, an observer, he had 'braved' danger to report honestly to his countrymen, and so was a hero. There were rumours of the Congressional Medal of Honour, given posthumously. (It eventually arrived and was mounted in Kevin's room at home.)

'Not all who die in the service of their country wear a uniform,' said the priest. 'There are heroes who serve as nobly . . .' Joseph thought of Senator Bassett. Bernadette was weeping and swaying beside him, and he put his arm about her absently. Once, in her grief she had said recently to him, 'The Armaghs brought disaster to the Hennesseys!' Then she had abjectly apologised and almost grovelled before her husband.

'You are all I have left,' Joseph said to Rory the night of the funeral. 'So all you do must be for us.' He had never seen Rory cry before, not even as a child, but Rory broke down and wept like a woman, his face in his hands.

In the second week of September Joseph came to Elizabeth. She held out her arms mutely to him, wise enough not to cry, not to ask, not to reproach, not even to console. She took him to her bed, almost without speaking, and held him close and kissed him and said nothing. She lay in his arms and felt his love and his grief and his anguish, and touched him gently – and still said nothing. She had the wisdom of a woman completely in love, asking only to give. It was enough for her that he had returned to her. There was nothing else.

It was almost dawn when he said to her abruptly, 'I asked you before, Elizabeth. Do you believe in curses?'

'No,' she said at once. 'If you are speaking of family calamities – they happen to all families, without curses, sooner or later. I believe in a merciful God. He would not permit any of His children to curse His other children. "Vengeance is mine," saith the Lord. "I will repay." '

That's what I am afraid of, thought Joseph, the wry Celt, who did not believe in God. He tried to smile at Elizabeth in the blue-grey light of dawn. 'Don't become mystical with me, Lizzie. There is no occult "vengeance".'

Then why did you ask? Elizabeth asked him silently. But she only kissed him gently. She said to him, 'I am not superstitious, and neither are you, my darling.'

They did not speak of their families. Joseph asked nothing about Courtney. Elizabeth held Joseph in her arms and felt she was holding her whole world. But a man with a woman did not feel that. This she knew. It was enough for her that she

336

loved and was loved in return, but a man never gave his whole heart to love and that was a fact with which no wise woman ever quarrelled.

Joseph, in Philadelphia, read the reports gathered by Charles Devereaux and his investigators regarding his son, Rory, and he felt a cold outraged anger. That damned young swine, secretive, wily. Why had he married the girl? To be sure, she was of a notable and aristocratic family, of much wealth and position. But why had he married her and so jeopardised his future?

'I feel that Rory has done himself well,' said Charles, looking at Joseph with curiously remote grey eyes. 'Marjorie Chisholm has an impeccable background. They married in secret because of possible opposition by their families. I am not going to question Rory's reasons for fearing you would oppose the marriage. I know the reasons of Mr Albert Chisholm. I think the marriage should be revealed. It will not do Rory harm. It might, indeed, do him a lot of good – married to the daughter of a distinguished family, of Boston.'

'You wouldn't understand,' said Joseph. 'He is going to marry the daughter of the Ambassador, Claudia Worthington, who is related to the British Royal Family.'

Charles said, 'No, I don't understand,' but he did. He, too, was partly of an oppressed race who longed for both justification and retribution.

'Write for an appointment for me with Mr Albert Chisholm confidentially,' said Joseph. 'In the meantime, talk to the minister who married them, and the town clerk who recorded the marriage. You know what to do, Charles.'

Unfortunately Charles did. He did not like it nor approve of it. But he was the son of his father and there were other things to consider besides emotionalism and what men called 'love'.

Mr Albert Chisholm, upon receiving Charles's cool and businesslike letter, thought to himself, 'No doubt that scoundrel, Armagh, is going to plead with me to allow a marriage between his son and Marjorie. I will soon put him in his place.' That night he called his daughter to him and said, 'Marjorie, my dear, are you ever seeing that young – Armagh, is his name? I truly hope not. You know I forbade you to see him again or to answer his letters and his impudent importunities.'

Marjorie's smooth olive face became very still. 'Why do you ask, Papa?'

The letter had been very confidential, from Charles, and Albert was too sensible a man, and knew too much of the Armagh power, to be indiscreet. So he said, 'I have noticed that you never accept the invitations of highly eligible young men, my dear child. So I have feared you are still thinking of that rascal's son.'

Marjorie dropped her eyes demurely. 'I go nowhere with Mr Armagh,' she said, and this was quite true. 'I am afraid that other young men do not interest me, as yet. They seem so callow – compared with you, Papa.'

Mr Chisholm bridled with pride and happiness, but he shook his finger archly at his pretty little daughter. 'But Papa cannot remain for ever with you, my love. You must really consider marriage. After all, you are going on twenty-one – in eight months.'

She suddenly sat on his knee and began to cry, and he was taken aback. He said, as he smoothed her thick glossy curls, 'My dearest child, I did not mean to make you unhappy. Marjorie, I would do anything in the world to give you happiness, in the measure allowed to human beings. You must never forget that.'

She put her small round arms about his neck and cried even harder and cursed Rory inwardly for his insistence on secrecy. She could no longer bear the deception on her father. She looked at him tearfully. 'Even if I wanted to marry Rory, Papa?'

He stiffened, and hesitated, then said with resolution, 'I pray, my child, it will never come to that. But, if it does, I will swallow my pride and permit it. But do not think rashly, Marjorie. Your whole future depends on one decision.'

Marjorie cuddled in his lap like a kitten, thinking furiously. Then, without any warning at all a terrible premonition came to her, of desolation and abandonment. It was silly. She was Rory's wife. It was true that his brother had been killed in the war, but nothing evil could ever happen to her Rory, nothing could ever separate them. Nothing.

CHAPTER FORTY-FOUR

MR ALBERT CHISHOLM had decided exactly how he would receive the swaggering and impudent Irishman, Mr Joseph Armagh. He would sit calmly in his office, behind the desk which had belonged to his grandfather, with the silver bowl made by his distant relative, Paul Revere, filled with fresh flowers – it was late September and the flowers were bronze and gold – and he would receive Mr Armagh with calm dignity and courtesy and offer him a cigar. He would speak in quiet and modulated accents – these Irish were so loud and noisy and obstinate – and so Mr Armagh would know that for the first time in his life he had encountered an authentic gentleman. Mr Chisholm had given orders to his secretaries. They would conduct Mr Armagh at once to his inner sanctuary, with discretion and soft footsteps, and would not converse with him.

Joseph entered the office and the secretary closed the door softly behind him. Mr Chisholm gaped. He could not believe it. Here was one not at all like the Irish Boston Mayors, such as Old Syrup, and sundry other politicians whom the fastidious Mr Chisholm had long deplored. Here was a tall, lean man impeccably dressed in dark, well-tailored clothing, his linen immaculate and beyond reproach, his few pieces of jewellery in excellent taste, his boots narrow and quietly polished. But it was Joseph's ascetic face which fixed Mr Chisholm's attention, that reserved, emotionless face, clean-shaven, stark and – yes! – aristocratic. The mingled russet and white of his hair had been expertly barbered, neither too long nor too short, and his expression was both controlled and formidable, and those eyes were the eyes of a most intelligent and immovable man. Something tight loosened in Mr Chisholm. Was it possible that this immigrant Irishman was a *gentleman*? Scots-Irish, perhaps, with a background of Covenanters? Mr Chisholm had such in his own family.

'Mr Armagh, I presume?' said Mr Chisholm in a carefully subdued voice and held out his hand. Mr Armagh took that hand briefly. It was long and slender, Mr Chisholm noted, and very strong and dry. Mr Chisholm had not intended to say this but he did: 'I was most distressed to hear of your son's death, ah, in the line of duty, Mr Armagh.'

'Thank you,' said Joseph. His voice, Mr Chisholm thought, might be a little too melodious, with a certain lilt notable in the Irish, but it was the voice of a *gentleman*! Neither too emphatic or dull, and very controlled. 'Please sit down, Mr Armagh,' said Mr Chisholm, a little shaken. Why, compared with this man, Rory Armagh, the son, was a hod-carrier! Still, blood told. The mother, perhaps, was a vulgar woman, and that explained Rory's sceptical wide laughter, vibrant colouring, vitality, and the cynical smile he bestowed on everybody, and his way of lightly mocking his elders. Still, blood told, and Mr Armagh was evidently a man of 'blood'. Mr Chisholm felt his vitals quiver with relief. Mr Armagh was also very, very powerful, and very, very rich. There might be a compromise ... It was rumoured that some of the Irish were descended from kings; landed gentry. Joseph had seated himself, one long lean leg over the knee of the other, and he was looking at Mr Chisholm, still not seated, with a most penetrating regard.

'I know you are a very busy lawyer,' said Joseph, 'so I will take up as little of your time as possible.' He had come swiftly to the conclusion that Mr Chisholm was not very intelligent, but was a gentleman and a slight ditherer, and a kind and somewhat hesitant man. Under other circumstances Joseph would have been inclined to look favourably upon him and think that Rory had not made too bad a choice in a family. He glanced quickly at a silver-framed photograph of Miss Marjorie Chisholm on Mr Chisholm's desk. A lovely child, with a fine bright face and mischievous eyes and a wide brow and a tangle of black curls: no one could quarrel with such a beauty.

He bent and opened his dispatch case and brought out a sheaf of documents and laid them on Mr Chisholm's desk. 'I have discovered, as no doubt you have, sir, that documents and evidence are much more telling than conversation, and save a lot of time. May I suggest that you read these?'

Mr Chisholm gaped again, and sat down slowly and then put on his pince-nez. He began to read. Joseph did not watch him. He looked about the room and thought how much this resembled his own rooms at Green Hills. However, there was no aura of power here, just meticulous and boring law, ponderous and dusty. Yes, a ditherer, poor bastard.

There was an ormolu clock on the mantelpiece, and its soft tick became louder and louder in the complete quiet of the room, and the small noise of the fire was the noise of an approaching holocaust. Joseph began to watch Mr Chisholm's face. Moment by moment, as he quietly turned page after page, his colouring dwindled, became very pale, then absolutely white, and his facial muscles sagged and twitched, and his eyes dropped, and a thin double-chin began to hang under the real one, like dewlaps. Suddenly, he was an old and diminished man, and his moustache quivered, and he sank deeper and deeper into his chair. His hands began to tremble, then increased to a palsy. His lips, under that pathetically groomed moustache, became purplish grey, and jerked. Joseph frowned. He had hoped not to encounter this. He had thought to face a very quietly pompous man of much composure and resolution, who would agree with him, or at least listen to his arguments.

Mr Chisholm slowly turned the last page. He looked at Joseph. Joseph had expected stricken and terrified eyes, but Mr Chisholm's were wounded and unafraid.

'So,' Mr Chisholm said, 'my daughter is married to your son, Rory. I forbade her to see him. I knew nothing but catastrophe could result. I was quite correct. Mr Armagh – it was not necessary for you to threaten me, and Marjorie.'

Joseph sat forward. 'I did not know with whom I had to deal, Mr Chisholm, or my approach would have been different. Let me be brief. I have other plans for my son. He is all I have left. He must make a name for himself. Your daughter cannot give him that name.'

Mr Chisholm said, as if he had not heard Joseph, 'If Marjorie, and I, do not give our consent to the annulment of this marriage you will shame my dear daughter as not being married at all – she was under age – and the minister was "deceived". In fact, the minister was a fraud, and not a duly ordained minister. The town clerk who recorded the marriage was deceived also. He never recorded the marriage. All records have been destroyed in that little village. There is no record. Therefore, Marjorie has been guilty of fornication with your son. You know these are all lies, Mr Armagh. You have used your influence. If Marjorie, and I, give our consent to a legal annulment, quietly suppressed so that no one will know, there will be no reprisals. Am I correct, Mr Armagh?'

'You are correct, sir,' said Joseph.

'If we do not agree' – and Mr Chisholm was taken by a violent spell of coughing – 'you will ruin me. You have done your research very well, sir. It is quite true that the Panic of '93 forced me into debt, and I have not recovered my finances. You own my paper at the banks. You will demand payment on that paper. That will reduce me to penury. I thought my bankers – were gentlemen.'

Joseph said, 'Bankers are never gentlemen.'

Mr Chisholm nodded. 'I know that now. I see terrible ramifications . . . My ancestors fought for America . . . No matter. That will bore you. Sir, if Marjorie quietly seeks an annulment of this fatal marriage, and it is granted without publicity, you will withdraw your threats against my daughter, and me?'

'Yes,' said Joseph, and he stood up and went to the windows and looked out.

'And if we inform your son, Rory, you will still take reprisals?'

'Yes,' said Joseph. 'He must never know. Your daughter must just tell him the marriage is over, for her own reasons.'

Mr Chisholm reflected. 'You love your son, and I love my daughter. I was willing that this marriage continue. But you are not. Mr Armagh, on second thoughts, I am desirous that my daughter should not be connected with you. With you, sir. Even through your son. She would not be able to bear it. She was brought up in an honourable family . . .'

Joseph swung to him so sharply that Mr Chisholm recoiled. 'So was I,' said Joseph. 'An honourable, God-fearing, decent, land-owning family. A family, a nation, a religion, ancient in history. But, sir, we were destroyed as ruthlessly as Russian serfs are destroyed by their masters. We were hunted down like animals, like vermin, for no reason at all but that we wanted to be free, as a nation, and to practise our religion. That was quite a heinous crime, wasn't it? To be free is to be condemned. To seek freedom is to be a criminal. To revolt against oppressors is to die. Yes, I know that. Your own ancestors left England for just the same thing. But you have forgotten. Your ancestors were poor driven English yeomen, who wanted nothing but peace and to serve their religion. This they were denied, as my people were denied. So they emigrated – here.

'Long before your ancestors were a distinct people, sir, the Irish were an ancient proud race. We were never slaves, as you Anglo-Saxons were, and never, by God, shall we be slaves!'

Mr Chisholm sat back in his chair and stared and his thoughts were jumbled. Then, still looking at Joseph he said, 'You are taking revenge.'

Joseph returned to his chair and sat down. 'You are very subtle, Mr Chisholm.'

'Mr Armagh, you have no religion at all, have you?'

Joseph was silent for a moment or two, then he said, 'No. I do not. I have not believed in anything since I was a young child. The world taught me that, sir.'

Mr Chisholm nodded. 'I so suspected. Mr Armagh, one of these days you will be driven to the edge.'

He stood up. He was stately again, but not with an offensive stateliness. He said, 'Mr Armagh, what you wish will be consummated. You may rest assured of that. I am not impressed by your threats against me and my daughter. I wish it ended. I hope never to see you again.'

Then Joseph said, 'I wish I had known your kind when I was a child, sir. We might have come to the same conclusion.' His face was full of regret, and yet he was coldly amused.

He left then and Mr Chisholm watched him go. Again he was swamped in pity, and again he was humbled. God forgive us, he thought, for what we do to each other.

Mr Chisholm said to his daughter, Marjorie, in his study at home: 'He will not only destroy us, my love, but he will destroy his son, Rory, also, unless we agree to this. It is for you to choose.'

'You mean, Papa, that you are willing to do as I choose?' asked Marjorie. She had not cried at all. She had sat near her father in his study, with his confidential secretary and personal lawyer, Bernard Levine, just behind her, listening. Bernard had been hopelessly in love with Marjorie for a number of years; he was a slight young man with a quiet, intelligent face, brown eyes and hair, who listened more than he spoke.

'I mean exactly that, my love,' said Mr Chisholm. 'No matter the result, it is yours to say and only yours,' and he

343

thought how much she resembled her mother as she sat before him in her blue serge suit and shirt-waist and neat little buttoned boots, her black curls vehemently bursting from her pompadour, her small face quickly changing with her emotions and her black eyes eloquent but disciplined. He had called her and Bernard into his study that night, and had simply given his daughter the papers Joseph had left with him. Only once had she exclaimed uncontrollably, and that was at the revelation of her marriage to Rory. 'Oh, Papa!' she had cried, in a tone of deep remorse and affection. 'I am so sorry that I deceived you. But it was for Rory's sake. His father . . .'

'I know all about Mr Armagh,' said Mr Chisholm, with sadness. 'I wish we had known each other earlier.' This was so enigmatic to Marjorie that she had stared at him and wondered.

Now he had given her the choice, to destroy him, and perhaps Rory, to save her marriage. She doubted that Joseph would 'destroy' Rory, his only remaining son, and in a way his only remaining child, out of disappointed ambition and his famous anger. He was not so womanishly capricious, as Rory had often remarked. His first rages, Rory had told her, were later modified by pragmatism and his own brand of reason. But still, Rory had not cared to risk that rage by revealing his marriage. Marjorie felt cold and sick and wild with anguish. Surely it was all a nightmare. She was not being asked to give up Rory, never to see Rory again, to permit the destruction of her marriage. Rory, Rory. She became incredulous.

'He, Mr Armagh, would not do what he threatened to do, Papa!' She clenched her little hands on her knee. 'Why, he loves Rory, and Rory loves him! Rory is all he has!'

Mr Chisholm noted, with sorrow, that Rory, not himself, was first in her thoughts.

'I am afraid, my dear, that he would do exactly that.' Mr Chisholm turned to Bernard. 'You saw Mr Armagh in my office today. You know, from reading the newspapers and the hints in them, what Mr Armagh is. Bernard, do you think that in this instance he would – er – mellow, come to terms, to acceptance?'

Bernard hesitated. It tore him apart, he thought, to see Marjorie so agonised, for all her calm. But he said, 'From what I know of Mr Armagh, and his history – the man has

344

fascinated me for a long time for some reason, and I have read almost everything concerning him – yes, I think he would do that. I read, on the occasion of his brother's murder, that he had, for many years, abandoned that brother before their reconciliation because Mr Sean Paul did not rise to his standards, and ambitions. There is also a rumour that he has a sister in a convent, whom he ignores. That may be only hearsay. And there has been gossip, newly revived, that he was the cause of the death of his father-in-law, long ago. Perhaps only malicious gossip, in *Life* magazine. I understand that he has ruined many men, in pursuit of his goals. That part is no mere gossip, or hearsay. It is a fact. He has stated in these papers before us that he has "other plans" for his son. I think we can safely say that if those plans are thwarted that he will do as he has threatened. I never heard that he threatened anyone without carrying it out. There is a great deal about Mr Armagh that I know from my long reading about him.'

'Just in newspapers, and magazines, Bernie?' asked Marjorie, and now she was even paler and more tense.

'No. There was something about international bankers which I read recently. Mr Armagh is a director of many large banks in the United States, so it is safe to say that he is in close touch with the bankers of America, and Europe. It was all in a – book. I hear it was suppressed, later, just when it began to be sold in quantity. I don't know if Mr Armagh is one of them, but he is certainly entangled with them.' He looked at Mr Chisholm, sitting in ashen misery in his leather chair. Mr Chisholm looked disbelieving.

'Bernard, what you are hinting? It is not to be believed!'

Bernard shrugged his shoulders, a gesture Mr Chisholm disliked, and spread out his hands in a 'foreign' gesture which Mr Chisholm disliked even more. 'I read, just today, in the *Boston Gazette* – a newspaper you do not care for, sir – that our government is in deep debt to the bankers for this past war, and that the US Supreme Court will soon declare the Federal Income Tax un-Constitutional again. The war, though short, cost several billion dollars. The bankers in new York hold the government's paper. In an interview with Mr Morgan he declares that the only way to be "solvent" is to have a permanent Federal Income Tax. In short, if we are to have wars – though he did not say that, of course – the people must be taxed for them. No taxes, no wars. I also read a privately circulated leaflet that there is something called a Scardo Society, formed of prominent American politicians and industrialists, who have already decided that wars are necessary for prosperity, in this increasingly industrial age.'

He shrugged again. 'There have been many hints of these things in New York newspapers, too. Whatever is going on, sir, is being kept very secret, and those who even slightly suspect are being ridiculed or ignored or suppressed. I don't know, sir. It is certainly very sinister.' Again he spread out his hands. 'I do know that reviewers in the newspapers ridiculed and violently attacked that book I mentioned, and called the writer a believer in bogeymen. There was a curious similarity in the attacks.'

Mr Chisholm sat in profound and shaken thought, and Marjorie thought, Oh Rory, Rory! Nothing must part us, Rory, never, never! The great cry in her swelled to her eyes, eyes dry and aching, and there was a choking in her throat. She was filled with desolation, rebellion, hatred, despair.

Mr Chisholm came out of his shock, shaking his head. 'I am glad I am no longer young, and have no sons,' he said. 'For the first time in my life I have a fear for my country. Still, I can hardly believe it. I am sure we will never have a Federal Income Tax on individuals; I am sure we will have no more wars. The Hague repeatedly says so . . . No matter. We must solve our own problem. Marjorie, my dear?'

'I cannot believe a man can be so monstrous as to threaten a harmless gentleman like you, Papa, and a harmless girl like myself – and his own son! His own son!'

Mr Chisholm could not bear to look at his beloved daughter, so pale, her face quivering, her eyes strained and huge with suffering, and so tense on the edge of her chair. Her mouth, usually smiling with mischief and affection and wit, was the mouth of a tormented woman, pleading for reassurance. No, after one glance, Mr Chisholm could not bear to look at his Marjorie, and now he hated Joseph Armagh with the first real hatred of his life. His thin hands clenched on the arms of his chair. He understood, now, why it was some men could kill, something which had made him incredulous before. Only madmen, only the deranged, the illiterate, the low-born, the ignorant and stupid and animalistic, killed, he had once thought. Now he could understand. The blood swelled into

Mr Chisholm's withered throat and engorged it. His face turned scarlet and broke into sweat.

But he said calmly enough, 'I am afraid he means what he says, Marjorie. I should not like to put him to the test. As for myself, I was not young when I married your mother; I am old enough to be your grandfather, my love. I do not fear for myself, for how much longer will I live? I will always have a little sustenance. But I do fear for you, my daughter. He would, indeed, ruin you, and your – your – husband.' He hated Rory now, who had taken Marjorie into this frightful situation, who had put her under threat from an evil man.

'Bernard, what do you say?'

Bernard looked down on his clasped hands. 'I agree with you, sir. We dare not take the risk. If Marjorie wants this marriage to continue she has only to say so. I am sure, in spite of what – he – says in those papers, that the legality of the marriage can be proved. It may be difficult. It may take years. But I think a court test, and a summoning of witnesses, would bring out the truth. After all, perjury is still a crime and highly punishable. Marjorie has her marriage certificate, with the names of witnesses, the town clerk, the minister. Not all of them would be able to lie in a court with conviction. Too, sir, you have a name.'

Hope flared in Marjorie's tormented young face and a glow filled her eyes. Now Bernard could not look at her any longer either.

'I don't think, however, that we should forget Rory Armagh, himself,' continued Bernard. 'He is not the character his father is. The pressure which would be put upon him might be unsupportable. From what I have heard of him, in certain places in Boston, he might remember his father's money, and that he is the heir . . .'

'No, no!' cried Marjorie, swinging to him eagerly. 'He has just this last year at law school! Then he would tell his father, upon his graduation, that he is already married! That is our agreement. Rory loves me. He will never give me up, willingly, and I would be prepared to put my life on that.'

Bernard said, 'But his father has threatened him, too, and his father is known to keep his threats. Nothing would stop him – to separate you and Rory. His father has enough influence so that Rory would never gain entrance to a law firm of any repute, anywhere. If he set himself up as an independent attorney – he would find few clients. Sir,' he said to Mr Chisholm, 'would you, yourself, risk taking young Mr Armagh into your firm, in the face of his father's opposition?'

Mr Chisholm thought. He thought of his partners, his associates. He became small in his chair. 'No, I wouldn't dare that,' he said finally. 'No, I wouldn't dare. Nor would my partners permit it.'

'But I have money, Papa,' said Marjorie. 'It won't be long before I am twenty-one. It is in your hands to permit me to have Mama's money at that time.'

Mr Chisholm's colour, in his wrinkled pale face, became ghastly. He averted his head. 'Marjorie, I must confess something to you. I – I had control of your mother's money, for she trusted me. During the Panic, a few years ago, I put up her money as collateral for debts, for borrowing . . . It is not lost. In a few years, I hope, I am sure to recover the full worth of my investments, and I will return the money to your – inheritance. But Mr Armagh has threatened to make that impossible – he owns my paper, from the banks . . .'

He put his hands over his face. 'Forgive me, my child,' he said, and his voice broke.

Marjorie was on her knees beside him, embracing him, kissing him frantically. 'Oh, Papa! Oh, Papa, it doesn't matter! I don't care! Please, Papa, look at me. I love you, Papa. It doesn't matter at all.' She was freshly terrified.

'In a few years – your inheritance will be intact, with interest,' said Mr Chisholm, and he sat in Marjorie's arms like an old child, his head on her shoulder. 'You would never have known, my love, if this had not happened.'

'It is all my fault,' said poor Marjorie. 'If I hadn't married Rory when I did, we should not be in this nightmare. Forgive me, Papa. If you can, forgive me. Oh, how could I have brought this down on you, threatened by a low and wicked man, you a gentleman, you, my father! I hate myself. I despise myself. I wish I were dead.' Now, for the first time, sitting on her heels, she burst into tears. She dropped her head on her father's knees and groaned.

'My darling,' said Mr Chisholm, 'don't reproach yourself. Your grandfather, your mother's father, opposed our marriage, too. I never did know why. But we married, just the same, and I never regretted it, and the old gentleman came around nicely.' He paused. 'But I don't think Armagh will do that.' He lifted Marjorie's face in tender hands and kissed her again and again. 'Hush, my love. I can't bear to hear – those sounds – hush, my love. You are young. There will be a way – you are young.'

Bernard waited, suffering with them, until Mr Chisholm put Marjorie back in her chair. He said, 'Mr Armagh has mentioned, in these papers, that Marjorie was under age and did not have her father's written consent when she "allegedly", he says, married his son. And that, apparently, the marriage has not been consummated.' Bernard coughed. 'It says in these papers that Rory Armagh and Marjorie Chisholm have never – co-habited.'

He looked at Mr Chisholm. 'So, we have a small choice. Marjorie can sue for annulment of her marriage, which was never – consummated, very quietly, in New Hampshire. No names will be mentioned in the press, says Mr Armagh. It will be secretly arranged. Very delicate, very refined, of Mr Armagh, isn't it?' Bernard's mouth twisted with disgust. 'That is to save, he says, Miss Marjorie Chisholm's reputation and any future marriage she might consummate. I think,' said Bernard, 'he has shown this "generosity" in order to avoid a court suit to maintain the marriage, which might – though it is a small chance – be decided in Marjorie's favour. In spite of all his power. Then, too, I think he wants to avoid an open confrontation in the courts, with the resultant notoriety and scandal. Mr Armagh, I have read, is a man who cherishes his privacy above all else.'

Marjorie sat in her chair, listening. Her face was very calm, very quiet, though the big tears rolled down her cheeks without stopping. She seemed unaware of them. Then she said in a voice without any emotion at all, 'I will seek the annulment. Papa, you must arrange it.'

'My child,' said her father, and could have cried.

'I am not going to think about it,' said Marjorie. 'At least, not yet. I am your daughter, Papa, and I hope I have a little of your courage, and fortitude. I won't think about anything, yet.'

Joseph had not mentioned anything in the papers about the secret little flat in Cambridge, but Marjorie had no doubt that he knew. Why had he refrained from speaking of it? To expedite the annulment of her marriage, for lack of consum-

349

mation? That was, surely, true. She thought of that blissful little place, which had always seemed so full of light to her in spite of its dinginess, and she felt something break and shatter in her. Never to go there again, and cook and wait for Rory. Never to see Rory again, never to hear his voice, feel his kisses, lie in that sagging bed with him, in his arms. She squeezed her eyes shut against the anguish. No, she must not think of that, yet. Otherwise she would die, lose her mind, betray her father. Oh, Rory, Rory, she said in herself, don't suffer too much, my Rory. She could see his face, his smiling sensual mouth, his eyes, his bright colouring; she could hear his voice.

'I will write to Rory tonight,' she said, and her voice had never been so calm. 'It will be easier than telling him. I don't think I could trust myself, if I did. No, I could not.'

She would never tell her father of that little flat in Cambridge. She must let him believe that the marriage had never been consummated. Were he to know he would insist the marriage be maintained, for he was an honourable man.

She wrote to Rory that night, her young face drawn and wizened and dry.

'I have come to the conclusion, after a lot of thought, my dear, that our marriage was doomed from the start. We both deceived our fathers, and so invited calamity. I am not going to lie and say that I have not had a considerable affection for you, but I must confess to you now that that affection has been steadily declining. I have tried to revive it, but have failed. Therefore, I will seek an annulment – no one need know that we had that flat in Cambridge. In mercy, my dear Rory, I hope you will not put me to mortification by appearing in any court and contesting me and my word. I should be for ever shamed and would not be able to take up my life again, as I must. We were full of folly, and our hopes were childish. I will remember you with affection, as a dear friend, as a brother. It was a mistake, from the beginning. We can only go on from this place, and I will remember you ever, with kindness. I am returning the jewellery you gave me, for I cannot keep it in all conscience, now that any love I had for you – or what I thought was love – no longer exists. Please do not try to see me. Please do not write. Nothing can change my resolution. If ever you loved me, please heed my wishes, and cause me no more pain.'

She went to the dark little flat that day and laid the letter and the jewellery on the pillow of the bed. Then she broke down. She flung herself on the bed and hugged the pillows to her desolate young heart and lay, stricken and silent, for a long time, trying to get strength to leave this place for ever. She found a tie Rory had left behind, a worn tie, and she took it with her and left the flat and never looked back.

When Rory read that letter he said to himself, 'It is a lie. It is all a lie.'

Only two days ago he and Marjorie had lain in this bed, clenched together in a joyful and passionate ecstasy of love, and Marjorie had cried again and again, 'Never leave me, Rory, never leave me! Take an oath, Rory, that you will never leave me! I should die, Rory, if I never saw you again!'

His Marjorie, his love, his darling, his little bright wife with her mischief and dimples and intelligent wit and laughter, his Marjorie who never lied: but she was lying now. In some way that old bastard, her father, had found out about them, had forced her to write this letter to her husband, had threatened her. Well, he, Rory, was not going to let this happen to him and Marjorie, no matter what it cost.

For six months, thereafter, he stormed the Chisholm house, the door resolutely unopened for him. For six months he wrote wild accusatory letters to Mr Chisholm, letters full of despair and denunciation, of hatred and threats. He wrote to Marjorie every day. His letters were returned unopened. He tried to waylay her, but he never saw her. He grew thinner and paler, and his bright colouring diminished. He thought of enlisting his father's help. The Armaghs, he thought vengefully, were more than a match for that old soft-spoken pecksniff of a Chisholm.

Then one day he received a sealed packet which informed him that the marriage between one Marjorie Jane Chisholm and one Rory Daniel Armagh, had been annulled in a small obscure court in New Hampshire.

'I was not even subpoenaed,' he said to himself. 'I never knew. Marjorie did this by stealth – her father forced her.' Then he began to vomit and for the first time in his strong young life he became ill and could not leave his bed for several days. He hoped he would die. In fact, he thought of suicide. He gave it long thought, for the dark impulse lurked in him as it lurked in his father.

A year later he was married to Miss Claudia Worthington in the Ambassador's private chapel. Miss Worthington made a spectacular bride and the gushing newspapers spoke of the bridegroom's famous father, his own handsomeness 'and serious demeanour during the ceremony, which was performed by his lordship the Catholic Bishop of London, himself, and three Monsignori'. There were nearly two thousand guests, 'all distinguished', and three Royal Personages, not to mention 'many of the nobility'. The Pope had sent a Papal Blessing for the Nuptial Mass. The wedding was the event of the year, both in America and in England.

When Claudia lay beside him in the marriage bed Rory thought: Oh my God, Marjorie. My little darling, my Marjorie. Oh, my God, my God!

A year after that his first son, Daniel, was born, a year after that his son Joseph, and two years later twin daughters, Rosemary and Claudette.

Claudia Armagh was a most delightful hostess, and all spoke of her charm and gracious personality, her style, her taste, her *savoir faire*, her fascination, her wardrobes, jewels, furs, carriages, and even her large and stately limousine, one of the first to be manufactured in America, her house in London, her house in New York, her villas in France and Italy, 'where the most distinguished members of international society gather for her fiestas and dinners and concerts, which are considered beyond comparison. The most famous singers and violinists appear at *musicales*, at the summoning of Mrs Armagh. She patronises only Worth for her wardrobe, and only Cartier for her jewels. Her taste is impeccable.'

Claudia liked Washington immensely, for now her young husband was a Congressman from Pennsylvania. It is true that there was some uproar about the election, the other party claiming that 'dead men in cemeteries had voted for Rory Armagh, and live men had been bribed'. Mr Armagh had been elected, however, by a majority of one thousand votes over his opponent, who seemed somewhat resigned and contented. After all, one does not quarrel with the generosity of an Armagh. Nor with their power.

Once Claudia said to her husband, pettishly, 'I know that gentlemen are not always faithful to their marriage vows. My father was not. I do not quarrel with this fact. But I do wish,

Rory, that you were not always so – so blatant – but a little more discreet.'

Rory looked for Marjorie in every woman. He never found her.

I am still Rory's wife, Marjorie would think in her lonely little white bed at night, in her father's house. The marriage was consummated. I don't care about courts and lawyers and annulments. I am still Rory's wife and always will be. He's married to someone else, but he is still my husband, before God if not before man. Rory, Rory, I know you love me, and will always love me, as I love you. You will never know that I watched you from an upper window when you banged on Papa's door, and that I had to hold myself not to run down to you and throw myself into your arms, no matter what happened. Rory, Rory, how can I live without you, my love, my dearest? Papa thinks I gave you up for him, but I did it for you. Perhaps some day you will know, though I will never tell you. Oh, my Rory, my Rory. My husband, my darling. There will never be anyone else.

There was never anyone else. Her father and her aunt pleaded with her to 'encourage' the young men who besieged her, but she would say, 'I am not interested.' How could a wife be interested in any other man but her husband? It was infamous even to think of it. It was adultery, even to think of it. She would hold Rory's old tie against her breast at night, and kiss it and fondle it, and then sleep with it under her cheek. In some way she knew that Rory was thinking of her also, and that in spite of what divided them their love reached out for each other and could never be destroyed. This comforted her. Rory was her own and she was his. Then she began a fantasy. One day, sooner or later, Rory would return. It helped her through the years.

CHAPTER FORTY-FIVE

JOSEPH ARMAGH built a magnificent mansion for his son, Rory, and Claudia and their children on a fine tract of land adjoining his own house in Green Hills. The property was known thereafter as 'the Armagh Settlement'.

Bernadette was queen of the 'Settlement'. She was the Empress, the ruling mistress of the dynasty. She boasted that her grandchildren adored her. If Daniel, as some people said, had the teeth of a chipmunk, it did not matter. If Joseph whined perpetually and sulked, it was just his way. If the little girls were rude and not very bright, they were at least somewhat pretty. They trailed her contentedly as her own children had never trailed her. For she was always indulgent, and always, especially before an audience, the doting grandmother. She would almost squat before them – before an audience – her enormous hams thrusting out behind her – and speak to them in a sugary rich fashion. Daniel, the most intelligent, was a born cynic, and he would smirk. But he would play this game also, for Grandma was always ready with an extra dollar, or a treat, if she were pleased. The children would cluster about Bernadette, before an audience, and everybody was deeply affected. Such a close family, such affection, such devotion and loyalty. In private Bernadette would admonish the boys: 'We have a Name to live up to. We must do everything correctly. You have a future.' To the girls she would say: 'You must make good marriages. You owe that to your father and your grandparents.' They hardly understood her, at their age, but they had some respect for her, which was more than they had for their parents. Bernadette still had a 'hard hand on her', as Joseph once said.

In September 1901 Harry Zeff suddenly died of a heart attack in his mansion in Philadelphia, leaving his beloved wife, Liza, and his twin sons, now both dedicated physicians and very upright if somewhat obtuse young men. Both were married to girls of sound family, and both had young children. Harry had been proud of them.

A week later, when Charles was on the way home from Philadelphia his train was derailed and partially wrecked. Three men died in it. Charles was one of them.

'Christ, Christ,' said Joseph, when he received the telegram from Philadelphia. He went upstairs to his study and stayed there three days and nights and did not come out. He never answered the door. He never touched the trays which were left at it. Whether he slept or not, no one knew. No one ever knew that for the second time in his life he got drunk.

CHAPTER FORTY-SIX

ANN MARIE was thirty-six years old, and her brother, now a Senator, came from Washington to Green Hills – the 'Settlement' – to celebrate their joint birthday. His wife came with him, querulous as always and expressing her opinion that this was a hardship considering that 'the Season was in full bloom, and you need to be Seen, Rory'. Her children, neglected and brought up by well-paid but indifferent servants and governesses, annoyed her. Mentally a child herself, she thought of them as rivals. She reminded Rory that her parents had planned a birthday party for him in Washington and now it must be postponed for several days. 'After all,' she would complain to Rory, 'you owe everything to the fact that you married me and I am of a Distinguished Family, and your father is only a businessman.'

She could not understand why Rory laughed himself almost into hysteria.

Ann Marie seemed more of a child than ever, rosy, fat, smiling innocently, babbling, playing with her dolls. Rory, her twin, sat in her rooms with her and tried to find, in that blank face and those luminous sherry-coloured eyes, some trace of the sister he had loved, and who had grown in the womb with him. Once, when they were alone, he said to her very quietly, 'Ann Marie? Do you remember Courtney?'

The rosy smile had widened. But all at once Rory saw, in those shining eyes, a shadow, a terror, an anguish which jolted him. Then it was gone. He was shaken. How much did Ann Marie remember? Was she lurking behind that plump and roseate façade, hiding? The soft lax hand in his had tightened, had grasped, and then it was limp again and she was talking about her new doll. When he stood up to go, sighing, she had looked up at him and the smile was gone.

She had recognised him, then, though when he had appeared only an hour ago she had looked at him questioningly, with a child's shy and wary smile, shrinking at the sight of a stranger.

He bent over his sister, himself resplendent and shining

even in the pale and bitter sunlight of March, and the icy reflection of the glittering snow outside. 'Yes, dear,' he said. She put her fat arms up to him and he held her, and he felt the trembling of her cheek against his. Then she moaned, 'Rory, Rory. Oh, Rory – Courtney.' She clutched him desperately, and he dared not move or speak.

Then she had dropped her arms and he had straightened up and she was giving him, once again, a very young child's wide-eyed stare. She giggled. She pushed a doll at him and said, 'Kiss, kiss.'

His mother said to him, with a weariness not entirely affected, 'I wish to God your father would permit her to go to a good private institution. You have no idea of the hopelessness, Rory, and the responsibility. Ann Marie is becoming so heavy that nurses complain, and leave, no matter what we pay them. She is walking less and less, and spends more and more time in bed, and she is so fat that I can't understand what the doctors mean by "atrophy". She certainly isn't wasting! She can't go for drives any longer. It is almost impossible to get her up and down the stairs, and now your father is installing an elevator for her. She looks like an infant. It is more than I can bear. Do talk to your father. When we have parties here, she sometimes screeches from upstairs and it unnerves people, and sometimes she fights with her nurses and is uncontrollable and shouts that she has to go to the woods. Really, Rory.' She sighed. 'Worse and worse. And Rory – sometimes the smell! It is disgusting, and I am ashamed to speak of it. The whole upstairs, sometimes . . . Complete degeneration, the doctors say, who agree with me that she'd be far better off in some institution.'

'She never speaks about – anything?' Rory asked.

'No. If I don't see her for a few days, and God knows I am always here now, and I go into her rooms she stares at me and whimpers and doesn't recognise me, her own mother. It is very strange. She does recognise your father, no matter how long his absences are. I feel there is a curse upon this family, Rory, a curse.'

'Now, Ma,' he said, but he frowned. He did not speak to his father.

Joseph tried to be in Green Hills at least one week in every month to see his daughter. She always greeted him with such delight that he would dare to hope, for a minute or two, that she had returned to this world, for she knew him and would hold out her arms to him and cuddle against him, shyly. But within an hour or two she was withdrawn, smiling that little childish smile, and babbling. He would smooth that soft brown hair, and notice the widening bands of grey, and the increasing wrinkles in the soft rosy face. Sometimes she seemed sixty years old, blubbery, almost massive in her fat, inert, blinking, not seeing, not knowing. But how can I send her away? he would think. This is all she has, her home, these rooms, her toys, her nurses. He would look into her eyes, childlike still, and try to find his daughter, to discover that 'soul' that had once inhabited this bloated flesh. But it was like peering down into a deep well where only reflections rippled the surface.

He came back to Green Hills on a June morning so warm, so radiant, so full of brightness, that it was like a promise of coming joy. The roses rampaged from every bed on the estate, red and white and yellow, and were full of scent under the blowing trees. He remembered that spring day when he had first seen Green Hills and had heard the peepers in the trees and had seen the shine of blue water and the brisk arrowing of birds from limb to limb. What had he told himself then, what had he promised himself? He could not remember. I am an old man, he thought. I am tired, and old, and my hair is white and it is a burden to wake up in the morning and confront the day. Yet I must. Why? I do not know. I have yet to find out what drives us. He suspected that the tiredness of his body came from his mind and not from his still vigorous lean body and his supple muscles, but that did not decrease the weariness, the mounting sense of futility that ran over him like a tidal wave when he was most vulnerable. He was no more interested in his grandchildren – about whom Bernadette was always prattling – than he had been when his own children were this young age. Their occasional presence in his house bored and annoyed him. The shrillness of their voices, the pounding of their feet on wood or marble, their empty faces, depressed him. There was a growing fad these days about 'The Children', and he found it obnoxious and irritating, and when his friends spoke of their grandchildren he thought them fatuous, and knew that they knew they were.

Daniel and Joseph, nine and eight respectively, were already attending boarding school ('thank God,' Joseph would remark). The little girls, pretty but vacuous of face, were still at home. Now this was June, and the boys were in Green Hills and shouting 'all over the damned place', thought Joseph. Why didn't that fool of a mother of theirs try to restrain them, or their governesses thrash them? When Joseph spoke of his grandchildren to their father, Rory, Rory would say with a curious smile, 'I don't think they are too bad. Of course, they are not very intelligent, but neither is their mother. And you *did* want me to marry their mother, didn't you, Pa? Matter of inheritance. At least they are equal to Claudia now in their minds, if that is any consolation, which it isn't.'

Marjorie's children, Rory would think, would be bright and witty and spirited, not 'lumps', as Joseph called his grandchildren. Marjorie's children would be full of radiant mischief, but gentle, kind, understanding, perceptive. Marjorie. Marjorie, my darling, Rory would think, looking at his children with their red hair and pallid blue eyes and big teeth. Claudette was certainly no more aware of life than Ann Marie. Sometimes she drooled. 'Blood will out!' Rory would say roundly to his father, with a strange grin. 'Claudia's blood.' But he could not understand why his father would then look so sombre and turn away, for never had he suspected that Joseph had had any part of the annulment of his marriage. You can't make a silk purse out of a sow's ear, Rory would think, contemplating his children and their mother. But he did not speak of this to Joseph.

If only I could get rid of Claudia and not endanger my career, Rory would often say to himself. That foolish woman with her big backside and fat bowed legs and airs and graces! He no longer saw her charm, her formidable power of entrancement. He did not particularly like his mother but he resented Claudia's malicious imitations of her, the Irish imitations. Once he said to Claudia, 'When your ancestors were grubbing for English squires and sawing wood my ancestors were noble in Ireland,' to which she had replied, 'Really! No one takes the Irish seriously. Hod-carriers, and such.' She loved wine. She was always complaining of Rory's vulgar whisky. 'Whisky is not civilised,' she would say. 'Only *brutes* drink it.' Rory would look pointedly at her hands and she would darkly flush and hide them.

Now it was June and Rory and Claudia were in Devon – 'to hear the nightingales!' Claudia would sing, throwing back her head and showing all her huge white teeth. (Horse teeth.

Bernadette would say.) Rory was in England for another matter. concerning the Committee for Foreign Studies, and was his father's emissary. 'Gentlemen's affairs!' Claudia would carol in her infant's voice, when Rory went to London each week. They rented an estate in Devon each summer, for Rory, for a reason he would not explain to Claudia, refused to buy a house in England, though he remained in his father-in-law's house in London when he was in town. Unknown even to his father he would manage to visit Ireland for a few days also, and went to Carney where Joseph had been born. The poverty and misery of the Irish drove clefts about his mouth.

His children remained in the 'Settlement' for the summer, ostensibly under the devoted care of Bernadette, their grand-mother, who loved to parade them briefly before her friends, but only briefly. 'I am not here very often,' Joseph would say to her, 'so is it necessary for them to be screeching in my house when I come? Send them home. I bought them a fine house, and let them stay there.' The children feared him; they would look sideways with sly eyes at him, and hate him, but they obeyed him always and never muttered as they did with Bernadette. He could not endure the constant grins of the little girls, which showed the great white teeth they had in-herited from their mother, and Daniel's whining and spoiled demands infuriated him. 'I am afraid the girls are idiots,' Joseph would say to his wife, 'and Daniel is effeminate and Joe is a boor. Keep them far from me.' But still, they were his grandchildren.

He came to Green Hills to be with his daughter, and with Elizabeth. when she was home. She did not visit him very often now in New York or Philadelphia or Boston. 'I am almost sixty, my dear,' she would say to Joseph, 'and I tire easily now and travel is wearing. I don't know how you manage the travel so much. either.' She had retained the figure of her girl-hood, graceful and lissome, and Joseph thought she still looked like a young woman though the fine silky pale hair was more silver than blonde now, and her complexion had faded. But her green eyes were pure and steadfast and calm. 'You are much younger than I am,' Joseph would say to her, holding her tightly in his arms. 'You should not be so tired all the time.' Neither of them spoke of Courtney, for he had become a monk in a cloister in Amalfi and seldom wrote to his mother and then only to thank her for a gift she had made to his monastery. But Joseph knew Elizabeth's grief that the estrangement between mother and son had never been healed. She would say to Joseph, 'I have no one but you, my dearest, no one in the world, no sister or brother or cousin or nephew or niece. I have only you.' Her exhaustion seemed more pronounced each time Joseph saw her and he was becoming alarmed. Elizabeth smiled. 'I am in perfect health, Joseph, after all I am not young any longer.'

It seemed to him this June that there was a transparency about Elizabeth which he had not noticed a month ago, a translucence in her face which made her appear ethereal. She had visited her doctor recently, she assured him, and her health was not impaired. Passion was not spent between them, but it had reached a stage of tranquillity, of profound acceptance, of absolute trust. They would sit, or lie, for hours, without speaking, their hands clasped together, and it was the only peace Joseph had ever known or would know. He thought of Elizabeth as his wife, and she thought of him as her husband. He was, as she often said, all she had in the world. Her one terror was that he would die and leave her. He had to reassure her over and over again that he would not permit this, and he would smile. He came of a hardy, long-lived race, in spite of the early deaths of his parents. 'You can't kill the Irish,' he would say, 'except with a bullet or far old age. We are made of steel and rope. We've had to learn how to survive.' Elizabeth thought of Bernadette, fifty-five, coarsely vital if enormously fat and lumbering, with her heavy red complexion and loud voice and hair just slightly grey. Elizabeth had seen women like her in the markets of Europe, as strong as men and as vigorous. Elizabeth would sigh. Bernadette would live to be a very hearty old woman, into her nineties, eating and sleeping with zest and animal passion. Elizabeth had never known of Bernadette's great love for her husband which had never weakened at all through the years.

'You spend more time with That Woman than you do with your own family,' Bernadette would complain to Joseph. 'Managing her affairs,' she would add hastily. 'Doesn't she have lawyers, for God's sake? Yes, I know my father made you one of the executors, with his bank, but still . . . She lives like a nun in Green Hills. Her old friends hardly see her. She must be getting very, very old, and a recluse.'

This June Bernadette said to her husband, making her voice regretful, 'I have heard that Elizabeth is not very well. Some say she looks like a skeleton. She doesn't go – to town – much any more. Really. Well, at her age . . . Yes, I know she is younger than you, my dear, but then she isn't Irish. The English fade early. No stamina any longer. They're really decadent, you know. All the strength seems to have drained out of them. They're as bad, now, as the French.'

Joseph thought of a recent meeting he had had with his colleagues in Paris. His face tightened. He said, 'I think, in a war, that the English, whom I detest, would do very well. Very well indeed. They are not so decadent as we'd like to believe they are. The Anglo-Saxon can be a tough old party. And the French, in spite of their everlasting wars, can be as bull-doggy as the English, if not more so.'

'Well, there won't be any more wars,' said Bernadette. It was nearly twelve years since Kevin had been killed, but she remembered. He had been the one child she had come close to loving, though she was proud of Rory and gloried in him. There were times when she was actually fond of him, for everyone spoke of his splendour and his glowing personality and his affable disposition and intelligence. 'He is just like my father,' she would say with pride. 'He was the handsomest Senator in Washington, and when he was Governor no one could resist him. Rory is the very image of him. We expect wonderful things of Rory.'

Bernadette could endure even Claudia when Rory was home, but now Rory was in London and Claudia was in Devon. That silly affected conceited creature! Bernadette thought. She gets worse every year. And that dark coarse complexion of hers, and her gloves! Common blood. Now she chatters all the time in French, to her children, and even her servants, and her accent is really abominable. Schoolgirl-ish. She may impress low and ignorant people, but not me, my girl, not me. And everyone knows how tight-fisted you are, except when it comes to your own clothes and jewels, and how you pare the cheese when you are here. Shameful. Self-indul-gent creature, with no more brains in your head than a peacock. At least a peacock's pretty, which you aren't. Poor

Rory. Bernadette knew that Claudia snubbed her. It made her at once hilarious and infuriated.

Ann Marie's doctors tried to soothe Joseph. It is true, they said, that she was degenerating physically, but she might still live for years. It is true, they said, that she had to be helped into chairs and bed now and could hardly walk. But her health was superb, considering everything. Her appetite was good, though her food was bland, like a young child's. But she thrived on it. Her mind, they would say, had not shown more degeneration, which was a hopeful sign. 'Hopeful for what?' Joseph had asked them with bitterness, and they had not answered.

The elevator had been installed, and Ann Marie was helped into it by panting nurses assisted by the butler and the handy-man, and she was taken into the gardens almost every day, to sit hugely in a chair, smiling in the sunlight and asking for flowers – which she promptly tore to shreds in fat rosy fingers, squealing all the time like an infant. She cried as easily and as loudly as an infant also, something which the doctors did not tell Joseph, and it was a mindless crying. It was only when she slept that she would suddenly awaken, wailing like a woman, and calling, calling in thick confused accents. Lately it had taken hours of cajoling – and sedatives – to soothe her back to sleep, and when she slept after the outbreak her face was the face of a heartbroken woman.

Joseph spent hours with her every day this June, reading books or newspapers in the shade of thick dark trees, some-times listening to his daughter's babble, sometimes taking her hand, sometimes talking simply to her. She basked in his presence, and smiled, and if he had to leave her for a minute or two she cried, big tears running down her face. It would demand much of his strength to pacify her, while she clung to his hand on his return. Was he imagining it or was she showing a new fear this time, a new awareness of her desola-tion? He could not tell.

When he came to Green Hills he would invariably bring his daughter a new doll, a new toy, which she would receive with delight and crows of pleasure. He had brought her a Teddy Bear this time, which had been created in honour of Theodore Roosevelt. She hugged it to her flabby breast and murmured to it, and Joseph, with his book in his hand, watched her with a despair that never lessened. He knew, this June, that the long hope he had had was finally gone. His daughter had left long ago, on that ghastly day in the woods at the top of the hill. But where had she gone? This piteous creature was not Ann Marie. It was only an animal which had long lost even a semblance of the slim shy girl of earlier years, except for the eyes. There, in those eyes, Joseph would often fancy, there was a distant tiny figure, the figure of Ann Marie, on a far plane, longing to leave, and as despairing as himself, lonely, isolated, existing in Limbo.

But still he could not bear the thought of this body dying, for the body held Ann Marie in thrall so that she could not leave her father. She lingered, at an immeasurable distance it was true, but she lingered. At least, this was what Joseph believed and wanted to believe. When he looked into his daughter's eyes he would hail the infinitesimal figure of her in the clear pupil, and often he thought that she hailed him back, young, sweet, full of love and that delicate tenderness for him which he had known for years too brief and painful to remember.

There had never been a June day so perfect in temperature and shining quiet and fragrance, and the glistening green lawns spread all about the estate and the gardens shouted with roses and there was a singing fountain nearby, rainbowed in the sun. Leaf shadows fluttered over Ann Marie's face as she alternately murmured to her new Teddy Bear or crossly slapped it or hugged it. Her dry drab hair had been braided and then tied with pink ribbons, and the plaits lay on her gross bosom incongruously. She was fatter even than her mother, but her muscles were soft and weak and flaccid. Her legs, covered by a light blue rug, did not move. The big mansion gleamed like alabaster in the sunlight, and shadows tossed themselves radiantly over white wall and red roof and polished pillars. There was a breeze, and it made the far distant trees run greenly and nimbly up the hills.

Not even a gardener was in view, and the sunlight lay blindingly on the windows of the mansion and all was brilliant silence and peace. Joseph tried to read, sitting near his daughter on the lawn. Her babbling, softer now, was the only sound in that radiance.

Then Ann Marie was quiet. Joseph read. It was a confidential letter from Rory, in London, and though ambiguously worded it was important. His writing was small but black and concentrated, and if dispassionate to the casual eye Joseph could read between the lines. He almost forgot Ann Marie as he read.

Then he heard her say, softly and clearly, 'Papa?'

'Yes, dear,' he answered, not taking his eyes from the letter. Then suddenly it came to him, piercingly, that there had been a strange new note in Ann Marie's voice, aware, quickened, understanding. The pages of the letter fell from his hands to the grass as he looked up. Ann Marie was gazing at him, not with the rosy foolish fondness of all these years, the childish fondness, but with mature and sorrowful love.

She was transformed. The fat cheeks had flattened, the features sharpening instant by instant. The eyes grew large, widened, and Ann Marie was there, imminent, within touching distance. She had returned, was inhabiting her body again. A middle-aged woman looked at him, completely conscious, completely in the world, completely adult. The soul had come forward from vast spaces into the present. The loose mouth had dried, and all its contours were womanly and intelligent, and it was trembling.

But she was very pale. There was no colour in her face now except for her eyes, those glistening and shimmering eyes which held Ann Marie.

Oh God, Joseph thought. Oh, my God. His body began to shake; sweat broke out on his forehead. He leaned to his daughter to make sure, daring to hope, daring to accept this miracle. And she gazed back at him, faintly smiling, her eyes brightening moment by moment. 'Papa?' she said again. The Teddy Bear slipped from her arms, her thighs, and tumbled to the grass, and she did not know it.

Joseph pushed himself to his feet, shaking like a palsied old man. He wanted to shout, to cry for help, to run for assistance. But he could only stand, clutching the side of his chair. It was a light garden chair and could not bear his weight, standing, and it fell away from him with a clatter, and he staggered.

He took a step to Ann Marie, his head roaring, his ears clanging as if with bells, and he did not look away from her for fear that she would vanish again. He fell on his knees beside her. She held up her hands to him and he took them and stared into her face.

'Ann Marie,' he said. 'Ann Marie?'

'Yes, Papa,' she answered, and smiled at him. The sorrow was deep in her eyes. 'Poor Papa,' she said. She took one hand from him and smoothed his white hair, and she sighed. Her pallor was increasing. There was a fine shine of moisture all over her face, and she had begun to pant a little, rapidly, with a shallow indrawing of breath. A deep pulse was thrumming in that massive throat.

'You've come back, my darling,' said Joseph. His voice was dry and thick and choked.

'I never went away. I just hid,' said Ann Marie. Her face was like white wet stone in the blowing shadows of the leaves. 'I just slept,' she said, and her hand gently smoothed her father's hair. 'But I always heard you, Papa.'

'You won't go away again?' said Joseph, and his heart was pounding so furiously that he felt faint. 'You will stay this time, Ann Marie?'

She was shaking her head slowly and ponderously, but she still held his hand, and it was cold and slippery in his. 'Courtney is here; he is calling me. I am going away with him, Papa. He's come for me. You mustn't grieve. I am so glad to go. I stayed just now because I wanted to say good-bye to you, and tell you how much I love you and how sorry I am that I've caused you so much pain. Forgive me, Papa. I couldn't help it, but forgive me.'

Then her face was brilliant with joy and love and ecstasy, and she looked beyond him and cried out, 'Courtney! Courtney, I am coming!' Her eyes were like the sun itself. She pulled her hand from her father's and held out her arms to something only she could see, and there was a murmurous sound of rapture in her throat.

'Ann Marie!' Joseph cried, feeling madness about him, and terror and coldness. 'Oh, Christ!' he almost screamed, and took his transfigured daughter in his arms and pulled her against his chest. There was a quaking in him, heightened terror, a furious denial, and the bright day grew shadowy about him. Ann Marie resisted feebly, then she was still, and she collapsed against him and her head fell to his shoulder. He could no longer hear her breathe.

Then she sighed, and quivered all over her body, a long deep rippling of all her flesh, a final convulsion. She uttered one last sound, a fragile cry like a bird.

Joseph knelt and held his daughter to him, heavy against him, heavy in his arms. He said, again and again, 'Ann Marie, Ann Marie.' But only the wind answered in the trees. He began to stroke the fallen head on his shoulder.

Ann Marie Armagh was buried beside her brother under the pointed shadow of the tall marble obelisk, and the priest intoned, 'I am the Resurrection and the Life . . .' The black grave yawned and the dully gleaming bronze casket was slowly lowered into it, sprinkled with holy water, and with earth. Bernadette sobbed beside her husband. Friends stood about them, mutely. They watched Joseph, so grey and still and stiff, but so indomitable and grim and they thought – and later said to each other – that he had shown no grief at all and had not tried to comfort his wife. Unfeeling, they said. Yet it had been rumoured that he had 'adored' his daughter. Ah well, it was merciful that she had died at last. Just a burden on her poor mother, who had been a slave to her all these years. The girl had never been very intelligent, and the accident had taken away her last glimmer of intellect. The roses, white and red and pink, covered the raw earth. Tombstones glowed palely all about them in the hot June sun. Leaf shadows ran over the grass.

That night Bernadette sobbed to her husband, 'Yes, there is a curse on this family! I've known it for years! Now we have no child left but Rory. My last child!'

There was more fear in her than sorrow, superstitious fear. She said, 'What will become of us if we lose Rory? I have such a feeling . . .'

'Damn you, and your feelings,' said Joseph, and left her.

She forgave him, as usual, for only she knew how distraught he was, and how he prowled the house and the gardens at night, and how often he went to the cemetery.

A few days after Ann Marie had been buried Bernadette came to him in his rooms, carrying a newspaper in her hands, and her face, though swollen with weeping, was portentous and even a little excited.

'It is in the newspapers!' she exclaimed. 'Courtney Hennessey, my brother, died of a stroke on the very day Ann Marie – passed away! Here, Joseph, read it for yourself! His mother was notified by cable. He's been buried in the monastery burial grounds. It's all here.'

He took the paper in a hand that felt paralysed and numb. He read, the lines blurring before his eyes. He said to himself, 'So it was true. He came for her.'

He threw the paper from him and turned away. 'I feel sorry for her,' said Bernadette. 'He was all she had. My brother. I suppose I should feel sad, and I will have Masses said for his soul, but I really can't feel very much. Not very much. Maybe Courtney, and his mother, brought the curse on us.' Joseph was leaving the room. 'Where?' she asked him, but he did not answer. She began to cry, for she knew where he was going.

CHAPTER FORTY-SEVEN

IT had been a hot July day and it was nearly sunset, but the sky was a darkish copper against which the trees were turned a fierce unnatural green, and the hills had become sharp and tawny. Everything stood out in that ominous light with a hurtful vividness and clarity and appeared too close, too insistent, too detailed. Every blade of grass was distinct, painful, like an emerald razor that could cut the foot, and the colours of the flowers in their beds had a nightmare intensity. There was a profound hush over all things; nothing moved, not a leaf, not a bud. Even the fountains in the gardens had become noiseless, and there were no birds in sight.

The countryman in Joseph knew that the absence of birds at this time of the day meant a storm. He went down the gravel path to the gate and then into the road, and down the road to Elizabeth's house. The copper of the sky had taken on a sheen, to the west, like brass. A hot breath, not a breeze or a gust, touched Joseph's set face, and it smelled of sulphur to him and burning dryness. He entered the gates of Elizabeth's house. He had not seen a carriage or a person on the road. All things had taken instinctive refuge. He heard, now, the explosion of gravel under his feet and it was like a shotgun being constantly discharged, the birdshot scattering.

There were white seats and tables under the heavy dark oak

near the house, and there Elizabeth sat in a white dress too bright in that sinister illumination. She had a white shawl over her shoulders. Her pale soft hair, so severely dressed, her face and her still body, might have been the figure of a seated statue. She did not stir when she saw him. She only watched him leave the path and come towards her. Then, when he was almost before her, she rose and threw herself soundlessly into his arms and they clung together without a word, held each other as if they were dying. Elizabeth's cold face was pressed against the side of his neck. His chest crushed her breast, his arms were like iron on her thin flesh. She held him as desperately. She did not cry or moan or utter a sound.

They did not even think of watchers, of curtains being held aside, of curious eyes looking. From her own window Bernadette could see those distant figures clenched together in an agony she was not permitted to share with her husband. She dropped the lace curtain and leaned her head against the side of the latticed window and cried silently, the slow and bitter drops falling one by one down her face without a sob. It was her child who had died, but Joseph had gone to a stranger for consolation, and was holding her as if they had become one motionless upright body, Elizabeth's white dress as still as stone. For the first time Bernadette knew that Joseph would never love her, and that he would most probably leave her. She let herself fall weightily on her knees at the window and bent her head on the marble sill and gave herself to sorrow as if she were a widow and her husband would not return. The tears made dark little stains on the marble and Bernadette pressed her open and tormented mouth against the sill, and she felt the slow agonised breaking of her heart. She had never known such abandonment, such suffering, such humble anguish, in all her life. There was no hatred in her yet, only a deep groaning.

A wild wind suddenly rose, and there was a flash of lightning, then another, and a stunning smash of thunder. The brazen light was swept away by the turbulence of black clouds. Lightning flashed again and again, and the trees shook their green manes at it in fury. Then the rain came, sheets of glittering silver in the glare from the sky, pounding, rushing, roaring. It shut off all visibility. Bernadette lay supine and dumb on the floor of her room near the window, staring blindly at the terrible radiance that flashed over her.

Joseph and Elizabeth sat in the darkness and white fire that invaded the morning room. They sat side by side, their hands held together, staring at nothing, only half listening to the howling and raving of the storm, the wind, the thunder. They felt comfort in their nearness, and yet grief divided them so that they wanted to console each other and draw even closer. So Joseph told Elizabeth of Ann Marie's last words to him, and how she had cried out to Courtney and had appeared to 'see' him, and that he had 'come' for her. Elizabeth listened in silence, and now her eyes fixed themselves with a mournful absorption on Joseph's face, alternately hidden from her in darkness, and then revealed in lightning.

'I am glad,' she said at last in her controlled voice which trembled only slightly. 'I believe – I want to believe – that my son came for your daughter. Is there any other explanation for Ann Marie's knowing, and, as you have told me, her almost joyful dying?'

Joseph gently kissed her chilled cheek. He told her then of how his dying mother had apparently 'seen' his dead father, who had come for her. Yet he knew surely that it had been only coincidence, the last desire of the dying. He did not tell Elizabeth this, but she sensed his resistance. 'Don't you believe Courtney came for Ann Marie, Joseph?' she asked. 'Don't you think your father came for your mother?'

He did not want to add to her pain. He hesitated. 'I have heard of clairvoyance,' he said. 'It might have been only that.'

'But what is clairvoyance?' she said. 'It is a word, and we do have a habit of covering the inexplicable with a word and then thinking we have solved the matter by giving it a name. We have only added to the mystery. I believe – I believe . . . For the first time I truly believe. I have been only a nominal Catholic, sceptical and aloof, smiling at reports of miracles and simple mysteries, and now I think I was a fool. A sophisticated silly fool, who was too stupid to marvel and wonder – and hope. You have given me hope, Joseph, and please don't smile.'

'I am not smiling,' he said, and she saw his face in another burst of lightning and she thought he looked very ill. He thought of the three graves in the family plot, Sean, Kevin, Ann Marie, and the black earth which had swallowed those he had loved and he knew that he could not believe that they were more than their dead flesh and that they were aware, still, and conscious in some unfathomable place beyond the stars. It was against sense, against reason. A live dog, King David had said, was better than a dead lion, for he had being, and Sean and Kevin and Ann Marie and Harry and Charles had no being any longer, and had ceased to exist. He thought of Harry, and all the vitality and zest that had been Harry's and he thought of Charles, educated and intellectual and urbane. All that had gone out in the blink of an eye and there was nothing left, and no knowledge in them that they had ever lived. A rational man had to accept that, and not reach for mist and myths out of the torture of his heart.

But women were different. They had to be cosseted by comforting lies and made to believe the irrational. So Joseph said, 'It may be true that they are together now, for Ann Marie had no way of knowing that Courtney was dead . . .' For the very first time Joseph thought of the mother of his children, and she had lost two of them, and she had loved Kevin and had been inconsolable for months, and he could hear her crying in the night, possibly not for her daughter but for the misery of the years of her daughter. Damn, he thought. I never even considered her. She knew, I am sure, where I was going tonight. Bernadette is no fool. Perhaps she has known about Elizabeth and me all the time. She would have had to be an idiot not to know.

He had felt compassion for Bernadette only on a very few occasions in their life together, a tight, sour compassion. But now he felt a sick deep spasm of pity for his wife. He knew that she loved him, and really loved only him, and he revolted, as usual, against that love but now it was with pity also, even if that pity was tinged with his usual impatience. He had a horror of returning to that house and his wife, and confronting his sorrow again, his unbearable sorrow, in the silence of his rooms. He knew he would find himself listening for some sound from his daughter's suite, some childish babbling, some childish laughter, some cry or a call for him, as he had heard it for many years when he was home. But only the night would answer him. The rooms had been dismantled of their hospital equipment and utilitarian furniture, and had become, again, a pretty young woman's suite, to which Ann Marie would never return laughing from a ride on her horse, or singing at her little white piano, or running lightly over the polished wood. All at once the poor existing flesh which had been his daughter for years vanished from his memory, and it was the healthy shy Ann Marie he remembered now, with her soft little touches on his arm, her uplifted gentle face, her questioning dark amber eyes. At least that had returned to him like a ghost, but it did not relieve his grief. It made it worse, for it was as if Ann Marie, in full health and youth, had suddenly died and then had vanished, with her very voice in his ears and the very scent of her about him, and a last flash of her face.

The goddamn earth is one tomb, he thought, and we the walkers on countless graves. We would have been better if none of us had ever been born, to go through this, and for what? So we can have a few days of laughing, of hope, of ambition, of striving, and then nothing? Are they worth living for? I don't think so. What had Charles called this? 'The dark night of the soul.' But we have dark nights of the soul for the most of our lives, and only a brief dawn or two, or a little music, or the touch of a living hand occasionally, and I, for one, don't think it is worthwhile considering the whole of existence.

'Come to New York next week,' he said to Elizabeth, but without urgency, for there was such a weight in his chest, such a despair.

'Yes,' she said, and she knew what he was experiencing, for she felt it herself.

The storm was passing. Elizabeth did not ask him to stay when he stood up. But she looked at him and prayed as she had not prayed since she was a child, that he would be comforted, for there was no comfort any human being could give him, just as she could not be comforted even by the tenderest words. Only the dead could comfort the living, and they were silent. But hope was like a flowering star in her. She would think for hours of Ann Marie 'seeing' Courtney and running out of her mountainous flesh like a bride to join him. She knew that Joseph had told her in order to comfort her, and she took his dropped hand and pressed it to her cheek and wished that he had this frail hope also. It was only a gossamer thread to hold on to in the dark whirlpool of grief, but it shone in one's hand and in one's heart and perhaps such fragility was the truth after all.

Joseph bent and kissed her with the gentleness of shared

anguish, and then he went out into the warm diminishing rain and the almost violent freshness and fragrance of the new night after a storm. A full moon was now racing madly through tatters of black clouds, and Elizabeth stood at her door and watched Joseph as long as she could see him in that mingled white brilliance and utter darkness. She had willed him to come to her that night for she had been in frozen terror and despair, and she needed comforting and consolation and promises never to leave her. For she had heard, just before the news of Courtney's death, that she had inoperable cancer and that she had, at the most, only six months to live. Had not Ann Marie and Courtney died when they did she would have told him, lying in the strength and surety of his arms. But now he was as desolate as herself and he could not bear more grief at this time. She was thankful she had not told him. She would never tell him. Shared suffering and fear did not decrease them; they only added to the burden, for then two suffered instead of one. I must have courage, she said to herself, as she saw that Joseph was no longer in sight. What has to be will be and there is nothing one can do. At the end, we stand alone, just as we are born alone.

There was no sound except of servants in that great white mansion in the new night, and Joseph went upstairs. He passed Bernadette's room. The door was open and there was no light inside. He paused. Moonlight ran into the room and then was obliterated, but not before he saw Bernadette lying on the floor near the windows, not stirring, not speaking. He went to her at once and knelt beside her and then when the moonlight flared again, he saw her wet and swollen face and the yearning and grief in her eyes.

He put his arms under her shoulders and drew her to him and held her, and she cried against him but said nothing, and he was ashamed and no longer impatient and he said, 'There, there, my dear, it was for the best after all. Don't cry like that.' But he knew that she was not at this moment crying for Ann Marie. He said, 'Believe me, Bernadette, I will never leave you. I swear to God, I will never leave you.'

The dinner bell rang softly, and at last they went downstairs together, hand in hand, and Bernadette's large red face was brighter and younger than it had been for years.

Joseph had sent a cablegram to Rory of the death of his twin sister and had urged him not to return at once, but to continue his mission. He had said in the cablegram that there was nothing Rory could do, and the death had not been unexpected, and that he was grateful that he had been in Green Hills when Ann Marie had died.

Timothy Dineen, solid, grey-haired, quiet and rock-like, had taken Harry Zeff's place in Joseph's affairs and now lived in Philadelphia. He had never married. He had loved Regina Armagh unswervingly all through these years, with the stubborn dedication of the Irish. He had not known until he was in Philadelphia that she had written to her brother twice a year, and that Charles had had to destroy the letters. He had not known, either, that Charles had taken to writing her briefly a few times a year, informing her of her family. As Joseph's confidential secretary as well as henchman and manager of the Armagh Enterprises now, he opened Joseph's letters in his absence. He opened Regina's, and after all this time he recognised the light delicacy of her writing. His heart jumped. He had thought of Regina as dead long ago, for Joseph had never spoken of her, and at first he could not think of her as Sister Mary Bernarde. As he began to read the letter, shamelessly, feeling the old pain and longing, he gathered that she had not known at all that Joseph did not read her letters. She believed only that he would not answer them, but delegated others to do so. Apparently, however, Bernadette as well as Charles had written to her, and Rory, her nephew. She addressed Joseph with deep love and devotion as 'my dearest brother', and begged, at the end, that he would eventually find it in his heart to forgive her for 'any inadvertent pain I have ever caused you, my dear Joseph, in doing what I had to do. You are always in my prayers.'

She wrote that Rory had written her of the deaths of Charles Devereaux and Harry Zeff and Ann Marie some time before, but that she, herself, had been ill for a number of months and could not send a letter of condolence. She did not mention the nature of her affliction, but here and there her writing wavered as if she were still weak and tremulous. Her whole letter was full of love and tenderness and consolation, and a simple faith which even Timothy found somewhat naïve and girlish. She did not mourn the dead, but only pitied the living for their loss. 'The souls of those we love have ascended into the care and mercy of God,' she wrote. 'We must not trouble them with our tears and our grief. We must only pray for them and trust that they pray for us.'

Timothy did not see the face of a woman of fifty-five, but the face of the young Regina, beautiful beyond believing, with that shining regard which was so moving and touching, and the mass of glossy black hair. He thought: She never lived in this world at all, at any time, and still does not live in it, but is kept from it not only by her cloister but by her innocence and faith. Perhaps only by her innocence. He saw that even if she had not lived in a convent when she was a child she would inevitably have been drawn to this life of seclusion – and flight. The world was no place for such as Regina Armagh. He thought of some of the nuns he had known during his own childhood, nuns like Regina. Perhaps the Church knew of these women and in mercy offered them a refuge from a battle and a struggle they could never have survived, for they were the eternal 'little ones', in spite of intelligence and resolution. So the chronic yearning Timothy had known all this time lifted at last, and he answered Regina's letter as if he were a kindly older brother and said that Joseph was well. He took the simple holy card with its prayer, which Regina had sent to Joseph, and gently put it in his wallet.

He leaned back in his chair cautiously, for he was portly now, and he considered a rumour he had heard recently, that the Armagh family was 'cursed'. He could not remember who had mentioned this, and had laughed at it. All families, as they matured, suffered misfortunes and deaths, except for the very fortunate who were few. He smiled as he thought – I only hope the 'curse' doesn't extend to me, as it seems to have done to Harry and Charles, who were outside the family! He chuckled as he blessed himself. As for Joseph, the extent of his fortune was staggering, even among his fellow 'robber barons'. That must be its own consolation, thought Timothy: to achieve what you have set out to achieve. It was probably the only consolation the world had to offer.

He considered again what Joseph had said to him a few days ago: 'It is not too early to begin a boom for Rory for President in 1911. So I want you to gather a competent staff in his behalf. No money will be spared. You have only to ask for it. You will manage his tours and go with him to the primaries. You will need several publicity men – hire them. And public relations men, too. Secretaries. Various subsidiary campaigners, who will arrange dinners, speeches, meetings with the public and politicians in all the big cities, and the smaller ones, too. Slogans. Posters. Interviews. Rory is personable. It is unfortunate that women can't vote, but men like him, too. He must be shown as the friend of the people – the brother of a war hero. Steve Worthington is boosting him from within . . .' Joseph paused and looked at Timothy narrowly, but Timothy's strong face was carefully bland. 'You know what to do,' said Joseph. 'Every Irishman instinctively is a politician.'

'It will cost a lot of money,' said Timothy. 'And you know, Joe, that the country is very "anti-Papist". Let just a whisper get out that Rory is going to strive for the nomination of our Party and there will be a national flood of vicious smears and hysterical accusations and denunciations. It will be worse than the anti-British propaganda in the country, and God knows that is violent and suspicious and hating enough. I've been doing a little quiet investigating myself, knowing that you've had the intention of Rory trying for the nomination of our Party. I've dropped hints here and there in Chicago, New York, Boston, Philadelphia, Buffalo, Newark, everywhere. And the response was very – shall we say – strenuous in opposition, even among the politicians in our Party, and even among Catholics. "Does Armagh want to ruin our Party?" I've been asked. I've even been asked if you want to precipitate a religious war in this free land of ours. The prejudice is now even worse than it was thirty, twenty years ago, but you know that. We just aren't loved, Joe.'

'I know,' said Joseph with impatience. 'But you've forgotten the priceless ingredient of any campaign: money. I'm willing to spend twenty, thirty, forty, fifty million dollars, and more if necessary, to make my son President of the United States of America. Even the Rockefellers wouldn't put up that much money for any of their sons. What do you think I've been living and working for?'

Timothy was startled at the angry question. He had often wondered what drove Joseph Armagh, and now he had an idea. It was a tight vengeful face that looked into his, the deep-set small blue eyes filled with fire and determination. Joseph's hair might be white, but it was still thick and vital, and the face was the face of a young man, and invincible.

'I have half of Washington in my hand,' Joseph said, and

smiled sourly. 'You know that, Tim. So let us get busy. Money can buy anything. Do you think I've been idle all these years? I know what I know. So get to work, Tim, and ask for anything you need.'

'The Mugwumps and the Populists in Washington don't like Rory,' said Timothy. 'They call him a Monarchist, and worse. He has never yet supported a measure "for the public weal", as the Socialists call it. He has been accused of being an aristocratic "member of the ruling classes". He opposed the Child Labour bill and the unions, among other things.'

'Now he is going to out-Bryan Bryan,' said Joseph. 'From this day on. Social legislation is going to be supported with zeal – and eloquence – by Senator Armagh. He isn't vulnerable like Bryan. He isn't a fool – and we have money. There is nothing about Rory which anyone can laugh at: he never makes an idiot of himself. He can't be lampooned; he lampoons back admirably. He has wit and appearance and intelligence – and money.

'Now, for our first move we will begin a campaign against prejudice – against any man by reason of race or religion. We will appeal to the famous sense of fair play in Americans. We will publish that Rory had been invited to meet the Pope – and Rory declined. Yes, I know that won't be true, but it will have an impact on Americans. Rory will mention that he is not in favour of "parochial education", though it should be tolerated in the name of freedom of choice. Rory will attack the men of great fortunes, "who have no sense of obligation to their country and The Poor". Rory will be the champion of the working man, and social justice. He will be fervent. The people won't laugh. He has money. He has learned much. It is time for him to help himself, according to the advice I have recently received.

'Rory,' said Joseph, looking aside, his voice neutral, 'will have the support of many of my friends. I can promise that. Rory will be more American than the average American. He will be as American as . . .'

'A five-cent glass of beer,' said Timothy.

Joseph laughed, his low hard laugh. 'Yes. Well, get to work as soon as possible, Tim. I've done a lot of the groundwork myself, over many years. Don't forget to mention Tom Hennessey, "the friend of the people, the enemy of privilege". Rory's grandfather.'

He stood up. 'I can tell you this again – my friends support Rory. They know what I want.'

Timothy had known Rory from early childhood. He wondered if Joseph Armagh really knew his own son.

CHAPTER FORTY-EIGHT

ELIZABETH HENNESSEY had not died in six months after all. She lived almost a full year.

She visited Joseph in New York and other cities only occasionally during the last few months of her life, for she was increasingly exhausted and neither lip rouge nor tinted powder could hide, any longer, the pallor that had come to her fine-boned face. Many lace ruffles at her throat and wrists, and the soft silk dresses she wore with their embroidered bodices, did not conceal too well her increasing thinness and fragility. The big hats, with their flowers and plumes, set high on her proud head, seemed too heavy for her strength. She endured the mounting and ruthless pain in silence, and when she met Joseph she was as reticent, calm and smiling, as always. She explained her few visits lightly. After all, she was growing old, and tired.

Joseph listened to all her explanations of her dwindling appearance, and her excuses, and insistently forced her to repeat what her doctors had said last about her 'condition'. She would lie easily then, saying that the 'condition' was only ageing, that she had never been of a strong constitution, but otherwise her health was reasonably good. He would listen, watching her closely, and then appeared satisfied. However, he would remark on her lack of appetite, apprehensively, and she would lightly change the subject.

She could never tell him, she thought. He had had enough suffering. She would die alone, and quietly. At the very least, that would be her last gift to him. She had never troubled him with her anxieties and her personal problems or her midnight fears, or any tempers or petulances or alarms, and she would not trouble him now.

Then it came to her one day in their suite in New York, as he sat beside her chaise-longue and held her hand, that he knew, and that he had known for some time. She was startled deeply. She looked earnestly at his sombre profile, suffused with the softened light that came through the lace curtains. He seemed sunk in himself. Yet she was aware that he was thinking of her with absolute concentration. The street noises were muffled; the shrieks and the howls of the elevated cars seemed far away. The hotel was quiet, for it was late afternoon and no one was dressing for dinner yet or had returned from outings and shopping. It had been a warm early spring day and Joseph had bought her a bunch of yellow daffodils and narcissi from a street vendor, and they stood in a green vase on the velvet covered round table where they often ate their meals together.

They had not spoken for some time. He sat like a devoted husband at her side, his opened book lying on his lean knee. He was staring at the opposite wall. Yes, he knew. She did not know how he had come to know, but he knew. The intuition of love had told him. It could never be deceived. Tears came into her eyes. But I am glad that I will be the one to go first, she thought. You are strong, but I am weak. You will bear this as you have borne other tragedies, but I could not have borne your dying. For that, if for nothing else, I thank God. All our lives are a giving up, one by one, of the things we love and enjoy, and finally there is the last abandonment and we are empty. But I have the memory of our love which I will take with me, if I may, for you are the only joy I have ever known, the only contentment and delight. And so, I am rich after all, richer than most. Others live lives of no colour or vitality, and their existence is like nursery porridge, and as bland. But I have known all the heights that can be possible for a woman, all the raptures and the faith and the trust, all the excitements and the wonders, and even grief was bearable in your presence, my darling. I must not be greedy and try to cling to what I have had – for it is all fulfilled, full and overflowing. Nothing can be added. Nothing taken away.

For the first time since she had known of her mortal illness she was resigned, tranquil, no longer rebellious, no longer afraid.

He turned his head and looked down at her then, as if he knew this also, and their eyes met and held and everything they had been to each other, and all the long years, lay between them. They did not look away. Joseph's fingers tightened slightly on her hand, and that was all. She had accepted. He had been forced to accept. There was the difference.

Finally he said, 'Elizabeth.'

No, he must not speak. She put her hand to his mouth lovingly, and closed his lips. 'It's all right, darling,' she said. 'Please don't say anything. It's all right.'

She was so relieved that she almost cried. There was no need any longer for her to pretend, to paint her face, to try for soft animation, to force herself to laugh when the pain sprang upon her. So she was granted this great mercy, knowing that he knew, and she no longer felt isolated in an iron cage of torture, afraid to cry out lest she hurt him. She had thought nothing could be added to what she had already had, but now she had this. She fell asleep, like a dying child who has been eased of suffering, blissful in the absence of agony, but prostrated, and he watched her until it was dark in the room and the street lamps outside began to bloom.

Her peace of mind made her seem stronger the next day, and they went to the opera for the last time together, and they knew it would be the last time, and so the music and the arias and the costumes were all the more intense to them and full of meaning. But they knew it was Elizabeth who sailed away in the swanboat and not Lohengrin, and they looked at each other and their hands tightened together. Yet never, not even in her youth, had Elizabeth looked so beautiful to Joseph, so translucent, so full of dignity and peace. He could not violate this courage by a single word, and he knew it.

He took her back to Green Hills himself the day following and she did not object, though this was the first time they had travelled home together on the same train. She was gathering last impressions as a gleaner gathers wheat against hunger and the night of hunger.

'In two weeks I will come back for a whole month,' he said, when he left her at her door and her maid helped her across the threshold.

'Yes,' she said, and her great green eyes were full of love and not sadness.

She had chosen her grave a month before, not near Tom Hennessey, who lay beside his first wife in a sunken grave under a heavy stone. She had bought a plot of land, and had even ordered her monument, to be engraved simply with her name, the year of her birth and the year of her death. Oaks had always been her favourite trees. One stood there, ancient and mighty, and its branches would bend over her grave. She stood in the spring wind and was at peace, looking at the place where she would lie and sleep. When she had been young she had been horrified that people could casually choose their graves and what would be on their monuments, and could visit the spot. But now she felt comfort. It was beautiful here, and quiet.

A week later she died alone in her bed, at dawn, as she had hoped, and no one was with her. As the light increased a bolt of golden shadow shot through the window and lay on her sleeping face, and it was the face once more of a girl who had come home.

Bernadette telephoned Joseph in Philadelphia, to tell him that Elizabeth Hennessey had been found dead by her maid, that morning, and that the funeral would be held on Thursday. Bernadette's voice was subdued, though she was full of elation. Would Joseph return for the funeral? After all, he was Elizabeth's executor, and had managed her affairs.

'Yes,' he said. 'I will come.' That was all. He began to work again. There was no feeling in him at all except a vast hollowness, a far desolation. He could not believe, in spite of all he had known for some time, that Elizabeth was dead, and that he would never see her again. His mind froze at the very approach to that reality, and then fell away. It was the way she had wanted it, he said to himself. He would go to Green Hills but there was no longer anyone there for him. Once he had been a stranger, staring at a stranger's house, and again he would be a stranger, and he would look again at a stranger's house, and as he thought that, he threw his pen from him and went to his apartments in Philadelphia and did not leave them until it was time to go to Green Hills.

CHAPTER FORTY-NINE

WHEN Rory returned from Europe, after his sister's death, he had a long and quiet talk with his father. 'I attended a session of Parliament in England, a full-dress session. It was said that Germany, with her superior industry and mechanical genius, was "invading" the British "traditional world markets".'

'Yes,' said Joseph.

'So,' said Rory, 'there will be a war.'

'Not immediately,' said Joseph. 'Perhaps by 1914 or 1916. I have seen the blueprints. But America can't be got into a war without money. So – there must be a Federal Income Tax. You have known this for years.'

Rory nodded. The under lids of his eyes relaxed, artlessly. 'The big move,' he said. 'Wars and taxes will create dissension in America, and weaken her. We've talked about this often, haven't we?'

'Yes,' said Joseph. He stared at his son gloomily and did not pursue the subject. But Rory said, 'And eventually we will be bankrupt. Very clever, isn't it?'

At the opening of the campaign to secure the nomination of his Party for the Presidency, Rory said, 'I know all the objectives. I agree with them without reservation.'

'Good,' said Joseph, and his face was gloomier than ever. 'I don't think I will get the nomination.'

'You will,' said Joseph. 'There are millions behind you.' And the Right People, thought Rory, and smiled at his father. 'Faustian money,' he said.

'Rory, remember this: no man ever failed by holding his tongue. You must accept things as they are.'

'Oh, I do, I do. I assure you, Pa, I do.'

He smiled at his father amiably. 'It is really a struggle between money and blood, isn't it? And isn't it fortunate that the masses will never know – fortunate for us?'

'No man ever died of a surfeit of money,' said Joseph. 'Remember that. In comparison blood is nothing – if it flows into money. Blood is cheap. Money is all-powerful.'

Claudia said to Rory, her greenish-brown eyes wide and stretched and glowing: 'Isn't it delightful? You will be President of the United States! We will live in the White House! I will give such galas, such dances in silver slippers, such artistic performances, they will dazzle everybody with their sophistication. After all, we are still a crude nation. It is time for culture in political affairs, and discrimination, and the encouragement of the arts.'

'I'm not even nominated yet,' said Rory. He rarely talked

to his wife. He was now as indifferent to her as his father was indifferent to his mother. At least Ma is not a fool, he would think. But my wife would take honours in a school for imbeciles. The Phi Beta Kappa of the feeble-minded. But Claudia was a marvellous hostess, gracious, charming, smiling, greeting, and she had fine taste and a certain shrewdness. She captivated almost everyone, including cynical politicians of the opposite party. She chattered in French to the French Ambassador, and delightfully tried to chatter in German to the German Ambassador, who was overcome by her charm, the scintillating aura that seemed to surround her. She wore gowns as if Worth had created only for her and no one else. At times she affected a beguiling shyness, and everyone spoke of her 'jejune modesty'. That all this concealed a powerful ego, a cold-blooded drive for eminence, was known to very few. Surely such a gentle lady, with such a flair for the fitness of things, incapable of being gauche though she was an American, refined, culti- vated, sophisticated and fascinating, must have the soul of a 'dew-drenched daisy'. When Rory heard this he would laugh inwardly, and then go off to his lady of the day, the week of the month, where he could be assured of honesty, at any rate. Even honesty could be bought with money, if there was sufficient money, and temporary fidelity. But Claudia was a fraud even if she did not have the wit to realise that she was fraudulent and merely an echo. *Papier mâché,* Rory would think of her. Nicely coloured and jewelled and with auto- matic gestures and graces, but *papier mâché* for all that, except for native greed and expediency. No one can match her for that!

He was too good-tempered and cynically tolerant to hate her, but he came very close. So long as she did not try to inveigle him into what she called 'significant conversation', he endured her. But when she pretended to intellect and serious- ness he would stare at her with crescent-eyed and smiling in- credulity, until even she was embarrassed and burst into tears. He had an idea that she loved him as much as she was capable of love, but that did not touch him. Claudia had few capabilities, and what there were were directed mostly towards herself.

Claudia was positive that he would be nominated as the candidate of his Party, though Rory was sceptical in spite of his father's power and money. But as the 'boom' gathered weight and persistence throughout the country, as the money was spent on scores of managers and other politicians, and dozens of newspapers hailed him nationally, Rory had to admit that his father's dream might be possible. Money was all. It accomplished miracles, even in a nation obdurately obsessed by 'Papism', and prejudice. The opposition newspapers began to mention his religion less and less, as if they were ashamed of their bias.

He began to be called 'the Senator of the People', though few there were who could recall and point out anything he had particularly accomplished. Rory, under astute direction, decided to rectify this. Timothy Dineen, with a wry and understanding smile, consulted with him constantly. Timothy said, 'I disagree with Abraham Lincoln. You can, if you are smart enough, fool all of the people all of the time, and they will love it. Don't smile, Rory. You are not the worst politician in America. You are not even a first-class scoundrel. You never stole anything or accepted bribes. Tut, tut.'

Rory had many consultations, too, with the Committee for Foreign Studies, the American branch of which he had come to call, in himself, The Conspiracy. They found him serious and apparently dedicated to their international aims, respectful, pliable, intelligent, and agreeable. 'We can make you President,' one of them said to him, 'if we find you reliable. So far, Rory, I believe you are more reliable than Old Joe, your father, who has a nasty Irish tongue on him, and an irony which is unpredictable – and unsettling. You must never upset our foreign friends, you know. They have no sense of humour.'

'Pa has a gallows humour,' said Rory. 'He likes to exercise it. But you've found him amenable, haven't you? Yes.'

It was then that they began to study Rory. The young man was intent on being nominated, and elected. The question was: why?

There was a private railroad car for Rory. 'The people affect to love rugged simplicity and democratic tendencies in their rulers and politicians,' said Joseph. 'But in fact if a man is simple and rugged and honest – and has money and position – they will despise him and consider him less than their equal. After all, they reason, would they be simple and rugged and honest if they were in his position? No. They would be ostentatious and grand and overbearing. This man is not so. Ergo, he is no better than they are, and why should they honour him?'

So Rory had his private railroad car, and another car for his managers and secretaries and publicity and public relations men. Cars on other trains were filled with his 'advance men', who went all over the country to prepare the way for whom they secretly called 'the young Master', with snide chuckles but also with fawning. They engaged halls, were interviewed by reporters as sceptical as themselves, bought full pages of advertisements in newspapers, had brochures printed and posters. Rory's colourful face appeared everywhere, on lamp-posts and on walls and on fences, smiling, twinkling, handsome, engaging. Recalcitrant County chairmen, State chairmen, Mayors and Governors and Delegates of the Party, were quietly bribed, threatened, promised, intimidated. The bribes were very large, the intimidations and threats not idle ones, as they soon learned. Rory had not one, but several campaign managers. They announced his intention of appearing in all the primaries. They talked of his personable appearance, his wit, his intellect, his devotion to The People, his determination to rectify 'all injustices', his detestation of exploitation, his contempt for 'men of great wealth who care nothing for their workmen but use them as cattle'. He, though the son of a powerful and wealthy man, sought public office not for gain but for 'equity' and a patriotic zeal to serve his country and his fellow American.

Fundamentalist parsons in many backwoods communities did not believe in Rory's sincerity. If he were to be elected President – 'God preserve us from that calamity!' – the Pope would take up residence in Washington, in the White House itself, and would soon dominate the Senate and Congress, and bring in the Spanish Inquisition and thumb-screws and the wheel, and within a year America, Protestant America, would be a satellite of the Vatican. 'Did not our ancestors flee such as these?' they cried from their pulpits. 'Did they flee that their grandchildren should be the slaves of Popism and idolatry and priests?'

Rory's men used this very wicked bigotry for their purposes with an artfulness that was admirable and subtle. They even publicised the ravings of bigots, however obscure, and countermanded them by asking the American people to feel shame that they had such in their immaculate and tolerant midst. Multitudes did, indeed, feel shame and on seeing Rory for themselves, felt an emotional surge of affection and protection for him, to prove to themselves that they were just men and not ignorant fools full of hatred and vindictiveness. The other Party, therefore, was disarmed. If they mentioned Rory's religion it was only in passing, but the newspapers excoriated them, at least many of them did so to prove their tolerance. The opposition Party was left almost without an issue. It did mention that Rory had done nothing notable in Washington as a Senator, but Rory's men cleverly used that very lack as propaganda. He had done nothing harmful to The People, though he had been in a position to do so!

A notable and famous minister in Philadelphia did timidly pose the question: Would Rory's first allegiance be to his country or to his religion? It had been put in private, but his colleagues publicised it. (They were amply rewarded.) The man had been notable for his intellect and integrity, his justice to all American faiths, his kindness and charity. It was unfortunate that he had slipped this one time, and he regretted it immediately as unworthy of him. But Rory's men blazoned it throughout the country via the press, and the minister was condemned vehemently. He was 'intolerant' and 'unAmerican'. His own people ostracised him. When he was approached sympathetically by sweating bigots he repudiated them with anger at himself and disgust with them, and so earned more enemies. He never regained the authority and status he had once possessed, and he felt it a just punishment for his foolish and private lapse. He had many friends who were Catholic priests, and they were indignant, but he begged them not to intervene.

Claudia and her children were pressed into service. She appeared with Rory and her brood on the observation platform of his private car, a delectable and modish sight with her children clustered picturesquely about her. Audiences were charmed. She had a natural flair for publicity, and so was in her glory. She preened, she smiled, she cast down her eyes modestly as befitting a woman; she breathlessly, in her infantile voice, said she was not a feminist and did not believe in votes for women, and was only a Wife and Mother. She would look with passionate love at Rory, beside her, and touch his arm gently with her gloved hand. But she never intruded, never asserted herself, never expressed anything but the most proper opinions. She asked for votes for her husband, 'because I know his deep love for his country and for Social Justice, and peace and progress. He has talked with me often about these things, after I have put the children to bed and heard their innocent prayers. We are simple people and speak to you simply.' It was excellent propaganda that this appeal for simplicity was not accompanied by drab clothing and simplicity. Having been tutored well, she spoke shyly with farmers, workers, employers and employees, about their 'problems'. Rory would rectify them. He would be no 'tool' of established and venal politicians. He would serve his Country and its Sons. He was beyond politics. He would be the President of The People, without distinction of Party, race or creed. He had taken on this burden not for money or position, for he possessed both in enormous quantity. He asked only to give his life and his talents to America.

Even the suffragettes, who resented her as an anti-feminist, were charmed by Claudia. She gave large teas for women, though they could not vote. Bernadette, too, was pressed into service. She was a far better politician than Claudia. No one had to tell her what to do. Fat, 'unpretentious', an obvious matron and mother, she was forthright and zestful, and appealed to mothers, who in turn appealed to their husbands and harassed them. (She never made the mistake of talking with members of Altar or Rosary Societies, and never talked with Catholic women exclusively, if ever.) She talked only of The Children to women, and told them of her son's concern about child labour and the exploitation of children. 'Men, with all their business affairs, are sometimes ignorant of these things. It is necessary for us women to advise them.' She hinted that Rory was really in sympathy with Votes for Women. Her teas were lavish and delectable and attended in mass, and her burly laughter and 'honest folksiness' was applauded in many newspapers. Her father's record in the Senate was mentioned, though vaguely, for no one could exactly remember his record. However, it was hinted that it had been exemplary and guided by his deep concern for the American Character and Justice for All. Mr Lincoln had often confided in him. (This little *bon mot* was not repeated in the South.)

If Rory ever talked – as he did privately – with members of the Holy Name Society and the Knights of Columbus, it was not mentioned in the press.

The duality of his nature was an asset to him. In speaking before exigent and brutal men he was honestly exigent and brutal. He could be rough, brutish and cynical when necessary, and even vindictive, and then with others he was suave, evasive, refined, casual, easy, intellectual. All his faces were equally sincere. His advisers admired this protean quality in him, but never let it be inadvertently displayed before the wrong audiences.

He was inexhaustible. He seemed never to tire. If his youth was sometimes mentioned doubtfully, he would counter that wisdom did not necessarily come with age and that perhaps this should be the Era of Youth. Freshness. A new approach. An awareness that America was a young country, and why should not youth speak, too, in the conclaves of national affairs? After all, he would say with a jocular twinkle, youth was a malady that time would cure. In the meantime youth had something to say to America. He would quote the Bible – carefully, the King James Version, to the effect that 'old men had dreams and young men had visions'. Both were necessary. America had been born of dreams and visions. Without them, a nation was dead. 'A people without a vision must perish.' This was Rory's own touch, and it aroused the increasing admiration of his cohorts.

He never appeared to weary. He might talk at midnight, and then be fresh to speak at dawn at railroad stations, on the platform of his private car, to hordes of farmers and workers. He was eloquent and fiery, humorous and cajoling, amused and concerned. Sometimes his own men asked each other, 'What is really driving him?' They never knew.

But there were those who suspected, knowing both Joseph Armagh and his son. These, however, were not among Rory's audiences. They met in New York and Washington. They read long obscure letters from Europe, and quietly discussed them.

There was seemingly no end to the millions of dollars Joseph poured out for Rory. They were not spent ostentatiously. But the power and weight of those pouring millions had their effect. 'We will win,' said Joseph to his son, and Rory began to believe it. 'I have nothing left but you,' Joseph would say. 'Nothing.'

CHAPTER FIFTY

JOSEPH said to his daughter-in-law, 'Are you going to Boston next week when Rory speaks there?'

'If you wish,' said Claudia, who found it all exhilarating.

'I don't know,' said Joseph. Claudia was far too stylish and sophisticated – at least in appearance and manner – for Boston. Boston was not susceptible to charm. It also did not like the Irish, though the Irish were growing in power and wealth in that city. But that very wealth and power was suspect. However, Claudia was not Irish, and she had manners. Joseph considered it. Joseph had begun reluctantly to admire Claudia, who had the genius always to say the right thing at the right time. The voters were devoted to her. Perhaps Boston, who knew her assumed aristocratic pedigree, might be influenced. It was worth the chance. There would be teas for the ladies. Men were never invited to them, of course. It was all so charming, so feminine, so delicately urgent, so unobtrusive. So appealing, so shy, so modest, with the ladies all in silk and lace, carrying parasols and wearing dainty slippers. Joseph decided that Bernadette was not to go to Boston. She was too earthy for the ladies of Boston, though those ladies were earthy and ruthless and greedy enough. Even Irish ladies might be offended by Bernadette, and if invited would consider themselves her equal and therefore not be taken seriously.

Then Joseph received an abrupt if courteous invitation to attend 'a very important meeting' of the Committee for Foreign Studies in New York.

He more than suspected that he had not been invited to the last four meetings, and to a certain extent he knew why, or thought he knew why. The Committee was apolitical. It supported any politician who would serve their purposes, and the purposes of their European colleagues. To them there were no Democrats or Republicans, no Populists or 'Wobblies', or Farmer-Labour Parties. There were only potential and obedient servants, whether Presidents or obscure Delegates, Mayors of big or small cities, Governors, Congressmen or Senators. Every man was carefully scrutinised, his past records studied,

his bent analysed. On their judgment a man prospered politically or he fell ignominiously. They had supported Rory for
Congressman and Senator, and had approved of him, or rather
had approved of his father, their colleague. They had said
nothing against Rory on his bid for the nomination of his
Party. But insofar as Joseph knew they had not overtly approved of this either. Their whole attitude had been tentative.
They had talked frequently with Rory and had been apparently impressed by him, and had complimented Joseph on
his splendid son. 'Nominal Catholic or not, he could be
elected,' they had told Joseph. 'If he is – correct.' Joseph had
no reason to believe they had suddenly found Rory 'incorrect'.

Still, he was apprehensive. However, his relentless drive
made him adamant, though he admitted he had no real reason
to 'set my back up'. Everything had been smooth and perfect.
A member of the Committee had even written a few of Rory's
most telling speeches, which he had delivered with eloquence
and elegance, and with spontaneity. Why the hell do I worry?
Joseph asked himself on the way to New York. If they have
changed their minds – which is not possible – it will mean
nothing to me. My son is going to be President of the United
States. He is all I have left. He is my justification.

'My son is going to be President of the United States,' he
said to his colleagues in New York, after the rich luncheon,
with the best French wines, in the building. 'I have nothing
more to say.'

He had stood up in the meeting room, tall, spare, ascetic,
with his severe and hollow face under the thick mass of his
white hair. His blue eyes were burning, and he had looked
at them all, man after man, and they had felt his force and
now his dominance.

'Who the hell is Woodrow Wilson?' he said, and he spoke
with cold contempt.

They told him again, reasonably, quietly, and without reticence. They never spoke in ambiguities.

Woodrow Wilson was an Innocent. They had watched and
studied him for many years. He was naïve and an idealist,
and an 'intellectual'. Therefore, he was their man. He would
never know who manipulated him. They had had many
talks with him recently, and had impressed him with their
solicitude for America and in turn he had impressed them
with his solicitude. He had quietly congratulated them on their

publications, 'concerned with the advancement of America'.

'I bet,' said Joseph. 'Did he ever guess who we are? And what we want?'

It was their intention that no Republican would be elected in 1912, and that no Democrat except of their choosing. Mr Taft was 'impossible'. He was not 'amenable'. He had quarrelled with Mr Roosevelt, who had recently shouted that Mr Taft was a 'hypocrite'. 'My hat in the ring!' Teddy had cried. 'The fight is on and I am stripped to the buff.'

'I know, I know,' said Joseph with impatience. 'We are to divide the Republican Party with two candidates: Taft and Roosevelt. And Rory, then, is supposed to win.'

They ignored him with elaborate patience. 'Mr Roosevelt will run on the new Progressive Party ticket. We coined a phrase for him, "the New Nationalism". The voters are intrigued. They love the word "new". Mr Roosevelt, himself, has said he wishes "a Square Deal". It is a poker expression, and liked by the voters. People love him. He has a marvellous grin. Infectious. We have suggested a phrase for him: "The Bull Moose Party". He is, to use his own words, "delighted".'

'Yes, yes,' said Joseph. 'This was supposed to be in behalf of my son.'

They pretended they had not heard him.

They recounted to him all they knew about Mr Wilson. He had established the first potent Socialistic cell in Princeton in the early 1880s, when he had been a professor there. A fairly rich man, and a scholar, he had been most emotional concerning Karl Marx and had understood all that was necessary for the emergence of an 'Elite' in America. He distrusted the common man, though he championed him, not having known, through all his six universities, in which he had studied and taught, any common men at all. He was an aristocrat by birth, and that made him respected by the common man. He feared and hated the 'common men' who composed Congress, and he had quickly taken up what had been suggested to him concerning the power reserved to Congress for the coining of money. 'Money trust!' he had proclaimed. He had declared himself in favour of an independent Federal Reserve System, a private organisation, which would have the supreme power of coining the nation's money.

'I know, I know,' said Joseph. 'We have been working a long time to take away the power of Congress to coin money, and give it to bankers, who will issue money by fiat. If you have anything new to tell me, please do so.' His heart was beating fast with rage.

'We made him Governor of New Jersey.'

'Really?' said Joseph, raising his white-russet eyebrows. 'I didn't know that!'

They sighed. They hated sarcasm. They particularly hated irony and had always deplored Joseph's tendency to that.

'Mr Wilson,' one gentleman said, 'understands that America must leave her traditional isolation from world affairs. We must now emerge as a world power.'

'In short,' said Joseph, 'he will help get America into a war.'

He was sorry immediately that he had said that, and many pairs of eyes looked at him in hurt rebuke as at a child who had been repeatedly told a self-evident fact.

'Mr Wilson,' said one gentleman, 'understands that America must no longer be indifferent to World Injustices.'

Joseph stood up again, and leaned his clenched fists on the table. 'So Wilson is to be our candidate, our mannikin. Our Little Boy Blue who blows our horn. Mr Wilson, the Defender of the common man, whom he despises. Mr Wilson, who never did an honest day's labour in his life, with his hands, and knows nothing of labour.'

He looked at them all. 'What do the Democratic bosses think about all this?'

A few gentlemen chuckled softly. 'We haven't yet told them what to think, Joseph.'

Then Joseph made a fatal mistake out of his anger. 'Perhaps Rory can tell them the truth.'

A deadly and absolute silence filled the great panelled room.

No one looked at him. The air became heavy, immovable, still. Joseph felt it. He began to sweat lightly. He felt a chill on his flesh. God damn me, for my Irish tongue, he thought. No one looked at him. He slowly sat down, but his clenched fists remained on the table.

He began to speak quietly. 'Rory has followed all orders. He is speaking all over the country in favour of the Amendments for a Federal Income Tax, a Federal Reserve System, and the direct election of Senators by the people, and not appointments by State Legislatures. You know that. You've read his speeches in the papers. He followed all your orders.

391

All your directives. He has never deviated. You have written speeches for him. You have never, until now, indicated that he was not acceptable. Why now?'

One of them spoke, after a glance at the averted eyes around the table. 'Joe, let us be reasonable. Rory is magnificent. But he is young. And the young are naturally rebellious – and have their own ideas. Mr Wilson will unquestionably take our orders, given discreetly through many politicians we know. For instance, Colonel House. He is our man, as you know. Mr Wilson has had a long apprenticeship – in Socialism. He is ripe for us. Rory is not. Joe, again, let us be reasonable. In eight years, most probably, we will reconsider Rory. That will make him a little more mature, a little more understanding of our aims.'

Joseph said, 'You've talked often to Rory. Why have you turned against him?'

Again Mr Regan consulted half-averted eyes. 'Joe, I hate to say this, but we have a feeling that at this particular time Rory is not quite – reliable.'

'And Wilson is, whether he knows it or not? To put it briefly, he is stupid enough, naïve enough, to swallow anything you tell him. Any noble phrase, any high-sounding aphorism: he will adopt them. You are afraid Rory won't. You think he will laugh, and then do what he 'wants.

'You've considered Taft. He is an old and able politician. He knows quite a lot about us, I have heard. He wouldn't be amenable. He would think, first, of America. He is suspicious. Teddy Roosevelt is too flamboyant. He might have individual thoughts, too. He is an internationalist, as he has proved. But still, he would think of America in sober moments, when he wasn't off hunting. So, Taft and Roosevelt won't be considered. They are, potentially, "unreliable". So is Rory.'

He stood up again, and gathered all eyes to him. 'I'm wasting time. I have only this to say: I am pouring out my whole fortune to get Rory nominated and elected. I don't give a damn for our European colleagues, who want Wilson, as you have told me. This time I will act independently. Rory is going to be President of the United States.'

They listened and there was another silence. Then one said, 'Joe, this is no time in history for personal vendettas. I know you have a vendetta. Wait, Joe. Suppose Wilson gets two terms

392

as President. Then we will heartily reconsider Rory. What more can we promise you, in all reason, in all justice? We haven't abandoned Rory. We ask only that he, and you, wait for eight years. Come on, Joe. Be sensible.'

He looked at them all thoroughly. He said, 'Compared with our European colleagues, we are little children. They have centuries of political manipulation, terror, revolutions and chaos behind them. They have centuries of tyrants. They are old. They are very potent, more potent than we are. They know what they want. It is you who are following orders, not giving them.'

They did not speak. Joseph drew a deep breath. 'When are they going to move against Russia?'

It was as if he had uttered an obscenity in the presence of clergymen.

'A silly question, isn't it?' he asked, when they did not answer or move. 'It is planned, isn't it? So I have been told. Yes, I am wasting my time and yours. But again I must tell you. Rory is going to be President of the United States, if it costs every penny I have, and even if I have to shout the truth from the roof-tops and alert America . . .'

'To what?' asked a gentleman in the softest voice.

'To you,' said Joseph. Without looking at them again or speaking, he left the room. He was sick with his rage, but not frustrated. He felt no fear. He knew what he knew.

No one spoke after he left. One gentleman gently ruffled some papers. Then he put out his hand in an old familiar gesture, one known to the ancient Caesars.

CHAPTER FIFTY-ONE

TIMOTHY DINEEN had kept Joseph well-informed and up-to-date on Rory's publicity tours throughout the country, via newspaper clippings, editorials, Rory's speeches and the public reaction to them. Rory, himself, had coined a phrase: 'The New Vision'. It had taken the fancy of tens of thousands of people. The New Vision was all things to all men. If some cavilled at this or that, they approved of other areas. The employer of many little children in mills and factories might purse his lips at Rory's demand that children not be exploited 'for gain and small wages and deprived of their childhood and education'. On the other hand that employer was appeased by Rory's fiery exhortations against 'governmental interference, growing ominous lately, in the realm of private enterprise'. 'Private enterprise has made us a great and prosperous country, for individual judgment is superior to the conclusions of cloistered bureaucrats.' He denounced the Trusts, and on the other hand he defended the right of companies to merge 'so that they may operate efficiently, increase employment, set standards that are just to the employed and the employers, widen markets so that all Americans can participate in a growing era of mechanisation and luxury, advance foreign trade and compete in world markets.' He expressed sorrow at the 'huge Tariffs which deny Americans foreign goods', and then he would suggest that Tariffs be lowered so that cheaper foreign goods would be accessible to the people at large. He laughed at the idea that lower-cost foreign products would put American workmen out of jobs. 'Aren't our American workmen superior in skill and productiveness to foreigners?'

He teased, cajoled, laughed audiences out of ill-humour and suspicion, was serious and sober and light by terms, depending on the temper of those he addressed – and he always knew in advance. He was controversial only when those who listened to him were controversial and agreed with him. He was pacific or denunciatory, abusive or placating, as the occasion called for, and his natural intelligence informed him what to say.

He always concluded in this fashion: if nominated and elected by his Party he would not hide from his people in the White House. He would be open to all suggestions, 'even from the most humble'. In fact, he invited suggestions from workers and farmers. 'All would be given the utmost and dedicated consideration. After all, aren't you the bedrock of America? Whose opinions are more valid?' He never failed to end with a passionate plea to patriotism, national honour, and power. The band that accompanied him everywhere would follow his last words with a joyous – and loud – flourish of trumpets, and a military march, preferably one by Sousa.

Rory always said, 'I appeal to the Conscience of the American People. I rely on their sound judgment, no matter their

394

religion or position in society. I appeal to no Special Interests, or Groups. I am an American.'

They were the words of a born politician. Only Rory knew that he meant them. It was not odd, considering human nature, that this sincerity had less weight than his adroit half-falsehoods, his appeal to local prejudices, his wooing of those he despised, his evasiveness, and his deliberate use of his innate charm and handsome appearance. For when he spoke sincerely he was too simple. When he used his actor's rococo dissimulation he was far more believable.

Americans loved to be told that they had pre-eminence in the world of today, though Rory knew quite well that America was still a second-class country, unsophisticated, naïve, innocent, childlike, the butt of the jokes of the British and Austria-Hungarian and German empires, the derision of France. She was as immured from reality as was the lowering Russian Empire and its Oriental splendour and lingering despotism. Americans knew little of Europe, but Europe knew a disastrous lot about America.

He knew that when he had been a child in school the British had been hated vociferously, and always suspected and lampooned in the American press. To some politicians it might have been strange – as it was – that in very recent years the British were no longer so compulsively loathed. But Rory knew. The 'hands across the sea' had been invented by the Committee for Foreign Studies, at the behest of their colleagues in all the European capitals. He also knew why, for his father had told him. I wonder, by God I do, what would happen if I told the American people the truth? Rory would think to himself, with deep wry humour. But he knew that no politician ever told the people the truth. He would be crucified. The people wanted fantasies and flatteries and dreams and excitements and colour. There was one thing on which Rory was determined: if he were to be elected President, America would not be engaged in foreign wars. But of that he did not even tell his father. Rory knew when to hold his tongue which unfortunately Joseph did not always know. Rory had no history behind him of starvation, exploitation, hatred, homelessness and oppression, and so he could easily refrain from lashing out at dangerous moments. Once Joseph had said to him, 'It is said that the happiest nations are those who have no history. That is true of individual men, also.' Rory had guessed the implications of that more than his father knew or understood. Joseph had manifold drives, many of them deeply and profoundly emotional. Rory had but one drive, not rooted in emotion but in reason and exigency. He could even be objective about the Committee for Foreign Studies. He courted it and deferred to it charmingly and obediently. He used its material. He thought he had deluded it.

He received a telegram from his father when he was in Chicago. Rory and Timothy Dineen were to meet with Joseph in Green Hills before the speeches and appearances in Boston. The telegram was urgent if terse. Rory raised his eyebrows at Timothy, and Timothy shrugged. 'Old Joe must have some information we don't have,' he said.

So they went to Green Hills.

Joseph had told Timothy something about the Committee for Foreign Studies, and here he had been discreet for even Timothy must not know too much. But Timothy guessed a great deal with his Irish intuition. He had 'felt' a certain subterranean stir in the world, a certain heightening and obscure and hidden movement. The resentment against 'the rich' in America had always been there, born of envy and inferiority and failure, just as it was naturally prevalent in other countries. That prejudice had given rise to the war 'against the Trusts'. (Timothy knew that the Trusts were not disturbed by this.) It was all talk, all propaganda, designed to soothe the envies of the proletariat and make them amenable. But now there was a quickening against 'the powers that be'. There were the Populists, the 'Wobblies', the I.W.W., and now the Socialists, who had elected a number of men, especially from the Middle West, to Congress and the Senate. Timothy did not believe in 'natural trends'. He knew such trends were always carefully and deliberately invented and manipulated by anonymous and faceless men. If there was growing Socialism in America it had not happened by itself. It had been intruded delicately, and successfully, for a purpose which was still obscure, though Timothy had some thoughts on the subject. He had mentioned them idly to Joseph, but Joseph's face had remained carefully non-committal. 'Don't look for bogey-men,' he told Timothy. 'Don't search under your bed of a night.' He had smiled dourly.

Rory and Timothy met with Joseph in Joseph's study, all doors closed, all voices quietly modulated. Rory, who had not seen his father for some time, remarked to himself how the Old Boy had not been diminished in his almost visible aura of potency and power, focus and implacable strength. He had suffered not only the loss of two beloved children, and his best friends, and the earlier loss of his brother and sister: he had had to endure the loss of his mistress whom Rory suspected had had more of his father's love than even his children. Yet, if he suffered the bright and inextinguishable agony of loss, which could never really be dulled, he did not show it as he greeted his last son and Timothy. He was as quiet and as contained as usual, and as direct, as undramatic and as ruthless.

The first thing Rory noticed on entering his father's study was the 'arsenal' on Joseph's desk. He knew his father kept guns but he had never known Joseph to wear one. Timothy looked at the array of very modern pistols on the desk but did not remark on them. He appeared to accept them as ordinary. There were a dozen of them.

There was brandy and whisky and beer laid out. Joseph waved his hand at them, and at the glasses. Rory and Timothy, suddenly subdued – and always eyeing the arsenal – filled glasses. Then Joseph filled one for himself, and squirted soda into it. This was most unusual. Joseph, to their knowledge, rarely drank.

'I wouldn't have called you here if it weren't necessary,' said Joseph. 'By the way, Tim, you are a genius. The way you have handled Rory's appearances has been masterly.'

Timothy, white-haired and stocky though he was now, blushed like a young boy. 'Joe, we Irish are born politicians. We have an instinct for it. It doesn't call for too much effort, you know. We love it. It's our climate.'

He toasted Joseph and his eyes were affectionate. 'I think we will win in the primaries,' he said, 'and so the Party will have to take due notice. We've had a little trouble here and there with County Chairmen and State Chairmen – always jealous of their tiny powers – but we – ah – overcame them. The picture gets clearer and clearer all the time.'

'Thanks to money,' said Joseph. Timothy momentarily looked pained. One knew these things but was it always necessary to mention them? Joseph's irony was sometimes misplaced and unsettling. Then Timothy laughed, and Rory laughed with him. 'Even Our Lord would not be heard nowa-

397

days unless He had a good press,' said Timothy.

Timothy did not always understand Joseph. Yet he did understand the sudden darkening on Joseph's face, the sudden instant withdrawal, which were the result of ingrained Irish prudery, and a hatred – even in Joseph, if unsuspected – of blasphemy. Rory considerately studied his glass. Timothy was abashed. He felt his own crudeness, though he had heard worse among other men. The three Irishmen were silent for a while. 'Sad but true,' said Timothy at last, and knew he was forgiven, and it amused his Irish irony. An Irishman might declare – and with full personal conviction – that he was 'no docile son of the Church', and that he was an atheist and thought 'tradition' amusing. He might declare himself emancipated from 'priestly superstition'. But let even a faintly blasphemous word be uttered, a single deprecation of that which was held holy by most men, and the atheistic Irishman bristled as if just that morning he had made his confession and had received, though probably he had not done this since childhood. It was not a matter of mere teaching. It was a matter of the spirit, to revere the unknowable, to give it silent honour even if the mouth declared it deserved no honour. It made even the churchless Irishman fight to the death against English iconoclasts and military might.

Joseph began to talk. 'What I must tell you now could be extremely dangerous if anyone outside this room knew of it. I repeat, it could be very dangerous, even fatal. So listen carefully.'

He told them of his meeting with the Committee for Foreign Studies. Rory listened alertly, with all his concentration. Timothy listened and thought: I suspected what they were, all the time, in spite of Joe's off-hand remarks.

Then Rory said, as his father stopped speaking, 'So I am now unacceptable to them. I would be unacceptable even eight years from now. They want Wilson – that innocent! – who will tamely dance to their music, even if he doesn't know it is their music. They are afraid I wouldn't. How they guessed I don't know.'

Joseph said, fixing his small blue eyes on his son: 'What do you mean? "Guessed"? Is there something you haven't told me?'

Rory said quickly, 'I am just conjecturing. I feel they would be doubtful of my – compliance. They ought not to worry.

You've read my speeches. I know they've read them too.'
He hated himself for that slip of his tongue. He smiled at his
father ingratiatingly. 'I've never been there without you.
Have I said anything "wrong" to them?'

'No,' said Joseph, but he continued to eye his son.

'It seems incredible to me,' said Timothy, 'that men in
London, Paris, Rome, Geneva, and God knows where else, can
decide who is acceptable as an American President!'

Joseph gave him a flashing and contemptuous glance, as if
an infant had babbled without knowing what he had babbled.
He said to Rory, 'So there it is. In 1885 Wilson attacked Congressional "power", as he called it, with contempt and aristocratic disdain, when he taught at Bryn Mawr. In his subse-
quent collegiate career he "democratised" learning and spoke
of "serious readjustments in national government". What that
had to do with academic learning and teaching – for which he
was paid – no one has as yet questioned. He has intimated
at all times that the American Constitution is "outmoded", or
at least needs to be "reformed". He is an open enemy of
conservatism, though he has not yet stated what conservatism
is, except that he apparently fears it is rule by the people and
therefore despicable. Champ Clark and Underwood, of our
Party, laugh at him, but I hear he has William Jennings Bryan,
that clown, behind him. Wilson knows no more of human
nature than do the dogs we have around this house. He has
eclectic notions, all rainbowed, and all unrealistic. Wilson
talks of a "national renaissance of ideals", but when it comes
down to it he also talks vaguely of "trusts and money interest
and privileged Big Business". Phrases. Words. The Party dis-
trusts him. They don't like prissy fuss-budgets, who don't
know what the hell they are talking about, and they distrust
large nebulous exhortations. All we know up to now is that
he is and always was an immured man, and is totally unaware
of practical issues. Therefore he will be amenable to suggestion, if it is high-flown in words and empty of real content. Therefore he is the ideal choice of our – friends – we
don't want men they suspect might think, and irritate them.'

'Do I understand that this is the first time they have
moved in the direction of electing our Presidents?' asked
Timothy.

Joseph hesitated. 'Well, they had something to do with
Teddy Roosevelt, who suddenly realised – something – and so

after that was not acceptable. This is their first bold move to elect an American President. They are putting a lot of money behind Taft and Roosevelt, to divide and weaken the Republican Party and assure the election of Wilson. Taft is against removing the power of Congress to coin money, against – to some extent – a Federal Income Tax, and the direct election of Senators. That was enough to assure enmity, and dismissal. So they're backing Roosevelt, so Wilson will be elected. It is that simple. He is their man, because he will never know who pulls the strings. He will be surrounded by his fellow "idealists", all selected by the Committee.'

'Will it do any good for you, Joe, and Rory, to expose this?'

Joseph looked at him incredulously. 'Are you out of your mind? How many of the Democratic Party know anything of all this, anyway? They would laugh. So would the country. What! A quiet non-political Committee in New York determining who shall be elected or not elected? No one would believe it, true though it is. Americans love fantasies, but they are suspicious of any mention of "plots". They think it is "foreign", part of old monarchial institutions. Why, aren't Americans free men, free to choose their Presidents? Don't they vote in primaries, and choose? The fact that they are given few to choose from doesn't disturb them; they don't even think about it. They are persuaded that these men are "the best the Party has to offer". Democrat or Republican: they have no choice. For God's sake, Timothy, where have you been all these years, when you have been working for me?'

'Touché,' said Timothy, wincing.

'If anyone told the American people that the Committee in New York – which is directed and ruled by the international bankers of Europe and America – chooses their rulers, they would say he was insane. Europe! Who cares for Europe, full of kings and czars? The new American arrogance is equal only to American naïveté and ignorance. And these things are encouraged.'

Rory had listened in comparative silence, frowning, bent forward over his glass. 'All right, Pa,' he said at last. 'Do you want me to withdraw, and the hell with the country?'

Joseph frowned deeply. 'I don't know what you mean by "the hell with the country". What has the country got to do with it? I want you to be President of the United States. I will make you President of the United States. That's what I told them in New York. I will spend the last penny I have.'

He touched the guns on his desk. 'I want you and Tim to carry one of these all the time. I want your immediate bodyguard to carry them, too.'

Rory sat back noisily in his chair and stared at his father in smiling disbelief, his eyes inverted crescents of laughing incredulity. 'For God's sake, Pa, who would take a pot shot at me?'

A heavy darkness spread over Joseph's face. He said, slowly and quietly, 'I don't think you've really listened after all, nor listened in New York, London, Paris, Rome, Geneva. I think it was all wasted. You are as naïve as the average American, I am sorry to say. Have you forgotten Lincoln, Garfield, McKinley, all shot by those the newspapers called "anarchists"? Did you think, as the newspapers said, that these murderers were insane zealots of something or other, and acted alone? Do you think these assassinations occurred in the tiny little minds of obscure little men, driven only by private individual passions? I thought you were taught better. The hand that fires the gun was directed from far away, perhaps in some European capital. When Czar Alexander was assassinated by an "anarchist", for God's sake, it was Communism which ordered it, and you've been told that a dozen times by me. It was planned months, years, before. He was a humane man intent on reforming and establishing the Duma and relieving the Russian people of tyranny and serfdom. So – he would remove the cause of catastrophic revolutions. So – he had to die. Christ! You knew that.'

' "Elementary, my dear Watson," ' Timothy murmured, and looked hard at the guns.

Rory studied his father. His ruddy colour had diminished. He said, 'Pa, if they want to get me, to kill me, they know they can surmount any guards or guns we have. They can kill me anywhere – if they want to. On the street, in halls, even in church, or in my bed.'

'Ah, so you've finally realised,' said Joseph. 'You've finally accepted what they are. But that doesn't mean they will "get" you, as you say. I hate slang. Forewarned is forearmed. I don't think they will dare . . . They will only move very soon to discredit you, to make fun of you, to pour out more and more money for Wilson, to use propaganda against you. Your religion, for instance. Or maybe not. There are millions

of Catholics in America, of every race. They will find some-
thing, no doubt, besides guns. You aren't the President, yet.
Still we must be prepared. Rory, take one of those pistols.
You've been taught how to fire.'

He remembered what Mr Montrose had taught him. He said,
'Never raise a gun unless you intend to shoot. Never shoot
unless you intend to kill.'

'Oh, Jesus,' Rory muttered. But he took a compact heavy
pistol and dropped it into his pocket. He felt foolish. But
Timothy seriously studied the guns and finally selected one.
Timothy looked straight at Joseph and said, 'I will watch
Rory every minute, Joe.'

'Good,' said Joseph. He did a rare impulsive thing. He
reached over and shook hands with Timothy and Timothy
reddened with pleasure.

CHAPTER FIFTY-TWO

JOSEPH had carefully refrained from appearing with his
son anywhere. Some newspapers might mutter about 'The
Armagh Enterprises, many of whose activities are reputedly
nefarious,' but they could never come out bluntly and say,
'Joseph Armagh travels with his son and finances his public
appearances everywhere.' No one doubted the truth, but as
Joseph appeared uninterested in his son's journeys all over the
country, made no telling comments which could be adversely
misquoted, gave no interviews and only smiled briefly at
reporters who sometimes waylaid him, and talked publicly with
no one, he could not be openly denounced. Only once did he
say to a Philadelphia group of reporters: 'My son, Rory?
Oh, he's a born politician. I find politics dull myself, now. If
our Party wishes to nominate him – after all, I believe he
made a good record as Congressman and Senator – that is
entirely in the hands of the delegates next year. No, I don't
at this time plan to attend the convention. No, gentlemen,
thank you. I have nothing more to say.' They did not believe
him, and he did not care. At least, they could not quote him.

This did not prevent a number of influential newspapers
from implying that millions of dollars were being spent on the

Senator in an effort to influence the primaries and the delegates the next year. Lately editorials had lost their usual American humour and had turned to rough derision and vicious cartoons. Joseph was not in the least surprised even when papers who had written favourably of Rory were now expressing 'serious doubts', as they called it, and some were definitely hostile. 'The Circle' had begun to work. The attacks on Rory, and his father; would increase in intensity until the nominations. On the other hand, various newspapers became warmer in their admiration for Rory. Two can play at this game, thought Joseph. Still it was not something to ignore, and Joseph prepared to take action, and began to plan. The bastards had not yet taken over America completely, though time was running out.

He decided that Claudia was not to accompany Rory to Boston. She was entirely too exotic for Boston ladies, after all. It was not that she was too stylish, too elaborate, or too obviously sophisticated: it was that she was too charming though she was incapable of summoning up that charm at will. It flashed out like an enthralment, when least expected, and dazed women as well as men. Boston ladies were a different breed.

'Thank God for small mercies, then,' said Rory piously to Timothy and winked. Timothy smiled at him warningly. 'No high jinks this time, boyo,' he said. 'We will be demure and serious as all hell in Boston, and high-minded, subdued, modulated, intellectual if you feel pushed, historical always, and above everything else, the Proper Little Gentleman.'

'You don't have to tell me,' said Rory. 'Didn't I live for years among them, at Harvard, and – and in Pa's offices? I'll convince the Brahmins that I do, indeed, wash behind my ears and can sip sherry as elegantly as they can – God damn it – and my boots can be as discreetly polished. But don't forget the Irish there, Tim. A few little airs, "When Irish Eyes are Smiling, Sure they Steal your Heart Away!" No, too brash, too much like Old Syrup, who dances an Irish jig on any table at the snap of a finger. How old is the old bugger now, anyway? He's got "Kathleen Mavourneen" for his song, and I favoured that for myself. How about "Killarney"? No. Something light and haunting . . .'

'Like "The Band Played On"?'

'Shut up, Tim. This is serious. How about "The Harp that

Once through Tara's Halls"?'

'A harp for a Harp,' said Timothy.

Rory laughed, his deep ringing laugh, and Timothy would always remember it, for it was musical and manly and without affectation. 'Now, that's it,' said Rory. 'Have posters made, strictly for the Irish section. "A Harp for a Harp." It's good, Tim, really good.' He sang a few bars, and for some reason Timothy's bright sceptical eyes became a little dim.

> 'The harp that once through Tara's Halls
> The soul of music shed,
> Now hangs as mute on Tara's walls
> As if that soul were dead . . .'

Rory said, 'Talk about the Israelites weeping in Babylonian captivity. Every Irishman always weeps for Ireland, and his "exile", but damned few ever go back, do they? But it does the heart good to mourn. All warm and sad and moist inside. The Jews and the Irish are the most sentimental people in the world, but you can't fool either of them. I've found that out about sentimental people. Yes, "a Harp for a Harp."'

The band went ahead to Boston. The proper audience was summoned to the train on which Rory rode – not his father's private coach. Men, women and children had been given small American flags. It was a hot August morning, glittering and pleasant, for there was a slight cooling breeze. The band clashed and trumpeted and drummed: 'The Stars and Stripes For Ever!' The greeters cheered. There were hundreds of Irish faces there. Timothy gave a signal and the band became soft and haunting as it played 'The Harp that Once through Tara's Halls'. Only half the Irish greeters had ever heard that mournful and moving song, but the music was familiar to their ancient spirits and some openly wept, and some who knew the song sang it in quivering voices.

They went to a fine almost new hotel near the Boston Common. Rory had spent many years at the university near Boston. He had spent weeks every year, until he was a Congressman, in his father's office in that city. Yet, since Marjorie had deserted him the city had become strange and unfamiliar to him, a photograph of a reality he had once known and now half-forgotten and which he regarded with indifference. He stood at one of the windows in his suite and looked down at the trees on the Common.

'Like old times, eh?' said Timothy, watching him.

'Not particularly,' Rory replied. He had been in good lively spirits, for he had inherited his mother's buoyancy. Yet all at once the sunlight beyond him appeared to lessen and the trees to turn cold and drab. He shook his head as if to shake a film from his eyes.

He and Timothy were alone in his bedroom, but in the rooms adjoining there were the loud and excited and burly voices of politicians, vehemently disputing, some shouting, some laughing. The smoke would be thick in there, and the whisky and gin illimitable. They had been waiting for Rory for hours, and soon he would have to go into those rooms and meet them in a hullabaloo of greetings, back-slappings, finger-jabbing, shouts, yells, cheers, rude questions, ruder jokes. Most of them were Irish, and they were in a happy mood. The door of Rory's room had a separate entrance from the hall, and he knew that stationed without there were two of his armed bodyguards, quiet watchful men who knew their duty. They irritated Rory. He was too sanguine by nature to fear danger, or objectively to accept its possibility. If an assassin went gunning for a man, that assassin got his man, even a President, and he, Rory Armagh, had not yet even been nominated by his Party. Sure and the Committee for Foreign Studies had declared their preference for Woodrow Wilson, and Rory knew that they would not stop at discreet violence if necessary. But they would first wait for the convention, wouldn't they? By that time he hoped to have had many primary victories. Then there would be time for armed bodyguards, in the event he was nominated.

His changeful nature now turned melancholy. Without looking at Timothy he said, 'I have the funniest feeling that I not only will never be President of this country but will not even be nominated.'

'What's the matter with you?' demanded Timothy, startled. 'Of course you will. Your Pa is putting out millions upon millions, and he's sure enough. Don't even start thinking of failure. That's fatal. Once you think you might get licked, you will surely be licked. And no Armagh ever gets licked, does he?'

'No. He gets killed,' said Rory, thinking of his Uncle Sean, and his brother.

Timothy stood up abruptly, and his square pleasant face, tanned by the Western sun, had actually paled. 'God damn it, Rory,' he said in a low tone. 'What's the matter with you?'

Rory himself was startled at the sombreness in Timothy's voice, and he swung from the window and began to laugh. But Timothy did not laugh. He was staring at the young man whom he had tutored as a child, and whom he loved as a son, and his broad features were working. 'What a hell of a thing to say!' he added.

'What? What did I say? Oh, about Sean and Kevin. And about the nomination. Well, I can have my doubts, can't I?'

But Timothy said, 'You're not sleeping in this room alone. I'm going to share it with you.' Rory burst out laughing. From far downstairs came the strains of 'The Harp that Once through Tara's Halls'. The men in the adjoining rooms began to sing, emotionally, passionately, and very loudly. Rory shook his head, his amusement growing. His mood had changed again from that nameless Irish melancholy to gaiety. 'Get me a drink, will you, Tim, but don't let any of that mob in here yet. I want my lunch first. Never trust a politician on an empty stomach.'

Timothy, in silence, opened an inside door and instantly everything was flooded in a tide of roaring, singing, laughter, shouts, and a flood of smoke. It was these men, the ward-heelers, the petty politicians, the chairmen of counties, the exigent rascals, who decided who would be nominated and who would not, and not State Chairmen or National Chairmen, for all their airs and urbane smiles and plottings.

Well, why not? thought Rory, comfortably. Democracy in action. Long may she wave. She may stink at times, and stink mightily, but she's the best we have and probably will always be the best. Someone knocked on the outside door and Rory instinctively went towards it. He would have unlocked and opened it had not Timothy re-entered the big sunlit room, with its massive rich furniture. Timothy bellowed at him, and Rory stopped with his hand on the door-knob.

Timothy put down the soda and whisky and the glasses, drew a deep breath and said, 'God damn you, Rory. Haven't you any sense? Did you think your father was playing settlers and Indians?' His face was pallid and enraged.

He went to the door and roughly shouldered Rory aside, then shoved him against the wall. He was powerful, though

Rory was a head taller than he. He shouted through the closed door: 'Who is it?'

One of the guards answered. 'It's me, Malone, Mr Dineen. Somebody sent a card up for the Senator. Want me to push it under the door?' Timothy gave Rory an irate glance, for Rory had begun to laugh again. 'Yes!' said Timothy. A slim envelope was slipped under the door and Timothy, grunting, bent down and retrieved it. Inside was a fine card, faintly creamy, and finely engraved. Timothy read, 'General Curtis Clayton, Army of the United States'. On the back there was written in precise wooden letters: 'I beg that Senator Armagh grant me a few minutes of his time. Urgent.'

Rory plucked the card from Timothy's hand and read it aloud. 'Well,' he said. 'The General, no less. What do you think he wants? Even the President's afraid of the old bastard.'

'Would you know him if you saw him, Rory?'

'Of course I would. We've been at parties together, though never talked. I gather he thought me just a boy playing at being Senator. But he liked Claudia all right. Well, let him come up.'

Timothy put the chain on the door and cautiously opened it. He said to the bodyguards, 'The Senator will see General Clayton – for a few minutes.'

'The Senator will graciously grant an audience to General Clayton – for a few minutes,' Rory mocked. 'Tim, that's the most powerful old boy in Washington, outside the President. When he farts bugles blow, drums rattle, armies come to attention, civilian "authorities" hide under tables, flags rush up poles. Even Teddy runs for cover, as he wouldn't run from a charging rhinoceros. The Cabinet quakes when he walks. He's got a Presence, Tim, a real Presence. An old warrior. And he hates civilians. He especially hates Senators who dispute his military budgets. He's Chief of Staff, by the way. Haven't you ever heard of him?'

'Yes,' said Timothy. 'Now that you mention it. If he's an "old warrior", as you say, why did he oppose the war with Spain?'

Rory thoughtfully bit a finger and raised his red brows. 'Well, so he did! I'd forgotten. Teddy practically called him a traitor, or worse. Since then, though, he's put the fear of God in Teddy Bear. I don't know how. Anyone who can do that to Teddy deserves the Congressional Medal of Honour for extraordinary heroism under fire, and whatnot. If the military ever has a Pope, General Clayton will be it.'

There was another knock on the door. Timothy opened it but left the chain on, and motioned to Rory, who could hardly keep from laughing out loud, and Rory peeked through the slit 'Well, well, General!' he exclaimed. 'This is indeed an honour! Come in, come in!'

General Curtis Clayton, not in uniform now, entered after Timothy removed the chain. He watched Timothy replace the chain and then said in a deep grave voice, 'An excellent idea, sir, an excellent idea.' Rory was astonished. He had been holding out his hand and the General had been meticulously watching Timothy. Then the General turned to Rory and ponderously took the younger man's hand and gave it a quick shake, military and precise. 'Senator,' he said, briefly.

Though not in uniform there was no mistaking the commanding presence of a man of discipline and order and assurance and superb strength. He was almost as tall as Rory, but powerful of build, if compact, and though he was in his late fifties, self-control, self-discipline, made him appear much younger and very quietly vigorous. His voice was deep and strong and meticulously controlled. He was somewhat forbidding, as befitted a man who gave orders.

'My manager, Tim Dineen,' said Rory. 'Tim, General Clayton.'

Timothy and the General soberly shook hands. The General's eyes studied Timothy quickly and apparently he approved of what he saw for he gave Timothy a slight smile. He accepted Rory's offer of a drink, and he watched Rory pour it and his eyes narrowed thoughtfully as they ran over Rory's face and beautifully tailored suit and athletic body. He had not been mistaken, he said to himself. The Boy Senator was a man, suddenly a man. The General smiled again and gave Rory a small bow on accepting the glass of whisky and soda. He sat down, and Timothy sat down near him. There appeared to be a warm confidence between them, a silent exchange. But Rory sat on the edge of a table and lightly swung an elegant leg and smiled sunnily. They listened for a moment to the increasing uproar next door. Rory said, 'My boys. Politicians all. They aren't listening to each other, just to themselves. If they sound like bulls smelling a cow in heat, it's just their way, General.'

'I'm well acquainted, perhaps too well acquainted, with politicians,' said the General. '"Civilian control of the military", as the Constitution says, and it's an excellent thing. Most of the time. But now I wonder . . .'

Rory waited for him to continue, but he had fallen silent, his eyes fixed on the glass in his hand. So Rory said, 'What brings you to Boston, General?'

The General looked up and his eyes were full on Rory. 'You, Senator.'

Rory was surprised, and he lifted his brows and gave the General all his attention. 'I? May I ask why?'

The General sipped at his drink. 'While we military men are under the control of the politicians, we are alert to politicians. We dare be nothing else. So I have been reading the reports of your speeches all over the country, Senator. I have had scores of clippings sent to me, and I have studied all of them closely. Very closely.'

Rory's brows again shot up, but Timothy became alert. 'General,' said Rory, 'the speeches are just for the troops, as you would call them, yourself. Happy generalisations. Handsome vague promises. Lampooning of Taft and Roosevelt. Issues, excitable issues, not too well defined.' He shrugged. 'As you have said, you know politicians. We dare not be too explicit. If we were, it would come back to haunt us. I cut my political cloth to fit my pattern, which is the pattern of all politicians.' He spoke disarmingly, and with humorous frankness.

'I know,' said the General. 'You are all genial frauds and expert liars. No offence, Senator. It is a fact. The public wouldn't have you anything else. Can you imagine a politician who was absolutely honest ever getting nominated, not to speak elected? The very idea is absurd. It has never happened but a few times in history, and those times were celebrated. But the reason I am here is because I think you will be nominated by your Party, and will be elected President.'

Rory grinned. 'I wish I were that sure, General, but thank you.'

The General studied his glass again, and Rory and Timothy saw that he was going over his words before speaking them. 'I am sure,' he said at last. 'The Republican Party is being divided by Roosevelt. So, if nominated, you will be elected.' He lifted his hand. 'Let me finish, if you please. You will be nominated. It is not just your father's wealth, though that is the main factor. No man was ever elected without the expenditure of a lot of money, sad to say. But you will be elected because the voters want something new, perhaps something more vital than the average politician, perhaps someone younger, someone more attractive and original. Frankly, the voters are bored. You are not a boring man, Senator.'

Rory looked at Timothy with amusement, but Timothy was listening sharply to the General. 'I wouldn't have taken this incognito trip to Boston if I did not think you would be nominated, and probably elected, Senator, in spite of your er – religion and origins. I should not have wasted my time. Delegates? Local politicians? Your father has already bought them. I see you are not surprised. So let us confidently assume you will be nominated and elected. I have my spies, too,' and he smiled his reluctant smile again.

Rory had begun to frown a little. 'I have heard a rumour,' he said. 'About the Governor of New Jersey, Woodrow Wilson, who may contest my nomination. Just a rumour.'

The planes of the General's face suddenly became stonelike and expressionless. 'Not a rumour, only,' he said. He put down his glass. Then the General said, 'But I feel you know that, Senator.'

Rory's face lost all expression. He looked at the General. 'I wish to revert to the clippings of your speeches, which I have read,' said the General. 'The major newspapers left out a very salient ending to your speeches. Only a few obscure and backwoods papers printed it. No doubt the major newspapers felt it irrelevant. I refer to your ending, which usually goes like this: "Above all, I will work for peace not only for America but for the world."'

The General's eyes became penetrating as they fixed themselves on Rory. 'Now,' he said, 'why should you speak of peace in a world at peace, except for a few minor skirmishes in remote parts of the globe, notably Mexico and perhaps in one or two small South American countries, which are always skirmishing? Even the Balkans are quiet. The Hague never mentions wars any longer, but only a hope for a future league of nations. Mr Roosevelt was highly impressed by the Kaiser. Russia is enjoying an unusual era of well-being, freedom and prosperity, thanks to Czar Nicholas and the elected Duma. The British Empire is well-ordered, the balance wheel of the world. Americans have no desire for conquest, for expansion, and are not warlike. In short, Senator, peace is now an acceptable and taken-for-granted state in the world. So why do you invariably speak of peace? What could less interest the American people than such an issue? There is no threat of any war anywhere. So, Senator?'

'Well, General, it does no harm to speak of peace, does it? A little flourish.'

'Senator,' said the General with the utmost quiet, 'I don't believe you. That is why I am here: I don't believe you. I have built my hopes on my disbelief. I think you know something, Senator, which only a few know.' He leaned towards Rory and again fixed him with his eye. 'Tell me, sir, have you ever heard of the Committee for Foreign Studies?'

Rory, before he could control himself, felt his face involuntarily change. He tried to recover his blandness. He gave the General his candid relaxed look. 'I may have heard of it — somewhere. Isn't it a private organisation devoted to the study of foreign trends, banking, tariffs? Boring things like that?'

The General smiled. 'And no doubt, too, you have only casually heard of the Scardo Society in America, composed of self-declared "intellectuals" and "liberals"?'

Rory shrugged. 'I might have heard,' he said. 'Politicians hear everything, but that does not mean to say they believe everything.'

But the General was still smiling. Rory felt a slight sweat between his shoulder-blades. 'Your father belongs both to the Committee for Foreign Studies, and the Scardo Society.'

'If he does, I don't know it,' said Rory. Timothy was studying his hands.

The General closed his eyes briefly. 'Senator, let us not play with each other. I am trying to be frank with you, but you are not frank with me. I hardly expected it. Not that you are a politician, but perhaps — perhaps you are afraid?'

Rory looked up suddenly. 'Afraid?' His face became quickly scarlet and angry. 'I am not afraid of anything, General!'

To his amazement the General again closed his eyes for a second, and said, 'Thank God for that, sir, thank God for that. For you have reason to be afraid — and yet you are not. Thank God.'

'Of what should I be afraid?' demanded Rory with increas-

411

ing anger, yet he felt the cold finger of fear on his neck. But the General stood up and began to pace up and down the room, slowly, heavily, his hands clasped behind his back.

He said, as if ruminating, 'There is no need for all this fencing. No. I respect your caution, your reticence, even your denials. I didn't expect anything else, of course. I only wanted you to know that I know what you know, also, and perhaps even more. I have been studying your father for a number of years. I know more about him, perhaps, than you do. It may astonish you to know that I approve of your father – not his business activities, no, who could? But because of what he really thinks.'

'You don't know my father. You've never met him. How can you know what he thinks?' Rory was still angry, and the cold finger was broadening on his neck, yet he was curious and vaguely excited.

'I know, or knew, one or two of his friends. Good men. Men devoted to him. I knew Charles Devereaux. Perhaps you never heard of Charles either, Senator?'

Rory was astounded, and did not answer. 'Or Harry Zeff, no?' said the General.

Rory drew a deep breath and said coldly, 'Are you implying, General, that my father's friends and associates betrayed him to you, and repeated private conversations to you? I thought better of them.'

The General said at once, 'They thought better of your father than anyone else in the world! They knew him like brothers, devoted brothers. They never betrayed him, or told me things which they should never have told. They only told me of his history, his character. That was sufficient.' He rubbed his forehead as if it ached. 'I knew them for years. I made it my business to know them, and they knew why.'

Rory was deeply offended, and his love for his father touched with jealousy. 'I think I know my father, better than anyone. I am in his total confidence.'

'Yes,' said the General. 'I know that, thank God. And that is why I am here.'

'Perhaps you had better talk to my father, if you really have anything to say, General. So far I haven't understood in the least. All this talking about a subject . . .'

'Rory,' said Timothy, 'suppose you let the General explain.'
The General was grateful. 'I can't be explicit, Mr Dineen.

412

You know that. If there was a real need to be explicit to the Senator I wouldn't be here. He knows what I am talking about, and so do you. So let us assume that we have a mutual base of knowledge. If only as a hypothesis.'

Rory nodded. 'As only a hypothesis,' he repeated. The General continued to march slowly up and down. His head was bent, as if he were alone, and reflecting to himself, and choosing his thoughts.

'There are those who believe that military men, like myself, can only be alive and functioning during wars, and that they are eager for wars. That is a fallacy. We do not make wars. We do not suggest them. That is out of our hands, and so we are not guilty. The function of a military man is to defend his country, when called on by the President of the United States, and the Congress, which alone has the power to declare war. As of now, gentlemen, as of now. I cannot guarantee the future . . . It is being said now, and I think I know the reason, that big military establishments "provoke" wars. That is a calculated falsehood. Or it is being said by the simple-minded. The civilian authority controls wars – or peace. Not the military. This is true of most European countries, also. It is the civilians who goad a ruler into declaring war, who arrange for munitions, who buy munitions, who supply munitions.

'Man is by nature a combative and lustful and envious and ruthless species, a predator. Not all the churches or religions in the world can overcome that reality. He might deplore wars, but it has been said that no government announced a war and nobody came. All men are driven by their nature.

'When I was a child my father took me to a small zoo. A tigress in a cage had recently given birth. I saw the cubs. They were like little children, harmless, playful, romping, innocent, wide-eyed with interest as they looked at the world, eager to explore that world happily.' The General paused for a moment.

'But in those cubs awaited the tiger nature. No amount of "education" would ever remove it, nor any soft words, or any "conditioning" by idealists and the "hopeful". The nature was there, inborn. It could never be eradicated, never be changed. The cubs were born in sunny captivity, with everything provided for their comfort. They had never known the jungle, or killing, or hunting. But the tiger nature was there. It waited.

413

It was a matter of maturity, of burgeoning, no matter the environment. The tiger cannot really be tamed. Man cannot be tamed. That is why we have to have laws. That is why we have to have the military: to carry out the mandates of human nature. A soldier is no more bloodthirsty than a civilian, or as innately lustful for combat. He is only the servant of the civilian. In fact, soldiers are often sickened by war, and silently revolt against it, after a battle. But a civilian rarely is disturbed.'

He suddenly stopped and looked at Rory with quiet ferocity. 'I think you know what I am implying,' he said. 'Let me put it a little more childishly, though you do not need it. Wars were once fought in defence of a country – but they are now deliberately instigated for conquest – at civilian behest. Of course civilians always speak of "defence", but never of conquest. That might make the multitudes wary and hostile.

'We come to modern-day war. No nation is threatening another nation, now. We can't – guarantee – tomorrow. Do you follow me, gentlemen? This is the twentieth century. No war will be fought in this century except by fiat of civilians. And not for mere conquest of territories, or even solely for world markets.'

He paused again, and said, almost humbly, 'Soldiers are not eloquent. We have a hard time with words. We are not politicians. Let me say this: wars of this century will be fought to control men's minds and souls, to dehumanise mankind, to make it subservient to world rulers, who will be but one body. That war will not be a war of soldiers against other soldiers, or against cities and nations. It will be a war of devils against humanity.'

He looked at them. 'Perhaps you believe I am full of delusions, and fantasies?'

They did not speak. He went on, 'Those wars have been long in the plotting. I am not repeating rumours or fairy tales or imagined nightmares. I know them for myself. You know of Cecil Rhodes? Of course. He is dead, but his ideas, and those of Ruskin, live on and are gathering force. The ideas appeal, not to military men like myself, but only to civilians. In a way, then, future wars will be civilian wars against civilians, and not military ones, as in the past. They will be wars of ideas, of slavery against freedom, of the imprisonment of men's minds in cages of Socialism and servitude, of free choice

414

against a planned society.'

He added in a low tone, 'Such wars will be hateful to military men like myself.'

He stopped in front of Rory and his light brown eyes were almost fierce. 'The wars won't be fought by one aggressive nation against another, though governments will tell their people so. They will be wars of governments against their own people, of ambitious men against their own neighbours, for tyranny over their own nations, though ostensibly they will be against "foreign aggressors".'

He threw out his hands. 'If I did not believe that you two gentlemen already know this I should not be here now.' He waited for their comment, but they had averted their brooding faces. He said, 'I was a Rhodes scholar.' He sat down, as if exhausted. 'Though you can hardly believe it now I was a dedicated scholar in those days. But one year in England, as a Rhodes scholar, was enough! I returned and went to West Point. It was my way of learning to defend my country against the men who had taught me.'

Rory and Timothy were looking steadily at him now, but still said nothing.

He went on, 'You probably don't know it, but the opening guns against mankind will be lifted in a few years, perhaps 1917, or 1918, or 1920.'

Rory's face involuntarily changed, as he remembered what his father had told him, and seeing this the General smiled and nodded.

'Perhaps sooner, Senator. At least my spy in the Committee for Foreign Studies told me that recently. What must we do to prevent it, or keep America out of it? "Eternal vigilance is the price of peace." I've told that to the politicians in Washington who control the military budgets. They laugh at me, both the ones who think I am looking for bogey-men, and the ones who know I am telling the truth. So America must arm herself to the hilt so that she may warn Europe not to engage in any wars on penalty of punishment, and to be so strong that her voice will have power world-wide.'

He stood up before the silent men. He said, 'Your friends in the other rooms have begun to shout for you, Senator. Now you know why I came to you today: I think you will be our next President. I think you will be able to keep our country out of war, or even prevent foreign wars. Diplomacy backed up by strength, and the willingness to use that strength. Even the threat, I hope, will be enough. And when you are President you can tell our country the truth.'

'You haven't told Mr Taft any of this?'

The General hesitated. 'I did, to some extent, but he does not know what you know, Senator. But Mr Taft will not be President. Mr Roosevelt has arranged to prevent that. Nor will he be President. No, I haven't forgotten Mr Wilson, and those behind him. But I think you can overcome them, if only by a threat to expose them.'

'My God, no!' exclaimed Timothy. 'That would never do, and you know it, General. Even as it is they suspect Rory, though God knows why. He's been amenable enough. If they hadn't suspected him – though they claim they are only "doubtful" because his race and religion might militate against him with the voters – they wouldn't be behind Wilson now. You and I know about *coups d'état*. Rory must wait until he is President, and even then he would be in the most desperate danger – and you know that, too.'

'A soldier is always in danger,' said the General. 'So is a man who insists on telling the truth. That is the unpardonable sin in public life. Well, you must use your own judgment.'

He held out his hand to Rory and now his smile was warm. 'My best men are Irish,' he said. 'Irishmen are rarely, if ever, traitors. They also know that only the strong can keep the peace, and not the sweet-sayers and the pacific. That's why they are drawn to the police forces.'

'Yes,' said Timothy. 'But Rory still has to get the nomination of the Party, you know, against very formidable opposition.'

'He will,' said the General. 'And that's why you must take the utmost care . . .' He hesitated. 'Would you accept a contingent of my men, in civilian clothes, in addition to your own guards?'

'Yes,' said Timothy, at once, but Rory laughed shortly. 'No,' he said. 'It's ridiculous. Here I am – just letting the people see me throughout the country and get acquainted with me. I have broadly hinted that I'd like to be elected President next year, but haven't entered the primaries yet. I still don't have the nomination, and until then I am sure I am quite safe. But thank you anyway, General.'

The General looked at him long and hard and thought how

splendid this young man was in both appearance and magnetism. He was to remember his last sight of Rory the rest of his life.

When the General had left, Rory said to Timothy, all his sunniness gone and his face as harsh as his father's: 'There are New York reporters downstairs as well as Boston ones. Bring them up here, Tim. I am going to tell them some of the truth.'

Timothy was stupefied. He said in a strangled voice, 'Are you out of your mind?'

Rory said, 'In spite of everything, I just don't feel I will get the nomination, let alone be President. I just feel it. But at any rate I can let my fellow-citizens know, and be forearmed. Go on, Tim. Bring them up here. I mean it.'

Later Timothy was to wonder whether or not that interview with the press had anything to do with what was to happen that night, or whether the course of events could have been changed at all.

CHAPTER FIFTY-THREE

IT was five o'clock before Rory could return to his rooms with the heavily silent and desperately worried Timothy. The turbulent, half-sneering, partially derisive, and sceptical and somewhat horrified press had departed, after a session of wild questions, of smothered hoots, of eyes bulging with incredulity and excitement. 'War?' one of them had shouted to Rory, waving both arms in the air. 'With whom? Why? Sir, are you serious?'

'I thought I explained all that, at least twice,' said Rory. Some of his splendour had dimmed during the past two hours and he had not once been jocular as was his custom, nor joking. He looked much older. He had not sat down once during the interviews, but had walked up and down in controlled agitation. 'I have said the "enemy" has not yet been chosen, but I think it will be Germany. "They" haven't told me too much, because they suspect me. Perhaps,' he said, 'you might consult the Committee for Foreign Studies yourselves.'

'But they are only businessmen and financiers and political

students and political scientists, a private organisation! Americans! They have no political influence . . .'

'You may eventually learn, to your death, that they have all the political influence,' said Rory.

'Are you, sir,' asked another reporter with a sly wink at his fellows, 'just trying to throw dust into the voters' eyes because your Party indicates it prefers Mr Woodrow Wilson, the Governor of New Jersey, to you? Or, at least, that is the rumour. Are you trying for a little personal revenge – or to influence the delegates, and the primaries to favour you and not Mr Wilson?'

Rory felt that unique and desperate impotence men feel who try to enlighten their people to the truth, and finally understand that the truth is one thing which will never be believed. It was a hopeless impotence. He had never experienced it before, and it shook him profoundly. He had expected some scepticism, some horror, some amazement. But the leering eyes below him, the knowing grins, the shaking of heads, the malicious glances, almost undid him. 'You don't expect us to report this seriously, do you, Senator?' asked a young man who appeared to have taken the leadership.

'I had hoped you would take me seriously, for I have told you the truth,' said Rory. 'I know there is nothing so incredible as the truth – but, strange to say, I have a feeling that some of you – perhaps only two or three – know that I have told you the truth, and you are the ones who pretend to take what I've said with the loudest laughter and the most contempt. I don't know who you are – but you know. Well, gentlemen, that is all.'

Timothy, very pale, stood up then and said, 'The Senator will speak fully on this tonight in the ballroom of this hotel. We have given you this interview so that you might make the morning newspapers. Essentially, what the Senator has told you will be repeated tonight and perhaps enlarged upon. That is all. Please excuse us. The Senator is very tired. He has been travelling strenuously all over the country, speaking and meeting tens of thousands of citizens, and needs to rest before the speech.'

They straggled to their feet reluctantly when Rory turned to go, and there was not a single hand-clapping or show of respect. One reporter muttered to others, 'What's he got against Socialism, anyway? "Slavery!" "Plotters!" "International bankers!" "Worldwide Conspiracy!" I heard the Armaghs were pretty level-headed bastards. All that money,' and he wet his lips with venomous envy. 'The Senator's gone dippy.'

'Wars!' laughed another. 'Can you imagine Americans agreeing to an international war, a war in Europe, for God's sake! "To advance Socialistic-Communism," he says. Who listens to Karl Marx, anyway? That boy Senator has hot water on the brain! Wars! Didn't Governor Wilson say only last week that the world has entered on a permanent era of prosperity, peace and progress? Now, there's a man- I could vote for!'

'Me, too,' said another. 'Well, anyone going to report this drivel?'

'Not me,' said still another. 'My editor would fire me after asking if I'd been drunk. Well, let's listen to him tonight, if you can stand it. Wars! He's out of his mind.'

Two or three only smiled, but they looked significantly at each other. Then one muttered, ' "The Golden Boy." Well, he might just as well go and bury himself in the Armagh multi-millions and forget the nomination. He's cut his throat as far as sensible men are concerned.' They marched out together chanting, 'War, war, war! To arms!'

Rory undressed in his room in the heavy silence. Timothy sat by the window, in despair. What had possessed the usually discreet and exigent Rory? Why couldn't he have waited until the primaries, at least?

'Because,' said Rory, behind the muffling silk, 'I don't think I will even make the primaries.'

The telephone rang and Timothy, cursing, answered it. There had been orders not to disturb the Senator, yet the damned phone was ringing. 'Who?' shouted Timothy. 'Never heard of her! Tell her to go away, Jesus! What, she insists? "Old friend of the Senator's?" Well, damn it, what's her name, and I will report this intrusion to the manager.'

Rory was sitting on the bed taking off his slippers. Timothy looked at him with sparkling eyes of rage out of proportion to the 'intrusion'. 'Some damned female demands to speak to you, Rory. She won't go away. The assistant manager says she is of an "old and notable family in Boston". Knows the family well, and he doesn't want to tell her to get off. Well? She's on the telephone. Shall I tell her to go to hell?'

Maggie, thought Rory at once, and his haggard face was excited and suddenly filled with colour. He trembled, staring, sitting on the bed. Maggie.

'Some female you've bedded in Boston, no doubt,' said Timothy with anger. He could not get over that infernal interview and took his rage out on Rory. 'Maybe she's got a wood's colt to try to saddle you with; make good newspaper copy.'

Maggie, thought Rory, and he pushed himself to his feet and took the telephone. He moved like one in a daze, and did not look at Timothy. He could hardly speak for a moment. Then he almost whispered, 'Maggie?'

'Oh, Rory,' she said, and her voice was filled with tears. 'Oh, Rory, Rory.'

'Maggie,' he said. The receiver had become wet in his hand. Her voice rang over the years, all those long years. And the years vanished. 'Where are you, Maggie?'

'At home, Rory. I don't know what made me call you, but I had to.'

Timothy could not believe what he saw. Rory's exhausted face was illuminated and smiling and shaken. He was a youth again, excited, bursting with joy, transfigured. He held the receiver in both hands, as if holding the hand of a beloved woman. 'Maggie, Maggie,' he said. 'Why did you leave me, Maggie, my darlin'?'

'I had to, Rory. Rory, I am still your wife. Your wife, Rory. I don't care that you married again. You are my husband. I've been faithful to you, Rory. I've loved you always.' Her voice broke, and he could hear her sobbing.

'It was your father who separated us, Maggie. He did it, the . . .'

She interrupted wildly. 'No, Rory! It's time you knew the truth. I don't care what happens now. Papa and Aunt Emma are dead. I am all alone – your wife, Rory. It was your father who did it, who threatened Papa and me – and you, Rory. I did it for you, Rory. He would have ruined you, thrown you out, Rory. Your own father. We knew he meant it. So I did it for you, more for you than for Papa and for myself.'

He stood in numb silence for a long moment or two. Then Marjorie said, 'Rory? Are you still there, Rory?'

'Yes,' he said, in a most peculiar voice. He was staring at the wall now, and his pale blue eyes were wide and fixed, with the whites brightly glistening under the iris, and his face slack. Nothing showed in his expression, yet Timothy, watching with sudden intensity, felt that he was looking at a dangerous and deadly face, a mask that was terrifying.

'You believe me, Rory,' Marjorie was weeping. 'I never lied to you, except in that last letter. I had to do it for you, my dearest.'

'Why didn't you tell me before, Maggie?'

'I couldn't, not so long as Papa and Aunt Emma were alive. Papa died a month ago. Rory, perhaps I shouldn't have told you after all. What good does it do? But I read you were here. I saw your photograph in the newspapers. Oh, Rory, I must be out of my mind to talk to you now! But I couldn't control myself; I had to hear your voice, for the very last time, Rory. It will have to content me the rest of my life, I am afraid. Oh, Rory.'

He shook himself all over, like someone shaking off dusty years and dead grass and rising from them, renewed, after a long and lightless dream.

'No, Maggie,' he said. 'Not for the last time. Maggie, I am giving a speech here tonight . . .'

'I know, dear. I am coming to hear you. I should have been contented with that and not have intruded on you now – at this late day. Rory.'

'Maggie, afterwards, come up to my rooms.' He paused. 'Will you, Maggie?'

For God's sake, thought Timothy, who was astounded at the part of the conversation he was hearing. A trollop, apparently. But Rory had a taste for trollops. This was no time in his career for a flaunting of strumpets in the face of public opinion. She must have been a memorable doxy to stir the experienced Rory like this. He was actually trembling. 'Rory,' he said. 'Not tonight, for Christ's sake, Rory! You're in Boston!'

Rory looked over his shoulder at him. 'I am talking to my wife,' he said, and his voice was full of a huge yet elated impatience. 'Shut up.'

Timothy had been half rising. He fell back weightily in his chair, his head humming. His wife! Timothy's thoughts rang with wild surmises of bigamy, of madness, of polygamy, of threatened scandal, of a brood of unknown brats, of blackmail. The press! He put his hands to his head and groaned.

421

Rory was giving the number of his suite. Now his voice was the voice of a boy, speaking with his first love, exuberant, joyous, excited. His face was the face of a lover. His weariness was forgotten. He was bending over the telephone as if he would kiss it, devour it. His eyes shone and glittered, became deeply blue. He glowed. He radiated delight. His voice was deep, shaken, stammering. Then he said, 'Until tonight, my darling.'

He hung up the receiver, slowly, lingeringly, reluctantly, listening to the last when only silence was there. He turned to Timothy. He tried to speak, then sat down on the bed, clasping his hands on his knees, staring at the floor. His throat worked. He said, 'It was Maggie. My wife.' Then his face changed, became savage and terrible. 'That son of a bitch. My father.'

Then he told the aghast Timothy. He spoke without emotion, but Timothy could sense the charge of rage and hatred that impelled his voice which was slow and without emphasis. 'All these years,' he said, and he seemed heavily indifferent. 'All these wasted years. I haven't been alive. Only partly alive. He did that to me, and I thought he – I thought he had some feeling for me. He did that to me. He must have known what that would mean, but he didn't care. I could kill him. Perhaps I will.' Now his look changed again, and his face was eloquent with sorrow and despair and incredulous acceptance. 'He did that to me, his son.'

'Now, wait a minute, Rory,' said Timothy, who was sweating with his own emotions. 'I've known your father a long time, since you were only a child. If he did that, then he did it for you. A nice Boston girl, who couldn't meet his ambitions for you. You had to have someone who was – important – and spectacular, though I hate that word. Someone who was known, who could do you proud, as your father would say. Someone perfect for your position. Claudia is that. Perfect for the wife of a politician. Come on, Rory. You are a man, not a boy in his first puberty. You must realise your father did it for you.'

'For me, for what?'

Timothy tried to smile, and it was sickly. 'You know what Kipling said about women. A woman's only a woman. But you are a man, with a future. Your father knew that. Give him his due, Rory. I know it must have hurt – when it happened.

422

But you aren't a kid any longer. You have to be realistic. If the young lady is – willing – well, romp a while with her tonight, though God knows how I'll manage it, to keep down scandal. She isn't a kid herself any longer. How old? Thirty-three? Thirty-four? She should have had better sense than to call you, you a married man with four children. Women! A middle-aged woman, older than Claudia.'

'My wife,' said Rory. 'I never had any other wife, all these years. I committed the worst kind of bigamy when I married Claudia.'

'Who happens to be devoted to you,' said Timothy, with pity.

'Claudia loves only her image in the looking glass,' said Rory, and so dismissed his wife. 'Maggie. Let her in tonight, Tim. She's the only thing I have, and I mean it.'

He threw himself down on the bed and moved restlessly, as if his thoughts were too tumultuous to let him be still. 'I'll take it all up with dear Papa, when I get home,' he said. 'I'll divorce Claudia. I'll marry Maggie again, and the hell with everything. Marry her again? Why, I was always married to her, my Maggie, my darlin'.'

'Jaysus,' said Timothy, and threw up his hands. 'All these years of planning, and it comes to this! Rory, think of your future for a minute, just a minute.' Was it really possible for a man to give up his whole life for a woman – a woman! Incredible, nightmarish.

'I'm thinking,' said Rory, and smiled, and turned on his side and slept like a contented child, satisfied at last after a long and weary day.

Timothy watched the sleeping man for some time and felt broken with hopelessness. The press, already hostile to Rory, would go wild. 'Jaysus,' groaned Timothy. It was all over now, as they said, except for the shouting. He could see big black headlines all over the country. He could hear the bellows of indignation and incredulity. The Committee for Foreign Studies would be coldly satisfied.

Timothy had a thought. It was very possible that that ambitious nobody had been induced to do this to Rory Daniel Armagh – for a great deal of money. Timothy tried to reach Joseph by telephone. He was not in Green Hills. He was not in Philadelphia. Where the hell is he? thought the desperate and sweltering Timothy. Where is he? No one knew. Like father, like son, said Timothy bitterly to himself: probably in some discreet hotel with a trollop, tonight of all nights. Timothy, to his shame, was taken with a childish desire to cry. He had served the Armaghs the greater part of his life, and he was full of grief for them, not for himself.

He could hear the distant band playing 'The Harp that Once through Tara's Halls'. All at once it sounded like a mournful dirge, of centuries of sadness. Why the hell did we pick that damned song? Timothy asked himself, and he wiped his eyes and cursed. All I need now, he thought, is to hear the banshees wailing the end of the Armagh ambitions – and a man's whole life. He was thinking of Joseph Armagh. Now he sniffled, and cried the bitter tears of a man, sparse and scalding.

CHAPTER FIFTY-FOUR

'TIM,' said Rory, with a kind and admonishing look, as he dressed. 'Don't take it so hard. Everything isn't lost, you know. What will be will be.'

'Don't be so fatalistic,' said Timothy.

'I come of a fatalistic race. Come on, Tim. Cheer up. Where's the Irish in you? Maybe what I say tonight to that big audience will – what is the phrase – ring round the world. Have a drink, Tim. This may even get me the nomination. I want a drink.'

'You've had enough. All right, it is half past seven. Let's go downstairs.'

Never had he seen Rory so confident, so alert, so colourful, so potent. He also appeared larger and taller than usual, as if some power in him was expanding. His eyes glittered with excitement. He even hummed a little as he gave a last pat to his tie and shrugged his coat into position on his broad shoulders. He had brushed his hair until it shone like a red-gold helmet. Timothy, in the face of all that youth and romanticism, let himself hope a little. It was unfortunate that women could not vote. They would go mad for Rory Armagh, mindlessly mad. The rougher suffragettes vowed that men thought through their bellies. But women thought with their organs of generation, and Rory was the erotic dream of women. 'For the first

424

time,' said Rory, as they went to the elevators accompanied by six bodyguards, 'I feel, I really feel, that I will capture the nomination. There's an old saying: "Let the people know." I have confidence in the American people and their common sense.'

The enormous lobby below was crowded from wall to wall with heads, really nothing but heads, Timothy thought, for the crush, shoulder to shoulder, above and below, obliterated body and feet. The heads moved constantly, wordlessly bellowing, back and forth, pouring into eddies, into torrents, into swirls and backwaters and whirlpools, into roaring brooks and rivers and tributaries, into seething clots that dissolved to become bigger clots, larger whirlpools, broader rivers.

The lobby had gold damask walls and half-columns of walnut or mahogany, and there were many scintillating chandeliers, all lit, all swaying as if in a tropic wind. Doors at both ends of the lobby had been left open, and through them poured more men intent on joining the congested and yelling throngs already there. Some carried banners and flags. There were many white silk flags with a green harp imposed on them with the legend: 'A Harp for a Harp!' 'Erin go bragh!' was also seen on banners. A band was playing somewhere, patriotic songs and marches, and Irish ballads, inspiring those nearest to sing and enhance the general confusion and weltering roar. There were stairs on each side of the lobby, one set leading to dining-rooms, the other to the ballroom. Men stood on them, brandishing whisky glasses and yelping jovially and laughing, and milling up and down, and smoking, happily pushing each other. All were sweating profusely and mopping foreheads with handkerchiefs like banners themselves.

Uniformed men in blue and purple, employed by the hotel, tried to coax those frenzied, drunken and shouting men up the stairs to the ballroom, and there was a large blue contingent of the Boston police also trying for the same end. They were frequently swept off their feet, helplessly. Glasses were pushed into their hands, and cigars.

'Good God,' said Timothy, half-pleased and half-dismayed. 'This is far worse than Chicago.' The elevators had opened on a shallow elevation above the lobby. The two men stood there, unseen for a moment or two, and surveyed the scene below. Hoarse voices surged up to them, clamouring, ebulliently babbling, and tumultuous pandemonium, senseless but

425

joyous riot, feverish hubbub. And the heads seethed with increasing excitement, and the mobs increased and men fought to enter through the jammed doors and the band, losing its mind, devoted itself mainly to drums and trumpets, possibly in a last effort to be heard.

Rory had to bend and put his mouth almost against Timothy's ear to be heard. 'How many do you suppose are here?' 'Thousands,' said Timothy. The gold-coloured carpet of the lobby could not be seen under that heaving carpet of heads moving in vapour. 'Shouldn't wonder they'll start climbing the walls next or swinging from the chandeliers.' Their bodyguard shifted uncomfortably close to them, in all that heat and stench, and new crowds were being disgorged by the elevators, all bawling, all waving to no one in particular, all bulging frenetically of eye, and all very, very drunk. To them the clot of men standing quietly close by was an impediment. They shoved against them, and cursed and glared, but did not as yet recognise Rory. 'No way into the ballroom but through this damned jungle,' said Timothy.

'Come on,' said Rory. 'You'd be first to complain if the place were half empty.'

Placards appeared, with Rory's over-coloured portrait on them, and a thunderous shout went up: 'Rory! Rory! Rory! Harp for a Harp! Long live the Irish!' They had been recognised at last. A tidal wave of wet men swarmed upon them, carrying them off their feet, bearing them with bellows and shouts and hoarse chanting into the centre of the lobby. The bodyguard struggled and punched to keep up with the two men. Rory's red-gold head bobbed, sank, rose, turned about around and around, and his flushed and handsome face was laughing automatically. Timothy was close by, but having trouble even touching the floor.

Another group was struggling towards them, flailing arms and kicking, and the hysterical band began to play, 'Kathleen Mavourneen' and hundreds began to sing the song of Old Syrup, former Mayor of Boston, former Congressman, former looter who had been discovered with both hands and both feet in the public trough. He had been consigned to 'private life', and had never remained there, execrated and adored, incredibly fat and gross and huge of red wet face, and genial and honey-tempered as always, and perpetually engaged in politics, always regrettable and enjoyed by his public. Though he was in his seventies, married and with ten burly sons – now surrounding him and kicking and pushing too worshipful citizens – he had his 'lady friend', as she was coyly called, with him, a tall slender woman with bright red hair and big protuberant green eyes and roped with pearls and pinned with diamonds and clad in her favourite virginal colour – white silk – and showered with lace and wearing a huge plumed and flowered hat. Unkind rumour said she had been the esteemed madam of one of Joseph Armagh's expensive houses of joy, but in fact she was really a burlesque queen from New York, though she had been born in Boston. At any rate, Old Syrup had been devoted to her for nearly two decades – she was now in her lush ripe forties – and her name was Kathleen, and he had adopted the old Irish song 'as her own', in her honour. What Mrs Old Syrup had to say about this was not recorded. Nor was the source of his wealth ever questioned. It was expected that politicians looted. It only became reprehensible when they were caught at it. Old Syrup was once reported to say, anent investigations: 'Reform movements? I love them, now. They make money for me. Couldn't buy that advertising.'

He and his sons, and his lady, fell upon Rory. Rory was wrapped in huge fat arms, encased in bursting broadcloth, and smacked on both cheeks. 'Jaysus!' shouted Old Syrup. 'And it's a gladsome sight for me, boyo, to see the son of that old rascal, Armagh, campaigning in me own town, then! Old Joe! God bless 'im! Never a better Irishman in this whole damned country, God bless 'im! How's old Joe?'

Rory had met Old Syrup many times before, and was always amused by him, and fond, for there was something charming about the old scoundrel, something both innocent and wicked, honestly good-hearted and kind, and ruthless, pious and blasphemous, ready to weep – and sincerely – at a story of want and suffering – and ready to exploit and rob the very same day, even those who were already exploited and robbed. 'An Irishman,' Rory once said to his father, 'never makes a good Machiavelli. He can't master either his heart, his emotions, or his lusts. Nothing devious about us, sad to say. Whatever we are, we are with full soul and bad temper and our very, very uncontrollable tongues. Saint or sinner – we go all out on it, hammer and tongs, in spite of a lot of us trying to act like High Church bishops with gaiters, drinking tea and eating crumpets in genteel society. It galls us, finally.'

Rory knew what Old Syrup was, and it amused him and he let himself be heartily thumped and embraced and knew that for this moment, at least, Old Syrup was passionately honest in his greetings. (What he would think the next day, and before the primaries, and in close consultation with his cronies, was something else indeed.) Tonight he loved Rory like his favourite son. Tonight he was bursting with affection for 'Old Joe'. Tonight he desired nothing more than to establish Rory as the idol of the Boston Irish, and make him President. It was evident. His vast face, like the face of a happy child with naughty blue eyes, looked up at Rory with delight and affection.

'Mr Flanagan,' Timothy said, and had to repeat it several times before Old Syrup heard him. 'Is there any way of getting Rory into the ballroom before he is stamped to death?'

'Eh?' said Old Syrup, and looked up at his mighty belligerent sons. 'Sure and we can. Bhoys, out with the feet and the fists.'

But the crowd had become fully aware of the presence of Rory, and the boiling whirlpool surged towards him with the banners and the placards and the heat and the smoke. His clothing was seized, his shoulders. Arms tangled with his: he would have fallen if there had been anywhere to fall, an unoccupied spot. But every inch had legs and feet in it, struggling for advantage. Screams, howls, yells, expletives concerning trampled toes, rudely affectionate greetings shrieked in the highest and most penetrating tones, ruder questions, demands to shake his hand, demands to be heard, hoots and general bedlam, surrounded him almost visibly. The band went mad, pounding out 'The Harp that Once through Tara's Halls' in the most antic ragtime, which Timothy admitted was an improvement. He was fighting, together with the Flanagan brothers, to prevent Rory from being enthusiastically mashed to death, smothered or crushed. Above all that welter and happy fury Rory's shining head rose and bobbed, was lost, rose again. The crowd was trying to bear him somewhere, and rival contingents were trying to bear him somewhere else, and a few fist-fights broke out merrily, to joyous cheers, and the smoke rose to the golden dome of the lobby and the heat became intolerable. Something fell thunderously somewhere.

to heightened cheers, but no one seemed to know what it was, or where.

'Ah, it's a grand day, then!' cried Old Syrup, hugging one of Rory's arms determinedly and kicking out dexterously and without malice against pressing adherents. 'God bless the Irish!'

'Somebody had better, or I'll be killed,' Rory shouted back. One sleeve had been torn almost free from his coat at the shoulder, and his striped shirt showed in the gap. His tie hung at the side of his neck like a hangman's rope, and he was afraid he would be strangled. His feet had been stepped on so assiduously that they felt both burning and numb. His carefully brushed hair was dishevelled, and fell and bounced over his wet forehead, which gave him a very boyish appearance. It was splendid to be hailed this way, but he wondered if he would survive. He was already drained, and he had an important and momentous speech to make, and the ballroom was hardly nearer than in the beginning, and the noise made his head throb.

Then the Flanagans, man and boy, stood together like a football phalanx, and charged those nearest to Rory, and many of the crowd, cursing and waving fists, fell back and challenged the Flanagans to 'come outside, then'. Banners and placards tossed crazily, the band was shrieking its heart out and the drums were like thunder. But Rory found himself propelled towards the ballroom, three or four of his bodyguard with him, and Timothy, who ran with water and was bedraggled. The whirlpools swung together again en masse, and surged after Rory, and everyone poured and struggled and pushed and hit to get into the ballroom to the best seats.

The throng came to a brief halt as two men fell before it and tried to scramble to their feet and were either kicked impatiently or thrown off balance. Rory drew a deep breath; his lungs smarted from all that smoke and heat. He looked aside, still smiling widely. And near him, very near, almost within touching distance, Marjorie Chisholm stood, laughing and dimpling.

She was thirty-three or more years old and she looked like a fresh girl in her grey linen suit and gay sailor hat with pink ribbons. Her black eyes were merry – he had never forgotten them – and they shone and shimmered with love and joy at the sight of him, and her red mouth pursed in a kiss which she blew towards him, and her black hair began to tumble from under her hat in the way he remembered so dearly, all curls and tendrils and polished waves. In that instant he was not Senator Rory Armagh any longer, a husband and a father, a man aspiring to the nomination of his Party. He was Rory Armagh, the law student at Harvard, and he was meeting Marjorie here and in a moment he would have her in his arms, and there was nothing else in all the world and never was, and his whole body began to pound like one gigantic pulse.

'Maggie, Maggie!' he shouted over the hubbub. They were pulling the fallen men to their feet, and cursing them, and there was a little cleared space, miraculously, about Rory, and forgetting everything he plunged towards Marjorie, calling to her again and again, and his face was the face of a youth who sees his love, and it was lighted and passionate and urgent. She took a single step towards him, her gloved hands outheld, and she too saw no one else and every sound died from her awareness except the sound of Rory's voice, and she saw nothing but his face.

Someone seized Rory's arm. He never knew who it was. He tore that arm away, and turned his head furiously. It was the last conscious gesture he was ever to make.

For a shot rang out, stunningly, shockingly, and for a moment or two the roaring stopped, and the seething diminished. Someone called plaintively, someone denounced firecrackers in this place. Men looked about confusedly, suddenly immobile, staring, glaring. There was another shot, a great cry, and then a milling, of terror, of panic, of an animal attempt at flight.

'My God, what was that?' asked Timothy. He turned to Rory, for it was he who tried to restrain the other man. But Rory was only standing there, blank and white and blinking, swaying from side to side, his eyes blind yet searching, his mouth open. Then he fell like a post falling, but he could not reach the floor. He fell into the arms of half a dozen men, and they held him and whimpered and called over and over, 'Are you hurt? Anybody hurt?' A terrible mêlée broke out. 'Murder!' howled hundreds of men, who still had seen nothing and had only heard. 'Call the police! Murder! Get that man! Who's this man, lying here? What – what – what . . .'

The former noise was nothing like the noise which now struck the lobby, wave upon wave of clamour, of curses, of struggles, of yells and imprecations. Every man tried to run in a different direction from his neighbour, and they collided, staggered back, fought, thrust, even bit, in their terror and panic, their eyes starting from their pallid damp faces, their mouths open and emitting grunts and squeals and shouts. The floor of the lobby trembled; the walls trembled. The flags blew straight out. Those who had sought walls for shelter huddled together, panting, arms fending off those who fell against them, feet kicking. Over it all came the hoarse and gasping cry: 'Who was shot? Who did it?'

Police were using their clubs, raising them and striking down without discrimination. Men fell; others piled upon them, wriggling like a heap of frenzied worms. The police climbed on them, over them, smashing down, and with the instinct of the law moving steadily to where Rory and his bodyguard and Timothy and Old Syrup had been standing. Their faces were fixed, not snarling or threatening. They stared only in Rory's direction, and made for him, their helmets invulnerable to blows, their arms rising and falling like the arms of machines.

They had cleared a spot to lay Rory down. His chest was pulsing scarlet. His eyes were open and vaguely searching, though dimming rapidly. Only his hair remained in its resplendent condition, falling back from his forehead. His face was the colour of wet clay. His mouth moved a little.

'Oh Christ, Christ, Christ,' said Timothy and knelt beside Rory and took his hand. He looked down into that dying face and he burst into tears. Old Syrup, his hands on his knees, bent over Rory, muttering, gaping. Then a cry rose: 'A doctor! A priest!'

'Armagh's down! Armagh's been shot! Armagh's dead!' roared hundreds, and they halted their flight as they realised, aghast, what they had said and what it meant.

'Oh, Christ, Christ, a doctor,' groaned Timothy. 'A priest. Rory? Rory?'

Several policemen had reached them and Timothy raised his distorted face and implored them, 'A doctor, a priest. He's badly hurt, Rory.' He repeated it over and over again and clutched Rory's hand and a nightmare dazzle began to blind him and he said, 'No, no, no.' A ring of faces, appalled, pallid, loomed over him and he begged them to help, and finally someone said, 'It's all right, Mr Dineen. A doctor's getting through, and a priest.' Hands touched him comfortingly, seeing his agony, but no one touched Rory. No one wanted to see what had been done to him, and many men about him began to cry like young children, turning aside, bending their heads, their features grimacing. Old Syrup staggered into the arms of two of his sons and he pressed his face against the chest of one and wept and whimpered, and they patted him, and were grim.

Timothy, who felt he was dying, himself, vaguely saw a woman kneeling beside Rory on the other side. She had lifted his head on her knee, her grey linen knee. Her hat was lost; her black polished hair fell to her shoulders. Rory's blood covered her gloved hands, her dress. She drew his head to her breast. She said, 'Rory. It's Maggie, Rory. Maggie.' Her face was white and petrified. She pushed back his hair. She bent her head and kissed his cheek, his fallen gaping mouth. 'Rory, my dearest, it's Maggie.'

No one tried to remove her. They were all struck by the sight of a dying man in the arms of this strange young woman, dabbled with his blood, holding him as she would hold all the world.

Rory was in a dark and swirling place, filled with flashes of scarlet lightning. He was being tossed about on a black sea, helplessly. He could see nothing. But he could hear Marjorie's voice, and he thought he replied to it: 'Oh, Maggie, Maggie, my darling. Oh, Maggie.'

But he made no sound at all. He died an instant later in Marjorie's arms.

A priest was kneeling now, beside them, blessing himself, murmuring the prayers for the dying, for the dead. And Marjorie knelt there and knew that all her hopes were finally as dead as the man she held, but to the very last she would not let them take him away.

CHAPTER FIFTY-FIVE

NEVER had Old Syrup been so magnificent, so theatrical, so eloquent, and such a delight to the press. Reporters came from all over the country to interview him, and then to write excited columns about him. The story was dramatic enough, but Old Syrup was not only a former Congressman – they always called him 'Congressman' – and very rich and politically powerful, but he was dramatically Irish and descriptive and never once did he repeat his story in the exact same words as before. There was always something remembered, something added, something imagined. This led to his later appointment as Senator the next year by the State Legislature, and to an increase in his fortune. Queenie, 'my lady friend', was his hostess in Washington, and a very discreet one. It was well-known that Mrs Old Syrup had no taste for politics, was very retiring, very charitable, and a joy to her parish, and disliked Washington. She was also a gentlewoman and never mentioned Queenie except as 'my dear husband's assistant'.

'There I was, with my bhoys, and my darlin' young friend, Rory Armagh, the Senator – like a son to me himself, then – and we were all laughing and the band was playing, and hundreds, perhaps thousands were struggling to get to Rory to shake his hand and shout their support of him, and there he was, shining like the damned sun, itself, now, and a sight for any sore eyes – his Dada was my best friend – and I tell you, gentlemen, that I'm a cynic, but there was tears in my eyes, with joy. I couldn't have been prouder or happier if Rory had been of my own flesh and blood. Knew him since he was a little boyeen, and always ready with a smile, a joke, a sparkle. A scholar and a gentleman, as well as a Senator. If Rory had lived to be nominated he would have been elected, yes sir, and he would have made the best damned President this country has ever seen. It's America's loss, gentlemen, even more than his parents' loss, and may God console them in His mercy.

'Well – you will excuse me a minute, now, won't you, while I wipe these old eyes? After all, it's a terrible thing, all that life and handsomeness and vigour, a young man, too, with a darlin' wife and four little children – my heart breaks for those little ones, and the young widow, so brave and beautiful and never breaking down, though you could see her heart was shattered, standing by the grave in her black veils like a statue, and never even shedding a tear. It's the easy grief that cries, not the deep one. Well, as I was saying, there we were in the lobby, and the crowds and the hails for Rory, and the band, and the people pouring in through the

doors just to look at the lad, and then all at once he moved —
he must have seen someone he wanted to shake hands with —
and he was exposed just for an instant, and me there with my
sons and his bodyguard, and then there was a crack — a loud
crack, like a firecracker. That's what we thought it was, for a
minute, and we cursed the fool who'd do that in such a crowd.

'Then there was another crack. We all stood there, gowp-
ing, not knowing where to look, then men started to run and
mill. Like hell, itself, yelling and shouting and pushing each
other and somebody screamed "Murder!" And, gentlemen, it
was.'

Genuine tears would stand in his crafty eyes for a moment,
because of the picture he had drawn. Emotion broke his
sonorous voice.

'Well, gentlemen, there was Rory on the floor — someone had
cleared a space when he fell in the arms of his men — and a
young lady, a most beautiful young lady — was kneeling beside
him, holding him in her arms. Now, I knew that young lady's
Dada well; an old and valued friend, a distinguished gentleman, Mr Albert Chisholm, a lawyer of an old firm in Boston,
honourable, upright firm. Miss Marjorie Chisholm. She'd
known Rory in Boston when he was at Harvard. Rumours,
there were, that they once was engaged, then. Young love.
Miss Chisholm never married.' Old Syrup would then look
about him significantly, sigh, and shake his head. 'I know,
gentlemen, that she was first named "the mystery woman",
but there weren't no mystery about Miss Chisholm. Belle of
Boston when she made her day-boo. The pleece knew her
at once. She wouldn't let Rory out of her arms for a long
time; had locked him in them, she had. It was pitiful. Then she
went with him to the hospital, with the priest, old Father
O'Brien, old friend of mine. But Rory was already dead.
You'll excuse me a minute, gentlemen. All Miss Chisholm
could say, again and again, was: "Rory, Rory, Rory." Like
a Litany. Her father's associate had to be called to take her
away, a Mr Bernard Levine, a lawyer himself — trusted friend
of the family.

'The murderer? Well, gentlemen, I never saw him, meself.
But they found the "black flag of anarchy", as they called it,
in his pocket, a little black flag, and a card saying he belonged
to the I.W.W. Now, sir, I'm all for Labour, meself. Didn't I
always fight for Labour when I was in Washington? Wobblies,

they called them. Gentlemen, will you believe me when I say it is my conviction, my heart's conviction, that that murderer was no member of the I.W.W.? Rory always stood for the working man, when he was Senator. Always spoke for the working man, all over the country. And another thing, gentlemen, there wasn't a single piece of identification on that foul murderer, not one. Even the name on the card was false. Never belonged to any union, and the I.W.W. never heard of him. And there wasn't a fingerprint of his on the card, neither! What more proof do you want, then? Card as clean as a babe's mouth, and new as if it just come from the printing press. Young feller, they said, with a beard. Not more than twenty-one, twenty-two. Never did find out who he was. Never will, I'm thinking.

'Who shot him, right after he shot Rory? No one will ever find that out, either. Rory's bodyguards' guns had not been fired. No pleeceman had fired a gun. It came, now, out of the blue, as they say. Well, there were hundreds, thousands, there. Any man could have killed the assassin. And then melted off, like butter on a hot plate, oozing out of the crowd. I've heard him called a "hero" by some newspapers, for killing the assassin, but if he's such a hero why don't he come forward to be praised? All I can say now is that that's the real mystery — outside the reason why Rory was murdered. If that assassin hadn't been shot, himself, we'd maybe have got the truth out of him. The pleece here in Boston, and I'm proud of the bhoys, have ways of making criminals talk. Now we'll never know the truth — who ordered Rory assassinated.' Old Syrup looked about him weightily. 'Maybe that's the idea, then, gentlemen, maybe that's the whole idea.

'What's that you say, sir? "Disgruntled youth?" Now, begging your pardon, what the hell does *that* mean? Just words, now. Empty words. Is it hinting at a plot I am? Gentlemen, I don't know. Who would "plot" against Rory? Finest young Christian gentleman I ever met, a lovely lad, never harmed a soul in his short life. Kind, charitable, full of fun, the best of sons and husbands. The whole Senate grieves for him, as well as his friends. You've read the eulogies. Weren't anything compared to what was said at the grave. In the family plot, in Green Hills, Commonwealth of Pennsylvania. Well, lots of you were there, too, so I don't have to repeat what was said. Assistant Secretary of State was there, and several

Senators and politicians, and two-three Governors. And,' said Old Syrup, impressively, 'Old Joe's associates, many of them, big feenanciers and businessmen and bankers – never saw such a gathering. Mr Jay Regan, himself, the big financier, stood beside Joe Armagh and held his arm, and I'll never forget what he said to Joe, in that deep voice of his, at the funeral:

' "Joseph," he said, and many of us heard it, "remember, you have four grandchildren." Now, gentlemen, I think that was touching, then, don't you? "Remember, you have four grandchildren." Consoling, now. Reminding Joe he still had obligations, though all his three children lay in their graves before him, his son, the war hero, Kevin, his beautiful daughter, Ann Marie, and now Rory. And there was his brother's grave there, too, Sean Armagh, known to millions as Sean Paul. Greatest Irish tenor in the whole world, and don't deny it.

'What did Joe say? Well, he just turned a little and he looked at Mr Regan and it was as if there was a fire on his face for a minute – he being reminded of his dear little grandchildren, and that he had a duty to them, even if his poor heart was broken. Joe's made of steel, gentlemen. As we always said, the same fire that melts butter hardens steel. And Joe looked right at Mr Regan, one of his dear friends, and he smiled. Comforted, right there at the grave, thinking of the little ones, Rory's children. He smiled.

'Rory's poor mother? Ah, there's the tragedy. Lost her mind. She's in a sanatorium now, in Philadelphia, poor soul. Sent there last week, right after the funeral. God send His angels to comfort her. They found her in the dark one night – wandered out of the house – and lying on her son, Kevin's grave. Not crying, just mute. Like a dead creature, poor lady. Knew her father well, the old Senator, when I was young. Wonderful man. My Dada took me to see him in Washington; couldn't have been more than twenty or so.

'Ah, and a tragedy it all is, then. Mrs Rory is with her parents, and the children. Under private doctor's care, in her father's house. Declared up and down, when she first knew that Rory had "died in the cause of Labour". The Rights of Labour, she says. Well, who knows her husband's heart more than a wife does? So who knows what Rory would have done if he had been President, for the Civil Rights of All Americans? Ambassador Worthington has hinted of them, himself.

'We mourn for the sorrow of the Armagh family. But, gentlemen, we should mourn for America, who suffered this tremendous – I say, tremendous – loss. God, in His wisdom, we say, knows best. We can only hope. And don't, gentlemen, out of mercy, repeat any more about "the curse on the Armaghs". What curse? They never did anyone harm, now.'

It was deep winter, but in Maryland it was dry and bleak and grey and black, the hills stark under a bitter sun. There was little snow, and these were in patches on the brown fields and in the ditches.

Mr Timothy Dineen sat in an austerely clean room smelling of wax and fern and incense. Light came in faint and feeble shadows through the stained-glass windows. Before him was a screen and behind it he could see only the dim outline of a nun. Her voice was low and clear, the beloved voice he remembered, the young voice unroughened by the years, the melodious Irish voice he had adored in his youth. It was firm and gentle with courage and faith and consolation. But, he thought, I am old, old, old as death and as weary.

'You say, Tim, that dear Joseph died of a heart attack a month ago, in his bed, at night. I think he died of a broken heart. You see, Tim dear, Joseph never lived a single day for himself. He never once thought of himself, in all his life. Is that a sin? We esteem self-sacrifice . . . but we also must remember that one has one's own soul to save, too. Ah, darling Joseph! He lived for Sean and me, and then for his children. I remember my young days in the orphanage. Sister Elizabeth would tell Sean and me of Joseph's sacrifices for us, his endless struggles for us, his endless devotion. Sean . . .' The gentle voice hesitated. 'Ah, we are often blind, and our ears often deceive us, or we deceive ourselves. But I always knew, even as a very young child, what Joseph was doing for his family, and how he denied himself the simple joys and pleasures of youth so that we could have safety and security and a home. He was very young when he became the head of our family. Only thirteen, dear Tim. But, he was a man. And that is something strange and rare and wonderful. A man. He never asked for pity or for help. He never asked anyone to be generous or kind to him. He didn't even ask Sean and me to love him! But he loved us. He dearly loved us. Ah, God forgive me that I did not entirely understand! My youth was no excuse, no excuse at all, dear Tim. I do penance daily for my lack of understanding. I was drawn inexorably to this life, and always was drawn since my earliest recollections. But perhaps I was too stupid to make Joseph understand. He thought always, that I had deserted him – as Sean had deserted him. I must do extra penance.'

Timothy felt old and broken. He remembered:

> 'The tumult and the shouting dies,
> The Captains and the Kings depart.
> Still stands Thine ancient sacrifice –
> An humble and a contrite heart.'

Then he thought: But the 'Captains and the Kings' haven't 'departed' at all! They were stronger than ever, since Rory Armagh's assassination. They would continue to grow in strength, until they had the whole silly world, the whole credulous world, the whole ingenuous world, in their hands. Anyone who would challenge them, attempt to expose them, show them unconcealed and naked, would be murdered, laughed at, called mad, or ignored, or denounced as a fantasy-weaver. The hell with the world, thought Timothy Dineen. Maybe these 'quiet deadly men' were all it deserved. It would deserve the wars, the revolutions, the tyrannies, the chaos. For wicked men there was always the hope of remorse and penance. For the stupid there was no hope at all. The stupid invariably sacrificed its heroes, and raised statues to its murderers. The hell with the world. He, Timothy Dineen, was growing old. He would see the beginning of the last battle of man against his assassins – but, thank God, he would not see the final *débâcle*. That was left to the coming effervescent and enthusiastic young, who would follow any banner and die in any carefully plotted war, and murder any potential rescuers.

He said, 'Sister, pray for me.' Then he was astonished, for the conviction had come to him that Sister Mary Bernarde's prayers might have some efficacy! She was only an immured nun, shut off from the world, living in an atmosphere of simple devotion and faith, unaware of the terrors outside her convent, unaware of all the ramifications of her brother's life of which he could not tell her, for she would not understand and be only confused. Yet he said, 'Pray for me.'

'I will pray for all the world,' she said. 'And especially for

Joseph, dear Tim, and you.'

He went out into the cold winter afternoon. The station hack was waiting for him. He heard the soft ringing of bells over the desolate landscape. The old bells, the ancient bells, the oldest voices in the world. Who knew? They might be eternal.

He leaned against the door which had gently closed behind him and he cried. But for what he cried he did not fully know.

Two months after Rory Daniel Armagh's assassination General Curtis Clayton attempted to address the Senate 'to reveal what I know'. He was denied. He wrote a book. It was never published, and never found after his death. He implored the President to see him, and the President never answered.

He tried the press and the reporters listened to him with grave faces and dancing eyes. They never reported what he said.

He died in the Army Hospital at Camp Meadows on the eve of the election of Woodrow Wilson. Some said he had committed suicide. His name was soon forgotten.

BIBLIOGRAPHY

Allen, Frederick Lewis, 'Morgan the Great,' *LIFE* Magazine, April 25, 1949

American Heritage, August, 1965

A Primer on Money – Subcommittee on Domestic Finance, Committee on Banking & Currency, House of Representatives, 88th Congress, U.S. Government Printing Office, Washington

Bryan, William 'John', *The United States' Unresolved Monetary and Political Problems*

Budenz, Louis F., *Bolshevik Invasion of the West*

Courtney, Phoebe, *The Council on Foreign Relations*

Dall, Curtis, *FDR, My Exploited Father-in-Law*

DeGoulevitch, Arsene, *Czarism and the Revolution*

Flynn, John, *Men of Wealth*

Forbes, B. C., *Men Who Are Making America*

Gitlow, Benjamin, *The Whole of Their Lives*

Groseclose, Elgin, *Money and Man*

Hansl, Proctor, *Years of Plunder*

Huddleston, Sisley, *The Tragic Years*

Hull, Cordell, *Memoirs*

Lundberg, Ferdinand, *America's 60 Families*

Mises, Ludwig von, *Human Action*

McFadden, Louis T., Congressman, *On the Federal Reserve Corporation, Remarks in Congress*, (Congressional Record)

Myers, Gustavus, *History of the Great American Fortunes*

National Economy and the Banking System, Senate Documents, Volume 3, No. 23, U.S. Government Printing Office, Washington

Noyes, Alexander Dana, *The Market Place*

Papers Relating to the Foreign Relations of the United States-Russia, House of Representatives, Document No. 1868, volume 1, U.S. Government Printing Office, Washington

Patman, Wright, *Newsletter*, June 6, 1968 – also Congressional Record, March 21, 1962, etc.

Quigley, Carroll, *Tragedy and Hope*

Rothbard, Murray, *Economic Depressions, Causes and Cures*
   What has Government Done to Our Money?
Senate Silver Hearings, *Testimony of Robert L. Owen*
Seymour, Charles, *The Intimate Papers of Colonel House*
Sparling, Earl, *Mystery Men of Wall Street*
Spengler, Oswald, *Decline of the West*
Sutton, Antony, *Western Technology and Soviet Economic
   Development*
Viereck, George S., *The Strangest Friendship in History*
Warburg, James, *The Long Road Home*
Warburg, Paul, *The Federal Reserve System*
White, Andrew D., *Fiat Money Inflation in France*

ESPECIALLY RECOMMENDED

Allen, Gary, *C.P.R., Conspiracy to Rule the World*
         The Bankers and the Federal Reserve
Skousen, W. Cleon, *The Naked Capitalist*, private edition
Report from Iron Mountain